The Three Queens of Richard the Lionheart

©India Millar 2016

Table of Contents

Chapter One

Chapter Two

Chapter Three

Chapter Four

Chapter Five

Chapter Six

Chapter Seven

Chapter Eight

Chapter Nine

Chapter Ten

Chapter Eleven

Chapter Twelve

Chapter Thirteen

Chapter Fourteen

Chapter Fifteen

Chapter Sixteen

Chapter Seventeen

Chapter Eighteen

Chapter Nineteen

Chapter Twenty

Chapter Twenty One

Chapter Twenty Two

Chapter Twenty Three

Chapter Twenty Four

Chapter Twenty Five

Chapter Twenty Six

Chapter Twenty Seven

"In Every Woman There is a Queen. Speak to the Woman and the Queen Will Answer"

Old Nordic Proverb

Chapter 1

"Mother, I'm not going to marry that woman. She is no more than a whore – the whole world knows and would laugh at me. Me! A cuckold even before I'm wed! A man whose own father has put the horns on his head! It's insufferable, I tell you. Not to be thought of."

He paused for breath, but continued pacing angrily, measuring the length of the room and back. The dainty Genoese greyhound cowering in Eleanor's skirts shivered, tail between its legs, as he brushed past, almost knocking the timid dog aside in his fury.

"My son." Her voice was calm but its familiar authority cut through his rage like a sharp knife. He paused before her in automatic obedience. "My son, for heaven's sake. Calm yourself. Sit, we must talk about this. Sit."

Sulkily, he slouched on to the stool drawn up beside her. Even perched on the little stool, he was head and shoulders taller than the old woman. For a moment she remained still, gathering her thoughts, then reached out and drew his head against her shoulder as she might to a child. He sighed and rubbed his face against her cheek.

"Your beard tickles," she complained, but allowed him to stay. "You don´t think, my dear Richard, that fate is laughing at your expense?"

"Laughter?" His voice rose, quick to anger. "What´s so funny about the fact that the King of England is about to be made a fool of? And a public fool at that! Would you have your favourite son made the butt of every joke told by the whole court? By the whole world, come to that?"

"Shush, my dear. Listen to me. For once. The irony in the situation is one you cannot miss; you deposed your father from his throne; now it appears he´s deposed you from your marriage bed. Tit for tat, it may be said. No?"

"Aye, I suppose so. If you say so." He muttered grudgingly. "But he deserved it, mother, you know he did. If we leave aside the insult to me, think what he did to you Eleanor, Queen of England and France; Eleanor of Aquitaine, the greatest, most beautiful queen the world has ever known." She purred under his praise, stroking his face tenderly. "How did you feel, Mama, when he flaunted Rosamund of Clifford before you? When he ran after that bitch and didn't even bother to cover his tracks? Rosa Mundi, Rose of the World indeed!" He sniggered. "Or Rosa the Unchaste, as some have named her! And he put you away from the world for her. Fifteen years away from your own throne, for a provincial nobody. And where is she now, the beautiful Rosamund? Saintly and shriven in some nunnery, while dear father rots in his grave."

"But we, my love, are alive and well and free." She smiled slowly "And you're crowned King of England whilst dearest Henry, as you say, rots in the grave. Strange you know – I believe he actually loved Rosamund, as much as he ever loved anybody other than himself, and she him. But Alice now, she was just one of many. Do you know, if he had been anybody but my own husband I could almost understand the silly little bitch's head being turned by his attentions – he was the King, after all, and many thought him an exceptionally attractive man. Damn it, I thought him an attractive man, before he turned against me, but I will never, ever forgive her for giving way to him. I bought her to the court. I treated her like my own daughter for years, and she betrayed me with my own husband. The pair of them – fornicating in my own bed, rutting like animals underneath my very eyes and I never even suspected!"

"She betrayed you, Mama, and me – you of all people know how long she and I were betrothed. I even believed the slut was in love with me. I was prepared to marry my dearest Alice as soon as the fuss over my coronation was settled. And now I find my own father has defiled her! She went from court in a hurry, Mama, and the rumours say she was with child – Henry's bastard! Is it true?"

"Henry's babe or some other knight's. Who knows? If she'll lift her skirts for one man, she could do it for another. But aye, the gossip named my dear husband and I have no reason to disbelieve it. I believe a child was born, a maiden, but it died soon after birth, thank God. Alice Capet, princess of France, is tainted goods, my son. And as you say, the world knows it." The greyhound whined, and she comforted it with a stroke. "I believe Juliet wants to go out."

"Can't it piss in the rushes like every other dog in the place?"

"Certainly not. I'm not going to have my solar stinking like the great hall. Isabel," the door opened so quickly the girl who entered must have been hovering outside, waiting. "Isabel, take Juliet out. And be careful as you go through the hall – I think she's coming on heat and if one of those slobbering great hounds has her, she'll surely perish from the consequences".

The greyhound capered out at once at sight of the girl, and pranced around her skirts as she left the room as silently as she had entered. Richard glared at her silently.

"You still have that Jewish thing around you, then" He complained. "I thought she'd perished with all the rest of her vile clan. You should exhibit her, Mama, for she's surely a rare thing – the only Jew left in London!"

"I've told you before, Richard, but you choose not to listen. Isabel is no longer a Jew. She embraced our Lord years ago. She's as Christian as you or I, these days."

"Aye? So you say, but born a Jew, always a Jew. She should have died with the rest of them in London as God's greatest celebration of my coronation. I tell you,

Mama, my people could have given me no greater tribute than rising up and slaughtering those beasts that killed our Lord. The streets were sticky with their blood, but I've been told that even the curs wouldn't lick it up, as if they knew it would poison them. I would have shouted my thanks to the mob from the bottom of my heart, if it wasn't for the fact that I had need of the services of the rest of the Jews left in the kingdom. As they say, one does not bite the hand that feeds you - or lends to you, in my case! But you managed to preserve your pet, didn't you? How you can tolerate her near you, I don't know. She reeks of the ghetto, like all the rest of them. I tell you Mama, one day, when I have enough gold myself, I shall cleanse my kingdom of the rest of them, and when that day comes even you will not be able to protect your dear Isabel."

"She's useful to me." Eleanor said patiently. "I took her in payment of a debt of mine – oh, don't look at me like that. You know full well every penny your father had went on the Crusade, and rightly so. But there were times when I had to look for every groat. I got her when we were in York – that cursed time when Henry first laid eyes on Rosamund of Clifford. He was besotted with her from the first, and nothing I could do or say would distract him – every time I asked him for money, he brushed me aside with false promises. I had hospitality to repay and not a farthing to do it with. So I did what every other good, impoverished, citizen does, and turned to the Jew King instead of the King who should have been by my side. Isaac of York was generous; instead of his money back and a usurious rate of interest beside, he put it to me that he was afraid for the safety of his family and asked nothing of me but that I take his daughter and keep her safe until he asked for her back. He's never asked, and I'm well content with my bargain. She's both quiet and discreet. The nobles talk freely in front of her, because they don't even notice her. The servants gossip to her, because she's as much beneath anybody's notice as they are."

"You mean she spies for you?" Richard spat incredulously.

"That she does. And well. She's my eyes and ears about the court. Her English is, of course, perfect, and her Frankish more than passable. What Isabel hears, I hear."

"A pity she didn't tell you about my father earlier, then! Mama," he moaned, recalled to self pity "What am I to do? Tell me! Philip of France is insisting on the marriage to his half-sister going ahead. He says that he refuses to believe the rumours about Alice and – insult upon injury! – points out that I have no other choice of bride anyway. But I cannot marry Alice. I will not!"

"But you must marry. You must have an heir, and soon, before your Crusade commence if at all possible. If anything happened to you, then John would inherit the throne. I know he's my son, just as much as you are, but I also know that dear John is the greediest man in the kingdom. He thinks of nothing but himself. If he was King, then he'd sell England if he thought it would do him any good. You must marry, you must get a son for England's sake, but not Alice, no. You could not countenance that conniving whore for a wife, and nor could I. In any event, the Pope wouldn't allow it. The Holy Laws forbid it, and rightly so. In Christ's name, if her bastard had lived, it would have been your half-sister!"

"Then if not Alice, who? Mama, you're smiling. Tell me!" Richard jerked to his feet and began to prowl the room again.

"Did you really think I've been idle, Richard? I may have been put away, but I still heard and saw through my friends, who are many. I knew of the rumours surrounding Alice Capet, before you did. So I made certain plans, should this terrible time come to pass. Richard, do sit down – you are like some great beast roaring about my chamber!"

"Your pardon, Mama." Immediately contrite, he resumed his place on the low stool. "Put me out of my misery and tell me!"

"Do you remember Pamplona?" Seeing his blank look, she prompted, "In Navarre?"

"Of course I know Pamplona is in Navarre, but it must be – Lord! – ten years since I was there. They held a splendid tournament in my honour, or rather, it should have been splendid but the whole thing was ruined by the mud. It chose to rain for the first time in months just before I got to the outskirts, and it was like riding through quicksand. My horse nearly threw me at my first joust when it got mired, and I wrenched my shoulder badly. It hurt for weeks." He added piteously.

"If you remember the tournament so well, then you must remember King Sancho's daughter."

Richard stuck out his tongue the better to concentrate. Suddenly, his face cleared.

"Yes, of course! A delicious little creature – face like an angel. Blanche! That was it, Blanche. As fair skinned and fair haired as her name, I recall."

"Richard, no. Not Blanche. Blanche is Sancho's younger daughter. I'm talking about Berengaria, his elder daughter. Not as quite as beautiful as her sister, but a divinely pretty child with great brown eyes and a sweet, retiring manner. Richard, you must remember her! You declared yourself in love with her, and paid her so many compliments she was at your feet and followed you around like a puppy all the time you were in Navarre."

"Did she? But Mama, I've paid compliments to every princess in Christendom, and no doubt meant it at the time. Berengaria, Berengaria. Ah, yes, I do remember her. A pretty girl, as you say, slim as a boy and tiny, but with a quick wit." Richard patted his mouth thoughtfully, unwilling to admit that all he could really remember of Berengaria was a full lower lip, a determined chin and a body as slim and sinuous as a fish. "I recall she carried her copy of the Roman de la Rose everywhere with her – I remember teasing her that it was time she found her own lover instead of looking to an old book for consolation. She's still unmarried, then, after all these years? What's wrong with her? Has she got fat since I saw her? Turned to religion as a consolation for lack of a man, or taken a lover or two? Or has Sancho been mean with her dowry? God help us, all of them?"

"Not at all. I'm assured that Berengaria is as pretty today as she was last time you saw her. She carries as good a dowry as could be expected, and she's still a virgin – trust my good friend Sancho to see to that. She is, of course, observant as a good Christian should be, but has none of the makings of a nun."

"Aye? Sure are you, Mama? Lies are always told about prospective brides, it's only to be expected."

"My *very* good friend Sancho assures me it's all true. Berengaria has met with ill luck; it had been planned that she was to marry but her suitor preferred Blanche, and would not be persuaded otherwise. I believe there have been others, but for one reason and another, the betrothals didn't come to fruition. I've kept in contact with Sancho for these many years, and we have whispered together in our letters across the miles. Now, if could say to Sancho that my dearest son, Richard of England, wished to take his daughter as his bride, there would, I assure you, be great rejoicing at the court of Navarre, and it would not come entirely as a surprise to him."

"Mama, you are amazing." Richard grinned. "But …. Berengaria. How old is she? She must have been – what – thirteen? Fourteen? When I last saw her all those years ago. Is she an old maid, left to whither on the shelf? I want a young bride, not an old woman."

"My son, if wishes were horses, then beggars would ride!" Eleanor said sharply. "I'm offering you a princess of Spain; pretty, witty and well educated. She comes with a good dowry and powerful relatives; Sancho has already pledged his support for the Crusade. She'll make an excellent queen for you. She is, admittedly, not young – all the more reason for you to marry quickly." Richard grunted and she continued quickly, "I think you forget that you are now thirty-one, and about to depart for a holy Crusade. Trust me, Berengaria will suit, I promise. Or would you prefer Alice, after all?"

Richard pouted.

"I'm between a rock and a hard place!" He complained.

"A place of your own making," she responded acidly. "If you had married Alice years ago, instead of whoring and fornicating throughout the continent, Henry would have been forced to look elsewhere to relieve his itch."

Richard pouted and rubbed his hand on her arm.

"Perhaps it runs in the family." He said slyly. Eleanor frowned and he added quickly, "There was so much to do for my kingdom before I could even consider marrying. But to business; you wish me to marry before I depart for Acre. I have no objection to Berengaria as a bride; I suppose I must marry somebody and she seems suitable enough." His face brightened. "Her dowry will help finance my Crusade, and if Sancho is willing to send men and money as well, then I'll welcome this daughter of Spain with open arms. But I have no time to marry before I leave, Mama, you must see that. My arrangements are made – my army is ready, my ships poised, my allies gathering!" His chin jutted and his eyes narrowed as if he could see the noble fleet already assembled before him. "The Holy Land awaits me! I can't put my own plans before the defence of God's realm, Mama." He glanced at her stony face and shrugged. "You know I intend to leave at the end of next month. But I'm perfectly happy for you to send a messenger to Sancho to confirm the betrothal. We can send a proxy if you like, and we can be wed in name if nothing else. She can travel here at her leisure, and we will marry formally as soon as I return to England from the Holy Land."

"No." The word was final. "No, my son. It will not do. England must have an heir, and quickly. So you must have a bride, and quickly. The devil only knows how long you might be away in the Holy Land. One year? Two? More? No. I have already written to

Sancho in anticipation of your happiness at my plans; by now he will have spoken to Berengaria and she will be overjoyed at the news of her betrothal."

Richard scowled and shrugged his shoulders.

"So? Mother, I haven't got time to go to Navarre to bring her to England. She must wait. God knows," he added spitefully "She's waited long enough already for a husband, another year or so won't hurt her."

"My son, my son. How foolish you are. Gather your army and make your plans and sail for Acre as soon as you're ready. You'll make land at Sicily, en route for Acre?" Richard nodded, watching her warily, suspicious of this sudden agreement with his plans. "Excellent. Apart from anything else, you know full well how the land lies with Johanna in Sicily. It's past time that that wretch Tancred learned that it's extremely silly to hold a Queen – a poor, newly widowed queen at that – to ransom, and to steal all she has in the world."

"I'm not entirely sure that I would describe my sister as "poor", Mama." Richard frowned. "Spirited, perhaps, if you're feeling polite about it. A damned bitch if you're not!"

Eleanor wagged her finger as if she was chastising a naughty child.

"Don't speak ill of Johanna, Richard. You may have always have argued like cat and dog, but she is your sister, and she is – or rather was – Queen of Sicily. Tancred's insolence is a personal affront to us, to the whole family, and I'm relying on you to put him in his place. It'll hardly slow you down; you'll need the time to gather your army together. You meet Philip of France in Sicily?"

Richard's eyes gleamed.

"I do. And I daresay I can take the time to ensure that Tancred realizes that it's not wise to trifle with Richard of England's sister. Now that I will enjoy. As you say Mama, it's an insult to all of us, and I can't let my poor sister linger in captivity another day." A thought struck him and he paused. "Is she actually in captivity, by the way? Last I heard, she wanted to travel to Rome, to petition the Pope on her behalf."

"Well, she might not actually be imprisoned, but Tancred has all her money, all her treasures, and he holds the throne, so she might just as well be behind bars. No matter. Explain to Tancred that you don't take kindly to him treating your sister in this disgraceful manner, and retrieve Johanna and her treasure both. What you do with Tancred is your own business. And after that, why everything is arranged." Eleanor shrugged. "I have done it all for you. Sancho expects me in Navarre as soon as I can undertake the journey. I'll leave England as soon as possible, certainly before you sail, and I'll escort your bride to Sicily where we'll meet you."

Richard's good humour vanished instantly. He retorted angrily:

"Mama! You can't mean that! This marriage must wait. I will not have you put at risk. You're too old for such a journey – it will take months. And the discomfort, the danger!" She shot him a look that could have fried snow. "No Mama, for once I will not be quiet. You're still the greatest queen in the world, but you're nearly seventy. The journey will kill you. I will not have it. I'm the king of England, and I forbid it. Forbid it, I say."

"Aye, and I, my son, am Queen of England. I remind you; I have married two kings; birthed ten children; been queen of two countries; sailed on Crusade with a

King of France. And I'm not nearly seventy; I'm little more than sixty. And I'm going to Navarre, and I will bring your bride to you in Sicily."

He stood, towering over her. The sun slipping through the arrow slit behind him turned his hair and beard to a golden halo. Eleanor remained seated; comfortable and relaxed. Richard glared; she smiled sweetly. Admitting defeat, he blew out his breath in a long sigh.

"As you wish, Mother. As you wish. Bring me my bride to Sicily, then, but bring yourself safely, above all."

She smiled and held out her arms in invitation. Richard slid down beside her and allowed his hair to be stroked rhythmically.

"You're hot, child." Eleanor rubbed his forehead tenderly. "When were you last bled? You're choleric by nature; a true Angevin. You have too much blood for comfort."

"Oh, I don't know. About six weeks ago, I think. But I wasn't bled, my surgeon prefers to leech. He says it gives him greater control. Perhaps you're right, Mama. It is time I was leeched again. I have a terrible headache, and that's always the result of bad humours in the blood, it's well known."

"Indeed, my son, indeed." She patted his head softly. Encouraged, he turned his head towards her breast and fastened his lips hungrily on her nipple, sucking at her through the cloth of her bodice. She allowed him to nurse for a moment or two then detached her breast gently. Richard pouted in disappointment, looking longingly at the wet patch he had left on the cloth.

Chapter 2

The news had come in a sealed packet at the beginning of December; Berengaria's father had called her aside immediately, and she had gone to him smiling, expecting some family news. Instead, he had taken her in his arms and embraced her, calling her his "Queen" and laughing at her bewilderment. Hardly able to credit his words, she excused herself quietly and went to her chamber, clutching the portrait of Richard, painted in miniature on ivory, which had been with the letter.

Once alone it was many minutes before she dared open her hand and look at the miniature; she had held it so tightly that the ivory had imprinted its neat oval shape on her palm. Her hand shook, but she could still make out his features and she dwelled greedily on the image. Just the same as if all the long years had never passed! Still blond, still impossibly handsome, still every inch the king. She could hear his voice, teasing, hear his laughter boom around her chamber, see his smile. She cried, without knowing why she cried. Laughed, but did not realise she laughed aloud. Slept, eventually, with the portrait clutched in her hand. Woke to find – against all the odds – that it was still there.

Even without the miniature to reassure her, she would have known that great changes had happened in her life. Courtiers swept her deep bows when she walked past. Suddenly, her small clique of ladies in waiting swelled dramatically as every unmarried woman in the court jostled to attend her.

Now, she stood still as ordered, and looked wonderingly at the seamstresses pinning and snipping and tacking around her. She closed her eyes slowly, and then opened them wide. A wedding dress. *Her* wedding dress. It was true, then. Not just a dream. She trembled with pleasure.

One of the youngest Court ladies looked at the dress with hungry eyes and moved closer, forcing the seamstresses to shuffle to one side.

"Richard the Lionheart."" Carmen whispered "I can't believe it. We all thought you'd been left on the shelf, and would end your days in a convent, and now look at you – Queen of England! Wife of the greatest prize on the marriage market."

The silence could have been sliced and served. Even the seamstresses paused with needles poised, their mouths agape.

Carmen drooped under their stares, wincing when Aunt Constanzia clicked her fingers and pointed at a chair at her side. Constanzia was the indomitable widow who had ruled the court with a rod of iron since Berengaria's mother had died, and now Berengaria trembled for Carmen. Nobody dared to upset Constanzia. The ladies sniggered with laughter, nudging each other in glee, as Carmen slouched, head down, to sit like a scolded dog next to Aunt Constanzia. Berengaria guessed that each and every one of them was relieved it was Carmen who was going to get the sharp side of Costanzia's tongue, and not them.

While their attention was diverted, Berengaria stooped and picked up a scrap of the silk, scrambling it in her hand. She felt slightly foolish, knowing perfectly well that she could have asked for some material, or simply picked some up in full view, but for the purpose she had in mind, it seemed more appropriate to slide some away secretly.

Later, towards dusk when the court was quiet and everybody was indoors, for approaching Christmas the days were short and chilly, Berengaria wrapped herself in a thick cloak and walked briskly across the courtyard towards the great outer doors of the palace. Reaching the soldiers at the gate where the men were clustered around an open brazier glowing with logs, she pushed her hood back and nodded at them; instantly, they sprang to attention and darted to open the small wicket gate for her. She guessed they were staring at her in surprise, leaving the palace on foot and alone at this time of day, but they didn't question her, even if they did tattle to their wives about it later. Perhaps, she thought, they wondered if she was stealing out to meet a lover?

She walked briskly in her little leather slippers, hurrying before the daylight failed completely. Skirting the palace walls, she watched the uneven ground carefully, shivering as a cold wind eddied around her legs and seemed to push her forwards. The path off to the left took no more than a few minutes to find, but from thereon her progress was slow as pine and carob trees skirted the path, their branches jutting at head height, A few seconds later, the bulk of the wishing tree blocked out the last of the light. The gusty wind rustled and blew the scraps of cloth tied all over it. Some still had traces of colour; others had been there so long they were gray and frayed at the edges. Others were so ancient the weft and warp of the weave was clearly visible, and the cloth was bleached to the colour of bone. Some said that the tree had been planted long ago at the place where a woman had been burned for witchcraft. The woman had been unjustly accused by a jealous wife; nobody remembered her name, but it was agreed that she had loved bright colours, and that her restless spirit would be appeased by the scraps of cloth. There were many who laughed at the old legend, but still tied their streamers to the tree, knowing that though they prayed to a Christian God an offering to older gods still might be a good thing.

Berengaria had no thoughts to either; she felt instinctively that she should offer something to ensure her continued luck. She stopped before the tree, her breath pluming in the cold.

Reaching up, she grabbed a branch above her head and dragged it down; grasping the rough wood, she inched her fingers along until she could clasp a higher branch still – that in turn was grasped and pulled down. Standing on tiptoe, she tied her scrap of silk firmly around the final branch and let go. The pennant of silk fluttered brave and alone, higher than any other.

Satisfied, she lingered for a second, breathing a final prayer.

"Please, make all well for me, Take my wedding gown and the wishes in my heart and give me happiness, please."

The wind gusted abruptly, making her own token stream out horizontally and she smiled, well pleased at the sign of good luck. She turned and followed the path back to the warmth and light of the great palace. As she banged on the wicket gate to alert the sentries, a cloud drifted across the moon and the first snowflakes of winter began to fall lazily, melting on her face.

Constanzia piled her trencher with the choicest pieces of meat, but Berengaria barely touched it. She drank a little wine, but pushed the food around her plate, afraid that if she tried to swallow any she would choke. She knew Eleanor was watching, and smiled timidly, her eyes downcast.

"The child eats little, Sancho." Eleanor frowned. "Is her appetite always so poor? That won't do for Richard – he appreciates his food and can´t abide women with sulky appetites."

"I think, dearest Eleanor, that my Berengaria is a little nervous tonight." He smiled fondly at his daughter.

"Aye?" Appeased, Eleanor smiled and reached across to pat Berengaria´s hand. The younger woman froze at her touch, good manners stopping her from snatching her hand away from the caress of old, cold fingers. "You mustn't be frightened of me, dear one. Shortly, I will be your mother. Come now – you may call me Mama from now on."

She nodded regally, certain of the great favour she was offering. Berengaria swallowed a gobbet of disgust, tempted to cry out, you're *not my mother! My mother was young and beautiful, her skin was golden, her hair black. My mother smelled of flowers, not dry, old bread as you do!* Instead, politeness got the better of her and she breathed,

"Thank you …. Mama."

Eleanor nodded regally and ripped a breast of chicken free for herself. She munched at the tender flesh with long, yellowed teeth, her receding gums clearly visible as her lips peeled back from the meat. Her mouth still full, she swigged wine and began to interrogate Berengaria, spraying a mist of flesh and wine across the table.

Finally satisfied, Eleanor turned to speak to Sancho.

"Do you dance, my friend?" She asked. Sancho rose immediately and made a deep bow to her, crooking his arm invitingly. "No, no, not with me. These modern dances are too vigorous for my old bones."

"Eleanor, you will never be old. It isn´t possible for one as beautiful as you to age."

She laughed, delighted with the gallantry. Startled, Berengaria realised that the old woman had accepted the compliment as her due, and believed it.

"Thank you, Sancho. But I do not dance tonight. But I'm sure Berengaria would love to tread a measure or two with her father."

Berengaria stood quickly and curtsied. Behind her smile, she clenched her teeth as she realised with horror that she desperately needed to pass water. But dance she did until she was satisfied that Eleanor was no longer watching her intently. Sancho would have led her back to her place at the high table, but she excused herself with a whispered explanation. He bounced his eyebrows in a gesture she remembered from her childhood and spoke softly.

"Don't worry. I'll keep the fair Eleanor amused – she'll not miss you for a few minutes. But don't be too long."

Berengaria slipped behind the dancers and out of the great hall door. The house of easement was too far from the hall for comfort, and to reach it she must pass in front of Eleanor. The courtyard would do. It would have to do. The hounds – ejected from the hall for the evening – immediately came sniffing around her, their doggy breath steaming in great plumes before them. She shooed them away and squatted in the gutter, holding her heavy skirts away from her thighs and sighing with relief as her bladder emptied. She leaned her burning cheek against the cold stone of the courtyard wall for a second, glancing up at the star strewn sky. The threat of snow had come to nothing, but there would be a frost by morning. Her veil cushioned her skin from the stone, but the cold seeped through and she shivered.

The panic came without warning. Still staring heavenwards, it seemed to Berengaria that the very walls of the palace were closing around her, sealing her in and refusing to let her go. Suddenly, the sheer impossibility of what was about to happen trampled over her former happiness as she realised that she could not go through with it.

"I'm nobody!" She spoke out loud. "A little, obscure princess from a provincial court. An afterthought, an old maid. I can't be Queen of England! I can't marry King Richard! I can't become a great queen like Eleanor. Not me, no. The English court will laugh at me; Richard will be ashamed of me."

The walls whispered her words back to her, agreeing with her. Tears stung her eyes. Even the great door opening and closing swiftly didn't make her move. She shrank back against the wall, invisible in the gloom. Two figures passed by swiftly, crossing the courtyard to the private chambers on the opposite side. Half way across, they paused, exchanging a succulent, sexual kiss. The woman laughed out loud; a high, breathy giggle that broke Berengaria's paralysis.

Carmen, Carmen and one of the knights, it was too dark to make out which one. Berengaria guessed cynically that there would be a spring marriage at court. A wedding she would not see.

For some reason, the thought gave her courage. At least she would never be like Carmen; a stupid girl who had nothing but her sexuality to entice and charm. She would be queen. She had dreamed of this for so long. She would not allow herself to fail. Not now.

Tugging down her skirts, she rose, lifted her head and walked back into the great hall, every inch as regal as the great Eleanor, even if all but a mite of it was pretence. Behind her, the hounds lifted their muzzles to the uncaring moon and howled their disappointment at being left out in the cold.

Chapter 3

"A few more days." Sancho pleaded. "Surely, waiting until after Christmas is finished can't make any difference. It would give you time to rest, to make sure all the arrangements are safely made."

Eleanor stared at him coldly.

"A few more days?" She echoed. "You mean until after Twelfth Night. No Sancho, I'm sorry, it will not do. I'm certain you can provision us with whatever we need, whatever will keep for the journey, in no more than two days, three at the most. My retinue, if you can call it that, is small, and apart from food we're well prepared for the journey. We need to be ahead of the weather, for one thing. More importantly, I know Richard will be on heat to move on to the Holy Land and press his Crusade and," she added hastily "of course, to consummate his marriage there. In any event, I have news that all is not well with my daughter, Johanna, in Sicily, and I need to spend some time with her as soon as we make landfall there. In any event, no doubt Berengaria is afire to begin her new life." She smiled benignly at Berengaria, taking her agreement for granted. Guessing her cause was lost anyway, she nodded reluctantly.

"Excellent, it's done, then. Sancho, we'll leave at first light the day after tomorrow. Berengaria, ensure that everything you'll need is packed by tomorrow, and I will order my men to stow it safely."

Later, she wondered how the days could have passed her by without her noticing it. The only moment that stood out clearly was a final trying on of her wedding gown and her father lifting her hands to his lips, telling her that she was beautiful, a true rose of Navarre.

Eleanor instructed that Berengaria was to ride in the carriage with her. She climbed in obediently, while Eleanor was helped in by two of her knights. Even with the two sturdy men to help her, Eleanor would have lost her footing on the icy ladder and fallen if Berengaria had not thrust out her hand to grab her sleeve. Eleanor grunted her thanks and settled in the corner snugly. Berengaria was grateful for her groti, the traditional

Basque sheepskin coat, thick and warm and soft. The sleeves trailed down to her knuckles, making it easy to tuck her hands inside for warmth. Berengaria's groti had seen many years wear, and was as supple as silk, the bright, oversewn embroidery to the skirts of the coat faded slightly. Sancho had gifted a groti to Eleanor, who pulled the hood so far forward for warmth that Berengaria could not see her face, and her words issued as if from an empty void, making the younger woman shiver. It was too like traveling with a skeleton for comfort.

"Pull the curtains across, child. It's freezing in here."

Berengaria hesitated. With the curtains drawn, there would be no chance for her to look back, to watch Pamplona retreating behind her.

"Mama." She faltered, "I had hoped to wave goodbye to the court and to my father and my aunt, especially."

"Nonsense, child. You should be looking forward, not back."

The carriage moved forward with a jerk and a frozen draught immediately capered into the interior.

"Dear God, this journey will be the death of me." Eleanor moaned. "For heaven's sake, draw the curtains before the good Lord calls me."

Berengaria stood reluctantly and drew the cloth across the gaping windows. Immediately, the carriage became quieter and dark. Eleanor blew out a breath of relief and a few moments later began to snore noisily.

Berengaria hunched into her own corner, trying to adjust her body to the sway and roll of the carriage.

"I'm going to be a queen." She mouthed the words silently, watching to make sure Eleanor really was asleep. "Queen of England. I have no need to weep, for my future is gold."

She pulled Richard's portrait from inside her groti, but in the dim light his features were blurred and unfamiliar. Deprived of her only solace, her tears fell and ran into the sheepskin drawn around her face.

Eleanor slept for most of the day. She awoke in late afternoon, yawned and stretched and shrugged her shoulders.

"Child, stick your head out of the window and ask where we are – if there's a village, or better yet, a monastery anywhere in view."

Dutifully, she asked the nearest out-rider whether there was any sign of shelter, but he shook his head.

"Nothing, ma'am. We topped a rise a few moments back, and I can tell you that this plain extends as far as the eye can see. Perhaps tomorrow there may be a village, but tonight we must make camp as best we can."

Eleanor grunted when Berengaria passed on the message.

"In that case, we stop now and pitch the tents while it is still a little light." She banged on the wall of the carriage with a force that belied her years, and the driver stopped immediately.

Eleanor pushed her hood back and stared at her. In spite of the dim twilight, Berengaria had the uncomfortable feeling that the old woman saw through her as if she was glass.

"You think me cruel, don't you?" She went on before Berengaria could answer. "Of course you do. I've denied you your last full Christmas with your family.

Believe me; it was for your own good. I remember when I was a young bride myself, no more than a child, torn from all I knew to be married to the King of France. It didn't matter that I had been raised to understand that I would make a good match. I was still terrified. I thought – they have made a mistake! They don't know I know nothing, nobody." Berengaria's mouth hung open in disbelief. Was the old queen looking into her mind, reading her thoughts and her fears? "I was driven away in the middle of the night, weeping until I ran out of tears. If I'd been able to see all I was leaving, I think I would have turned and ran and refused to go. You're a good girl, at least you didn't cry too much. Trust me, child, trust me. If I'd granted you a few more days, a final glimpse, your last memories of Navarre would have been clouded by tears and sorrow in parting; as it is, you'll remember only the joyous times."

Berengaria drew in a deep breath. She wished she hadn't; the stale air in the couch was foul, and she queasy.

The bivouac was a good one, cushioned by trees but in an open space that provided ample room for the tents, horses, carts and cooking fires. Eleanor leaned on Berengaria's arm and allowed one of the knights to show them to her tent; she dismissed the man with a nod and beckoned Berengaria inside.

"Thank you, child. You may come in for a moment, but I will have no further need of you tonight." The tent flap opened, and Berengaria glanced up to see a young woman enter, a bowl of water steaming in her hands. "Ah, Isabel, good. You've made yourself useful already, excellent." Eleanor frowned suddenly and both younger women stiffened, responsive immediately at the slightest sign of her displeasure. "Berengaria, I gave you no option to bring your own ladies, did I? No, of course not – you would only have had to abandon them in Sicily. Take Isabel, then. She will do until you can get yourself organized with your own court ladies. She's a servant, not a lady, but she's genteel enough. My own ladies are far too old for you, you wouldn't be happy with them, nor they with you." Berengaria sensed self-justification in her words, but didn't care. Eleanor's ladies terrified her almost as much as Eleanor herself. "Isabel is much your age, I think." She added, and flapped her hands towards the tent entrance. "Go, go, both of you. Isabel, take your lady to her tent and look after her, and on the way send Maria and Amalia to me."

Isabel bowed silently and turned, holding the tent opening ajar for Berengaria. Berengaria gestured to her.

"Go before me, Isabel, if you will and wait by my tent. I'll be with you shortly."

Eleanor pursed her lips in disapproval as Isabel disappeared.

"No need to be polite to her," she said. "I told you, she's not gentle."

"Is she dumb, Mama?" Berengaria wondered. She had not heard the girl speak.

"Dumb? Isabel? Indeed not!" Eleanor cackled. "She's my eyes and ears, and so useful I regret gifting her to you already. She's been my body woman for many years, and understands my needs better than any other. But, youth calls to youth and she will make you as comfortable as it's possible to be on this dreadful journey."

To Berengaria's relief, the next day Eleanor decided she would ride with her ladies. One of the knights helped

Berengaria into the side pannier on her palfrey, and Isabel adjusted her new mistress' skirts carefully, pulling the groti tight across her legs and tucking the sheepskin behind Berengaria's thighs for warmth.

As they moved north, the scenery changed. Berengaria rode with her hood pushed back, staring round her with deep interest. The rolling pine woods and gentle hills of the Basque country had given way to a greener landscape, scattered with great, black cypresses and patches of cultivated fields. She was deeply grateful to be able to see the world going past, rather than being contained in the closed carriage with Eleanor.

The strangers arrived as the knights were pitching camp for the day. They were greeted with bows drawn and ready to fire; hands lying ready on sword hilts. Eleanor's retinue had been warned that bandits roamed the area, and the knights were taking no chances with their precious cargo. To their exasperation, Eleanor poked her head out of the carriage window to see what the commotion was and immediately called out that she was to be helped down.

"My ladies, my lords." The taller and younger of the men paused and made a flourishing bow, cap in hand, the feather in the cap nearly brushing the dusty ground. He beat it against his slashed sleeve before replacing it on his head. "Have no fear of us, for we're nothing more than poor travelers. I'm Jack; I play and sing for my supper," Turning slightly, he indicated the lute strapped to his back. "And my friend Michel, here, will be pleased to cast a horoscope for anybody who desires it done. We ask nothing more, good gentlefolk, than to be allowed to share your food and the warmth of your fires." He smiled winningly and the knights glanced at each other before lowering their guard grudgingly.

"Who is it? Who are these men?" Eleanor's imperious voice carried clearly on the still air.

"Traveling people, ma'am." Sideberry, one of the knights shouted back. "This one says he's a troubadour, that one a fortune teller. The troubadour is English. I think." He added dubiously.

Eleanor clapped her hands with pleasure.

"Excellent. We shall have some amusement tonight, then. Feed them, Sideberry. When we have dined, bring them to me."

Jack was reasonably skilled on his lute. In addition, he had a fine, forceful tenor voice and amused Eleanor mightily with his songs. Berengaria blushed at some of the lyrics, and found it difficult to share the Queen's robust pleasure. Finally bored with the entertainment, Eleanor gestured to the silent Michel to step forward.

"Tell futures, do you?" She demanded abruptly. The man nodded but Jack spoke for him.

"He's dumb, ma'am." He said. "A nasty accident in Castille that resulted in him losing his tongue." Michel smiled, and Berengaria prayed he would not open his mouth.

"And I wonder what sort of accident that was?" Eleanor said archly. Both men grinned. "If he can't speak, how can he cast a fortune?"

"He can write, my lady." Jack said eagerly. "Before his ... accident, he was an educated man. An astrologer, skilled with the astrolabe as well as an adept at telling fortunes by the hand and the bones."

"Indeed?" Eleanor gestured at one of the servants to give the men more wine. Berengaria tried not to listen to Michel slurping from his beaker, but it was difficult not to hear. The dumb man sounded like a large dog drinking from a small bowl. "You're English, Jack?"

"Aye, ma'am. Or at least, I was once. I've been around the world for so long; I doubt any one nation would own to me now. Michel, here, is from Granada. But he speaks – or rather spoke – many languages."

"Do you know who I am?" Eleanor asked curiously.

Jack's eyes slid from side to side as he considered his answer.

"I don't know your name, my lady. But I can see from your great beauty and elegance that you're of high noble birth." He looked at her, grinning, obviously hopeful that he had given the right answer. Eleanor simpered.

"Good. Then your mute friend can cast me an honest fortune. No, not for me, I'm too old. It would be wasted on me." She gestured Michel away. "For her."

Michel took her hand in a firm grip. Berengaria was reluctant to allow him to touch her, but under Eleanor's gaze could not refuse. He examined her right palm closely, tracing the lines back and forth with his finger tip and then beckoning her to show him her other hand. Finally he shook his head and glanced at Jack, holding his finger and thumb together and making writing gestures. Jack nodded.

"He wants to make a written horoscope for her," he explained. "Can you give him the young lady's place and exact time and date of birth?" Eleanor raised her eyebrows at Berengaria and she gave Michel the information. He patted her hand gently before releasing it.

"He'll work through the night, and have the fortune ready for you in the morning, my lady."

Eleanor nodded and yawned widely, not bothering to cover her mouth. She gestured to her hovering ladies to help her to her feet, and took herself off to her tent.

By morning, both of the traveling men had vanished. Sideberry was beside himself with fury.

"They stole away like rats, ma'am." He growled. "Took a full wineskin with them, as well."

Eleanor shrugged, unconcerned.

"A pity. I would have been interested to see the child's fortune." She glanced at Berengaria. "I'm unfortunate with horoscopes. I had Richard's cast when he was a child himself, and the answer came that no good would ever come of him. Absolute rubbish, of course. I daresay yours would have been just as silly. Well, Sideberry, we had better move on."

The stop at a great Cluniac priory was a rare treat. They were welcomed with ceremony, the awed Abbot bowing to Eleanor and welcoming her in to the abbey. She swept in with as much assurance as if she owned it. Eleanor had the Abbot's cell, and she looked around the room with satisfaction, pouring wine for her and Berengaria with a lavish hand.

"The old man does himself well, I think." She said cynically. "I came this way many years ago, when we were on our way to Louis' crusade." The old woman's voice softened with the memory. "So many, many years ago now. You're a lucky child, Berengaria. You'll see things that not many ladies have seen, when you get to the Holy Land. You have no idea how much I envy you."

"I can barely wait, Mama." Berengaria said, truthfully. "I can't wait to see Richard, and I long to see the Holy Land, perhaps even Jerusalem."

"Ah, the names bring back such memories for me!" Eleanor stared into the fire, her face lost in old dreams. "I remember the colours of it all; the smells; the sheer difference of it. It was hot, and dry and dusty. The sun shone on stones so white your eye streamed but I could hardly blink for fear of missing something. I remember bringing back chests of spices – pounds upon pounds of pepper, and cumin, caraway seeds and ginger. Packets of myrrh and frankincense. And the silks, oh the silks! I was the envy of the court. Such colours as we could only dream of – scarlets and yellows and blues in all shades from nearly black to lightest turquoise. And only fancy – so cheap! Barely anything cost more than the tiniest bit of gold."

Berengaria stared at her, puzzled.

"But, the Crusade, Mama? What do you remember about the Crusade? About Jerusalem? You saw the Holy City"

"The fighting, you mean? Oh, Louis took care of all that, of course. I was allowed nowhere near the battles. The whole place stank, I remember. But then, spilled blood and guts always do. And there was a lot of noise. And the Greek fire was a wondrous sight. At least, it was if one was not on the receiving end of it! But the Saracens, Berengaria, them I remember. The Saracens. Such men! Great eyes as dark as Hell, and noses like hawks. Tall, they were, tall and proud and dark. They looked at one as if measuring one's worth with their glance and when they approved of what they saw," She drew a great shuddering breath, as if the memories were of yesterday, not years ago. "Why, then I knew what it was truly like to be a queen. I met with Nur Ad-Din, the greatest lord of them all, and what a man! Not even a Christian, but no matter. Had Louis won, I would have told him to bring the man back with him and put him in a cage so I could have looked on him every day."

She fell silent, and Berengaria sipped her wine quietly before curiosity overcame her, and she prompted Eleanor gently, thinking the old woman had lost track of her words.

"And Jerusalem, Mama? What was the Holy City like?"

"A great city, I suppose. Or as great as any of the so called cities were in the East. I´m sorry child, but it was all so very long ago. It all merges into a memory of heat and colour and smell in my mind, and at this distance in time it´s impossible for me to pick one from the other."

Deeply disappointed, Berengaria nodded and Eleanor was silent for a few minutes. She spoke abruptly.

"The whole world tells me I´m still the most beautiful woman in Christendom. The greatest, most noble queen the world has ever seen. The men still look at me with hungry eyes; the women compare themselves to me, and find they are wanting." Berengaria stared at the old woman in surprise; could she really believe what she was saying? "Would you exchange places with me, Berengaria? Become the queen of the world? Have everybody bend their knee to you? Only say the word, and it shall be yours! In exchange for one thing and one thing only." Eleanor stared at her intently. "One thing – take everything I have, but only give me your youth in exchange!"

"Mama, that I can't do." Berengaria mumbled, embarrassed.

"Do you think I don't know that?" Eleanor tugged fiercely at the loose skin around her neck, stretching the wattles and throwing back her head to force the skin back into shape. She massaged her neck hard. "Oh God, that I should have lived to see this old age come upon me! I tell you, child, I wake in the morning, and every bone in my body aches. I cannot see as I used to; even colours seem to have lost their brightness. I can no longer climb steps with ease; I have to be helped into my bed at night. What use is beauty, what use is greatness, when I can no longer put it to good use? Give me a grandchild, Berengaria; give me a grandchild after my image, so I can see my youth in your child, so I can live again!"

"Mama, I shall do my best." *I will,* she thought fiercely, *oh, God I will.*

"Aye." Eleanor paused, and Berengaria got the impression that she was choosing her words with care. "Berengaria, you must understand, Richard can be … difficult. He's not as lesser men."

"He's the King, Mama." Berengaria said simply. "He could not be as other men."

Eleanor stared at her. Berengaria thought she was going to say more, but she shrugged.

"Leave me child." She said abruptly. "Send Amalia to me, I would go to bed now."

"Mama." Berengaria paused by the door and spoke softly, "May you live a thousand years, Mama, and always be as beautiful as you are today."

Eleanor cackled with laughter.

"Is that a benediction, child, or a curse?"

Berengaria closed the door quietly behind her.

The good Cluniac monks stocked Eleanor's supplies well and added a warning – they would find there was little for them in Lombardy, for the Crusades had ravaged the countryside, taking supplies and peasants alike off to battle these many years past. The countryside had never recovered; the peasants who were left were themselves hungry, and there were no further substantial monasteries for many miles. Eleanor shrugged, uncaring. The peasants must fend for themselves, her expression said. What was it to her?

The landscape itself seemed to echo the forlorn words of the Abbot. For the first time, wolves followed them; long, rangy beasts that slunk after them like hungry shadows. A well aimed arrow from one of the knights caught the lead beast in its ribs and the pack immediately disintegrated in confusion. But Berengaria cringed when she heard their cries, echoing like lost souls.

It was Isabel who noticed the change. She made a noise, and Berengaria turned to look at her, wondering what the matter was. Isabel's head was up. She was sniffing the air like a dog.

"Can't you smell it, ma'am?" Berengaria sniffed, and shrugged. "Listen." Isabel urged.

Berengaria tilted her head, straining her ears. Far off, she could hear something like the sound of drums, beating out of rhythm.

"The sea, ma'am. It's the sea."

She could have sworn that Isabel had tears in her eyes.

Chapter 4

Berengaria leaned against the ship's hull. The deck creaked and moved gently beneath her feet. She knew she was in the way; knew that the sailors were shooting her sideways glances, wishing her below with the rest of the women, but she also knew that they dared not ask her to move. She wished them well in their work, but she was going nowhere. Everything was so rich, so strange, and so very foreign. And apart from that, she could not stand the noisome stench below decks.

 The sailors were different to any men she had seen in Navarre, or throughout France for that matter; they were taller, leaner, darker. Like well-trained hunting dogs, she thought. She watched them, fascinated, as they moved in seeming chaos. Ropes were hauled and stowed in piles as neat as embroidery threads. Baskets and chests and nets were dragged over the bows and packed away as quickly as they arrived. The billowing sails, pulled and tautened by many skilled hands, began to puff out.

The weather was pleasant, almost warm, and Berengaria decided to spend much of the journey on deck rather than in the cabins with their stink of vomit and close-kept bodies. Once the frantic activity of departure eased, the sailors accepted her presence with resigned shrugs. She leaned on the hull, staring up at a sky as blue as the inside of a robin's egg. The sky stretched over her, rounded like a bowl and she wondered, fascinated, why it should appear to curve when everyone knew the earth was flat. A shout from one of the sailors broke her serenity and she blinked about, startled and then abruptly shocked.

Land. One day had merged unbroken in to another, and she had simply lost track of time. Now, she realised that for the first time since they had left the harbour at Brindisi, the horizon held more than the unbroken blue of sea and sky. Land. They were approaching the island of Sicily, at last. Richard was here, waiting for her. She drew a shuddering breath, her stomach clenching in a mix of terror and anticipation.

Suddenly, the deck was once more a bustling city of activity. She was elbowed aside with great gentleness by the sailors, who darted everywhere. Sails were raised, other sails lowered. The hull creaked like an old woman with rheumatism as the boat's direction was turned, water-logged ropes twanging and chains rattling. And all the while, Messina harbour loomed larger and larger until, in no time at all, it dominated her world.

Although no larger than Brindisi, this harbour was a world apart. Every inch of shoreline was with ships; not the innocuous little fishing boats she has seen in Brindisi, seeming to rub together at anchor like friendly cats, but great vessels, decked out ready for war. Ugly ships, wallowing low in the water, ships that were built to inflict pain and, to Berengaria's startled gaze, ships that actually seemed to look forward to war. Other vessels, equally large but lacking armour, she guessed to be supply ships to support their warrior kin. As her own ship approached the harbour, she began to see people, clustering along the landing. Gradually, the crowd grew larger and larger, until she could hear the hum of their voices, rising like the random noise of bees. At the very last moment, a narrow berth appeared between the great warships and their smaller vessel pushed in slowly, dwarfed by the greater ships to each side.

"Sicily, at last." Startled, Berengaria realised Eleanor had appeared by her side. "And where, I wonder, is my dear Richard? Late as usual, I suppose."

Berengaria licked her lips.

"The crowd is so thick, Mama, he could be anywhere." Or nowhere, she thought, her heart sinking in disappointment. After so very long, he wasn't here. Had she ever really thought he would be? In her dreams, at least.

As the boat made its final approach, a great cheer rose from the crowd. At the same moment, it parted abruptly. A cloud of white dust rose from the hill leading down to the harbour and Berengaria saw a troop of horsemen galloping down, the mounted men cheering and yelling, waving their caps in the air like madmen. They thundered towards the harbour and reigned in sharply, making the great war horses rear and snort. Each rider was dressed entirely in white, all but one wearing a blue band of leather around their right thigh. Berengaria felt sick with excitement as the lead rider dismounted, throwing himself casually to the ground and landing with the litheness of an athlete, striding towards the boat and leaping over the prow almost before the ship had touched harbour.

"Mama!" Richard knelt before Eleanor, gathering her hands and raising them to his mouth to kiss the skeletal fingers. "I have prayed for your safety daily, and at last, you are here."

"Richard." Eleanor loosed one hand to stroke his head tenderly. "Can you do nothing quietly? Must it always be show and noise?" Her fond smile betrayed her words.

He grinned boyishly. Berengaria watched, hardly able to breath, her gaze raking Richard from head to toe, taking in his great height and strong body, the red-blond hair and fair skin. Just the same as she remembered. Tall and handsome and every inch a king.

"My son." Eleanor tapped Richard on the shoulder. "Your pleasure at seeing your mother does you nothing but credit. But I think you forget your bride. Berengaria," she beckoned her forward. "Can you do anything with this great fool, this son of mine?"

Richard sprang to his feet immediately and bowed deeply to Berengaria.

"My Queen." He murmured. "My bride." Just as he had with Eleanor, he sank to his knees before Berengaria, but instead of taking her in his arms, to her disappointment he gathered the hem of her skirt in his hand and raised it to his lips, kissing it repeatedly. "I'm at your feet. At your command."

The crowd yelled their approval. The white knights shouted again and again, setting their mounts prancing. Berengaria's murmured reply was lost in the noise.

Richard threw back his head and laughed loudly. Ignoring the frantic activity of the sailors, intent on making the ship secure, he stood and scooped Berengaria into his arms and jumped onto the shore with no apparent effort, landing as lightly as a cat. Once on land and greatly to her relief for she was hanging on to him for grim death, he set her down carefully and beckoned to one of the white-clad knights.

"Take great care of my lady, Rafe." He commanded. "See she is safely taken to the fort. I will follow with the Queen."

Mounted on a docile mare, Berengaria was led through the crowd by the knight, who forced his way through before her on his huge warhorse. The beast showed its great yellow teeth in a snarl of fury at those foolish enough to come close but still the crowd jostled around her, hands reaching out to touch her, their strange English voices sounding pleasant enough, although after the sweet sea air, Berengaria found the stench of so many unwashed bodies hard to take. She was deeply relieved to reach the fort.

The knight helped her dismount with a delicacy of touch that surprised her.

"Ma' am." He bowed deeply. "I'm Richard's man, and now your most obedient servant. Only ask, and if it's in my power it will happen."

"Thank you." She swayed slightly, confused that the ground appeared to be rocking under her feet in exactly the same way as the ship's deck had done. "Please, take me to my lodgings and bring my servant to me when she arrives. I need nothing else."

He offered his arm, and she leaned on it, grateful for the support.

"It's the sea.". He explained. "It gets into your legs in some way, and for a while your body thinks it's still on water. Were you sea sick?"

"No, not at all. I enjoyed the voyage."

The tall knight had an easy and pleasant manner. Berengaria found him agreeable and was almost reluctant to part with his company when he bowed her into her apartment. To be alone after being surrounded by constant company left her fidgety. She sank on to the prie-dieu, but her mind was whirling, and prayer was the last thing on her mind.

"Richard." She whispered. "Richard. My king. My husband."

The great hall of the fort was smaller than she had expected, but even so the walk to the high table took all her courage to manage. Every head turned to watch her progress and the movement of the men as they rose and bowed seemed to her to be like wind rustling through a field of ripe corn.

She took her place at Richard's left hand. Eleanor was already seated at his right, with a younger woman at

63

her side. Berengaria knew immediately that this must be Eleanor's daughter, Johanna. Eleanor had talked about her repeatedly on the journey through France and Spain, but even without that, she would have known that this woman was Richard's sister. She was the feminine reflection of her brother, her features softer but still every inch the proud Plantagenet. She made Berengaria nervous as Johanna stared at her with frank curiosity. Berengaria tried a smile, but Johanna shrugged and turned to speak to Eleanor.

Remembering Eleanor's warning that Richard had no time for picky eaters, Berengaria tried as much of the food as she could force down. Richard ate heartily, and drank more heartily still, as did Eleanor, but Johanna, Berengaria noticed, ate in slivers but sipped constantly at the strong, sweet wine. She peeked round at Berengaria from time to time but said nothing to her directly, instead chattering away happily to Richard, who responded with laughter and shared jokes, obviously born of a lifetime's acquaintance. In the midst of the throng, Berengaria felt intensely lonely.

"Berengaria, do you care to dance?" Richard stood, abruptly towering over his bride.

Immediately on cue, the musicians struck up and Richard led her on to the floor. After the first dance, Richard gestured for the rest of the company to join in and smilingly passed Berengaria's hand to one of his knights, who had hovered eagerly, waiting for his chance. Richard danced with Eleanor and Johanna, and then took his place at the table in the midst of his womenfolk.

"My God, mother," Richard smiled widely, speaking between clenched teeth. "What have you condemned me to? What happened to the little, slim fish you promised me? This is no bride to bring to my bed. She's fat and old and her skin is mud."

"Only think, brother "Johanna interrupted eagerly. "Those child bearing hips will give you a tribe of children, and with breasts like that, she can suckle twins with no problem!"

Eleanor smiled and bowed her head graciously, as if Johanna had amused her. She spoke quietly, but her voice was acid.

"Peace, my children. Richard, I think perhaps you're blind suddenly. Or is it that you've taken too much wine? Berengaria was little more than a child when you saw her last, now she's a woman, and a lovely woman at that."

"She's fat." Richard muttered sulkily.

"She isn't fat." Eleanor hissed, her smile unmoved. "She has a beautiful figure – look at that tiny waist. And she's deliciously pretty, with those great eyes and that wonderful hair. Her skin is gold, not dun. And just look at her neck, so gracile, so elegant."

"Aye, Mama." Johanna interrupted, almost hiccoughing with suppressed laughter. "But I fear my dear brother must take care. If he were to get into one of his tempers and put his hands around her neck, he might find a corpse in his bed rather than a bride!"

Richard roared with amusement.

"Johanna, I think you're jealous of my bride!" He teased. "As Mama says, she has in abundance the curves that you lack." Johanna pouted, and Richard was immediately apologetic. "Sweet sister, you know that if only you were not my sister, then I would have eyes for none other. Mama, it's no good you railing at me. I like my women slender as boys, and that's all there is to it. I suppose I'll manage somehow, but God help me! I know not how."

"Aye?" Eleanor nodded towards the dancers. "Don't you find it odd that all of your knights who are men, rather than women in men's clothing, are dancing such eager attendance on her?"

"Ah, Mama." Johanna interrupted gleefully. "Don't you know it's fashionable for the men to show their feminine side? It's all part of this new fashion for courtly love."

"Courtly love, my arse." Eleanor muttered robustly. "In my day, men were men and when they made love to you, you damn well knew about it."

Richard ignored both women. Frowning, he stared down his nose towards Berengaria, dancing lightly on the arm of one of the courtiers. The music ended as he watched, and immediately another knight stepped forward, begging for her hand.

"Of course they're queuing for her attention." He said doubtfully. "She's my bride; it would be disgracefully impolite for them not to pretend they find her beautiful."

"They do seem to be falling over their own feet to dance with her, brother." Johanna teased. "And I suppose she is very graceful."

Berengaria laughed at a remark from her partner, and the man bent to kiss her hand. Richard erupted in fury.

"How dare they? How dare she flirt like this? In front of me, as well." He sprang to his feet and Berengaria found her partner thrust aside by Richard. "My dear. You have danced long enough with my men, now I claim what is mine."

In spite of his words, Richard was bored quickly, and he led her from the dance floor and handed her back to her chair. Berengaria caught a flash of movement at his feet and craned her neck, expecting to see one of the hunting dogs that haunted the hall, hoping for scraps of food. Surprised, she realized that the figure was actually a young boy, sitting cross-legged at Richard's feet. Richard dropped his hand and fondled the child's hair.

"My troubadour." He murmured. "Shall you sing for me, dear one? Shall you play for your lord?"

The boy rubbed against Richard's legs with insolent familiarity, and reached behind him to produce a lute. He cradled the belly of the instrument in his lap and began to pick out a gentle, melancholy tune.

Richard hummed along for a second or two, and then began to sing, his deep tenor soaring above the lute. The boy joined in immediately, his much higher voice wandering above Richard's own. Berengaria swallowed the lump of jealousy in her throat and forced a smile.

Johanna spoke to Berengaria directly for the first time, her lip curled in disdain.

"His name's Blondin. Meaching little toad." She whispered. "I can't stand him, but Richard dotes on him. Lord knows why."

Their song at an end, Richard reached across the table and selected a sweetmeat, which he held out to the boy teasingly, inches from his lips. The boy made no attempt to grab for the sweet with his hands, but instead leaned forward, puckering his lips in a coquettish kiss. Richard roared with laughter and pushed the sweet between the boy's lips.

"Toad." Johanna said between tight lips. "He plays the child, but he's been around the court for so long any innocence he might ever have possessed was misplaced long ago."

Both women glared at Blondin, united in their dislike of the musician.

Berengaria's unease at the play with the young troubadour quickly evaporated as Richard slapped the boy's legs and sent him away. The child went sullenly, with many a backward glance, but Richard had already turned to talk to Johanna and ignored him.

Eleanor broke up the gathering shortly afterwards, obviously tired of the men's rowdy jokes and laughter. Johanna rose with her, glancing pointedly at Berengaria who followed them quickly out of the hall.

The ever present Isabel helped her into her nightgown. She sat up in bed, weary but on edge. She pleated the sheet between her fingers repeatedly.

"Blow out the candles and go to your cot, Isabel. Don't worry about me."

Both women paused, heads up like startled cats, at the growing sudden noise outside the apartment. Feet shuffled on bare flags; masculine voices hushed each other drunkenly; a cough, a laugh, quickly stifled. Silence, and then a tap on the door, repeated quickly and louder when there was no an immediate response. Isabel rose, and then hesitated, glancing at Berengaria for guidance. The door swung open before either woman could move or speak.

"My bride!" Richard was framed in the doorway, a wide grin stretching his lips, his hands clutching each side of the arched entrance, as if he needed the support of the stone. Behind him, Berengaria saw wraiths of figures as his companions fled. "My wife! My ... What the hell is she doing here? Out!"

Isabel ran, ducking under Richard's arm as he turned and aimed a kick at her fleeing backside. The movement almost threw him off balance and he grunted in anger.

"My love, why do you keep that Jewish bitch at your heels? Eleanor dotes on her as well, I can't understand it. Get rid of her, I beg of you." Recovering his temper, he smiled fondly. "Never mind – we'll have no unpleasantness tonight. Tonight, all will be joy as I welcome my queen." He walked carefully toward her bed. Berengaria watched him uncertainly, torn between delight that he was there and wondering how much, exactly, he had had to drink at dinner. And after.

"My lord," she whispered shyly, her eyes downcast.

The rope keeping the mattress tight creaked under Richard's weight as he sat heavily on the side of the bed.

"Do you have everything you need? Have I forgotten anything?"

He jumped to his feet, startling her, and began to prowl about the apartment. The sturdy oak table and a chair got in his way, but he seemed not to notice, heaving the chair aside with his thigh and banging off the table. A hot wind from the unglazed window stirred the candle flames and in the flickering light his face seemed demonic; his eyes glinting red, pouches beneath his eyes appearing as smudges of black. Even his beard glinted like fire.

He wheeled in mid stride and turned back to her, looming over the bed, staring down at her intently. Even though he towered over her, Berengaria could feel the puff of his breath on her face. And smell the wine, heavy on his breath.

She licked her lips, searching for the right words, but was spared the need to answer as Richard spoke again, not bothering to wait for her answer.

"There's nothing – there can be nothing. I've made the fort fit for a queen, just to welcome you. Dedicated twenty-four of my bravest, most noble knights to your service. All sworn to guard you, to care for you, to die for you if need be. What more could any woman ask?" He paused, staring at her as if she had spoken. Thrust his chin out aggressively. "Well, is there anything else?"

"Sire, I ask for nothing. Nothing except for my king."

Berengaria whispered the words. If Richard heard her, he made no sign. She had the disturbing feeling that, although he was looking straight at her, he was not actually seeing her.

"I have everything I need." She spoke louder than she had intended, and cringed at her own shrill voice. Dear God, he would think she was nothing but a fishwife! Anxiously, she smiled to soften her words.

"You do not know what I have done for you, my wife." Richard swayed, grabbing the bed hangings to steady himself. He wagged his finger in her face for emphasis. "You do not know how I have humiliated myself for you. Me! The greatest king in Christendom. But it was necessary. My soul must be without stain, my conscience shriven, before we marry."

She shook her head, bewildered. Richard lost his grip on the hangings and slumped beside her, slithering from the bed to the floor and sprawling in an untidy heap on the rushes. Raising himself on one elbow he leaned on the mattress, peering intently into her face. Miserably, she realized that he was drunk. Probably too drunk to even realize what he was talking about.

"I will show you! You'll see what I have endured for you!"

He jerked backwards and tore at the lacings on his tunic, ripping the cloth in his haste. Berengaria gasped and put her hand in front of her mouth. She stayed still, rigid with nerves, certain that whatever she said or did would be wrong. He finally succeeded in tugging the tunic open and yanking it down from his shoulders. Abruptly, he turned his back on her, twisting from the waist and turning his head to watch her reaction.

"See!" He hissed. "See what I've done for you! Would any man, man I say! Man, not king! Would any man do more?"

Her mind spinning, she leaned forward tentatively, ready to spring back if Richard made any move. He grunted encouragement, so she peered carefully at his exposed back. His skin was white like the breast of an egret, strung with faint pink lines, as if he had scratched angrily at a particularly irritating itch.

"You see?" He panted eagerly. "You see how I've suffered for you? Suffered to redeem my sins? For I'm deep in sin."

"Yea, though your sins be as scarlet, they shall be as white as snow; though they be red like crimson, they shall be as wool." Berengaria recited softly.

"Aye." Richard threw his head back, eyes bulging. "White! Aye, white as snow! For I have been shriven and my sins forgiven. I – the King of England – I stood penitent and barefoot in the great doorway of the cathedral in Messina and confessed my wickedness and begged the Bishop scourge me for my sins. He whipped away my sins, everybody saw. I'm purged, purged of any hint of earthly wickedness."

Shaking, Berengaria stretched out and traced one of the pink lines tenderly with the very tip of her finger. Richard grunted and flinched; terrified that she had hurt him, she immediately snatched her hand away.

"Nay, nay, my dove." Richard grabbed her wrist in a painful grip, forcing his back against her nails. "I deserve to have pain inflicted upon me. It's the only way I can find forgiveness." He writhed against her touch, grinding his skin against her palm, her nails. She stared at him in mute horror, thinking how strange it was that a trick of the light could cause his open mouth and wide eyes to appear as if he was in the grip of ecstasy, rather than remorse.

"Scratch me! Use your nails to scourge me as the whip scourged our Lord!" She ran her nails down his back and Richard howled. "Ah, white! Yea, my sins shall be white!"

He drew a shuddering breath that Berengaria felt under her hand and was suddenly still. A drool of saliva hung from the corner of his mouth, speckling his fair beard like a pearl. Suddenly, his eyes focused on her.

"My beloved." He whispered hoarsely. "Shall I come to you now? Would you welcome me into your bed? Shall I truly be your husband?"

She shuddered with excitement; excitement that was tinged with fear. Richard reached out and caressed her neck. The pads of his fingers were very rough against her skin, rough and oddly arousing. Her mouth opened and closed, but nothing came between her lips but a deep sigh.

"Ah, do I frighten you?" Richard´s eyes gleamed; in spite of her terror, she knew instinctively that the idea aroused him. "I do, don´t I? Well, we shall soon put your fears to rest."

He slid fully on to the bed, shucking off the remains of his tunic. Lay down beside her in his breeches and smiled.

Berengaria could feel her heart thumping, so hard that she thought her ribs must be vibrating with its pounding. The noise filled her head.

"My love. Have no fears. Tonight is the first of many. I shall do my best to make you happy. To be a good husband to you."

He spoke so earnestly that she managed a smile, and his response was instant. The hand that had caressed her neck slid onto her breast; made a fist so tight that she yelped in pain.

"Please." She whispered, not even sure herself if she was asking him to stop, or squeeze even tighter. She trembled, shuddering as if she had a fever.

"Please? Oh, yes. I will be pleased. I promise you."

Even in her turmoil she wondered at his choice of words. He would be pleased? Did that mean that he wasn't pleased with her already? And then sheer fear pushed everything thought out of her head.

"Tell me what to do." She whispered. "I don't know. I don't know anything." She added pitifully.

Richard chuckled. He didn't answer, but guided her hand down his belly, thrusting it briskly into his breeches. He took his own hand away and simply waited. After a moment, when she did nothing but leave her hand where he had put it, he cleared his throat and bucked his hips at her.

"Take hold, dear." He seemed to feel that was explanation enough. Utterly bewildered, she groped about and her delving fingers encountered something that made Richard gasp. With pleasure, she hoped.

"That's it. Just.... just wrap your fingers around him, and rub."

Him? Richard kept something in his breeches that was alive? She risked a glance down, and suddenly was so relieved she almost laughed aloud. *That.* That was what all the fuss was about? Biting her lip, she began to move her hand slowly, desperately trying to remember the last – the only – time she had seen a man's private parts before. Or rather, not a man's, but a boy's.

Cousin Paco had mooched into the solar one hot, overcast afternoon when the castle had been largely asleep. She and Blanche had welcomed him as a diversion. He prowled about, restless, finally standing in front of both girls, grinning at them.

"Want to see something I've got that you haven't?"

"You're a liar, Paco." Blanche retorted. "What have you got that we haven't?"

"This." Paco said simply, pulling his erect cock out of his breeches so quickly, he must have had it all planned. Both girls looked at it with interest.

"Oh." Berengaria reached out and gave it a tug, more to see if it would come loose than anything. Paco's reaction took her by surprise. He moaned loudly and thrust his hips at her, much as Richard was doing now. "What is it?"

"It's my carajo." He muttered.

Both girls looked at each other, and back at Paco. He was sweating, his face bright red.

"What does it do?" Blanche asked.

"Give it another pull or two, and you'll find out."

Berengaria pulled a face. Paco's carajo hadn't felt very nice at all; it was rubbery and hot and moist, all at the same time.

"If you like it that much, you do it." She said firmly.

So Paco did. For fully five minutes, he stood in front of the girls sliding his hand up and down his cock, while they watched at first fascinated and then bored.

"What's it supposed to do?" Blanche asked eventually. To their surprise, Paco – who must have been all of twelve at the time – burst into tears, his cock shrinking so rapidly it slid out of his grip.

"You did that!" He shouted. "You're not supposed to laugh at it."

But laugh both girls did, even after he had run out of the solar, slamming the door behind him. They talked endlessly about it, and eventually Berengaria decided they should ask Aunt Constanzia what Paco's toy actually was.

Berengaria was sure Constanzia was trying not to laugh when they told her what Paco had shown them.

"He did that, did he? I think I had better ask Sancho to have a word with him."

"Yes." Blanche said patiently. "But what was it, Aunt? Do all boys have one of those? Why haven't we got one?"

Costanzia's face was suddenly serious.

"Well, girls. Yes, all men have one of those. It's what makes babies."

Both girls' jaws dropped. No! But Constanzia was nodding her head.

"You see, the man puts that inside your private parts and after a while it spits white milk into you. That white milk has the seeds for babies in it. Once the seeds are planted inside you, they grow into a baby."

Berengaria thought about this, and then shook her head.

"Paco´s didn´t do anything at all." She protested.

"It will when he gets a bit older." Constanzia said firmly.

The sisters talked about it endlessly, wondering why Paco had been so keen to show them when it didn´t do anything. At the time, Berengaria had been full of questions – prime amongst them if it was nice, this business of making babies – but she had been far too shy to dare go back and ask.

Now, looking at Richard´s flushed face, she guessed that it must be a pleasant thing. For the man, at least.

"Harder." He snapped. His carajo was much bigger than Paco´s, she thought, and blushed richly as she wondered what it would feel like if – when – it was inside her. The idea made her glow, and a tiny flare of pleasure began to take the place of panic.

Richard juddered and her hand slipped; losing her prize, she flirted about in his breeches, desperate not to upset him. Finding flesh again, she gave it a really good squeeze in her relief. Richard moaned loudly, and at the same moment she realized whatever was actually nestled in her hand was not his carajo, and nothing like it. Frantic and bewildered in almost equal measure, she pressed the strange, slippery eggs of flesh again, and was surprised when whatever was under the baggy skin seemed to move to one side. Had Paco had these? She had certainly never notice them.

"Again." Richard's voice was hoarse, although with pleasure or pain she had no idea. She took a firm grip on this strange baggage, tugging and twisting them in her fingers.

Richard shrieked, almost like a woman, and then bucked against her.

Berengaria could not let go, his body was bent almost double over her waist, trapping her hand firmly in his groin. Then his movement slowed and stopped and abruptly he was standing, firmly pulling her hand away. She watched his face for some signal, and was deeply relieved when she realized he appeared to be happy.

"Forgive me." He cleared his throat and smiled down at her. "I was overwhelmed by the intensity of my feelings." He held his hands open and then bowed before grabbing for his tunic and shrugging it on. His voice was muffled as he pulled it over his head. "My love, I withdraw. Sleep well."

He lifted her hand to his lips and kissed her bunched fingers tenderly.

The draught from the closing door blew the final candles out, and Berengaria was left in darkness. She lay on her back, her hand caressing the warmth in the bed where Richard had lain. A fleeting thought troubled her; and she frowned; was this normal? Was this how all men behaved before their wedding? But she pushed the anxiety away with a shrug. This was the King. Hadn't Eleanor said she mustn't expect him to be as other men? Of course not, what was she thinking of?

In any event, he had seemed pleased with her fumbling efforts, and that was all that mattered. It would have been nice if she had found any pleasure in it, but perhaps it would be different when they did the thing that made babies.

She hoped so.

Chapter 5

"Mama, this is nonsense. Am I King everywhere except in my own family? Do my wishes count for nothing? First you tell me I must marry Berengaria in a disgraceful hurry. I agreed to that, but now you say we can't marry here so she can go back to England with you, but instead I have to take her to the Holy Land with me, and marry her there! I'm not doing that, it's too much to ask!" He wiped his hands over his face, and shook his head. "Anyway, she can't travel with me without a duenna – it would be scandalous! Her reputation would be ruined; I might as well have married Alice. You must see that. In any event," he added sulkily, "It just won't do. It's notoriously unlucky for women to travel on board a warship, everybody knows that. The men wouldn't stand for it. I'd have a mutiny on my hands before we even reached the Holy Land."

Eleanor set her lips tightly.

"My son, how many times must I tell you? It's Lent. It's no one's fault that our journey took much longer than I expected, but the truth of the matter is that neither you nor anybody else can wed in Lent, no clergyman would do it. Not even the Bishop, and not even for you. You can't wait for another thirty days before you sail, I understand that – you must catch the spring tides, or wait here for another three months. But I'm telling you, I can't wait for another – how long? One year? Two years? More? Before I see you wed and a grandchild in the cradle." She drew a deep breath, tears glittering in her eyes. "I'm an old woman, my son." Her voice wavered suddenly and she clutched her hands in front of her breasts, as if to contain pain. "Grant me this, my son. It may well be the last thing I ever ask of you."

"Mama." Richard sank to his knees and grabbed her hands, holding them against his own breast. "Mama, that's nonsense. You're not old. You could never be old. I would do anything for you, but this thing isn't within my power. Leaving everything else aside, Berengaria can't travel without a duenna, you know that. None of your ladies would make the journey. Perhaps you could, but the Holy Father is expecting you in Rome. It's impossible, you must see that."

"No, my son. Berengaria has a duenna. Johanna will accompany her."

"Johanna?" Richard's chin sagged foolishly. "Johanna's to go to the Holy Land on Crusade? But I thought she was going to Rome, with you, to petition the Pope."

"So she was." Eleanor picked at a thread on her gown, avoiding his eyes. "But now you have sorted out that wretch Tancred, and won back the treasures Johanna's husband left for her in Sicily all her troubles are over and there's no need at all for her to ask the Holy Father to intercede for her. She's got everything she lost when her William died - thanks to you, my dear son - and Berengaria could have no better duenna. They're much of an age and Johanna's a queen in her own right. She's longing to see the Holy Land. She still wants to go to Rome, that's true, but there's no urgency now. It can wait. It's an excellent solution to the problem."

"So now I have two women on board my ship, not one! I tell you Mama, the men will not have it, it's knocking on the Devil's door and asking him in."

"Superstitious rubbish. Anyway, Berengaria and Johanna will not travel on your ship with you – that wouldn't be proper at all. And far too dangerous. They'll travel apart from you; one of the supply ships will be more comfortable for them. If you like, you can leave one of the Blue Knights to look after them. And this business of women bringing ill luck on board ship is pure nonsense – I travelled with Louis to Jerusalem, and I certainly didn't bring him any bad luck. Quite the opposite."

"Apart from the fact that his Crusade was lost." Richard pointed out tartly. "Very well, Mama, I'll do this – for you. For you alone."

Eleanor patted her son tenderly on the shoulder.

"Not for me, but for the sake of my grandson, my love." She said gently. "Never forget that."

Johanna chattered non-stop. Everything her eyes saw, she commented on. Berengaria nodded and smiled;

relieved she need do no more. The great supply ship was comfortable – far more so than the little vessel that had brought them from Italy across the Straits of Messina to Sicily – and the two ladies had their own cabin. Rafe, the Blue Knight who had escorted her to the fort at Messina, had been assigned to look after them.

"You two must have so much in common." Johanna commented. "Rafe, doesn't your family come from somewhere in one of the Spanish countries?"

Berengaria stared hungrily at him.

"Is that so? Your family is Spanish?" She asked, hopefully.

"No, ma'am." He smiled. "My grandparents came into Gascony from Valencia, long before my parents were born. The only thing that is Valencian about me is my name – Rafael de Valencia."

"Oh, sweet Christ." Johanna said abruptly. "Forget it. We're moving, already. Oh. The motion of the sea. I had forgotten how much I hated it. Oh, God. I must lie down, before I die."

Glancing at Johanna's green face, Rafe excused himself hurriedly.

Good sailor though she was, even Berengaria soon found the rough seas difficult. The ship pitched suddenly and violently so that she could hardly stand, and there was no chance to go on deck. After the first day, the sailors lashed down their hatch to keep out the waves from going below, and the only light in the women's cabin was the grey glow that filtered between the ill-fitting planks in the hull.

Although at first she could not believe that the storm could get worse, the rock and sway of the ship soon became increasingly vicious. Johanna wept, muttering prayers and curses in turn, glaring at Berengaria as though the weather was her fault. Rafe – his face tight with worry – helped the women to tie themselves into their beds.

"How close is Richard's ship?" Johanna whimpered. "Hasn't he sent a message to ask after us? Doesn't he realize how wicked this is for me? Can't he change course, get us away from this storm?"

"Mistress." Rafe stared down at the deck, avoiding Johanna's eyes as he hung tight to the hull to keep himself upright. "Mistress, I'm afraid that we've lost sight of the rest of the fleet." Johanna shrieked, pushing her fists against her mouth. "The storm has scattered them. The supply vessels left harbour last, as they're heavier and slower than the fighting ships. Our vessel is the heaviest and slowest of all, so we've drifted away from the rest."

"We're going to die!" Johanna screamed. "We're going to drown, aren't we? It's all her fault." She pointed an accusing finger at Berengaria. "If it hadn't been for her, I'd have been on my way to Rome by now. If Mama Hadn't insisted I had to look after her, I would have been safe on dry land. Oh, Mama, how could you do this to me! As if it wasn't bad enough when William died and left me at the mercy of that wretch Tancred. Now this! What have I done to deserve it?"

Johanna screamed again as the boat shuddered and tipped suddenly, throwing Rafe to the floor. His head banged hard against the oak bulwark, blood spurting from his scalp immediately. He sprawled where he had fallen, the movement of the ship rolling his body like a child's toy.

"He's dead!" Johanna pointed at him. "Now Rafe's dead, as dead as my poor, dear husband. He's dead and it's all your fault, Berengaria. Oh God, what's Richard going to say?"

"If we are all going to die anyway, what does it matter?" Berengaria snapped tartly. Johanna stared at her and then burst into tears, mucous running from her nose to mingle with her tears and drip from her chin.

"You are a cruel, unfeeling woman." She choked. "If God spares us, I'll tell Richard what kind of woman he's taken for a bride."

Isabel, summoned back into the berth at Berengaria's shout, took in the scene at once. Not bothering to try and keep her balance, she slid to the floor, crawling on all fours towards Rafe.

Berengaria saw Isabel's lips move, but could hear nothing for the storm. Isabel flung her hands to the deck to stop herself landing on top of Rafe, and screamed out loud as her wrist bent backwards painfully. Nearly mad with fear, Berengaria tore at the knots that held her down and was thrown to the floor to skid on the stinking bilge water that washed the deck. Good luck slid her across and jammed her between Rafe and the hull, shielding him from further harm. Blood flowed freely from his scalp wound and splattered across her neck and throat. Isabel stumbled across and grabbed Rafe's arm, pushing against his chest to stop both him and Berengaria coming to further harm. Johanna howled non stop, her voice rising even above the din of the storm.

"He's dead. He's dead. Don't bother about him, Berengaria, He's dead."

"He isn't dead. Dead men don't bleed." Berengaria shouted.

"He is. He's dead and we're all going to die." Johanna screamed, and for the first time, Berengaria believed her. "I'm going to join William before my time, I know I am!"

The ship rolled, righted, rolled again. The two women clutched Rafe's limp body as the terrible sound of the screams of grown men, shrill over the storm, came clearly below deck.

"Help us, Lord. Help us." Berengaria whispered. Johanna screamed again and again and again. Ignoring her Berengaria jerked her head towards Isabel, mouthing words that were inaudible in the din. Isabel nodded her understanding and dragging Rafe with them, the two women sidled crab-like across the deck. The ship's violent motion pitched all three of them to the floor, sending them crashing helplessly towards Johanna, still laced into her berth.

"Never mind him! Help me!" Johanna shrieked, leaning down and grabbing Berengaria by the hair. Caught between the dead weight of Rafe and Johanna's mad woman's grasp, Berengaria took a deep breath and leaned against her hair, using Johanna's grip to right herself and somehow lugged both herself and Rafe on to the berth. Isabel heaved his legs up and, ignoring Johanna's never ending protest of shouts and moans, Berengaria wrapped her arms tightly around all three of them, and closed her eyes, praying for the strength to hang on.

Above them, the crew howled and screamed, bellowing oaths and swearing in English, the language unknown to Berengaria but the meaning only too clear. Johanna wept and moaned and wept again. Rafe breathed loudly through his open mouth, his wound still sheeting blood.

The storm died away quite suddenly. One moment, it seemed, the wind and water competed to wreak the greatest havoc, the next it was relatively quiet.

"Thank God. Thank God. Thank God." Johanna muttered. "We're going to live. Thank God."

Berengaria started to answer her, but her words were lost as the ship screamed as if in pain. The deck rose up, bashing their feet against the hull and then terrifyingly suddenly there was no movement at all. No sound other than the sea slashing at the battered ship. Berengaria trembled, suddenly more frightened than she had been even at the height of the storm.

She exchanged a glance with Isabel, who shook her head in obvious puzzlement. Even Johanna was silenced as they heard a sound that was like somebody tearing a cooked chicken apart, only much, much louder.

"We're moving again." Berengaria said softly.

Only this time, the movement of the ship was odd. It no longer whirled and pitched, but seemed almost sedate, as if it was a dog taken for a walk on the end of a leash.

In the relative silence, the sound of the ropes that had secured the hatch being hacked apart by axes seemed unnaturally loud.

"Oh, thank God." Johanna whimpered. "We're saved. Richard's come for us. At last, my dearest brother. At last. I knew he wouldn't leave me. I knew."

"Hush." Berengaria tried to say, but her mouth was so dry the word emerged as a single, hissing syllable. She stared upwards as the hatch creaked and groaned and was thrown aside. The sudden light was blinding and the women closed their eyes in pain.

"My ladies." The voice spoke Frankish, but with such a thick accent it was difficult to make out the words. "Isaac Kommenos, King of Cyprus, at your service."

Berengaria shielded her eyes with her hand and peered through her fingers. A man's head was silhouetted in the open hold, but other than that he was very dark skinned, with black hair beneath a velvet cap, she could make out nothing of him. She was about to speak when Johanna kicked her ankle and she turned the words into a cough.

"Where in Cyprus are we?" Johanna demanded. Berengaria stared at her in surprise; she had spoken rudely to the man who had called himself King of Cyprus.

"Limassol harbor, madam. You have been unlucky. Three of the ships in your fleet were wrecked in my harbor. The men who were saved are now my guests, shall we say? You are anchored well off shore; you were lucky not to be wrecked yourself." He smiled winningly. "Your captain tells me you are desperate for fresh water. I think myself the best thing is for you both to come ashore, and join me in comfort in my palace. You can wait for King Richard there."

"You know who we are?" Berengaria asked.

The man sniggered. A nasty sound, as though he was laughing through a mouthful of mud.

"The bride of a King, and the sister and widow of a King. Which is which, I neither know nor care, but I will be honoured to have you as my guests until the great Richard arrives. Will you come ashore, ladies? He coaxed. "My palace is at your disposal."

"No." Johanna spoke firmly, and Berengaria stared at her in amazement. "We'll stay here, all of us, until Richard arrives. Which I hope will be soon."

"As you will." Kommenos shrugged. "The ship's safe at anchor. I would tow you in, but I have to admit I have no ship large enough to do the job. But just to ensure your safety, I will leave a few soldiers on board with you."

His head withdrew like a tortoise retreating into its shell. As soon as she was sure he was gone, Berengaria turned to Johanna, questions tumbling from her lips.

"What was so bad about going to his palace?" She demanded. "If he already has some of our sailors there, why is it a problem? Surely, it would be better than waiting here? Poor Rafe needs some attention, if nothing else."

Johanna pulled a face.

"Listen to me. I know him. Or at least, I know about him. Calls himself king, but he's not. He was just a provincial governor, until he staged a coup and took control. That was when I was still in Sicily. We heard all about it, at the time. The man's a bandit, pure and simple. Once he got us secure on land, he would put us in a dungeon and leave us to rot, until Richard got here to ransom us. Or worse. And he certainly wouldn't worry about Rafe. Trust me, Berengaria, we're better off here."

"Oh." She blinked. A tug on her skirt made her glance down. "Dear God, Rafe. Isabel – can you help him? Is," She paused, dreading to say the unthinkable, "Is he going to die?"

"No ma'am, he's not going to die. Not if I can help it. If you could hold him in place for a few moments, I'll bring my things through."

A sharp blade made short work of Rafe's black hair, leaving a furrow of inflamed scalp an inch wide across his scalp. Isabel threaded a needle with a length of thread and looked appealingly at Berengaria.

"Ma'am, I can't sew the wound and hold the flesh together at the same time. Can you pinch his skin together for me?"

Berengaria carefully put her fingers on each side of the gaping wound, shuddering as she pulled Rafe's skin together. Isabel sewed quickly, probing the wound gently as she worked, feeling cautiously for splintered bone and finding none. Finished, she applied a sticky yellow salve to the entire length of the wound, rubbing it in firmly. Rafe moaned in his sleep.

"Oh, my poor, beautiful Rafe!" Johanna groaned. "What have they done to you?"

"Saved his life, I hope." Berengaria pushed her hair back, wilting in the heat.

After a couple of days, it began to seem to Berengaria that she had always lived in the fetid hold; that the past she thought that she remembered was nothing more than a dream, likewise that there was no future. Perhaps she had died in the storm, and this was purgatory; the idea appeared to make perfect sense. She tried to whisper a prayer, but her lips were too sore to frame the words.

The captain advised them to stay below; he didn't trust the soldiers left to guard them. He doled out water and food as if both were precious, and hungry and thirsty all three of the women finally gave in to sleep.

Berengaria slept uneasily, dreaming she was in a strange country. A green and pleasant place, where all the men looked like Richard and all the women like Johanna.

Strangely, try as she might to get their attention, none of them seemed to see her. Still sleepy, she was grateful to be shaken awake by Johanna from the disturbing dream.

"Berengaria! Wake up, for God's sake! There's fighting. Close by. Listen, will you!"

"Who is it?" She mumbled, still groggy.

"Richard, my dearest brother. It must be him. He's come for us, at last! Isabel, shout, damn you! Shout, and let them know where we are or Kommenos's men will get to us first and kill us and hide our bodies so they can get away with it. Shout, woman, shout!"

Confused, Berengaria muttered,

"Why would he kill us now?"

"Because if he doesn't, Richard will kill him, I tell you! His only chance is to kill us all, and get rid of our bodies."

Johanna shrieked piercingly. A man – so bloodied it was impossible to even see his features – tumbled backwards over the hatch and crashed to the ground. Rafe struggled to rise, but was held back by Isabel. Berengaria opened her mouth to speak, and was surprised to find she was screaming instead, although the noise seemed small over the terrible commotion on deck. The women huddled together; arms around each other and sheltering Rafe with their bodies, and did what women have done since the beginning of time – waited.

Arrows fell into the hold every few seconds. Now and then, the light was blotted out by men struggling together. Johanna sobbed, but her tears went unnoticed. Slowly, the sound of the fighting changed and it was possible to make out individual voices, roaring and cursing and screaming in pain. A rough wooden ladder nosed into the hatch, caught, twisted, was withdrawn and pushed forward again. Johanna's tears hitched in her chest as the women waited to see who the victor was. Berengaria's lips moved in a soundless prayer as she spoke Richard's name, over and over and over again, willing him to be the winner.

A body moved to climb down the ladder, but was grabbed by the shoulder and roughly thrown aside. A man hooked his foot over the hatch cover and placed his feet on both side of the ladder; sliding down. Reaching the bottom, he swung round and all three women screamed in terror. Tall, broad and covered in blood and dirt, the figure swung a two-headed battle axe in its right hand, the haft matted with hair and flesh. A sword hung half out of its scabbard at his waist, the blade caught in its own leather bindings. A dagger appeared to be protruding from his right shoulder, but when he moved it fell free from where it had caught in his tunic.

Rafe was the first to find his voice.

"Sire." He croaked, raising himself on his elbow. "I've failed you. I'm so sorry."

His balance lost, he fell to the floor at Richard's feet.

Richard stared at him, moved his gaze to the women, and then looked down again at Rafe. Stooping, he traced his finger along the length of the terrible wound in his skull.

"Sweet Christ." He hissed, "Someone will pay for this, and dearly."

He shouted angrily, and within moments Berengaria and Johanna were hoisted out of the hold in makeshift panniers. Rafe was hauled out, unconscious again, strapped to a wooden pallet. Isabel clambered up the hold via Richard's ladder, as anxious to get away from Richard as she was to follow Berengaria.

The rest of the fleet assembled in the harbor at Limassol. Richard smiled as he counted in his lost lambs. Glorying in his victory, he beamed at Berengaria.

"All's well that ends well, eh? If that stupid bastard Kommenos hadn't made the mistake of trying to keep you and Johanna prisoner, then we would never have taken Cyprus. Now, I have the best staging post in the whole of the Mediterranean. My fleet can stop here at will to take on supplies. We have a refuge with an excellent harbour. Could hardly be better."

And me, she thought? *What about me, my husband? And Johanna? Aren't we even worth you asking whether we're alright? Whether we suffered at that man's hands?* She shook her head slightly, trying to dislodge the thoughts.

"What will you with Kommenos, then?" She said quickly, annoyed at the way her voice wavered. "Let him pay to retain his throne? Wouldn't that be dangerous?"

Richard laughed, spluttering wine on his tunic. He wiped it away impatiently with his fist.

"Isaac Kommenos has been at pains to tell me how poor his country is, how he only dared to take my ship because he was in dire need of any treasure it contained. His country can't afford a ransom, he says. If he had only known that all of Johanna's silver plate was in the hold, he would no longer have been so poor! Although I'm beginning to think Johanna's treasure is cursed – first Tancred poached it off her, and now Kommenos has narrowly missed the opportunity to do the same." He snorted. "Perhaps I should keep it safe myself; no doubt once away from Johanna, it will no longer be unlucky."

"What will you do with Kommenos?" Berengaria repeated. *He kept me prisoner, remember? Me and your sister both. Don't you care?*

"No idea. At present, he is in one of his own dungeons, loaded with chains. His daughter is with him. I may behead them both for the effrontery they showed to you and Johanna, and the injury they inflicted on my poor Rafael. Show these islanders what kind of man their new king is."

Just for a heartbeat, Berengaria thought, *good. Serve him right.* Then pulled herself up in shock. *Dear God, I've been close to Johanna for too long. I'm beginning to think like her! And Kommenos has a daughter? What has that poor innocent, little thing ever done to deserve this?*

"Richard, why not spare him? Them, I mean? Nobody would expect it, not even from a great king like you. But it would be such a merciful gesture. You could say you had done it for me, given their lives to me as a wedding present. The whole world would be in awe of your mercy."

Richard stroked his beard thoughtfully.

"You think so? You don't think it would appear as weakness on my part?"

"Never. If Kommenos can't be ransomed, then he's of no use to you. Send him into exile and let it be known that you acted out of the great bounty of your heart, gave him his life as God spared Abraham's son."

"As God, eh?" Richard smiled, obviously pleased. "We'll have him up here, I think. Him and his wretched daughter. See what he has to say for himself when he's in front of you and Johanna. If he's properly penitent, I might spare him."

All the nobles of the Crusade fleet crowded into Richard's hall for the show. Playing to his audience,

Richard pretended to be interested in no more than his game of dice with Philip of France, postponing the moment to glance at Kommenos until he had thrown and lost.

Kommenos made a miserable figure, shackled wrist to ankle, as he hobbled in. Johanna glared at him, trembling with rage.

"The bastard!" She hissed to Berengaria. "Look at him! Weighted down with chains and he still has the cheek to smile. If he's not worth a king's ransom, then Richard should behead him. Show the world he takes no nonsense from the likes of this worm."

Berengaria shook her head and watched Richard carefully. He seemed amused by Kommenos's defiance and leaned towards Philip to whisper something close to his ear. Both men laughed at the shared joke and she relaxed a little, whispering a silent prayer. *Please God; I do not want the death of this man on my conscience. Please God, let Richard be merciful.*

Both kings continued with their game, ignoring the prisoner. Richard bellowed with laughter as he won the pot back from Philip.

"I shall win it back," Philip said with supreme indifference. "You don't have the patience to make a successful gambler, my Richard." He nodded towards Kommenos. "So my old friend – what do we do with this one? Shall I keep him – send him back to France to play at being my court jester? My fool? Hey, Kommenos? Would you be happy to continue your existing role in a different court?"

The assembled nobles sniggered at the witticism. Kommenos drew a deep breath and tried to stand upright but was stopped by the heavy chains. Berengaria saw that his wrists had already been rubbed sore by the manacles.

"I would rather die." He spat.

"Fine." Richard waved a languid hand. "He's made his choice. Take him out and behead him. Him and his daughter both."

"My lord," Kommenos flicked his head up. "Me, yes. My life is yours to do with as you wish. But not my daughter. She is but an innocent child, a lamb of God. She's my only child. You would not kill a child, sire."

"Normally, no. But in your case I would be happy to make an exception."

Philip sniggered, rolling the dice idly in their cup.

"Why not bring this lamb for us to have a look at, Richard?" He suggested. "If she's presentable, which I very much doubt, looking at her father, we could perhaps make something of her." He smiled slyly. "If she takes after her sire, then she could make a half way decent scullery maid, with a bit of training."

"As you wish." Richard said indifferently. "Bring her up, let's get it over with. I become bored by the whole thing. Throw the dice, Philip, I want to take as much money as I can off you, before we separate his head from his shoulders. What do you think to a small wager on how many strokes it will take to do it?"

"Richard!" Berengaria reproved. Richard pouted, glancing at Philip and shrugging his shoulders as if to say; *the ladies. What can one do?*

"You have a tender heart, Berengaria." Philip smiled. "It does you great credit. But you must remember, Cyprus has great strategic importance. But whilst ever their King – and his daughter – live, then there's always the danger of a revolt, an attempt to return his line to the throne."

"I understand that," Berengaria said urgently. "But to consider killing an innocent child…..!"

She broke off as the nobles craned their heads to watch the progress of Kommenos's daughter through the court. Several of the knights stood on tiptoe, leaning against the great trestle tables the better to see. Bundled up in an old, grey cloak that was many times too big for her, she made a tiny, pathetic figure.

The gaoler who had escorted her came to a halt in front of the high table and bowed clumsily. Irrelevantly, Berengaria noticed that his leather jerkin creaked with the movement.

"Prisoner, my lord." He said briskly.

Richard glanced up from his dice and waved his hand lazily.

"Unwrap the parcel, then, man." He called, to shouts of laughter from the nobles. "Can't see a thing in that awful old cloak. It could be a monkey in there for all I know. Probably is, if she takes after her father."

The gaoler promptly reached out with fingers like sausages to tug at the ties holding the cloak in place.

Once the knots were undone, he peeled the cloak away and folded it into a bundle beneath his arm.

"Prisoner, my lord." He repeated.

Kommenos's daughter stared round wildly before focusing on Richard. She ignored everybody else and immediately sank to her knees before him, manacled arms held up pitifully, tears running down her face. She tried to speak but her voice choked with sobs and she fell forward full length to the stone floor, lying shuddering and mute at Richard's feet.

Richard paused in mid throw and then abruptly threw the dice cup to Philip.

"Here, Philip, take care of those for a minute. I want to have a better look at her."

He vaulted athletically over the trestle, clearing goblets and food alike, to the murmured applause of the nobles. Falling to his knees, he raised the terrified girl to her feet; standing, she barely reached his shoulders. He peered into her face and then patted her body up and down and up as if he were searching for broken bones. The girl wept soundlessly, her mouth wide open in terror.

Berengaria rose and walked quickly around the table towards them, her heart wrung with pity.

"Oh, God." Johanna put her head in her hands. "He's taken one of his fancies to the child. God help us all."

"I believe he has." Philip agreed. His face was stony, but his voice shook. Johanna glanced at him sharply, wondering if he was angry or if some other strong emotion was making him shudder.

Richard shouted sharply to the gaoler to remove the girl's shackles, at once. The man pulled a chisel and small mallet from his greasy leather belt and, as Richard held the iron away from her wrists and then her ankles, hammered away the bolts that held the heavy cuffs in place.

Phillip leaned forward and spoke quietly into Johanna's ear.

"Your new sister is not only a beautiful woman, but I think she is also an angel of mercy. She is very innocent, is she not?"

"That she is. As innocent as a newly hatched chick. Give her her due, I thought she had the way of managing Richard, but I wasn't expecting this." Johanna responded grimly, watching Richard kissing the raw flesh on the child's wrists. "Do something, Philip. Distract him."

"Too late, I think." Philip frowned. "If Richard is really taken with that wretched child, he's going to be diverted until he gets tired of her, and God knows how long that will take. We must move now. Much longer and Saladin will have all his defences in place and the spring storms will spit in our faces. I think, Johanna that it's past time Richard and Berengaria were wed. The quicker the better." He groaned as Berengaria put her arms around the child, trying to comfort her. The girl immediately wriggled free and turned back to Richard, burying her face against his chest. "At once, in fact."

"You surprise me, Philip." Johanna said acidly. "I would have thought Richard wed to Berengaria was the last thing you would have wished. Apart from anything else, weren't you insisting that your half-sister had been wronged by all the gossip, and was still a spotless virgin?"

Philip grinned wryly and shrugged. He drew his finger through a puddle of wine on the trestle and avoided her glance.

"Aye, but needs must, my dear Johanna. Between the two of us, Alice was a damned fool. She made her bed, and must lie in it, quite literally in her case. I have found a very minor nobleman who is willing to turn a blind eye to her past, in exchange for a handsome dowry. In any event, the Crusade must move, and your dear brother must get him an heir. I cannot face the thought of dealing with John as king. Richard must be distracted from this scrap of nonsense. For all our sakes."

"You'll speak to him, then?" Johanna said anxiously. "He'll listen to you, if nobody else. Lent is nearly finished, there's no reason why the marriage couldn't take place here on Cyprus, and soon. Once wed, Berengaria and I could sail for Rome to meet Mama, leaving you men to fight your battles in peace. And you would have dear Richard all to yourself again." She added casually.

"I will speak to him. Richard," he called, "How is the child? Do we take her head off, or what?"

"Take her head off? What on earth are you talking about? She's wonderful. Just look at her, Philip. That combination of blonde hair and black eyebrows –

irresistible! How old are you, dear?" Richard enquired tenderly. The girl spoke into his chest. "I think she said ten. Is she ten?" He asked Kommenos, who shrugged and bowed his head in response. "My God, if she looks like this when she's filthy from the dungeon, what will she look like cleaned up? Berengaria, isn't she delicious?"

Berengaria nodded, bewildered but grateful for Richard's change of mind, and mood.

"She's very pretty, Richard. But she's also terrified. Come child." She held out her arms enticingly, but instead of moving towards her, the girl burrowed against Richard as if he was her only hope on earth. Which, Berengaria conceded to herself, he probably was.

"She likes me." Richard said triumphantly. "Sweet child, what is your name?"

"Agnes, my lord." The girl whispered breathily.

"Agnes? Ah. Never one of my favourite saints, that. And an ugly name as well. No, it will not do." Richard thought for a moment and then his face brightened. "From this day on, your name shall be Angela, for you are truly angelic."

Philip drew a deep breath.

"I shall speak to him tonight Johanna." He promised. "The wedding will be arranged for Sunday, and it will take place on Sunday, I promise you."

Chapter 6

Berengaria's thoughts wandered to Angela. She should, she knew, feel sorry for the poor child, but there was something so *knowing* about her. Something that troubled her instinctively. She could not put her finger on it, but Angela, she thought tartly, was trouble, pure and simple. She realised suddenly that the girl reminded her strongly of Carmen, and the thought made her hiss in annoyance.

The knock at the door shook her out of her reverie. Isabel backed in clumsily, tugging the rope handle of a large wooden chest that trundled behind her like a large dog. Straightening, Isabel gestured at the water-stained and paint-peeling chest, her face working with distress.

"Ma'am," she wailed. "I'm sorry, I'm so very sorry".

Confused, Berengaria shook her head.

"Isabel, what is it? What's happened?"

For answer, Isabel stooped and threw back the lid on the chest. She snatched back wafer thin layers of cedar wood, stained and corrupted with sea water, and held up a shapeless, grey garment, cruelly patterned with salt and stiff with water damage. Berengaria shrugged.

"The sea water got into some of our clothes, then? It's not so great a problem is it? We must have some left, and if not, we shall borrow something that fits from Kommenos's ladies."

Isabel shook her head, a huge tear trickling down her cheek.

"Mistress, you could never borrow, beg or steal anything like this, anywhere. It's your wedding gown, your beautiful, beautiful wedding gown. All of the other trunks have taken some damage from the storm, but nothing like this, nothing as bad."

Horrified, Berengaria stretched out a trembling hand to touch the ruined gown. Gold thread and seed pearls nubbed under her fingers and she rubbed the cloth gently, willing Isabel to be wrong even when she knew the truth in her heart. Taking the dress in her arms, she held it against herself. The water damage had corrupted the very shape of the gown; one shoulder hung below her elbow, the waist was beneath her breasts. Instead of the rustling cream silk that had looked so wonderful against her olive skin, the cloth looked like an old grey rag, fit for nothing more than washing the floor.

"No." She whispered, "Oh, no. Isabel – there's nothing good that hasn't been ruined? Nothing?"

"A few plain gowns, ma'am. Nothing – nothing at all – that a lady, never mind a queen, could wear to be wed in."

Berengaria's eyes swam with tears. Vaguely, she heard a man's voice in the open doorway but ignored it, her only thought that she must see Richard. He could do nothing, she knew, but her heart ached for his comfort, for a kiss from him to help make the hurt go away. She pushed past Isabel and brushed aside the man who blocked her way, groping blindly down the corridor that led from her apartment to Richard's – once Kommenos's – quarters. Behind her, she heard Rafe's bewildered voice and was thankful that Isabel would deal with him.

Richard's door was firmly closed with two of the Blue Knights standing guard outside, one in front of each of the massive cedar door posts. Both knights sank to their knee as she approached.

"The King is here?" She demanded. The men glanced at each other. One licked his lips and cleared his throat noisily before replying.

"Your Majesty, the King is in his apartments, but we have been given strict instructions that he isn´t to be disturbed on any account."

"I think you forget, sir," Berengaria drew herself upright and took a deep breath to steady her voice, "I think you forget, I am the Queen."

Both men hesitated, but Berengaria had had enough. She stepped between them and rapped smartly on the door. When there was no response, she knocked harder.

"Who the devil is that? Have the Saracens invaded?" Richard sounded furious. "I said I was to remain undisturbed. I will have your lights out for this, you men!"

Berengaria made shooing motions with her hands and the two knights scuttled away quickly. She twisted the great iron ring on the door and stepped inside Richard's apartments, expecting to find him deep in conference over the coming campaign. She stopped short just inside the doorway, an apology dying unspoken on her lips.

Richard was seated in front of one of the narrow arrow slits, a lute on his lap, his right hand plucking lazily at the strings. A shaft of sunlight lit his blond hair and fell across his white tunic. For a fraction of a second, Berengaria thought he was alone then as her glance followed the line of light down Richard's body she saw Angela curled at his feet, seated on a low stool. The girl's head was resting on his knee, her flaxen curls draped across his hand, his fingers wound possessively into her hair. As Berengaria stared, she chose a honeyed apricot from a silver bowl at her side and popped it languidly into her mouth, licking her fingers afterwards lazily, as if she had all the time in the world. She smiled and Berengaria felt jealousy punch her guts. For a second, she had no idea whether she hated Angela or Richard most. She shook with fury, and was astonished at the strength of the emotion.

"Agnes. I mean Angela." Her voice lashed like a whip. "You will leave us. I wish to speak to my husband."

The girl pouted and turned her head into Richard's leg, her curls falling forward to hide her face entirely.

"Angela." Berengaria snapped. "Out. Now." She jabbed her finger out of the room. Angela shook her hair back and turned a sulky face towards Richard. He hurriedly untwined his fingers from her hair and pushed her away. But gently.

"Angela, my dear. You must remember, you are no longer a princess." She pouted, the scowl darkening her pretty face, "And you must learn to obey the Queen, as well as you do me."

Angela scrambled to her feet and strolled towards Berengaria, lingering only long enough to look her up and down insolently. Berengaria put her hand in the small of the girl's back and shoved her out of the room, closing the door firmly behind her.

As she turned, Richard walked briskly to the great oak table, where he turned over densely written parchments and maps as if he had a sudden urgency to find a particular document.

"My dear Berengaria, such an unexpected pleasure." Realising the unfortunate choice of words, he flushed an ugly red. "Poor Angela was really quite distressed – I was trying to comfort the poor child. But never mind her – what can I do for you, my dear one? What brings you to me with such secrets that can't be shared with our new sister?"

"Richard. Sunday." He frowned absently, toying with a gorgeously coloured map. Mermaids decorated the four corners of the parchment, and the prevailing wind direction was indicated by a cherub blowing a kiss of air. "Sunday." Berengaria repeated. "Sunday, Sunday, Sunday! Our wedding day."

He looked hurt.

"Of course, my dove. No need to remind me. Is there some problem with the arrangements? Surely not. Philip assured me that he would take care of every detail. Not every bride is fortunate enough to marry one king, and have another prepare the wedding for her, you know!"

He smiled, already sure of himself again.

"The problem is, Richard, that we can't marry on Sunday. I must have more time." Her voice shook.

Richard's smile faded slowly as her words sank in. He shook his head, frowning.

"More time? How now, wife? Are you nervous, dearest?" He brightened as the thought occurred to him. "No need to worry, it will be a wonderful marriage." Berengaria shook her head. "What then? Have your courses started unexpectedly? No need to worry about that. I've seen enough spilled blood on the battlefield. A little more isn't going to worry me."

He grinned. Berengaria flinched at the crudeness of his words, wondering if she had imagined hearing pleasure in his voice. She held her hands out to him, begging him to understand.

"I have nothing to wear!" She almost shouted. "My wedding gown – the sea water got into the trunk and it is ruined, totally ruined. A milk maid wouldn't wear it to clean out the cowshed!"

"You have nothing to wear?" He repeated slowly. "You've been rescued from obscurity to marry me, your wedding has been arranged by the King of France, you were brought to me by the greatest Queen in the whole of Christendom, and you dare stand before me and say we can't wed because you have nothing to wear! Have you run mad, woman?"

His face had flushed a dark, ugly red and she could see he was trembling with anger. For a second, she thought he was going to actually strike her, then his fingers balled into fists and he planted them on the table and leaned towards her. So close that spittle sprayed her face as he shouted.

"Hear me, Berengaria. I've had enough of this nonsense. We marry on Sunday or not at all. We marry on Sunday or you can go back to Navarre, with your tail between your legs. I have my choice of any princess in Christendom; all I need do is to click my fingers," He did just that, holding his hand aloft with a flourish, "And I can take my pick. Wed in what you are standing up in now, wed me stark naked – it doesn't matter a damn to me."

Sick with distress, she somehow found the strength to stand up to his fury.

"It does matter, Richard." She spoke strongly, refusing to look away from him. "It may not matter to you, but it matters to me. I can´t marry you in a second-hand gown, in somebody else's cast off."

"Do as you like." He shrugged, his mood changing abruptly. "Marry me in that gown; marry me in your nightgown for all I care. All eyes will be on me, anyway, I don´t know why you're so bothered – nobody is going to notice you, you know. Or don´t marry me at all, it´s up to you. You´ve upset me, Berengaria. I have one of my terrible headaches now, because of your nonsense. As you go out, ask one of the knights to send for my surgeon for me. I will be leeched, that always makes me feel better."

He turned his back on her and slouched across to slump in his chair, fingers pressed across his eyes. She watched him for long seconds, waiting for him to say something more.

Tears – of pain or anger, she had no idea which - spilled down her cheeks and she walked to the door blindly. She would not let him see her cry, no matter what. She groped for the latch without seeing. It snicked suddenly and she almost fell out of the door. A hand caught her arm, steadying her; pulling the door closed behind her.

"He wants his surgeon. Please see to it." She spoke quickly, her head turned aside to hide the tears.

"My lady." She gestured with her hand – leave me alone – but the man was at her side, his hand beneath her elbow, his pace matching her shorter stride. "My lady, wait. What is it? You're upset, what's happened?"

She stuttered for breath, tears sliding down her cheeks.

"Go away. Leave me alone."

"No. I can't leave you like this."

His voice was gentle, caring. She wiped her face on her sleeve and peered blearily up at him.

"Rafe. I thought you were one of the knights who were on guard when I went in. I'm sorry I was so abrupt."

"Richard is in a bad mood?" He said bleakly. She nodded, and shrugged helplessly. Voices came from the end of the corridor and he slipped her hand quickly in the crook of his arm. "Walk with me. The garden's warm and very pleasant, and I think it will be quiet at this time of day."

She allowed herself to be led outside. He steered her to a carved stone bench, shaded by a rose arbour, and fussed around until she was comfortable.

"What happened to the men who were on duty outside Richard's apartments?" She asked, distracted. "He wants his surgeon - he says he needs bleeding."

"The men made themselves scarce. I bumped into them biting their nails with fear. That's how I knew where you were. I'll arrange for his surgeon to visit him. Trust me, a good bloodletting followed by some stinking concoction to make him feel he's been given medicine, and he'll be happy." She set her teeth, frowning at the thought that a surgeon could mend Richard's mood so easily. "I came to find you to thank you for saving my life – ironic when it was me who was supposed to save you. I would have come to you much sooner, but the damn surgeons wouldn't let me use my own two legs until today." He slipped to his knees before her, raising the hem of her gown to his lips. "My lady, I was your servant before – now I'm your slave."

Berengaria bit her lip, cut cruelly by the contrast between Rafe's sweet words and Richard's indifference.

"You have Isabel to thank more than me." She said wearily. "If she hadn't tended to your wounds then it would have been very bad for you."

"I have already thanked Isabel." He rose and sat beside her, smiling. "She's an excellent surgeon, better than those imps of Satan who've kept me prisoner in my own bed for so long." He paused. "Isabel told me about your wedding gown. It's totally ruined, isn't it? You must be so disappointed."

"Disappointed? Aye, you could say so. I went to tell Richard. I went to explain to him that we must postpone the wedding, that I couldn't be married in a rag, and he raved at me. Told me that we would be wed on Sunday, or I could go back to Navarre." Once started, she couldn't stop and words came in a flood. "I thought he was in conference about the campaign, but only Angela was there with him, cuddled up to him like some little harlot he'd picked up in a back street. And her gown, her gown! It was embroidered all over with little rosebuds, it was beautiful. I would have been wed in that gown happily. But Richard didn't care – he said I could be wed in my nightgown, it didn't matter. I wanted him to say it didn't matter if I was married in a dish clout, because it was me and …. and I was who he wanted. But he didn't say that, he didn't mean it like that at all."

She stared into space, choking back sobs.

"He didn't mean it, I promise you." He said gently. "He was angry, that's all, and ashamed you caught him with Angela. When he's angry, he says things he doesn't mean. As soon as he gets over his temper, he'll be sorry, you'll see. That's just the way he is."

"And what about Angela?" She said stiffly.

Rafael waved his hand contemptuously.

"He has a fancy for her. She came to him as a damsel in distress. In his own mind; he thinks he's rescued her. It never crosses his mind that the only danger she was in was from him. It will pass. He'll get tired of her fawning on him, soon enough."

"Will it? You didn't see how he was with her. The way she was cuddled up to him. It made me feel sick. I'm beginning to think that I would be better to accept Richard's invitation, and return to Navarre." She laughed bitterly. "Life as an old maid in a nunnery might be preferable to this humiliation from my own husband."

"No." He took her hand and held it to his lips, kissing the tips of her fingers. "You were born to be a queen, not a nun. And queen you shall be. You´ll be married to Richard on Sunday, I promise you. And not in your nightgown, either." He stood and in spite of the warmth of the sun, she was cold without him next to her. "Please, wait here for a few minutes. I´m going to find Angela." She frowned and shook her head. "I know, but I have a use for her. Wait for me, please."

He walked off briskly.

Angela was sitting in the great hall, feeding scraps from the table to a small dog lying on its back on her lap. Rafael guessed that the dog had been her pet before Richard's arrival, and had now been restored to its mistress. It appeared as spoiled as she was. Angela brightened as Rafael approached.

"Has Richard sent for me?"

She made to stand, but Rafael sat on the bench beside her, pressing her down with a hand on her shoulder.

"He has not." She pouted. "It's the Queen who has need of your services."

"Her?" Angela sniggered. "What does she want me for? Doesn't she know that Richard likes me better than her, or is she blind?" Rafael stared at her in blank amazement, unable to believe her smug self-confidence. "He does." Angela persisted. "He calls me his little blonde angel, and says he wishes it was me he was marrying, not that old woman. I bet he's never so much as kissed her, but he touches me." She smiled slyly and leaned towards him. "Do you want to know where he touches me?" She whispered breathily.

"Thank you, no." He said quickly. Curious, he asked, "Angela, what do you think you're going to gain from Richard? If you're lucky, he may take you as his leman, for as long as the fancy lasts. But what will you do when he tires of you? You'll be ruined; no decent man will look twice at you, the King's off cast."

Her face darkened with childish fury.

"You don't know what you're talking about." She spat. "He says she's old and fat. He doesn't want her – he wants me. Me! He'll be lucky if he gets an heir off her – she's too old. I'm young, and prettier than she is, and he likes blonde women. I tell you, he can't keep his hands off me. He's not married to her yet, he could put her aside and marry me, instead. I'm just as royal as she is."

Rafael shook his head in disbelief.

"You're a fool, Angela. Once he's had you once or twice, he'll be tired of you. I've seen it a hundred times. And as for you being as suitable a bride as Berengaria – don't deceive yourself. You're the daughter of an obscure usurper who's not even a king anymore. And in any event, you're only a child! How old are you? Ten?"

"Thirteen. Nearly fourteen." Angela's lower lip jutted sulkily. "I told Richard I was ten, because I thought it would make him feel sorry for me. But thirteen is well old enough to be wed. Many girls of my age are married, or at least betrothed."

"Ten or thirteen, it doesn't matter. Listen to me, you little idiot. Berengaria is the daughter of Sancho of Navarre, Richard's ally. Her father has sent men and money to support the Crusade, he's key to Richard. England needs Navarre as an ally. They will marry on

Sunday and you'll help, like it or not. If you don't help, I shall tell the king that the rumour is that your private parts are so well used that you drip black bile from them – see how much he wants to touch you then!"

Angela bared her teeth in a snarl and bent to tweak the dog's tail savagely, taking her fury out on her pet. Rafael stared, fascinated, at the crown of her head. Parted in the centre, her hair showed a black strip, startling against the pure blonde. He licked his finger and rubbed at her parting, wondering if the black would rub off. It did not. Good humour restored at his interest, Angela tossed her head and simpered, widening her eyes. Her lashes, he noticed, were as black as her eyebrows.

"Fooled you, didn't I? I was blonde when I was very small, but as I got older it went black, like everybody else. I hated it – I wanted to be fair. You think I'm stupid, but I'm not. I thought about it, and thought about it until I had an answer. I took a hat – the kind the peasants wear made of plaited straw with a hard, wide brim – and knocked the crown out. I put the brim on as if I was wearing the full hat, and then pulled my hair over the top. I poured lemon juice on it, and then went and sat in the sun, oh, for hours! I was very clever – the hat stopped my face from darkening, but the lemon juice lightened my hair beautifully. All I need to do now is put some more on when it grows out a little, sit in the sun and I'm blonde again! See? Beautiful, isn't it?"

"You amaze me, Angela." Rafael said honestly. "You are very clever. Clever enough to realise where your future lies. Richard will marry my Lady Berengaria, come what may. You may distract him for a while, but she'll be his wife. And you could be one of her ladies in waiting. Come now," he coaxed "Would that be so bad? You'll be taken to the English court; you'll mingle with the greatest in the land, in any land. As a princess in your own right, it's entirely likely that you'll make an excellent marriage. But you must help us, now."

Angela nibbled her lower lip, assessing her chances. Finally she made her mind up and smiled sweetly.

"What would you have me do?"

Rafael told her quickly, and she stared at him in amazement.

"Is that all? I thought it would be something difficult. They'll be here this afternoon. There's a sewing room here in the fort; it should be full of materials. She shall have her gown, I promise you. Just as long as it's not prettier than anything I have."

The seamstresses crowded around Berengaria. Angela sat on a comfortable chair, the dog asleep with its head on her foot. She translated briskly, but without interest. The ruined gown lay on the long table; from time to time, the seamstresses walked across to it, to finger the material or try to tug it into shape. Failing, they shook their heads in shared disappointment.

"They say it must have been a beautiful gown." Angela said, "They think the embroidery's exquisite."

"Can they make me a wedding gown by Sunday?" Berengaria asked dully. She turned to order, held out her arms dutifully, but felt able to take little more interest in the proceedings than Angela was displaying. A sudden sense of déjà vu made her turn her head sharply, certain that she had heard Aunt Constanzia and Carmen squabbling, somewhere close by. Her thoughts were far away, back in the palace at Navarre when she had had such radiant hopes for the future as she was measured for the ruined gown. How, she wondered sadly, had such joy turned to despair? She sighed heavily, remembering her father's gentle rebuke when, as a child, she had nagged for something – "If wishes were horses, then beggars would ride."

Angela stared at her, obviously surprised.

"By Sunday? Of course they can." She said rudely. "It won't have as much fine embroidery as the first one, but it will be beautiful. They know what will happen to them if it isn't." The head seamstress sat back on her heels and said something; Angela frowned as she translated. "She says it's a pleasure to sew for someone with your figure, that every eye will be on you on Sunday, and that you'll be lovely. Do you want cream or white silk? She advises the cream, as it will have some gold thread embroidery around the neckline, and that will show better. She also says it will be more flattering to your complexion. Do you want me to have her whipped for impudence?" Berengaria hardly heard her as her spirits began to lift.

"Cream." She said, and Angela translated quickly.

"Cream it is, then. And pearls sewn into your veil, with gold thread around the hem."

The woman reached into her apron pocket and produced what looked like a handful of small sausages, tightly wrapped in dull thread. She said something in rapid Greek and Berengaria raised her eyebrows at Angela, waiting for the translation.

Angela tutted impatiently.

"Silkworms." She explained. "This woman makes the best silk on the whole of Cyprus. When the little beasts are nearly ready, she carries them about with her so the warmth of her body ripens them, or something. It's a great secret how she gets the silk from them, only a few women on the whole island know how to do it, and none of them will tell. The secret came out of China, they say, and they reckon that if the Chinamen find out that their secret is lost, then they'll all be murdered in their beds. She's not very bright, but she is a good seamstress and she says her very best silk will go into your gown, and you'll be pleased with it."

Berengaria was stiff by the time the women had finished their measuring and snipping. Angela drifted away as soon as she could, the dog snuffling at her heels. Isabel helped her back into a borrowed dress. At the door, Berengaria turned to smile her thanks at the seamstresses and raised her eyebrows as she saw Isabel tucking a thin strip of silk into her bodice. Pretending she had not seen, she turned away, wondering. She caught up with Angela quickly.

"Angela, do you have wishing trees here?"

"Wishing trees?" Angela stared at her, clearly bewildered. Berengaria explained.

"Special trees where maidens can tie cloth, to wish for a husband. Widows for another beau."

"Oh." Her face cleared. "You mean a Joshua Tree. Of course – but people don't just wish for a husband on a Joshua Tree, they tie their tokens in hopes for prosperity, or a good harvest, or a release from disease. We have a very fine cedar tree just outside the palace gardens that people have wished on for years. Why? Do want to see it, to make a hope for the future?"

"No. I don't need it." She said with more confidence than she felt. "I just wondered."

She allowed Angela to drift off, the girl's interest immediately switching to the yapping dog. Berengaria returned to her apartment, her thoughts wondering.

"What's the matter with your face?" Johanna greeted her. "I thought Rafe had got the wedding gown all sorted. Something else gone wrong?"

"No, not at all. The seamstresses assure me the dress will be ready. I think Angela has put the fear of hell into them if it isn't."

Johanna giggled. "Oh, the girl has got her uses, then?" She said slyly.

"Aye." Berengaria agreed. "It appears so."

She moved to the trestle and sat, her elbows on the smooth, cool wood, as she let Johanna's chatter wash over her. Her heart went out to Isabel; instinctively, she knew that the silk from her own wedding gown was destined for the Joshua Tree. Had Isabel got herself a beau, then? She shook her head slightly in disbelief at the thought. Taking it as a response to an unheard question, Johanna rambled on happily. How could Isabel have met somebody worthy of a wish and a prayer? The girl was between a rock and a hard place; she could hardly marry a servant, but neither was she noble – none of the knights would look twice at her, pretty and gentle mannered as she was. She could, perhaps, receive an offer of sorts, but it would not be better than an invitation to be some nobleman's leman and surely she would not even think of accepting that. Poor Isabel! I will think of something, Berengaria decided suddenly, I will find someone for you, Isabel. Some sturdy merchant with a good living who will make you the best of husbands, or perhaps – if Richard could be persuaded to change his views – even an ambitious younger son of some very minor noble from the provinces, desperate to do anything to court the royal favour.

"I said, what about your ears?" Johanna repeated.

"My ears?" Rudely distracted from her thoughts, Berengaria blinked at her, sure she must have misheard.

"Your ears." Johanna said again. "They need piercing. You should have had them done years ago."

"I did." Berengaria protested. "I had them pierced when I was a child, but they bled and hurt when I tried to wear earrings, so I didn't bother and they healed up again."

"We'll soon see about that." Johanna advanced and placed a firm hand on her shoulder. "Your earlobes are very long, you know. Perfect for earrings."

"Most women from Navarre have long earlobes" She said defensively. Are you trying to tell me I have big ears?"

"Not at all." Johanna said soothingly. "Now just sit quiet, this won't hurt a bit."

Berengaria screwed up her face as Johanna raised her other hand with a fine flourish, revealing the fat bodkin and cork she had concealed in her palm.

Richard was in fine mood at supper. Noticing her red, sore ear lobes he clucked solicitously, offering to send his surgeon to attend to her. He patted her hand fondly, kissing her fingers and comparing them to the buds of a white rose. Angela was seated far from the top table, flirting ostentatiously with one of the Blue Knights. Bewildered by the change in him, still Berengaria could not help her spirit rising in response.

"You are better, Richard?" She enquired carefully, sure that an interest in his health would be happily received.

"Surely." He nodded seriously. "I was leeched thoroughly. I felt a little tired afterwards, but it was worth it. I'm choleric by nature, and my blood sometimes contains ill humours that are best treated by letting a little out. And is all well with your gown, my dear?" He enquired with apparently genuine interest. "Rafe said he was going to arrange things for you."

Seated at Richard's left hand, Philip broke off his close conversation with Johanna and reached across for a peach. He inspected it critically, rubbing the downy fruit softly with the ball of his thumb.

"A good man to have about one, Rafael." He said nonchalantly, biting into the peach. "I have half a mind to steal him from you, Richard."

"I think not, my old friend. I think not. Rafe is my man, not yours."

Berengaria stared from one King to the other. Despite the casual words, there was some underlying tension in the exchange she did not understand. Buoyed up by Richard's good mood, she ignored it and smiled playfully,

"Nay, my lords. I'm afraid that neither of you can lay any claim to Rafael de Valencia, for he is my bondsman, not yours. Richard, didn't you say that all of the Blue Knights were mine to command?"

"So I did." Richard said slowly. "So I did. There Philip – Rafe is safe from your predations, after all. Safe in the hands of my lovely wife." Philip raised his eyebrows and both men laughed as if at some good joke. Berengaria joined in the laughter uncertainly.

"Richard, will you not show your lovely bride her wedding presents?" Philip said. "Or did you think to wait until you were alone together?"

Richard smoothed his beard with his hand, smiling.

"I can wait no longer. Berengaria – see what I have for you!"

He bent beneath the table and produced a velvet bag. He placed it on the table before her and nodded encouragingly.

"You may open it now." Berengaria reached inside, her groping fingers finding something smooth and cool.

She pulled her find out carefully and her mouth opened wide with pleasure.

"Oh, so beautiful!" She said, breathy with delight. Richard smirked and took the bag off her.

"And there's more." He shook the bag out onto the table, and two cream-coloured pearl earrings fell beside the wide collar of pearls that rested in Berengaria's fingers. The jewels were perfectly matched, mounted in fine gold that glowed softly in the glittering candle light. "Your poor little ears may hurt now, dear, but only think how happy they will be to wear such treasures!"

Berengaria smiled, sparing only a passing thought for the pain the pearls were going to cause to her newly-pierced earlobes.

"Richard, they are exquisite. Beautiful. The loveliest things I have ever seen." Richard puffed with each extravagant phrase.

"Nothing is too good for you, dear. Only the very best is fit for my Queen." He purred. "Of course, once we are wed the jewels of England, the jewels of the Queen of England, will be yours to wear. But these little keepsakes are for you alone."

Berengaria smiled at the same time as she wondered how long it would take to prise the royal jewels from Eleanor's firm grasp. Richard beamed and shouted for more wine and for the musicians to strike up. Rising to his feet he bowed with a flourish and led Berengaria in to the centre of the hall. Philip inclined his head politely to listen to Johanna, but his eyes followed the royal couple.

"You're paying me no attention whatsoever," Johanna tweaked his tunic coquettishly. "Do you have eyes only for Berengaria and Richard?"

"My apologies," Philip said smoothly. "What do you think, Johanna? Will she tame your brother? Will Richard Coeur de Lion become Richard the Lamb?"

"If you had asked me that a few months ago, I would have laughed. But now, I don't know. She may be quiet, but I think there's iron in her core. But," Johanna smiled. "She will have her work cut out for her. I think my dearest brother has his own plans, as always."

"Perhaps so, perhaps so. But she is very lovely, isn't she?"

"Richard says she's fat and old. I suppose she's pretty enough if you like that dark, lush style of woman." She added spitefully, and cursed as she trailed her sleeve in a pool of spilt wine. Philip lifted the sleeve to his mouth and sucked the wine from it, licking his lips sensuously.

"My dear Johanna, how delicious you taste." He whispered "But strictly between old friends such as us, your dear brother can sometimes be a fool. And who would know that better than me? But I, Johanna, am not a fool."

She pouted and leaned towards him.

"Dearest Philip," she said softly. "Perhaps there are certain things that we should talk about, alone?"

Philip glanced at Richard and Berengaria, waving gaily at them as the rhythm of the dance turned them to face him.

"Your servant, sweetheart." He smiled. Beneath the table, his fingers travelled slowly up Johanna's thigh. She rubbed her legs together like a snake twisting, pressing his hand hard between her thighs and gasping as Philip nipped the tender flesh, twisting skin and cloth cruelly between his fingers.

"You should be careful who you invite in, my dear Johanna." His smile widened even as his grip tightened,

"You might find you do not care so much for your visitor as you expected."

"Dearest Philip." She hissed. "I think you forget, I'm Richard's sister. We have much in common." Her hand clasped in a fist around Philip's fingers, squeezing them ever tighter.

"Amen to that." He smiled.

Chapter 7

In the grey, bleak times that were yet to come, she found that if she could recapture the memory of that day, then there was always the will to continue, to get through somehow, no matter how impossible dream happiness had become.

 Isabel roused her early, to bathe and dress her. The new wedding gown made her cry for memory of the ruined gown, but the tears soon dried as she determined to look forward, not back. Ready at last, Isabel held the precious Venetian mirror up and down, so Berengaria could see every detail of her dress and mantle. The pearl-encrusted veil sat lightly on her hair, held in place with a simple gold diadem. Long, flowing sleeves of silk rustled lightly against her arms, pointed cuffs falling past her hips. As the seamstresses had promised, rich gold thread decorated the round neck of the gown, reflecting the glow of her skin. Richard's pearl collar encircled her slender throat, the rows of pearls cool against her flesh, the earrings nipping her tender lobes.

She smiled at her reflection.

"Isabel, you will come to the chapel. I have asked Rafe to ensure that a seat is kept for you."

Isabel licked her lips, caught between surprise and pleasure and fear.

"Ma'am, if the King sees me, he will not be pleased."

"Follow." She said simply. "Follow a few moments after I leave. There will be a seat for you, in the last row of the chapel."

Johanna, impatient as ever, poked her head around the door.

"Ready?" She demanded. Without ceremony, she paced around Berengaria, inspecting her critically.

"You're glowing." She said grudgingly. "That dress suits your colouring. Hurry up, they're waiting for us. Richard left a while ago. It's only a few minutes journey to the chapel, but it may take a little longer if we have to force our way through the mob. It seems as if the whole of the island is mad to see you."

Berengaria drew as deep a breath and lifted her head.

"Then we go." She said simply.

The early May sunshine was already pleasant. It seemed to her that the whole of the island, noble and commoner, English, French and Cypriot alike, had taken to the streets to see her. The sea of people parted to let the bridal train pass through, closing again behind them. Berengaria smiled and waved, a sweet-smelling posy held to her face to mask the worst of the crowd's stink. Her heart missed a beat as the chapel of Saint George came into view.

Richard's towering war horse was held by a groom at the chapel doors. It tossed its head and neighed as Berengaria and Johanna approached; the groom immediately tugged on the great beast's bridle, forcing it to its knees in an equine bow. Johanna clapped her hands and laughed at the trick, and Berengaria beamed her pleasure.

The congregation for the wedding mass held the greatest nobles in Christendom. The banner of St. George was held high above the heads of kings and princes; knights Templar and Hospitaller; knights of

England and France. At the end of each aisle, a knight of the Blue Thong knelt on one knee. The air was thick with the scent of precious incense, swung in a thurible over the congregation. Huge candles flamed on the great altar, itself spread with a magnificent embroidered cloth and strewn with jewel encrusted chalices and dishes. Richard stood before the altar. She walked slowly down the aisle, praying her trembling legs would carry her. As she approached Richard, the knight kneeling at the end of the final pew raised his head and smiled; Berengaria's jittering nerves calmed slightly as she thought that if the worst happened and she fainted, at least Rafe would be there to catch her.

Her footsteps sounded unnaturally loud in the dead silence that had fallen on the chapel. Just before she drew level with Richard, he turned and smiled at her and the sun shone suddenly through the great window of the chapel, lighting his golden hair and beard with flame. He drew himself erect, his chest puffing out his rose coloured woolen tunic and the movement setting his silk cloak rustling, the decorations of gold half-moons seeming to swirl with a life of their own.

"My Queen." He bowed over her hand and turned her to face the altar.

Chapter 8

Feasting began as soon as the royal couple reached the palace. For what felt like the first time in months, Berengaria was ravenously hungry. Seated beside Richard, her stomach growled as she watched the servants parade the rich dishes around the high table before placing them with a flourish before Richard. Pride of place went to a peacock, roast and stuffed carefully back in to its own plumage, tail erect and quivering as if it might leap off its dish and strut around the table at any moment. Beside it, a feathered swan, beak tucked beneath its wing, was bedded carefully on a ground of tiny white, purple and green aubergines, cunningly designed to resemble a nest of eggs. Further along still, a smoking hot boar, tusks gilded, sat on glowing pomegranate seeds stacked and banked to mimic smouldering embers. A great pie, glossy with egg, nestled next to a haunch of venison.

With a gleeful, "every man for himself", Richard leaned across and speared a great slice of the peacock, munching on the tough flesh with apparent relish.

Berengaria hesitated, feeling suddenly queasy, overwhelmed by the plenty. As she hesitated, Philip leaned across Richard towards her.

"You do not eat, Berengaria? I understand – these viands are too gross for your delicate appetite." He glanced sideways at Johanna, who was tearing into a huge slice of venison with her knife, stuffing the meat into her mouth with her fingers, grease running down her chin. "I have a special dish for you."

He clicked his fingers and a servant hurried forward, offering a dish to her.

"What is it?" She asked, the savoury smell making her mouth water.

Philip nodded and the servant placed the dish on the table before her. The pantler carved the succulent golden breast of the bird, his sharp knife cutting wafer thin slices which he placed on Berengaria's trencher, fanning each slice so she could see the intricate marbling of the bird.

"A special dish, fit for a queen. I had my cook prepare it himself. One takes a good goose, and removes all the bones. Inside that goes a capon, skinned and boned. Within the capon a pheasant. Within the peasant, a partridge. Within the partridge, a quail. And last of all, a lark. A great dish, but the greatest trick of all is in the carving, to ensure that each slice contains a little of each bird. It's good?"

"Delicious." Berengaria assured him, fighting the urge to copy Johanna and stuff the slices whole in her mouth. His attention caught, Richard leaned across.

"What have you got there, my rose?" He demanded, and speared a slice from her trencher, ignoring the wobbling mound of flesh on his own plate. "This is a wonderful dish, Philip. I shall have some, and you must tell your cook to show my kitchen how to prepare it."

Berengaria smiled at his childlike greed and Richard laughed out loud, a thread of saliva glinting between his teeth. She had a sudden image of herself as a morsel of food caught between those teeth, and she swallowed as her head swam with desire. He reached for her hand and licked each of her finger tips clean in turn, and she wondered why he couldn't feel her trembling.

"Eat well, darling." He murmured. "Eat well, for tonight we shall surely dine on each other."

She blushed and looked down at her plate, grateful for the sudden distraction of the jugglers swooping around the tables throwing and catching platters, goblets, even pieces of meat snatched from beneath diners' noses. Richard watched for a moment and then – quickly bored – threw a coin to the leader who caught it deftly before retreating, bowing from the waist. A stir from the back of the hall proclaimed the entrance of the next entertainment, the group of mummers clomping down to the high table with stolid lack of grace. The men clattered to a halt before Richard and bowed clumsily, the leader announcing their play. Richard shrugged and waved a hand to them to continue.

Berengaria kept a straight face for a few minutes, and then broke into helpless giggles. She had persevered in learning to speak English with Isabel and knew enough to follow the action of the mummers' terrible acting. Two of the youngest men – little more than boys themselves – were dressed in maidens' clothing, and she quickly realised that the two pretty boys were supposed to represent her and Johanna as they clung together, uttering high, falsetto shrieks at intervals. A number of men wearing rusty armour mooned about in the background, growling fiercely. But it was the two main actors who had her in fits. The smaller of the two was obviously meant for Isaac Kommenos; he wore a parchment crown on his head which persisted on falling down over his ears at every movement, and a sword which was so long it trailed on the ground at his side. Every time he attempted to draw his weapon, he tripped over it instead. The mummer who was portraying Richard was, in contrast, most splendid. A head taller than Kommenos, his height was helped even more by thick wooden clogs. His crown was painted gold, his armour almost new. A becoming wig of yellow wool topped his head, falling in curls to his wide shoulders and what Berengaria hoped was chicken blood streaked his face. As Kommenos shouted defiance, the counterfeit Richard chased him around the hall, thwacking his backside with a broadsword until the smaller man fell at his feet and mumbled a prayer for mercy.

Richard was delighted. Tears of laughter ran down his face as he stood and gestured the mummers to him, leading the applause. A purse of coins chinked enticingly in his hand. He spoke, loudly, and Berengaria craned her neck to listen, her brow wrinkling as she realised she could not understand a word he was saying. Neither, she saw, could the mummers.

The lead actor bowed and shuffled, his head modestly lowered as he accepted the purse and backed away quickly. Too quickly; he trod on the diminutive Kommenos, who was standing close behind him and for a moment the two mock kings were locked in each other's arms, doing a sprightly dance as they fought for balance.

Richard screamed with laughter and mopped at his face with his sleeve as he gasped for breath.

"See how they adore me?" He boomed. "Good, decent, honest Englishmen to the core. Peasants perhaps, but loyal to their King, and happy for the world to see it.

I tell you, I do believe they appreciated a word from me even more than the gold."

Berengaria murmured her agreement, grateful that Richard had not realised the men could not understood a word he had said.

Gradually, the dishes emptied and the richly-laden tables degenerated into a mess of grease and strewn food. Voices rose as more wine was drunk and the laugher rose higher and higher still. Ladies stumbled at the dance and the gentleman took their chance to allow a hand to linger at breast and thigh. Through the flickering candle-light, Berengaria saw Angela, her face flushed and blonde hair trailing in rats' tails around her shoulders, rubbing sinuously against one of the younger knights. Richard laughed at some remark she didn't hear and she smiled nervously, desperate to please, but his eyes were elsewhere and he didn't notice her.

As if at some signal, Johanna rose abruptly and bowed to Richard and Philip. Gesturing to Berengaria, she swept her out of the hall. Behind them, the voices stopped for a second and then began again, even louder.

"Not that way." Johanna tutted as Berengaria unthinkingly turned toward her own lodging. "This is your wedding night, for the Lord's sake – we're going to Richard's apartment."

Berengaria's mouth was suddenly dry. Moths fluttered in her stomach. She wanted to explain to Johanna, to say to her that none of this was right, not how it should be. Since she had been a child, she had known exactly what her wedding eve would be like. At a signal from Aunt Constanzia the ladies would leave the room in a graceful procession whilst each man in the company bowed before her.

Clustering around her, the company of women would escort her to her new husband's apartment. Each woman would try to be one of the favoured few who helped her to disrobe; comb out her hair; passed her nightgown to her; settled her in the marriage bed. Until her husband arrived, the women would stay with her, chattering to distract her. A knock at the door would herald the bridegroom, ushered in to the room in the midst of his retainers. The greatest men in the court would surround their lord; the most favoured would pass him a basin of water for the ritual cleansing of face and beard; possibly the pot to piss in. Just as her own ladies had done, the men would jostle for the privilege of disrobing their Lord and helping him into bed beside her. Then and only then would the ladies and gentlemen of the court withdraw, pulling the curtains of the bed closed behind them. And in the morning would come his triumphant exit, after which she herself would rise, and make her way to her own apartment. Only then would the throng be allowed to enter to be shown the tumbled and bloodied bed sheets, and to cheer the event.

Tongue tied, Berengaria tried to find the words to explain all this to Johanna. The other woman stared at her impatiently.

"Oh, I daresay that's how it should have been." She said. "But don't forget, We're camped in some bloody foreign little island, you can't expect things to be perfect."

Drooping, Berengaria allowed herself to be bundled out of her wedding gown and into her nightdress. Johanna inserted her between the scratchy linen sheets neatly and efficiently, and then stood back to stare at her sister in law critically.

"You'll do." She said grudgingly. She began to wander aimlessly about the room, adjusting the hangings on the bed and humming tunelessly to herself. She was making Berengaria even more nervous, and she began to pray that Richard would arrive quickly.

The knock at the door was so soft that Berengaria thought she had imagined it. Johanna heard the scratch and immediately brightened.

"Sire!" She called loudly. The formality of her tone terrified Berengaria and she began to shake, immediately changing her mind and wishing Johanna would stay; that Richard would go away; that it was already morning.

The door creaked open and Richard stood alone in the doorway, smiling slyly. His fair hair was neatly brushed, his hands twined before him so that he looked like a sheepish schoolboy, caught out in some childish prank. Berengaria took a deep, shuddering breath, wondering suddenly if by some miracle perhaps Richard might be as nervous as she was. She managed a shaky smile.

Already, Johanna was curtseying, taking her leave of her brother with great solemnity. Richard leaned down and kissed her on both cheeks; Johanna said something very quietly and he smiled, standing aside to let her leave. She closed the door behind her and Richard stood straight and tall in front of her, the most perfect knight in all Christendom, staring at his bride as she sat bolt upright, cocooned in the great marriage bed.

Alone, Berengaria thought. Alone and it was her wedding night and this was her husband and she had waited for this day for so very, very long. And she loved him so very much. Nothing else mattered.

Richard laced his hands behind his back and strolled forward, sitting on the edge of the bed. The mattress sagged and groaned beneath his weight, just as it had done on that almost forgotten night when he had last come to her. Only now, he was truly her husband and nothing could come between them.

"Well now, little Berengaria" He said softly. His voice sounded wrong, as if quiet words were strange to him. "You look like a frightened little girl – are you not pleased to welcome me? I like your hair braided like that

– suits you." His gaze slid down the pleated front of her nightgown and the muscles in his face and neck bunched; surely, she thought, it was a trick of the wavering candle flame that made him look as if he was grimacing. "That sweet nightgown; I like it hugely."

He stretched out a long finger and tilted her chin up. She trembled helplessly.

"My dear, no need to be frightened of me." He cooed. "You know, you look like the little girl I remember so well, with your hair all tied up and your nice, neat nightgown hiding your treasures."

She tried to smile, but achieved nothing more than a grimace. Richard leaned forward, his weight dimpling the mattress so she was moved abruptly and the kiss aimed at her lips hit her nose instead. She moved quickly, trying to bring her head around to find his lips but to her horror, the movement unbalanced Richard and he bashed his forehead against the bed post.

"My lord!" She shrieked and leaned forward to gather him to her. "Oh, Richard! I′m so sorry!"

Richard rubbed at his forehead with his fingers.

"No need to apologise, my bride. You are nervous – I understand that. Of course you are. And so am I." He added honestly. "Come now, let's finish that kiss."

His hands slid to her shoulders and gripped tightly as he pulled her towards him. His lips pressed on her neck, smoothing up to her lips. At the same time, his fingers caressed her neck, running up and down her spine.

As he stroked and caressed, some of her nervousness seeped away, slowly being replaced by rising desire. With no idea of whether she was doing right or wrong, instinct made her try to get ever closer to him; she felt her nipples harden painfully as her breasts moulded to him like warm butter. The sensation was too much, and she groaned aloud against his lips.

His hand fell to her breast and for a few seconds, he paused, his mouth suddenly immobile. At a loss as to what to do, she simply waited, willing him to move. To speak. A candle guttered and went out with a splutter, casting new shadows across the room. Richard sighed and pulled away from her, licking his lips. Berengaria stared at him, willing him to tell her what to do, to tell her what he wanted her to do. She wanted to cry.

"Ah." He cleared his throat with a sound like gravel shifting. Turning his head, he hawked phlegm into the rushes. "Take if off." She stared at him, dumb, not understanding. "The nightdress. Take it off."

He nodded encouragement and she hoiked the nightdress up to her waist. Crossing her arms, she tugged the hem over her head. At a loss what to do next, she began to fold the fine linen carefully, hugging it to her breasts. He leaned across and snatched at the garment impatiently, throwing it on the floor. Ludicrously, Berengaria found herself hoping it had not landed on his spittle.

Shuffling forward, he snuffled at her neck, sounding more like an animal than a man. The idea excited her hugely.

"You smell… very sweet." He sounded almost disappointed and her hands balled into nervous fists. "I mean, you smell lovely. You must remember my dove that I´m more used to the smell of battle, of sweat and fear. Your fragrance is so very, very different."

She stared at him from lowered eyelids, her pulse singing so violently that she was sure he must hear it. He traced the outline of her right breast with a ragged finger nail; it caught and stung and she hissed with pleasure at the sensation. He pursed his lips, nodded as if he had come to some decision and stood, looming over her, blocking out the candle flame.

"Richard." She whispered, the words catching in her throat. "Richard, my husband."

He threw the bedclothes back with a grunt. His shoes followed awkwardly and then – without bothering to take off any of the rest of his clothes – he slid in beside her, pulling the sheets back across them both. Berengaria wriggled towards him, feeling for his warmth. She touched him shyly, on his chest and shoulders and face, anxious to please but terrified of disappointing him.

"Show me." She whispered. "Show me what I should do. Please. I don´t know."

Richard grunted and his hand enclosed her breast briefly, tweaking the nipple between finger and thumb. The same hand moved quickly down to her belly, his fingers running over her ribs as if he were playing an instrument. Oddly, Berengaria remembered that it was said that Richard could play all know instruments. The thought excited her greatly; she wanted him to take her in his hands, to play her like a lute, to pluck at her senses. His fingers slid to her spine and ran up and down her behind, nails sliding between her cheeks. His other hand was tugging at the laces of his breaches; hesitatingly she reached to help and he immediately closed his fingers hard around her hand, his huge fist enveloping her completely.

"Like this." He hissed, loosing her hand to fumble at his groin. She shook her head helplessly, unable to either see or feel what he wanted. "Here." He pushed her hand hard, forcing her to rub against him. Remembering, she slid her hand inside his breaches and ran her finger hesitatingly up and down his penis, very gently.

"Harder." He mumbled into her neck. She licked her lips and increased the pressure of her fingers slightly, terrified she might hurt him. "God's wounds, woman, not like that. Hard!"

His fingers were closed around her hand like a vice, crushing her. He grunted as he jerked her hand back and forth, back and forth. He had liked her doing that before, she thought. Suddenly, he jerked away and abruptly rolled on top of her. The same ragged finger nail that had scratched her breast earlier shoved into her sex, making her shout out loud with pain and surprise. He raked at her for a few seconds with his hand; muttered something she could not make out and then he was moving jerkily on top of her, his elbows uncomfortably shifting into her ribs, his knees forcing her legs apart.

She felt his penis probing for her, and moved her legs as wide apart as she could manage. He grunted and shifted; she shifted with him and then felt a shock of pain as he finally found his target and slid inside her.

She moved with him, desperately trying to follow his rhythm, but missing. She felt pleasure in his touch, rough as it was, and knew that she loved him beyond anything. She wanted to shout in triumph, to tell the world that this was her man, her king, her husband and that nothing could take him away from her. And then there was a desperate longing in her belly that made her want to laugh and cry at the same time. Still trying with half her mind to concentrate on pleasing Richard, she suddenly became aware of a strange, but totally pleasurable sensation that was beginning to blossom deep, deep inside her. Now, she wriggled with him, push for shove, searching for something she could neither name nor understand.

Suddenly, Richard moaned and shuddered, taking her unawares so that she continued to writhe beneath him until she realised that he was not just unmoving, but rigid. She whimpered with deep disappointment as his body flopped loosely and he slid bonelessly on his side, panting.

She lay dumb, her whole body tense as a long bow strung ready to fire. Bewildered, her hands hovered over Richard's belly, not daring to touch, not knowing where to touch. Within a minute, his laboured breathing slowed and he started to snore. Helpless, she whispered his name over and over in the darkness, praying he would wake and take her in his arms, call her his love, his wife, his queen; do something – anything – to quench the screaming desire in her belly. But Richard never stirred. Dazed, she ran her helpless fingers over her own body, searching for some sign that she was different, changed. She found a mass of sticky wetness at her groin and jerked her hand away in disgust, only to return again in helpless fascination. She rubbed her fingers together, feeling the warm, syrupy fluid slippery on her skin. Blood. It was done, then. She whimpered with fear and excitement; finally, unable to stand the suspense a moment longer, she raised her hand to her nose and sniffed carefully. Expecting the coppery smell of blood, she flinched in surprise when instead she scented something more akin to salt cod. She sniffed again and bit her lip to stop hysterical laughter, as she realised what the sticky mess on her hand actually was. Not blood, not her blood, but rather Richard's seed. Carefully, she wiped it away on a corner of the sheet, and then used the same sheet to clean Richard's semen from her body.

That was it, then. They had done the thing that made babies. It wasn't blood at all. It was part of Richard. Part of her, now. She glowed at the thought.

"My king." She whispered softly, "My king, my husband. My lover."

She lay back on the pillows, blowing a goose feather loosened from the mattress gently away from Richard's forehead. For what felt like hours, she simply looked at him, watching the rise and fall of his breath, reading his dreams in the brief changes of his expression. She pushed sleep away, wanting to be sure that he was there, that she could feel him beside her.

She lay awake in the moth-coloured darkness, feeling Richard's warm bulk beside her. Her fingers hovered uncertainly over the skin of his arm, but she dared not touch him for fear of his anger if she woke him. Eyes wide open, but seeing nothing but darkness, she finally drifted into sleep so deep that she never felt Richard climbing out of their bed. Never saw him pause to lean over her; never saw his expression as he crept out.

Chapter 9

"Oh, God's teeth." Johanna cursed as her needle jabbed her full in the plump cushion of her fingertip. Furious, she threw her embroidery frame away from her and stuffed the injured finger in her mouth. Berengaria picked up the trailing tapestry and brushed it down carefully. Johanna thanked her grudgingly.

"I hate this." Her mouth puckered angrily and Berengaria saw how her pretty sister-in-law would look twenty years along, when time had deepened her expressive face into sour wrinkles. She raised her eyebrows enquiringly. "This. The sea. Ships. All of it. Richard knows how I suffer from seasickness, how ill it makes me, but still he insists I come."

"I thought you wanted to see the Holy Land?" Berengaria said, surprised.

"I do, I suppose. Mama always made it sound so fascinating. But I don't want to see it that much that I must suffer for weeks on this wretched boat. I hate it, I really hate it."

"But what else could you do?" Berengaria asked mildly. "With Eleanor already gone, you couldn't stay in Cyprus, on your own. It could have been months before you got a ship back to France. And even if Richard had let you stay, the sea journey would have been just as long as it's going to take to get us to Acre."

"I know. Go, stay. I'm damned either way." Johanna bit her lip and added, "It's not just the seasickness, now. Every time a wave hits us, I remember being shipwrecked in Limassol, and I'm terrified."

"It's very calm at the moment." Berengaria soothed "Perhaps it will stay like this all the way."

Johanna shrugged off her words, obviously near tears. Berengaria sat down next to her, putting her arms around her and cuddling her like a child.

"Doesn't it worry you?" Johanna rested her head on the other woman's shoulder, and sighed. "Don't you think about the storm? I do. I have nightmares about it. We were nearly killed!"

Berengaria wet her lips, relieved Johanna couldn't see her face. Had they been that close to death? She rather thought they had. But, as well as it being frightening, she had found it hugely exhilarating. Even the battle afterwards, waiting and wondering if Richard was going to win, had been thrilling. She admitted to herself that the whole experience had left her shaking, but with excitement as well as fear. She chose her words carefully, knowing that if she told Johanna the truth she would think she was mad.

"But we didn't die, did we?" She said finally. "We're safe. And lightning doesn't strike twice in the same place. We'll be fine."

"Oh, God. I hope so." Johanna jabbed her needle in and out of her work without pulling the silk through. "We're bound to have at least some rough weather. We're going to be at sea for weeks. It's alright for you though, isn't it?"

"I can't help it if I don't get seasick." Berengaria said mildly.

"Yes, but it's not just that is it?" Johanna bridled. "Not only do you not get seasick, but you look like the cat that got the cream. You've got it all, haven't you? You've got my great, stupid, dragon-killing brother mewling over you. As if that wasn't enough for anybody, the delicious Rafe is throwing himself at your feet as well. It's not fair!"

Berengaria hid a rueful smile. *Ah, Johanna!* She thought. *If you only knew the truth of it.* Before the Crusade had set sail, Richard had appeared to dote on her. But only in public. He had spent every night in her bed, as well, but more often than not he declared himself too exhausted by the demands of his campaign to do more than sleep as soon as he lay beside her. Bitterly, she remembered how her hopes had risen when a couple of times he had made the effort to push her hand to his private parts and had shown her how to please him. At first, she had taken her own pleasure in knowing he was happy, but it wasn't long before she began to wonder if there was ever going to be any more. Had the one time they had made love been enough to make a baby? She thought not, and worried.

But she had been delighted when Richard had released Rafe to sail with them. She liked him and had to admit that there was a certain smug satisfaction in knowing that Johanna was jealous of his attentions.

As if reading her mind, Johanna spoke suddenly, startling her.

"You haven't fallen on already, have you? You look so well, I wouldn't be surprised. "

"What?" Berengaria blinked, embarrassed.

"You haven't started a baby, have you?" Johanna sighed impatiently.

"I don't know. No, I don't think so." Berengaria shook her head, uneasy at how closely Johanna was echoing her own thoughts. "How would I know?"

"Well, it's too early for you to have missed your courses, isn't it?" Berengaria frowned, counting on her fingers. Shook her head. "Have you been sick in the mornings?" Another shake. "Felt like eating strange things? I had a lady in waiting once who wanted to eat earth when she fell pregnant, and I heard of one lady at court," although they were alone in the closed cabin,

Johanna still lowered her voice, "Who craved nothing more than to eat her husband's seed."

"No!" Berengaria's mouth fell open in disbelief.

"It's true!" Johanna nodded vigorously. "And the strange thing was, before she conceived she was the straightest-laced thing you've ever seen, spent hours praying, never missed a mass. Couldn't even take a joke. Makes you wonder if God's got a sense of humour, doesn't it!"

Both women giggled, grievances momentarily forgotten.

"I don't think I can be." Berengaria said eventually. "I don't feel any different at all."

Johanna shrugged.

"You've got plenty of time yet." She said grudgingly. "At least you've got a husband. Not like me – a widow with no children alive, nothing." Her voice was bitter. "All I can hope for is that dearest Richard will win this damned Crusade quickly, and then find me a husband. I'm not going into a nunnery, no matter what. He can't make me, can he?"

"No, of course not." Berengaria soothed. But there was no getting away from it; Johanna was older than she was. Already a widow and with no children alive to convince a suitor that she could bear children, it would be difficult for Richard to find her another husband. "Anyway, there's no convent on earth that would be mad enough to take a she-devil like you."

Johanna pulled a face.

"They would if Richard told them to." Her lips puckered as if she was on the verge of tears. "I'm not going to let them. They're not going to lock me up. They did it to Mama, you know. Locked her up in a confined order in Winchester for years and years. Only let her out under close guard, when father allowed it. To do that to the Queen of England and France! My God, if they could do that to the great Eleanor, then they can surely do it to me."

"You're forgetting" Berengaria said firmly. "Eleanor isn't closed up now. She's in England and free. Do you really think she would let anybody inflict on you what she had to suffer?"

Johanna considered her words and brightened.

"Aye, that's true. If I don't annoy Richard too much, and keep out of Mama's bad books, I should do well enough. So, I must find me a husband. Who do we have?"

Berengaria entered into the game willingly, happy to keep Johanna in a good mood. Some they agreed were too old, or lacking in enough fortune. A couple was grudgingly dismissed as too young, being still in the nursery. Some were rendered ineligible by inconvenient wives. When Johanna finally fell on Berengaria's father, and looked at her hopefully, Berengaria decided she had had enough and excused herself, leaving Johanna picking idly at her sewing.

She found her favourite place on the foredeck and made herself comfortable with her back against the warm wood, careful that her arms and face were out of the sun. She had come to envy deeply the court ladies' white skins and wished her own golden skin tones could have been as pale as theirs.

She took a deep breath, savouring the smell of the ocean. Johanna was right, she reflected, life at sea did suit her – she thought that she had never felt so alive, so happy. She shrugged away a moment's guilt at the knowledge that part of the happiness was caused by Richard's absence. Isabel, she reflected, seemed to mirror her mood, she was all smiles. Either that or she too was simply happy to be away from Richard.

"It's unfair."

A shadow fell over her and she smiled as she saw it was Rafe.

"Unfair? What's unfair?" She waved her hand at the bench beside her, inviting him to sit, but instead he slid to the deck at her feet and sat cross legged.

"The sea is unfair. A human rival I could defeat. If my rival was a man, I would find some way to get the better of him. But I can't fight the sea."

She laughed and shook her head.

"Rafe, you talk nonsense. How is the sea your rival?"

"You think better of it than you do me." He said promptly. "That's what's so unfair."

"Aye? At least the sea is constant, Rafe. For all your fine words, I've noticed your absence on this voyage."

"You've missed me, then?"

"No, not at all. I've been far too busy enjoying your rival, the sea. And watching for the others."

"The others?"

Berengaria waved her hand at the horizon.

"The other ships. Which one do you think carries Richard?"

"The first ship, of course," Rafe said simply. "He would always be at the forefront. I doubt we'll be able to see it from here. Richard will be in the vanguard, with the rest of the fleet strung out slightly behind him. We bring up the rear."

She nodded, and smiled. Rafe blew out his cheeks, looking so like a disappointed child denied sweetmeats that Berengaria took pity on him and stroked his hair, much as she would have done to a pet. Immediately, he caught her hand and pressed it to his lips. She tugged it from his grasp laughing.

"No, no Rafe. You can't expect my favour when you've neglected me quite shockingly. It's too calm for you to plead sea sickness, so you've no excuse at all."

"I have sought you out, believe me. But," He shrugged and stared at his finger nails and Berengaria sensed that the flirtatious game had ended for the moment.

"But what?" She demanded curiously.

"But you're always with my Lady Johanna." He said finally. "I'm sorry, it isn't a courteous thing to say, and I shouldn't say it, but she looks at me as if she would eat me up, and I have no taste for such a meal."

"Oh, my poor, poor Rafe! Frightened by a lone woman, what am I to do with you?"

"Anything you wish to do with me, anything at all." He spoke so quietly that she had to bend her head to hear him. He lifted his head to stare at her and the look in his dark blue eyes stopped the words in her throat. "I'm sworn to you. Anything you ask of me, anything, I'm at your command."

She shivered, the hairs rising on the back of her neck. Rafe reached up and smoothed his fingers down the side of her cheek, his touch barely there on her skin.

"Anything." He whispered. "Anything. I'm yours to command."

Berengaria shook her head. His touch aroused an ache that was too deep, too intimate to be comfortable.

She stared at his lips and immediately wondered what it would be like to be kissed by him. Richard, she realised suddenly, had never kissed her properly. And she wanted to be kissed. Kissed and held and caressed and touched. For hours upon hours. Rafe was so close that she could feel his breath on her face; smell the scent of the sea on his flesh. He said something, but she couldn't hear his words for the drumming of her own pulse in her ears.

A seagull skimmed across the deck, screaming raucously. The harsh noise broke the enchantment and she stood abruptly, pulling her skirts close around her.

"I'm sorry my sister- in- law doesn't meet with your approval." Her voice trembled. She couldn't look at his face. "Perhaps if you spent more time with her, you might find her more to your taste?"

Rafe closed his eyes as if she had slapped him. Jumped athletically to his feet, only to sink immediately on one knee before her.

"My queen." His voice was hoarse. His back was rigid, his head bowed. "I'm at your command, as always. May I walk back below with you? The stairs are very steep."

"Thank you, yes." Berengaria spoke softly, knowing that Rafe was only too aware he had overstepped the mark, that he had taken the unwritten, forbidden step from courtly flirtation to real desire. It would not happen again, she knew. And wondered at her disappointment at the knowledge. She allowed Rafe to take her fingertips to guide her down the companionway.

As soon as she was safely below decks, Rafe bowed and left her. She stood for a moment, touching her cheek, knowing Johanna would want to know why she was blushing. She took a deep breath, straightening her shoulders as she pushed open her cabin door. And stopped dead.

Angela was sitting beside Johanna on her own berth, the two women's heads almost touching as they giggled over something held in Angela's lap. Anger bubbled bright in Berengaria as she saw the object of their amusement was her treasured Roman de la Rose. She glared and cleared her throat noisily and Angela jumped to her feet, her expression mulish. Berengaria flicked her finger at the girl and stood to one side pointedly to allow Angela to shuffle past her.

Johanna's face was set in a sullen pout, her arms crossed defensively over her breasts.

"Mine, I think?" Berengaria said icily, moving forward to take her book.

"We were only laughing at the antics of the Rose." Johanna snapped.

"Really? And I could have sworn that I had left this safely packed in one of my trunks. Have you and Angela being rifling my belongings, sister?"

"Oh, for the Lord's good sake." Johanna jumped to her feet, arms akimbo. "It's only a book. Surely you don't mind me looking at it."

"Not in the least." Berengaria said coolly. "But I would have liked you to ask. And did you have to invite her in here?"

"Her? You mean Angela, I suppose? Honestly, sister, can you really be that... that selfish?" Berengaria jaw dropped in shock as Johanna ranted on. "Oh, it's alright for you, isn't it? You can sit for hours staring at the stupid sea, watching the sailors working. Straining your eyes to see if you can see your precious Richard. And if you get tired of that, why all you have to do is click your fingers and Rafe is mooning at you feet. But how often do you take time to talk to me?" Her voice changed to a pitiful whine. "You know how much I hate the sea. You have everything, everything! – Richard, Rafe, babies to come, a throne – everything to look forward to. And what do I have? A barren belly, no husband, no kingdom, nothing but relief that the sea is quiet. At least Angela wants to talk to me. Nobody else does! I could be dead for all you care about it."

"Oh, my dear." Stricken with guilt, Berengaria rushed forward and wrapped her arms around her sobbing sister-in-law, hugging her tightly. "I'm so sorry, I didn't think."

Johanna disentangled herself and wiped her face with her sleeve.

"You'll stay with me, then? Talk to me?" She asked tremulously.

"But of course I will. You're right, I have been selfish. I'm so sorry. "

Johanna smiled through her tears and sniffed nasally. She started to speak, and then stopped abruptly. The sudden change in the sound, in the rhythm, of the ship made both women's heads jerk up. Berengaria stared around, puzzled, not understanding what was happening. Johanna moaned, clutching Berengaria uncomfortably tightly.

"What's happening?" She shrieked. "Are we sinking? Have we been attacked? What is it?"

The ship lurched and then rolled, rocking the two women from side to side. The sound of the drum beat for the slaves who rowed the ship day and night, so constant that it had become unnoticeable, was now shockingly loud, the beat urgent and fierce. Berengaria shrugged helplessly.

"I don't know. We must be turning, I think."

The ship rocked again, seeming to shake itself like a dog coming out of water. She could sense the power of the rowers' labours as the timbers creaked and the vessel surged forward.

Johanna screamed, shrill as a whistle. Berengaria could feel her trembling and she fought down her own panic, guiding Johanna to the nearest berth and forcing her to sit down. She sat down beside her, and put her arms around her sister, hanging on to her shoulders to make sure she did not try and stand. The ship rolled and swayed beneath them and Johanna's face promptly turned green.

"My ladies." Rafe had opened the door without knocking, but Berengaria was too relieved to see him to reprove him. "My ladies, we have had a signal, passed back. Richard's ship has sighted a Saracen supply vessel, and he's giving chase. We follow." He said the last two words sourly, and Berengaria guessed that he longed to be at the forefront of the action.

"We're not going to be involved?" She asked, more for Johanna's sake than anything.

"No." Rafe shook his head glumly. "We will be onlookers, well away from any danger. "

Berengaria glanced at Johanna's pinched face and made her mind up.

"Sister, you'll be safe down here. I promise. I'll send Angela to look after you."

She pushed Rafe in front of her, moving quickly before Johanna could protest. Angela was in the corridor, swaying towards the cabin, her face ugly with terror.

"We're following Richard's ship." Berengaria told her crisply. "I think there's going to be a battle. Go in and look after Johanna. Stay with her no matter what happens."

Angela's face turned the colour of gone-over milk and she lurched into the cabin without a word. Berengaria guessed that nothing less than the ship sinking would prise her out of the comparative safety.

"Come on to deck with me." She grasped Rafe's arm for support, shoving him forwards.

He stared back at her, his expression horrified.

"You can't! Even though we will be far from the battle, I think – I know! – Richard would want you safe below. He would not want you to see."

"I don't care." She almost shouted. "I don't care what Richard wants for me. He isn't here – he's out there, and I must see what happens. Don't you understand? I must see that he's safe."

She realised as she spoke that the words were ridiculous. Safe? How could Richard be safe, in the middle of a battle? It wasn't what she meant, at all. She looked up at Rafe, and saw understanding in his expression.

"Come, then." He said simply.

She leaned against him as he led the way on deck. Once into the sunlight, Rafe barred her way with an outstretched arm, holding her back. She pushed against him angrily, trying to force her way through, and then realised that he was trying to protect her from the chaos on deck.

Sailors were scampering with the unseen control of ants, answering the call of commands she could not understand. As she watched, sails were raised and adjusted; ropes thrown accurately across anything that was not already fastened down. When he decided it was safe to move, Rafe guided her across to a niche at the foot of the fo´castle

"Stay there." He commanded. "Whatever happens, don´t move unless I come back for you. I´ll be close. Do you understand?"

Her jaw dropped as she suddenly understood that the ship could still be in danger, away from the action as it was.

Suddenly far from excited, she whispered her thanks, but he had already gone, staggering towards the prow and out of her sight. Her thoughts whirled like a flock of starlings at dusk, from Richard to Rafe and back again. If they got close enough to the battle, would Rafe literally leap to the defence of his King? Might she lose both of them, her friend and her husband alike? She leaned forward cautiously, jerking back as a sailor passed at a run. She heard his mumbled prayer as he passed.

For minutes, nothing seemed to happen. Even the deck crew's activity had stopped, and there was no sound except the relentless boom, boom, boom of the drum beating the pace for the rowers below. For the first time, Berengaria wondered about the chained men doomed to row to that beat. The rowers were slaves, she knew, captured in some battle or other and forced to labour in return for their lives. Every nation had slaves; every nation had slaves from every other nation. But until that precise second, she had never spared a thought to what it meant to be a slave; to be made to do exactly what another man told you. Now, she shivered, thinking how bad it had been in the comfortable cabin when they were not allowed on deck because the weather was bad. How much more terrible must it be to be manacled in the darkness below decks, rowing constantly to a shouted command, without hope? She shook her head, her gorge rising at the thought.

Then the ship seemed to turn on its own axle, staying still by some miracle of steering, and all thought of the slaves who were fighting with their oars to achieve that miracle fled. This isn't a game. She thought. The mummers are not going to unmask to applause and laughter. Richard could die, while I watch. What possessed me to come up here? Was I mad?

"No." She spoke out loud. "No. He will not die. I will not die. Richard will win. I know it."

She drew a deep breath. And waited.

A yell, seeming to come simultaneously from all of the crew together, made her jump. She leaned forward, peering around the bulwark.

They were much nearer to the rest of the fleet than she had realised. Though still in the rear, she could see – perhaps a hundred yards away – the other supply boats, waiting behind the fighting ships. Richard's great warships, dark and ugly, were strung in a semi-circle around a huge Saracen ship that floated low in the water. As she watched, the lead ship in the Crusader fleet unleashed a hail of arrows. At that distance, nothing was clear. Figures appeared as blotches against the sunlight, the flow of arrows seemed almost a solid wall. She heard screams, wild yells; not English, not any language she had ever heard.

As if the Saracen ship held a magical attraction, the English vessels drew closer and closer to it. Arrows sang from all directions, followed quickly by spears. Suddenly, Richard's vessel was close enough to board the other craft, and sailors swarmed across the narrow gap, scrambling over each other in their eagerness to reach the prize. Berengaria opened her mouth wide and screamed as she saw an English sailor miss his footing and slide between the two vessels; in spite of the distance, she was sure that she could hear his bones crunch as his body ground between the hulls.

"Take it, take it, you fools!" She heard Richard's distinctive voice howling over the chaos. "Let it get away and I'll crucify the lot of you. You hear me!"

Berengaria fumbled for the crucifix at her own throat and breathed a prayer for his safety. As Richard's words sank in, she dropped the cross in sudden revulsion.

A contrary wind took her vessel, turning it so that she could no longer see the battle. She could hear though, still, and the shrieks and howls of pain and fear and the smells of blood and much worse made her feel sick. She covered her face with her hands, and was barely aware that there was a body pressing against her, shielding her from the worst of the hell.

"You should have stayed below." Rafe shouted, his words almost lost above the row of battle. "This is not for your eyes."

"And will it be any better in the Holy Land?" She sobbed, ashamed of her weakness but unable to stop herself. "Are all battles like this, Rafe? Is this my life from now on – to spend all my days worrying and wondering if Richard will come back to me?"

"Nay, Richard is safer than any man on the sea today. Do you think anybody would dare lift a hand against the king? Friend and enemy alike will look out for him, trust me." Berengaria stared at him, hoping he was speaking the truth. He nodded, his face open. "Trust me". He said again. And she realised that she did.

Chapter 10

Berengaria longed for the blessing of sleep, but it would not come.

Scenes from the battle flared in her mind endlessly; the sailor who had been crushed between the vessels; strange, dark faces screaming defiance from the Saracen ship; Richard's threat of terrible vengeance on his own men; and above all, the stink. Sweat and blood and terror and the disgusting reek of bow strings soaked in urine to keep them supple. Her stomach churned at the memory and even the rose water that Isabel fetched for her could not remove the stench that seemed to have settled in her mouth and nose. She felt sick to her stomach, and spared a moment of sympathy for Johanna, who even in her sleep moaned at every movement of the ship. As soon as dawn came, Berengaria rose and shook Johanna awake.

"Come take a turn on deck with me." She coaxed. "The sea's flat as a millpond and some fresh air will do you good."

"I could, I suppose." Johanna said grudgingly.

Both women leaned on the deck rail, watching the sea rush past. Joanna clutched a handkerchief fiercely in her hand, raising it to her lips at intervals. Berengaria thought she was determined to be seasick, and cast around for something to distract her.

"Look." She pointed "Dolphins. I've seen them running in front of us before. Do you think they do it for the sheer joy of playing?"

"The sailors say they're the souls of drowned sailors, trying to entice the living to their death to join them for all eternity."

"Oh." Berengaria felt deflated, all joy in the sleek dolphins evaporating. The two women lapsed into silence.

"I think," whatever Johanna was about to say was drowned out by a shout from one of the sailors, the words ringing down from the crow's nest perched precariously at the top of the rigging.

"What did he say?" Johanna demanded. Berengaria shook her head, and the two women suddenly clutched at each other in terror as the rowers' beat changed, the drums becoming urgent and fast, and the ship responding at once.

"Oh, dear God, no. Not again. Please, not again." Johanna wailed. "Not another battle. I can't stand it."

Berengaria shaded her eyes with her hand, concentrating on making out the rest of the fleet, bobbing like leaves before them. Each vessel was turning to the right, and very faintly across the gentle waves she could hear the drum beat of their own vessel repeated and repeated and repeated from every ship.

She grabbed at Johanna's sleeve, shaking her sister-in-law to make her listen.

"Johanna, I think we're close to land. Be quiet."

Johanna moaned, refusing to be comforted, but over her groans Berengaria made out the voice of the sailor in the rigging overhead. His accent was so thick she couldn't understand him, but she was sure she was right; the man's voice was excited, not fearful.

Rafe bundled them both below. Isabel and Angela were ordered to put up all and anything that was not to stay on board. Isabel responded with a smile, Angela a grimace and a muttered comment about being treated like a servant. The two queens sat together on the berth, Johanna chattering endlessly, her sea-sickness forgotten.

The rhythm of the sea itself changed subtly. The waves became subdued, the motion of the vessel slower, more cautious. When they were almost at a standstill, there came the grating of hull nudging hull.

"We're there," Johanna breathed. Berengaria nodded her mouth too dry to form words.

After the endless weeks of waiting, it seemed as if the final hours and minutes would never pass. Berengaria became certain that something had gone wrong, that they would not land, but rather would leave harbour again, to sail – like the spirits of the dead sailors – forever, never touching dry land again.

She felt sick; anxiety drew all the air from her lungs and she yawned wide, snatching for breath. At her side, Johanna shuffled, fidgeting like a bored child.

Hulls bumped against them again, and finally, an eternity later, the door was opened and Rafe bowed low.

"My ladies." He said formally. "The Holy Land awaits you."

After so long, after such expectations, Berengaria stared in bitter disappointment at a ragged port, backed by dull, sand coloured buildings. The sun shone with unmerciful heat, but even the brightness could not make the filthy dock, smeared with fish guts and scales and things Berengaria didn't want to think about, look clean. Even the sea that lapped against the sides of the moored vessels was dirty grey; thick with greasy wastes whose stink caught in her throat and made her retch. Beggars, their faces disfigured by sores, some missing an arm or a leg, some drooling in idiocy, clustered on the port, hands held out in urgent supplication. Children clustered amongst them, huge eyes staring from dark, dirty faces as they regarded the great Crusaders' fleet solemnly. As Berengaria watched, one of the children fiddled in his robes and casually turned aside to pass water, splashing the beggar next him. He clouted the child's ear before resuming his constant appeal for alms, cupped hand held out suggestively, the other hand fastidiously twitching his rags away from the puddle of urine.

Berengaria swallowed a bitter mix of bile and disappointment, searching the quay side for sight of Richard. Where was he? In the throng dragging their mounts to shore? Surely, he could not care more for his horse than he did for her? The thought made her want to cry.

At her side, Johanna jabbered with pleasure. A commotion parted the stinking crowd before the ship; Berengaria's hopes rose and then fell abruptly as she realized that the horsemen pushing through were led by Philip, with no sign of Richard. One of the great warhorses stood on a beggar's foot, and the man howled and hopped away with surprising nimbleness for one who had been bent and stiff a moment before.

Philip shouted orders and waved his arms and within moments the gangplank was made fast between their ship and the shore. Berengaria stared uneasily at the narrow, rough-hewn plank, worried by the foot-wide gap between boat and plank that appeared at every movement of the ship. But Philip was already bustling up the plank as if it was nothing.

"My ladies," he bowed low. "It is my pleasure to welcome you to the Holy Land. To Acre. Berengaria, will it please you to take my arm?"

Philip grasped her arm confidently, but the plank was as narrow and slippery as she had feared. She hesitated, and her foot slipped, her silk slipper dangling for a moment before it slid in to the depths of the harbour. Philip's hand steadied her immediately, but Berengaria hardly noticed as she watched the shoe slide through the depths, supple and slippery as a fish. Tears trickled down her cheeks.

"My shoe." She whispered, feeling ridiculously foolish but still unable to stop the tears. "My shoe."

Philip shrugged indulgently, as if to say, "The ladies and their fripperies!"

"My lady, the silk makers of the Holy Land are famous for their skills. You'll have a pair of shoes for every day of the year, if that's your wish."

She smiled through her tears, unable to explain that the shoe had nothing to do with her tears, really. Nothing at all.

Chapter 11

The summer unwound with terrible slowness. Eventually, Berengaria adapted to the rhythms of the East, understanding instinctively that this was the only way to survive. The heat was enervating, constant and unyielding. And the flies; flies everywhere. Flies that wanted to crowd into her mouth with every bite of food; flies that feasted on her sweat day and night. Flies that bit and nuzzled and irritated, making her scratch until her skin was raw. Isabel made a potion that smelled strongly of citrus fruit, and that, when smeared on all exposed flesh, helped a little. But Berengaria often found that on going to bed she had bites in places she would have thought it impossible for even a fly to find.

Weeks passed that had no more texture than the dust.

Richard appeared at irregular intervals; sometimes weeks went by before the noise of his horses disturbed their routine. With his coming, the palace sprang to life. While he was there, there was music and laughter and conversation. Angela flirted with him outrageously, and Richard responded, taking her on his knee and calling her his favourite niece. Johanna fawned on her brother, to the extent that is seemed to Berengaria that she was competing with Angela for his attention. She watched both women coolly, not caring greatly. It saddened her, but she admitted the truth to herself, grieving more over her loss than the cause of it.

She no longer loved Richard. The all-consuming passion she had once felt for her husband had withered and died to a husk in the heat of the Holy Land. She examined her own feelings carefully, probing; expecting pain and not finding it. Where once she would have itched to have taken Angela by the hair and thrown her aside, now she simply watched, barely irritated by the girl's antics. And she knew now that Richard had never loved her. That the marriage – for him at least – had been one of convenience. The one thing that did cause her pain was the understanding that not only had he never loved her, neither had he ever desired her.

It annoyed both her and Johanna that Richard had left Blondin with them. He wandered in and out of their chambers unbidden, perpetually sure of his welcome from both women. Berengaria still disliked him, and Johanna hated him with a passion, but Johanna warned her that he was Richard's favourite, and it was better to tolerate him. Blondin told her without being prompted that he had been born in the court in France.

"How old are you?" She enquired idly, watching as he plucked at his lute strings. The instrument never seemed to leave his hands. He was, she had quickly realised, much older than she had first thought. Not a child at all, but probably eighteen or nineteen.

"I don't know." He said pettishly. Not for the first time, Berengaria wished she didn't have to tolerate his lack of respect. But he loved to talk about himself, and he rambled on happily. "I remember being in the kitchens in the palace when I was so big," Blondin held his hand about two feet above the floor, "And being fed by the kitchen maids, and sleeping in front of the fire."

"Didn't they make you work?" She asked in surprise, knowing that any and all hands were put to work in everybody's kitchen. Blondin looked at her sulkily from beneath his thick eyelashes. His hair, she thought, was barely darker than Richard's own, but straight and silky where Richard's waved and curled riotously. The boy always seemed quite extraordinarily clean, to the extent that he made her feel quite grubby.

"Nobody could make me work." He said arrogantly. "I went anywhere I wanted at Court, and one day I heard some of the knights playing and singing. I thought, "I could do that, I know I could", so I waited until there was nobody there, and started to play on their instruments when they left them lying about. One of the knight's caught me with his lute one day, and he was so impressed with what I had taught myself that he said he would help me to learn to play properly, and he did. Soon, I could play the lute better than he could, better than any of them, except for my Lord Richard, or course. And then one day Richard heard me singing and playing, and he told the knights that I was to be his troubadour, because I had the voice of an angel." He finished triumphantly.

Berengaria blinked at him, taken aback by the sudden ending of the tale. Before she could comment, Johanna came in and Blondin rose to his feet immediately, making a deep, somehow insolent, bow.

"My ladies." He smirked. "I will leave you now,"

Johanna watched him go, tight lipped, and closed the door firmly behind him.

"I hate that brat." She said. "If Richard didn't love him so much, I would turf him out on his arse like that." She clicked her fingers.

"I know, I don't like him either." Berengaria agreed. "He sets my teeth on edge. But I suppose he's harmless enough, and he is very talented. And it was very clever of him to learn to play on his own."

"Learned on his own?" Johanna raised her eyebrows and blew out her cheeks in scorn. "What tale has he been spinning you? The one about him being raised by the kitchen wenches and him finding a knight to be his protector?"

"More or less, yes." Berengaria said. "It isn't true, then?"

"My God, no." Johanna laughed. "I told you – he's a poisonous little toad; don't believe a word he says. Ever. He was born at court, probably the bastard of one of the servants, and he did have the run of the place, but only because nobody could catch him and make him do some work. Mother found him in her solar one day and for some reason I have never been able to fathom, took a fancy to him. She's as bad as Richard, sometimes. She made a pet of the brat, and when she found out he had a good singing voice, she made him take lessons from her favourite troubadour. She thought it was funny that he dared to defy her, and tried to run away from his lessons, but even Blondin couldn't get the better of Eleanor, and she had him turned into a halfway decent musician in no time. Richard found him hanging about Mother, and of course, if he was Mother's pet, then Richard loved him as well. Mother got tired of him eventually, and turned him over to Richard."

Berengaria bit her lip, reflecting silently that if Blondin had the ear of both Richard and Eleanor, then it would be better to have him as a friend than an enemy.

When Richard was with them and she could get him on her own, she questioned him closely about the progress of the Crusade, desperate to know how close he was to victory. How long before they could go home, to

England. The thought of England as "home" still seemed strange to her, but she forced herself to think of it so. *My country,* she thought proudly. *My people.* Sometimes, he would shrug her questions away in irritation, snapping that he had come away from battle and had no need to be reminded of what he had left. At other times, he spoke as if to himself, rambling of pain and blood and death. Of fallen comrades and near misses, and Berengaria's stomach soured as she listened. On those occasions, it seemed to her that he came to her bed gladly, as if he needed her, at last. When it was too late. His love making was always harsh and hurried, so quick that she had no time to think about taking any pleasure herself.

Was this normal, she wondered? Were all royal marriages like this? She remembered the intense love that had been so obvious between her own father and mother; a love that had been so strong that her father had refused to re-marry when her mother died, and she sighed, saddened by the knowledge that it didn't have to be like this.

Once, when Richard came fresh from the heat of battle, stinking of horses and sweat and dust, he took her by the arm to her apartment, tearing her clothes aside and mounting her without preamble and then, almost immediately, turning her over and forcing himself into her back passage. She cried out with pain and shame, but the louder she cried and tried to struggle, the harder Richard pumped into her. After a few moments, she laid still, her teeth gritted, and tried not to hear his guttural grunts of pleasure. When he had finished, he rolled aside and wiped himself absently with his sleeve before falling into a deep and apparently contented sleep.

She turned her back on him and lay still, tears of pain and humiliation running into her ears. He grunted in his sleep and pressed against her. She felt that he was half erect again, and unable to bear his touch she slid out of bed.

The candlelight glinted on Richard's sword and dagger, discarded the moment he came into the room. Half crouching in her anxiety not to make a noise, she walked across and fingered the sword, trying to lift it. Even with both hands, it was too heavy for her to more than hold it steady, and that with a huge effort. The dagger, though. That was light, and wickedly sharp. It seemed to sparkle, to invite her to take it up. To walk back to the bed with it, to press it against Richard's throat, and just lean against it, quite gently. It was so sharp, she was sure it would be ridiculously easy. And then all she had to do was to raise the hue and cry. To scream of an assassin who had slid in to the apartment, taking Richard when he was asleep, and disappearing as silently as he had come.

She thought she would have had the courage to do it, as well, but Richard snuffled softly in his sleep, speaking quietly. She leaned towards him, listening, and then lowered the dagger, biting her lip.

In his sleep, Richard had called out for her. A single word; "Wife".

But it was enough.

She slid back beside him and closed her eyes, barely flinching when his hand found her breast and fastened on to it tightly.

She watched him ride off next morning, and smiled when he turned in his saddle and waved. Smiled again when she found Angela behind her, scowling.

As the heat progressed from hot to hotter to unbearable, Johanna came down with a quartern fever. She tossed and turned, mumbling in delirium and Berengaria watched in horror, frightened she might die, and sick with misery for her own helplessness. Isabel took command firmly. In spite of Johanna's curses, she dosed the sick woman repeatedly with a rancid smelling green concoction. She forced Johanna to drink every hour; finding she spat out the concoction when it was mixed with water, she added a little wine to it and coaxed the result down her throat. Johanna would not eat, but Isabel assured Berengaria that is did not matter, as long as she drank. Concerned that Isabel had dark bags under her eyes and looked more tired than her patient, Berengaria told her to sleep and tried to look after Johanna herself, but Johanna decided to be contrary and pushed her away and threw her medicine on the floor, mewling pitifully that Berengaria was trying to kill her, and that she needed Isabel.

Terrified that Johanna might indeed die, Berengaria sent word to Richard. His response came immediately; Johanna was to be left at Haifa, and Berengaria was to join Richard outside Jerusalem. The fighting had slackened at last, Richard wanted her away from Johanna's sickness and anyway, she had always longed to see Jerusalem, now was as good a time as any. Rafe delivered the message awkwardly, giving as much grace as he could to Richard's blunt command of, "Oh, go fetch the silly woman. I don't want her coming down with whatever Johanna's suffering from. In any event, she's always whining on about wanting to see the Holy City, so let her come now. We may have to retreat any day. At least she can see it from a distance. Johanna can manage with that Jew bitch to look after her. But mind Rafe, look well and make sure she has no sign of the fever – if she has, leave her there."

"Jerusalem." She breathed the word, giving shape to each syllable. "I'm to go to Jerusalem." She licked her lips, hardly able to believe that after so many hopes, so many dreams, she was to see the Holy City at last. Then reality intruded harshly, and she shook her head. "I can't, Rafe. I can't leave Johanna. She's so ill. How can I leave her?" She scrunched her lips together, fighting back tears. For a bitter moment, she hated Johanna, the spoiler of her dreams.

Rafe stepped forward, his hands outstretched pleadingly.

"The King commanded that you come. He is, of course, concerned for his sister, but I think she is in the best of hands with Isabel." She stared at the wall, desperate to be persuaded. Rafe repeated, "Richard has commanded," and she crumbled.

Johanna ranted. She screamed insults at Berengaria, accused her of running to Richard and leaving her to die. Berengaria found her response comforting; surely she couldn't be that ill, if she could be so noisily angry? Isabel spoke to her quietly, assuring her that the worse was over, and that she would return to find Johanna well. Guilt piled on guilt as Berengaria realised she was far more unhappy to leave Isabel behind than she was to leave Johanna. But Richard had commanded. And Jerusalem called.

Jerusalem! She pushed aside Eleanor's less than ecstatic description and in her mind overlaid it with childhood tales of the city of Christ, shining in the sun, basking in almost a thousand years of devotion. And at last, at long last, she was to see her dream.

The smell hit them before she could even see the city walls. Riding into a slight dip as dusk fell, her horse shied and shook its head, nostrils flared in disgust. Berengaria wrinkled her own nose in sympathy.

"What in the name of God is that stench?" She demanded of Rafe. He stared at her puzzled for a moment, and then laughed shortly.

"That smell is Jerusalem. Jerusalem the Golden, they used to call it. Nowadays, it's more like Jerusalem the Rotten. You'll find you get used to the stink, and don't notice it so much after a while"

Before she could reply, the horses breasted the rise and the city was suddenly spread out far beneath her. She gasped, but in horror rather than awe.

The city walls still stood, but were pockmarked at irregular intervals where they had been thumped with siege engines, blackened in others where Greek fire had done its worse – or best, depending which side you fought on. In places, the wall had been breached and the holes stuffed with any old rubbish – masonry, wood, ship's timbers and – Berengaria swallowed hard – in other places what looked like human bodies. Huge siege towers, draped with wet, stinking hides to keep out the heat were lined at irregular intervals along the wall. Between the towers and the walls, further bodies – men, women and children - lay where they had fallen, some little more than bones in rags of clothes, others knights till wearing the remnants of armour. Rafe kicked his horse forward and Berengaria followed automatically, choking down a surge of nausea as their approach disturbed a flock of vultures which rose in to the air, only to fall back again on a heap of carcasses a few yards further away. A miasma of dust hung over the whole city, blessedly obscuring any worse horrors.

"Not what you expected?" Rafe spoke kindly.

"Why? Why didn't you tell me? Warn me? This …. This charnel house isn't the city of Christ!"

He shook his head.

"What could I say? Would you have believed me? Nay, better to leave your expectations intact until the last minute. I'm sorry, but Jerusalem is no longer a holy city. It's no more than a stinking shell of what it used to be. It is a prize, to be fought over and taken and kept by the strongest. And may the Lord grant that that will be Richard!"

Leaning across, he grabbed her horse's reins and led her in a wide circle away from the Holy City. Within a minute, it had vanished from view. Only the stink stayed.

Richard expressed his delight in his wife's presence by sweeping her into his arms and giving her a smacking kiss on both cheeks. The sun had wreaked havoc with his fair skin; ulcers were split all around his mouth, and his eyebrows were puffed and swollen to the extent that they were hidden entirely by proudflesh. His nose was a drinker's red blob, and his hair hung lank, uncombed and unwashed, so greasy that the mark of his helmet was clearly visible around his skull. His clothes were meshed to his body by sweat and dirt.

"Well, wife?" He bellowed. "Jerusalem at last, eh? Not quite what you expected?" He roared with laughter. "No need to worry, once we oust the Saracens finally, we will ensure that the City of Christ is made fit for our Lord once again. I promise you, every trace of the Saracens will be removed and we will worship in Solomon's

Temple again. But in the meantime," he winked at Rafe. "In the meantime, it is many weeks since I saw my dear wife, and I think it is time we got to know one another again."

She could not help it, no matter how she tried. She could not make herself respond to him. She lay as unresponsive as a log as Richard pulled and tugged at her clothes. His nails were jagged, and scratched her flesh unmercifully. His beard rubbed her cheeks raw.

Her stillness aroused Richard far more than her fumbling attempts at passion had ever managed. His breath came in short pants – ha! ha! ha! – like a dog exhausted from running. His breath smelled of wine and onions and garlic

Berengaria turned her head to one side, and Richard promptly bit her exposed neck. Hard. She bleated in protest and he raised his head to look at her; it may have been a trick of the light, but she was sure she could see blood at the side of his mouth. If her arms hadn´t been pinioned beneath his body, she would have found the strength from somewhere to push him away, husband and king or no.

Richard grinned at her and slowly poked his tongue between his lips. Leaning forward, he licked her face from between her eyebrows to her mouth. He paused there for a second and then rubbed his dry tongue around her lips, finally forcing his way into her mouth. She had no will to resist, but simply opened her mouth and let his tongue explore her gums and teeth. Weary of his amusement, Richard drew back and slid down her body. His filthy beard and hair scratched at her skin until she wanted to claw at herself to find relief, but she couldn't move. Finding her nipple, he suckled on it contentedly, snorting like a baby. That, at least, was pleasant, and she felt the very first stirrings of pleasure.

She made a small noise and immediately wished she had kept quiet. As if she had disturbed Richard, he bit her nipple hard enough to hurt and tossed his head, muttering to himself. For a second, she thought he had had enough but no. He rested his head on her shoulder and his hand moved over her belly, rubbing it in exactly the same way she had seen him caress a favourite dog. But not for long; his nails gouged a line down her stomach, tangling in her pubic hair where he scratched quickly for a second or two. For a moment, she thought this was some new love game he was playing, and then realized he was simply trying to find his way into her. She shifted slightly and Richard's hand found her sex, ducking inside and pawing at her, clenching his fist against her tender flesh.

Unaroused by his actions, she was dry and screamed out loud at his attentions.

"Ah. You like that, wife?" Richard mumbled into her shoulder.

Berengaria blinked back tears of pain and said nothing at all. What was the point? If she said yes, he would do it all the more. If she said no, he would sulk and still probably carry on.

Richard seemed to take her silence for consent. Abruptly, he shoved his whole hand into her sex, stretching his long, thick fingers as far as he could reach. The pain was too much; hardly able to move, Berengaria managed to turn her head and bit savagely at the only thing she could reach. His ear.

He screamed like a girl and she tensed, expecting a blow in return. Instead, Richard snatched his groping hand away from her and rolled over on top of her, his cock probing frantically to get inside her. And he was erect. Unlike the normal, floppy erection that jabbed at her half-heartedly this was thick and strong, rearing and probing as if it had a life all of its own.

She grunted in surprise, and was even more surprised to find that the feelings Richard was arousing were suddenly pleasurable. Timidly, she began to move in time with him. Closed her eyes and let her body take over. Began to pant, to grab hold of Richard's shoulders to try and stuff even more of him inside of her.

And moaned out loud with disappointment as Richard gave one final thrust and then rolled off her to lie shuddering at her side. Nearly crying with frustration, she turned her head and closed her eyes, wanting only for him to sleep, as he usually did soon after making love to her. But after a moment she felt his hand on her stomach, the calluses left by his sword rough against her skin.

"Wife, you must give me a baby. You understand that? A boy child. England must have an heir. If there's no babe from you, then my brother John will take the throne." He turned his head and spat, as though he was getting rid of a bad taste. "True enough, I have said that I would sell London if I could find a buyer, but John! My dearest brother would sell the whole country if he thought it would keep him in luxury. Come now, Berengaria, what do you say?"

She shook her head, close to tears.

"A baby – our baby – there's nothing I want more. Nothing. You must know that?"

"Aye. Or so I thought. But that Jew bitch who waits on your every whim. She hates me, I know she does. And I have heard these people know things that decent Christians do not. She has not persuaded you to take anything? Some potion she has concocted for your own good – or so she says? Something that would do you no good at all?"

Berengaria laughed shortly.

"No, nothing. Not so much as a draught for a chill. Babies come in their own good time, so my mother always said, and not before. Perhaps when we reach England, and we can be together more, it will be better?"

And do I really believe that? She thought sadly.

"Maybe so." Richard said grudgingly. He sighed, dropping his head heavily on her shoulder. "I have never been gifted with good luck. Never. It was foretold that it would be so. Mother told me that she had my fortune cast when I was born, and the seer said so then. A great king, he said. A great soldier. But one without luck. Do you know, at my very coronation in London a bat flew into the hall – in broad daylight! – and circled around my throne. No one could catch the damned thing. A bad portent if ever there was one. London – ha! I hate the place. I would sell it to any man on this earth, if only I could find one stupid to make me an offer. It's London that has bought me such ill luck."

"Superstition. No more." She said firmly "You are a great King, and all great men make their own luck."

"You think so?" Richard nodded. He smiled at her and then yawned widely. He was asleep almost as soon as he had stolen more than his share of the mattress.

Chapter 12

The knocking on her door kept on. She had been dozing away the heat of the long afternoon and at first she thought the noise was part of her dream. It had not been a good dream; Richard was shaking her and shouting at her and telling her she had bought him bad luck. Yelling that if it hadn't been for her wanting to come to Jerusalem, he would have been able to take it back from Saladin.

She was grateful for being woken up until she remembered that it hadn't just been a dream. Richard had been furious with her. He had ranted and raved and shaken her like a terrier with a rat, until she was so terrified that she shouted back at him, and he had dropped her then and stalked off with a face working with rage. She knew, instinctively, that he had left her before he could lash out at her. Take out his anger on her.

Now, she wanted only to be left alone. But the banging would not go away, would give her no peace. Eventually, it stopped – as she had known it would - but the relief was short lived as the door latch snicked and Rafe walked into her chamber.

"Go away. I don't want to see anybody. You least of all."

"I'm sorry." He knelt at the side of the bed. "He didn't mean it, you know. He had just heard that we had lost yet more men – Saladin sent a messenger to tell him they could be ransomed back, at a price. I think it was the last straw for him. He took it out on you because you were there, that's all."

She thought about it for a moment, and spoke bitterly.

"Is that supposed to make me feel better, Rafe? I just happened to be handy for him to shout at? You're saying I might just have well been one of the servants? Or one of Richard's favourite hounds? That doesn't exactly make me feel any better." She set her lips tightly to keep the tears back. "And now I'm never going to see Jerusalem, am I? It's lost, isn't it? And I don't care what you say, Richard thinks it's all my fault."

The tears rolled down her face. They stung and she wiped at them fiercely with the back of her hand. It was a while before she realized what Rafe was saying.

"It isn't your fault. When Richard is less furious with himself, he will apologize to you. But trust me, you were better facing Richard's temper than seeing Jerusalem as it has become. Some dreams are better left as dreams."

His voice was so peculiarly bitter that she blinked and tried to focus on his face. Her vision was smeary, but she could see his expression was an odd mixture of sadness and anger.

"How do you know what Jerusalem is like?" She asked curiously. "I thought no Christian had been inside the walls this last five years? Not since Saladin retook it."

"I was there. Last year." He closed his eyes and Berengaria resisted the urge to shake him to make him go on. "I'm dark enough to pass for Saracen; in the right clothes nobody would look twice at me. I speak Arabic with an excellent local accent. Richard decided he needed to know what state Jerusalem was like inside, so he sent me to look for him."

."You would have been killed if it had gone wrong." She said incredulously. "Richard was willing to lose you?"

"It was worth the risk." Rafe shrugged. "We both thought so. And I'm here to tell the tale. But Jerusalem as you think of it isn't there anymore. I promise you, you're better off not knowing."

"Tell me." She demanded. "Tell me, Rafe. I know what it was like. Tell me what it is like now. I need to know. Please."

He stared at her face and nodded, as if he had made his mind up. Didn't look at her as he spoke. Quietly, with no emotion in his voice at all.

"You saw the outside of the city walls?" She nodded. "The inside of the city is a hundred times worse. The streets run with filth. There are more people crammed in there than you would believe possible, most of them very poor, none of them with anywhere else to go. They keep their pigs in the Temple of Solomon, live alongside them. Why not? The Temple means nothing to them. Every other child is a beggar. Give alms to one, and there are a hundred of them following you about until you give the nearest one a punch out of desperation to get rid of them. The streets are littered with the bodies of animals who have dropped and been left. There are dead bodies there as well, bodies that once were people but had nobody left to bury them. All of it stinks. The Jerusalem you treasure has not been golden for at least the last five years. It's a war site, nothing more. I told Richard that. I also told him how many men Saladin has there. How well armed they are. How the walls have no weak spots that I could see. He thanked me, but he didn't listen to me."

"He sent you there, knowing you could be going to your death, for nothing?"

"Yes. But if you care, care about me, then it was well worth it. A thousand times over. Please. Please don't cry."

Until he spoke, she had no idea she was crying again. He reached out with his finger and wiped the tears away. The gentleness of his gesture unleashed something inside her. Suddenly, the tears were not for Jerusalem, not even for Rafe, but for another dream equally lost. The dream that had been Richard and her marriage to the man she had loved for so many years. The man who had destroyed all of her dreams, without even noticing.

Feeling as though her body was acting against her will, she raised her arms and held her hands out to him like a frightened child. As if it was the most natural thing in the world, Rafe took her hands and raised them to his mouth, kissing her palm delicately. She whimpered and he leaned forward, smothering the sound with his lips.

She simply stayed still, having no idea how to respond. What to say, or do. His mouth was gentle, as if he knew she was frightened. When he moved his head, her lips felt cold without him.

He sat back, looking at her. It occurred to her that Richard had never actually looked at her like that, as if she was something worth gazing at, and the thought made her want to cry all over again. She was grateful that Rafe didn't give her the chance.

His kisses were tender. He kissed not just her lips, but her whole face. Her earlobes were still sore from Johanna's rough piercing, and as if he knew, he took each one in his mouth and sucked it gently. She hissed with pleasure at the feeling. Hissed again when his lips moved down to her neck, plucking gently, licking and nibbling in places that were suddenly exquisitely pleasurable. She closed her eyes and felt rather than saw him unlace her dress and slide her gently out of it.

"Oh, but you are beautiful." He breathed. She laughed shortly and then realized with huge amazement that he meant it.

She was shy, and tried to hide her breasts and her sex with her arms and hands, but Rafe was having none of it. He moved her arm away from her breasts carefully, and he wet his finger in his mouth and rubbed the wetness on her nipples. They hardened at once and she gasped at the pleasure the simple action gave to her.

He waited, and after a while she guessed he was waiting to see if she would tell him to stop. But the moment for that was long past, and she could not.

But neither could she bring herself to touch him. Not that she didn't want to; she simply had no idea what would please him, and was too worried that she would disappoint him, as she had Richard. So instead, she simply lay still and let Rafe make love to her.

His roving hands slid down her belly and lingered at her sex. She wanted desperately to part her legs, to invite him in to her body, but to her horror she felt her private parts clench tight. It was the same every time Richard came to her bed, but he barely noticed, simply forcing himself in to her when he felt like it, not caring about the pain he was causing her. And now she was doing it again. She screamed at herself to relax; this wasn't Richard with his clumsiness and greed. This was Rafe, who found her beautiful and was caressing her as if it was the most natural thing in the world. She trembled under his touch, but nothing could make the tightness inside of her unknot.

And then Rafe was touching her pubic hair, so gently he might have been stroking a timid cat. Softly, so slowly it tickled. She laughed in spite of her distress and he smiled at her.

"What do you like?"

"I don't know." She said sadly. He bit his lip and she was sure she saw pity in his face, just for a moment, then it was gone and he was smiling at her again.

"Ah, then we shall enjoy finding out!"

One finger probed gently at her opening. She tensed, her hands arching into claws. *I'm sorry.* She thought. *I'm so sorry. I can't help it.* She cleared her throat, trying to find the words to explain, but Rafe spoke before she could.

"Shush. I´m not Richard. I´m not a king, who has to be obeyed. I´m your friend. Your lover. And I will not hurt you. Ever."

She stared at him amazed that he understood. And in that second of distraction, his wandering finger slid into her and began to stroke her, gently. She stiffened, then realized that she was actually wet. That the normal dryness that made making love with Richard so painful was gone. She stared at him in disbelief.

His erection was pushing hard at her thigh. Daringly, she slid her hand down to it and grasped it, nearly exclaiming with shock at its size and thickness. Even at his most passionate, Richard had never had anything like this for her. A new worry immediately began to nag at her; could she possibly take this inside her? But Rafe was obviously enjoying her attentions, he began to move in her hand and she could hear his breath quicken.

Almost automatically, she tightened her grip and began to haul fiercely on his cock. She heard him gasp, and then his hand was on hers, but pulling her fingers away rather than clamping them closer.

"Gently." He said softly.

She shook her head in amazement.

"But Richard likes that."

"I'm not Richard." He said simply, and took her fingers away altogether.

He laid her back gently on the bed, and without taking his hand away from her, began to kiss her breasts and belly. His head moved lower and lower, and it was only when his lips and mouth pushed into her sex that he slid his hand away, and then only far enough to part her sex.

She screamed out loud. Let the servants hear her, she didn't care. Let Johanna come running, it didn't matter.

He raised his head, and she saw with a kind of wonderment that his lips and chin were glistening with her juices.

"Now? Now, my love?" He said and she nodded.

He slid into her effortlessly, and she almost laughed aloud. Why had she ever feared that she couldn't take this? It was easy. The easiest, the most wonderful thing in the world.

"Finished?" She gasped, and wondered why Rafe was laughing at her and shaking his head.

"Not yet. Not for a long time."

And however long it was, it couldn't be long enough. And then, what seemed like a minute later, she felt pleasure rise in her sex and spread to her belly in waves of delight. She raised herself up to him, desperate to get every last morsel of him inside her; she wrapped her legs around his back and her mouth opened in a silent scream of pure ecstasy.

When he had gone, she lay still on her bed, amazed at the wonder of it. In the distance, she could hear Johanna scolding Isabel for some fault, real or imagined. A fly buzzed at the sweat on her forehead and she batted it away, hardly able to summon the energy to shoo it off. Her arms and legs felt leaden, her whole body deliciously heavy with remembered pleasure.

She was about to drowse off to sleep when a thought occurred to her and she frowned. Something had been different about Rafe. Not just his tenderness, nor his determination to give her pleasure – although the memory of that made her smile – something had been physically different to Richard.

Next time, she decided; and the idea that there was going to be a next time delighted her, next time, she would ask Rafe about it. Better still, she would take a good look first. And then ask him.

She slid into sleep with a smile on her lips.

Chapter 13

Isabel wrung out a cloth and wiped her forehead with it. Berengaria wriggled, trying to avoid the annoyance.

"Leave me alone. There's nothing wrong with me."

Isabel shrugged and dipped the cloth in a bowl of flower-scented water, wringing the cloth out firmly before dabbing at Berengaria's forehead again. Absently, Berengaria thought how red, how large, Isabel's hands were. She had never noticed before and it made her sad. Would it really be possible, she thought again, to find Isabel a husband from the court when they eventually – please God! – arrived back in England? Surely there must be some younger son of minor nobility, who was desperate for preferment and would do anything to gain it. Anything, even marry a Jewess. She was a good girl, she deserved some happiness.

"Ma'am, the fever is everywhere. You must take all precautions that you can against it. This will help."

Berengaria sighed and gave in. Isabel was gentle, and the concoction smelled very pleasant.

"What's in it?" She asked drowsily. With her back turned as she wrung out the cloth, Isabel muttered a list of flowers and herbs. Berengaria noticed she repeated "lavender" twice and raised her head to watch the maidservant as she moved about the room. Isabel moved slowly, langorous in the sodden heat. Her hair was braided untidily, almost as if it was trying to come loose under its own length and weight, and her expression was abstracted, dreamy. Oh, oh, Berengaria thought. What have we here? Has my little maidservant found herself a man, without me to help her? Memories of Rafe instantly jumped in to her mind and she smiled; how could she even try to deny Isabel a fraction of the joy she had found? If Isabel had found somebody she fancied, then she would do all she could to help. Why should Isabel be doomed to an unhappy marriage, just as she had? No matter if the man was totally unsuitable, if Isabel wanted him, then she would have him.

Isabel turned as if she had spoken out loud.

"Ma'am?" She said, but Berengaria waved her away.

"Leave me. I'll try to sleep a little until it gets cooler." A thought occurred to her and she propped herself up on her elbow. "Doesn't the heat bother you, Isabel? Was it so hot where you come from?"

Isabel giggled.

"No, Mistress. I come from York, many miles further north than London. It was rarely very hot in York, and in winter it snowed from November until March. We were more often cold than hot, but I like the heat, better than being cold, for sure!"

"Are your family still there?" Berengaria asked with lazy curiosity.

"Aye. So far as I know, at any rate. My mother died when I was young, but I live in hope that my father and brothers and sister have been spared and are still alive and well."

Her curiosity piqued, Berengaria asked,

"So how did you come to be in Eleanor's service? Does she have property in York?"

"My father," Isabel paused, rubbing the moist cloth between her fingers. She cleared her throat nervously and glanced around the room before continuing. "My father is a Usurer, Mistress."

Berengaria shrugged, puzzled. Of course he was; Eleanor had borrowed from him, hadn´t she? Where else was she to go, only Jews were allowed to lend money. And everybody used them in times of hardship; there was no shame in that. Even Richard, she knew, had had to borrow heavily to finance his Crusade, and God knew when his Jews would get any money back, if at all.

"Yes?" She probed "Your father indentured you to Eleanor as a servant, didn´t he?"

Isabel flushed a deep, mottled red and shook her head.

"No. He asked her to take me. He gave me to her."

Berengaria blinked in surprise. Slaves, of course, were part of life. She remembered that her own mother had kept a little Moorish boy as a slave, and had treated him like a toy; dressing him in bright colours and having him perform acrobatic tricks for her amusement. But Isabel was white, or as near white as made no difference.

Her skin was dark, but in truth only a few shades darker than Berengaria's own olive complexion. And she was English by birth, and Berengaria thought uneasily that she had not known that the English made slaves of their own people.

Realizing that Isabel was deeply embarrassed, she waved her away. Now she came to think about it, she remembered Eleanor telling her much the same thing before they had parted. Isabel, she had said, is my eyes and ears, and more valuable than rubies. Look after the girl, she had commanded. Take good care of my hidden jewel and you will find she has hidden uses.

As the heat and humidity descended with the persistence of a cloud of flies, she forgot about Isabel and slid into a doze, more asleep than awake.

"My love, you called for me."

"That I did not. How could I, when I was asleep?"

"Then perhaps you called out to me from your dreams?"

She smiled; perhaps she had, at that, when her last waking thoughts had been of Rafe. Of her lover. Her stomach lurched with pleasure at the thought.

He sat on the bed at her side, his fingers stroking her neck. She stretched with pleasure and sighed. Wrong, she thought. This is wrong. I'm wife to the King of England. Wife to Richard the Lionheart, the man I loved for so many years. But how could I love him now, when he has no love for me? When I know that he must have taken lovers, lovers he no doubt cares far more about than he ever cared for me. She frowned at the thought and Rafe paused.

"That doesn't please you?" He asked.

"No. I mean, yes, of course it does." She caught his hand and brushed it against her lips. "It's just … I was thinking about Richard. I know he has had lovers, probably many lovers." Rafe shrugged, watching her quietly. What a serene presence he was, she thought, this man who could bring her alive with nothing more than his gentlest touch.

"He is the king." He said simply. "The normal rules of life don't worry him. The world is his for the asking, and – remember! – you're the woman he did ask for. You're not his merely his lover, you're his queen, his wife."

"In name, at least." She said bitterly. "I know about Alice, Rafe."

He started to speak, stumbled over his words and stopped.

"Everybody knew about her." She said sadly. "We even heard what had happened in Navarre. I didn´t believe it at first, I thought it was just a nasty rumour. And then people started saying she had left court in a great hurry and had vanished, and the gossip started in earnest. About her and King Henry being lovers. I can remember as if it was yesterday the ladies sitting with Aunt Constanzia and chattering about who was left for Richard to take as a bride. It was a very short list, and it´s ironic, really, I think I was the only possibility that wasn´t mentioned. I spent hours on my knees, praying that he might choose me, but even when it happened I couldn´t believe it. Papa always said you should be careful what you wished for, in case you didn´t like it when you got it, and he was right. I loved Richard, you know."

"I´m sorry." Rafe said helplessly.

"I know I should still be grateful for all Richard has done for me, I know all that. It's just when I think of the way he looked at Angela, I just wish he would look at me in the same way, just once."

Rafe shook his head, his lips tight.

"You really believe he took Angela to his bed?" He said. "Really? For myself, I would have thought he would have had better taste than to touch that little trollop. Unless he had a sudden taste for the gutter, perhaps, for certain sure that one was no maiden."

Berengaria laughed shakily.

"Rafe, don't. I should have more sense than to even talk to you like this. What right do I have to criticize Richard, when I'm lying next to my own lover? Anyway, she's gone."

"Aye. I believe Phillip spirited her away to some provincial court or other in France." He paused, and she wondered if Phillip had got rid of Angela to get her away from Richard. Probably, she decided.

"God knows what havoc she's wreaking there." She smiled briefly. "What happened to her horrible father? Is he still a prisoner in his own dungeons?"

Rafe grinned and shook his head.

"You underestimate Isaac Kommenos. I heard that he managed to bribe himself free not long after we left Cyprus, and he's now trying to drum up support for another attempt at the throne. The man's a fool. He should know that what Richard gets, he keeps. Mostly." He added softly, and kissed the end of her nose.

She lay still for a moment, leaning against him in pleasure.

"I expect Johanna will be gone soon, as well." She sighed. "Off to Toulouse to wed her Count. And what shall I do when I'm all alone? When I don't have a friend left in the whole world?"

"You'll always have a friend, for you'll always have me."

"You're more than my friend, you're my lover." The word sounded wicked in her mouth and she tingled with pleasure. "But how can I talk to you about women's things? You're used to the battlefield, to death and glory, not babies and gossip."

"I do my best." Rafe shook his head in pretend sadness. "Now you've told me you want me only for tittle-tattle and baby talk, I'll keep my ears open for all the juicy gossip, and learn to swaddle a babe as well as the next."

"Fool!" She poked his ribs and Rafe snuffled her hair, pushing aside her veil with his nose. His fingers danced against her shoulder, sliding down to her breasts, his lips following.

"Ah," she exhaled softly, "Ah".

"No more talk, dear one." He said hoarsely, his mouth mumbling at her nipple. "We'll forget Angela and Richard and Johanna, for they are not here. But we are!"

"The door?" She whispered in a last attempt at sanity.

"Locked and barred. The whole world can knock and bang on it, but we'll not let them in until we're ready."

She moved against him, taking pleasure in the sensation of the rough cloth of his tunic. It seemed that there had never been a time when she had not known this man, not known the sight of him, the feel of him, even the smell of him; an earthy amalgam of leather and wool and fresh sweat. And yet, each time he touched her, each caress was a new sensation, a new arousal.

He helped her to wriggle out of her gown and would have taken off his own tunic and hose, but she stopped him with a touch to his arm.

"Leave it on." She said "I want the feel of it against me. On my skin."

He nodded and ran both his hands over her ribs, cupping her breasts. Straddling her hips, he rubbed against her nakedness with his clothes and she screamed softly with pleasure at his touch.

It had been like this, from the very beginning. He had been able to arouse her effortlessly, leaving her breathless with lust. All she had anticipated, all she had hoped for, with Richard she had found in Rafe. And more. Much more.

At first, she had worried how she would be able to hide her new knowledge from Richard. Surely, he would see and feel the difference in her? She could hardly believe that everybody couldn't see the change in her, and daily expected Johanna to challenge her, to demand to know what she was up to that made her so happy? But Johanna was purring at the news of her new marriage, and noticed nothing.

"Better bargain as a husband than that brother of Saladin, eh?" She laughed. "The Lord only knows what Richard was thinking of, when he proposed that idea. Mind you, as it turned out, it seems he didn't fancy me for a bride either. Cheek of the brute, turning down a queen for his wife."

"From the way Eleanor talked about the Saracens, I thought you might have made a good bargain there." Berengaria said slyly. "A handsome man, I imagine, from all I have heard about his brother, and so exotic! You would both have been joint rulers of Jerusalem." And, she thought silently, there would have been peace at last and the Crusade could have ended and Richard and I could have gone home. I could have been Queen of England, in truth as well as name.

"Exotic my left foot." Johanna responded huffily. "All men are the same when you get their clothes off. No, I'll take my French Count, thank you, and back to Toulouse it is for me. Back to civilization! And I'm never, ever going to set foot on a boat again. Mind you," she added wistfully "I did think at one time that perhaps Philip himself was more than a little interested, it seemed he had something of a tendresse for me, but apparently it was too close for comfort, his father having been married to Mother at one point."

Berengaria frowned as she attempted to work out what relationship that would have meant for Johanna and Phillip and Johanna glared at her.

"Think yourself lucky." She snapped "If it hadn't been for the Holy Laws forbidding it, Richard would have married Alice and where would you have been?"

"In a nunnery, probably." Berengaria said bluntly, and Johanna immediately hugged her in an attack of remorse.

"Oh, I'm so sorry. I'm nothing but the worst kind of bitch. Take no notice, you know I don't mean a word of it. I just open my mouth, and out it pops. Eleanor is for ever saying I don't think before I speak, and I suppose she's right. You'll come and visit me, won't you? In Toulouse? Bring Richard if you must."

Berengaria assured that she would visit, often.

"You'll be tired of me, and wishing me back here in a week."

"Let's persuade Richard to let me go now. And you can come with me, as well." Johanna begged. "Leave Richard here, to get on with his battles. This is no place for you, or me. Before I marry Toulouse, I'm determined I'm going to Rome, to seek an audience with the Pope. William always promised he would take me, but then he died and that wretch Tancred took me prisoner. I've always wanted to see Rome, and now I'm going to Toulouse to a new husband, it may be the only chance I get. Come on, you would love to go to the Holy City, you know you would." Berengaria shook her head, remembering that other Holy City that had been such a bitter disappointment. Admitting defeat, Johanna stuck out her tongue and flounced off.

At one point, Johanna had thought she might take Isabel with her, and Berengaria had been plunged into deep gloom at the thought of losing both her sister-in-law and treasured servant. For once, she was grateful to Richard, who had vetoed all of Johanna's fantasies with callous bluntness.

"You're not taking that penniless Jewish bitch with you." He snapped. "What would Toulouse think, if I sent you back with the likes of her as a serving maid? Not only English, but a heathen Jew, as well. A pretty start, to be sure. She stays here – we can always leave her behind when I'm victorious. Anyway, it doesn't matter because neither you nor Berengaria are leaving the Holy Land yet. I've got far too many problems ongoing to even think about finding safe passage for two queens. It would be inviting trouble – think of the ransom the pair of you would bring. Didn't you learn anything at all from that wretch Kommenos?"

Not even Johanna's petulant sobbing, a noise that hung on the air like the plaintive cries of cranes, would move Richard.

His visits to Haifa had become more and more frequent as the summer progressed into autumn, and Berengaria sensed a change in him He spent hours closeted with Rafe, and curious she had asked him;

"How do you cope with it? How do you manage to be with him, without being overcome by guilt? Without worrying you'll say something wrong? Don't you worry he'll notice something? I do. I worry every second I'm alone with him; I think twice before I open my mouth."

Rafe shrugged.

"He's my Master, just as you are my Mistress. I love you both."

As the autumn advanced and the weather became almost bearable, Richard took to coming to her bed almost each night he spent at Haifa. His lovemaking was more perfunctory than ever, for which Berengaria gave thanks. She accepted him simply as part of her duty as wife, as Queen, and slowly it seemed to her that their former roles were becoming reversed.

Richard clung to her like a drowning man desperately trying to grasp a slippery rock. He lay beside her, stroking her hand, rubbing the fabric of her gown between his fingers and talking, talking, talking. He whispered to her of battles, of men dying, of atrocities that she did not want to hear, but could not refuse to listen to. Told her that the city of Jerusalem was lost, probably forever. Eventually, sure she would awake insane if his voice repeated in her dreams, she lay with her head cradled in the bedlinen, eyes tightly closed as she tried to think of anything to distract her from his words.

Often, he talked of his brother, Prince John.

"Don't trust him." He warned. "Don't listen to his fair words – they'll all be lies. John wants nothing but my throne. He cares for nothing, except himself. King John, that's how he sees himself." He put his hand behind her head and pulled her face so close to his that she felt his breath warm on her cheek. "Whatever he tells you, whatever he promises, don't trust him."

She shrugged.

"Why do I need to put my trust in him, Richard? You're the King; he's nothing more than your younger brother, looking after the country until you take your rightful place."

"Don't trust him." Richard repeated. "Don't trust him. Eleanor will tell you. Eleanor will look after you, if I'm not there. But even Eleanor can't live forever."

Even though the sun was less fierce, Richard's fair skin was terribly damaged. His eyelids were red raw, the skin on his cheekbones constantly peeling. His lips were a mass of cold sores, vivid against his beard. Berengaria undressed him firmly, refusing to listen to his complaints that he did not need washing, that water was – as everyone knew – injurious to the skin. His clothes were stiff with dirt and patches of stain that she did not want to identify, and she simply threw all of them out of her chamber, knowing that Isabel would pick them up and launder them before Richard left. Naked, Richard seemed terribly vulnerable and she was moved by his pathetic attempts to hide his body from her.

Gently, refusing to listen to his grumbles, she bathed him from head to foot in water scented by pungent herbs. She washed his hair and beard with soapwort, and marveled at the red-blond hair revealed by the herb. He winced and sucked his teeth as she tried to bathe his face.

"Isabel could make you an ointment for this," she suggested. Richard glared at her.

"Isabel? She would kill me, given half a chance."

"Not if I tell her it's for me." She coaxed.

"It is very sore." He mumbled. "Perhaps it would help if I was bled? It must be months since the leeches had a go at me. Bad blood, bad blood. That's the trouble."

"No, Richard." She shuddered. "Enough blood has been spilled on the field of battle. No more, please. Let me speak to Isabel."

Grudgingly, he agreed and Isabel promptly produced a pot of ointment. Berengaria guessed she had been waiting for the opportunity.

"It… it will not hurt him, will it?" She asked reluctantly.

"It may sting a little at first." Isabel replied, either misunderstanding her question or pretending to misunderstand. "But it will soothe his skin very quickly. But I can only help a little. To make a proper recovery, he must stay out of the sun."

Berengaria nodded, knowing that Isabel was asking the impossible.

She rubbed the ointment gently into Richard's skin, beginning with his startlingly red, sunburnt ears and progressing over his face. He lay inert at her side, sighing with contentment occasionally. Slowly, Berengaria realised that the love she had once felt for this man, love she thought had gone for ever, had not gone completely, but rather had changed. Gone was the fierce, all possessing romantic love she had felt for her bridegroom. Gone the agony of wishing him to love her, and none other, the agony she felt when he looked at any another woman with interest.

Instead, she cared for him almost as if he was the child she longed for. She took pleasure in caring for him, in soothing his wounds. She rubbed Isabel's cream into what looked like suppurating insect bites on his chest and when he winced, she stopped and stroked his arm gently until he relaxed. The more he clung to her, the more she felt pleasure in his neediness. Slowly, she understood that her love for Richard had become the love of a mother for her child, and that he, in his turn, now depended on her and needed her.

She had thought him asleep, soothed by her ministrations, and was startled when he spoke.

"Philip's seriously thinking of withdrawing." He said abruptly. "He can't, he says, afford to go on. France is bankrupt, his people bled dry. He has no money to pay his soldiers, his people have no crops to harvest, no food to see them through the winter. Berengaria," He propped himself on his elbow and grasped her wrist fiercely,

"Berengaria, what can I do? If Philip runs, I can't re-take Jerusalem alone. I don't have enough men, it's impossible. As soon as Saladin hears I'm deserted, he will attack and attack until my men die where they stand. Damn Johanna! If she had been more compliant, if she had been willing and accepted Saladin's brother, all would have been well. But now, there's nothing. Nothing but defeat and ruin. What am I supposed to do? Run away with my tail between my legs?"

Tears leaked from his eyes and ran down his cheeks, leaving angry red steaks where they irritated his inflamed skin. He looked at her imploringly and Berengaria pulled him gently into her arms, nestling his head against her breasts as if he were a child. Richard sighed heavily and slowly fell asleep. Berengaria let him lie until her legs went into cramp and she was forced to slide away. Richard stirred briefly in his sleep and then began to snore.

He remained at Haifa for the whole of September. Deprived of sun, his skin began to heal dramatically and Richard, contrarily, gave all the credit to Isabel.

Strangers came, day after day. Tall, grim men clothed in white tunics with a red cross, the colours stained and faded, but still obvious. Men who walked with the assurance of royalty: men who were ushered into Richard's presence by Rafe, who then found the door closed against him. Other men, dressed in quiet robes; men who smiled and nodded and walked as if they wished not to be noticed. Men with olive skins and aquiline noses, men who reminded Berengaria of Isabel.

"Templars." Rafe said bitterly. "So called Poor Fellow Soldiers of Christ and of the Temple of Solomon. Poor! I tell you; those men could buy and sell Richard. The Jews will lend Richard his money, and tell him what they want in exchange, and stick to it. But the Templars… call themselves Christian men." His face reddened with anger. "They'll give Richard his money, and afterwards Richard will find that somehow he's managed to pledge his entire kingdom to them. Do you know that they own most of Acre? We are only here at Haifa by their grace and favour – they even own this palace."

"I understood that they were good men." Berengaria said cautiously. "They've fought bravely in all the Crusades, haven't they? My father said that without them, none of the Holy Land would ever have left the Saracens' hands."

"Aye, good men they were, in our grandfathers' times. But now they have power, Berengaria, power and great wealth and many great friends. Even Richard dare not cross them." Rafe lowered his voice to a whisper as if he feared he might be overheard by some invisible presence. "I told you what the Temple of Solomon was like. Did you think it was the Saracens that caused that? That took the treasures of the Temple? Oh no. It was the Poor Knights, I tell you. Their Grand Masters know where the Treasure is, but they will never tell. If they speak of it at all, they say they guard it for the glory of Christ. Glory of the Poor Knights, more like." Seeing her expression of disbelief, he leaned forward until he was almost touching her face. "I know Berengaria. I don't know where the treasure lies, but I know about the Poor Knights. I had a friend, a good friend, who sat at the right hand of the Grand Master, and I know their dirty secrets. But I tell nobody, not even Richard."

Instinctively, Berengaria knew there was more to Rafe's outburst than he was prepared to say. Quietly, she said.

"What happened to your friend?"

"He died." Rafe said bitterly. "They said he died at the Battle of the Horns of Hattin, but they lied. He died because he knew too many secrets. He died because he told me."

Berengaria quickly forgot Rafe's outburst. Richard's machinations held no interest for her, apart from her hope that no money would be forthcoming, from either Jews or Poor Knights. If Richard could only acknowledge that Jerusalem was lost to him, that his Crusade was at an end, then they could go to England, and she could take her rightful place at his side, as his Queen. Of course, there would be much work to be done. If France had been bought to its knees by the Crusade, then England was even worse. But once Richard returned then surely all would be well again. If only she could persuade him that the future lay with his own country, not here. Not with a cause that had been lost already.

But the autumn was gilded, and thoughts of politics had no place for her in the gentler sun. September bought a great harvest of fruit, and Berengaria became greedy for the golden bounty. Oranges, apricots, persimmons, pomegranates; the wonderful fruit reminded her of Navarre and she ate her fill. Rafe laughed at her, accusing her of turning into a glutton and telling her that she was getting fat. Fat, and as glowing as the fruit. She flicked him away with a gesture of her hand, called him a pestiferous fly, and he laughed with her.

It seemed to Berengaria that she could not satisfy her appetite, both for fruit and for Rafe. She was as greedy for the one as for the other, and no amount of fulfillment could satisfy her. She resented every moment that he was away from her, and demanded that he be with her every moment that Richard would release him. If Richard himself, or Isabel, or Johanna noticed she cared not at all.

Now without either Rafe or Richard, and with Johanna wrapped in one of her extended sulks, alone and bored and unable to settle, she rummaged through her chests and came upon her long neglected copy of the Romance of the Rose. Indulgent, she turned the pages and smiled as she recalled her lost innocence. This sweet allegory had once been all she had known of love, of life, but now it seemed a lifetime away. She put the volume down and stretched, running her hands down her ribs and across her stomach. And frowned. Had she really got fat? She could barely feel her ribs and her stomach, too, was rounded where it should have been flat. Cautiously, she cupped her breasts in her hands and winced as the fabric of her gown irritated her nipples.

After a moment, she rose to her feet and wandered across to the chest where she had unearthed the Romance of the Rose. In a line to one side, she found the layer of clean clouts left ready for her monthly use. She fingered them uncertainly and took up a handful, returning to sit on the mattress. Counting on her fingers, she thought – how long? How long since I last had need of these? Isabel would know. Almost, she shouted for Isabel to ask her, but caution stayed her tongue at the last second.

She sat for almost an hour, in turn fingering the cloths and running her fingers over her body. Did she feel different, she wondered? Had she been sick in the mornings? No, not at all. Did she desire strange foods? No, fruit could hardly be called strange, and in any event, she had always adored fruit. And her desire for Rafe had increased ten-fold; even thinking of him made her stomach clench with lust. No, apart from her missing monthly courses, there was nothing. But …. Four months? Four and a half months? She had never, ever been more than a few days late before. Could she really be pregnant?

Rafe had teased her about putting on weight. Richard hadn´t even noticed. The thought of Richard made her groan out loud and she stuffed her knuckles in her mouth, rocking back and forwards in terror. Was the baby even Richard's? How was she to know? Slowly, she began to gather herself together. Did it really matter who the father was? Richard would own it as his own, no matter what. Would have no idea at all that the baby might not be his. A memory from Navarre came to her suddenly; one of the ladies at court had had a baby who everyone knew was not her husband's. A first child, as well. The child had had bright red hair and green eyes, and very white skin. Rumour had it that the mother had fallen deeply in lust with one of the servants, and that the baby was his. In any event, her husband had been perfectly happy, and had even accepted compliments on the paleness of the baby's skin. Had simply accepted the child as his.

"I don't care. It's my baby." She whispered over and over again. "Mine, mine, mine."

She wouldn't tell Richard yet. She would wait until the date for her next courses had come and gone first. Then she would be really sure.

She was sitting by the window, her hands clasped over her belly, thinking of names for the baby, when Isabel spoke, startling her.

"The money men have gone, ma'am." She said quietly.

"The money men? Oh, you mean the Poor Knights and the Jews. So they have. Have they come to an agreement with Richard, I wonder?"

Isabel paused before answering.

"The word is that they did not." Berengaria watched her curiously. Isabel would know, of course. She always did. "The rumour is that terms could not be agreed with either the Knights Templar or," she paused and then shrugged "Or the Jews. They asked too much, it is said. It seems that King Philip has kept to his word, and has started to take his men away. And so now there's nothing."

"What do you mean, 'nothing'?"

"If Philip has withdrawn, and the King has no money, then," she frowned and spoke slowly, as if to a child. "Well, then he can't fight any longer. That is all."

Berengaria stared at her as thoughts tumbled across her mind. No money to fight. No support from Philip. No way for Richard to continue his Crusade.

"Then," she whispered, "Then we can go…. Home."

"Aye, mistress." Tears gleamed in Isabel's eyes. "We can go home. Back to England. You'll be Queen, take your rightful place. And I will be home. Home!"

Berengaria stared, unable to say anything. Soon, she thought, she would be happy, would feel overjoyed at this sudden news. Her baby, her precious heir to the

English throne, would be born on English soil. For the moment, she was numb. She waved Isabel away and the servant girl left silently, glancing back over her shoulder as if she expected Berengaria to say more.

She stared into space, seeing nothing. Richard was here, he had appeared with Rafe before dinner yesterday, had spoken a few words to her, but she had seen neither man since. The two had dined alone together, closeted in Richard's chamber. She must see him, tell him about the baby. Persuade him that she must set out for England now, as soon as possible. For her safety, or if that meant nothing to him, for the safety of the unborn child. Johanna could travel with her and go on to Rome from England, if that was what she wanted. In any event, she would be overjoyed to leave the Holy Land. Eleanor, she thought cynically, would welcome her with open arms once she heard the news.

She climbed to her feet and thrust her feet into her slippers. The corridors were empty; it was the dead hour in the early afternoon when even the servants had an hour or two to themselves. Berengaria pattered noiseless as a ghost along the passage, moving from dark to light as she passed shuttered and open windows. As she walked, she rehearsed over and over what she was going to say to Richard, anticipating the happiness on his face, not even allowing herself to think that the baby – her son – might not be Richard's child, as if the very thought might betray itself on her face, as if Richard might suspect. She shrugged the idea away angrily. Of course he could not know. Any anyway, there was nothing to know. It was Richard's babe. Of course it was. Of course *he* was.

Richard's door was closed, without its usual guards. Wondering if he was there, she pressed her ear against the oaken door. She could hear nothing, no murmur of voices, nothing. She pushed against the door and it opened silently, swinging into gloom.

The shutters were closed against the heat and glare, and she walked in uncertainly, pausing to allow her eyes to adjust to the darkness. A sound somewhere between a deep sign and a groan made her head come up quickly and as her sight grew used to the gloom her mouth dropped open in a silent scream. She shook, trembling like a sapling in a high wind. If her hand had not been clutched on to the doorframe, she would have sunk to her knees.

Richard lay on his bed; the sheets flung back to reveal his naked body. Sweat had dried on his skin, caking in little patches of salt on his chest and thighs. His head had fallen back, his eyes closed, his mouth parted in pleasure or pain or both. At his side, Rafe lay with his body flush against the other man's, his nakedness all the more shocking as Berengaria knew every curve of rib and thigh, every finger, every inch of skin. As she watched in horror Rafe opened his eyes and gazed lovingly at Richard. He moved his left hand and ran it over Richard's ribs, stroking his body in a way that was so familiar to Berengaria that she felt his touch on her own skin. Richard lowered his head and the two men kissed; a deep, succulent kiss that excluded the whole world from the two of them.

"My lord." Rafe whispered "My King. My own love."

Richard stirred and rolled over, his body engulfing Rafe and hiding the other man from her gaze. He began to move, slowly at first and then with increasing urgency and Rafe moaned, bucking against him. Richard shouted with pleasure, and Berengaria was filled suddenly with a great sadness, smothering her shock and horror like a black wave. She had never been able to give Richard such pleasure, pleasure that made him scream aloud with happiness. Never would, she understood now. She shook her head helplessly as tears rolled down her cheeks and she backed away from the door silently.

Out of nowhere, a memory came of Richard calling to her in his sleep. "Wife", he had said. But suddenly she knew it had not been her he had been calling for, but his lover. She had heard the word she wanted to hear, but now she was sure that Richard had not called for her, his wife. He had called for his lover. For Rafe.

Her vision swimming, she swayed back to her own apartment, rocking from side to side of the corridor and using the walls to support herself. She found her way through her door more by luck than judgment and fell on the bed, the sobs she had held back tearing out of her throat. She cried until her chest and throat were sore, until there were no more tears left to cry.

The pain had become harsh before she even noticed it. Her mind was numb to anything but the thought of Richard and Rafe together. Her husband and her lover. Together. A deep, deep tear in her belly jerked her upright and she clutched herself in shock. She propped herself on her elbows and dragged her gown aside, staring in disbelief at the bloody fluid between her thighs.

She screamed out loud then, again and again and again and eventually, after a lifetime had passed, Isabel was by her side. The girl was there, then gone, and then back again and Berengaria clutched at her, her nails biting deep into her arm.

Isabel pushed her back on to the bed gently.

"Let me see." She demanded, forcing Berengaria's gown above her breasts. She pressed one of Berengaria's clean clouts between her legs, throwing it away almost immediately and replacing it with a fresh one.

"My baby." Berengaria mewed, "My baby."

"Aye." Isabel responded grimly. "It's trying to come now. I don't know, I don't think we can save it. It's too young and labour's gone too far. Why didn't you call for me earlier?"

Berengaria shook her head, unable to speak. The pain rolled over her and she sat up, her arms around Isabel, holding her tightly, rocking to the rhythm of her agony. But the pain was welcome. After a while, it became so deep, so enduring, that it even drove out the memory of Richard and Rafe, happy in each other's arms. Happier than she had ever been able to make either of them.

That knowledge hurt almost as much as the physical pain.

Vaguely, Berengaria was aware that it had been light, and was now dark. And was light again. The pain came and went, ebbed and flowed. Although it never diminished completely, eventually she felt a dull acceptance of the agony and felt that she wanted nothing so much as to sleep, to sleep until it went away.

"You're wishing it." A firm voice snapped from somewhere close at hand. "Stop it. If it's God's will to take this child, then let it go."

Vaguely, Berengaria thought the voice was that of her mother, dead so many years past but back now, in her time of need.

"No." She whispered "No, it's my baby. Mine. Nobody else must have it. Nobody. Not even God."

"Let it go." The voice demanded. "Give in to your body. Let it go."

"No. No, you don't understand…" Berengaria whipped her head from side to side in pain and panic. Suddenly, her face was cradled in a strong hand and a cup pressed to her lips. The drink was syrup sweet, but even the intense sweetness could not hide the underlying bitterness.

"Drink." Her mother's voice said gently "Drink and the pain will go."

So she drank, and the pain fled and she slipped into the sleep she had craved.

Chapter 14

Berengaria opened her eyes to light. She stretched and winced at the pain in her belly. For a moment, her mind was filled with pleasure at the cool of the day and the golden light flooding through the window and she had no other thought. Someone put a cup to her lips. She raised her head obediently and sipped, drinking greedily as she realised how thirsty she was. The liquid was cool and pleasant, smelling and tasting of fruit. She lay for a second, and then memory flooded back.

"My baby." She shouted. "My baby. Where is he? My baby?" She struggled to rise, but was pushed back, gently but very firmly.

"Mistress." Isabel said softly, "Be still, please. You'll do yourself damage. Be still."

"My baby." Berengaria repeated. Her hands grabbed Isabel's shoulders, and she hauled herself up to a sitting position. "What have you done with him? Where is he? What's happened?"

Isabel spoke quietly, persistently. Repeating the same words over and over, but in different order, until – unwillingly – Berengaria was forced to listen to her. To listen, and understand.

"There is no babe. Your baby came too early, much too early. You were barely more than five months gone I think. If that."

Her mouth opened and closed, but only a croak came from her lips. Even so, Isabel seemed to understand the unspoken question.

"It was a girl, ma'am." She said quietly. "Tiny, no bigger than this." She held her hands about six inches apart, "But a girl, for sure."

"Her hair? Her eyes?" Berengaria croaked.

"I could not say. She was not old enough to have hair, and her eyes were not opened."

"Where… where have you put her?"

"I buried her myself." Isabel said softly. " In the Christian cemetery. I can show you where, when you're feeling stronger. At the moment she has no stone or marker."

"Thank you." Berengaria whispered hoarsely. *My baby*, she thought. *My poor baby, condemned to purgatory forever. Isabel had not understood that giving the baby a Christian burial meant nothing, for it – she – had died unshriven. How could she have known? The girl had done her best, she should be grateful for it.* She lay still for so long that Isabel was reassured and was about to rise when Berengaria's hand clamped around her wrist.

"Richard?" She asked. "Richard. Why isn't he here? Where is he?"

"He's gone." Isabel said bluntly. Berengaria shook her head in bewilderment.

"Gone? Where has he gone? What do you mean?" And then, "How long have I been asleep? What potion did you give me? Why has Richard gone? I don't understand."

Isabel spoke gently, talking slowly and clearly, as if to a child.

"The Crusade is done, ma´am. King Baldric came, and was closeted with Richard for half a day. That was not long at all after you went into labour. After that, all hell was let loose. Rumour said that Philip had decided that he must withdraw, and he would not change his mind. Baldric could not persuade my Lord that he could regain Jerusalem without Philip. After Baldric had gone, the Saracens came very soon after and the King was close with them for many hours. And then when they left, it was said that my Lord Richard had decided that he had no hope. I think myself it was six of one and half a dozen of the other. King Richard could not hope for victory with his supporters running away, and Saladin in his turn was undone by the Christian victory at Jaffa. I heard that in return for peace, and the Christians relinquishing any claim to Jerusalem, Saladin agreed that unarmed Christian pilgrims would be allowed free access to worship in Jerusalem and that Richard and his men would be allowed to go in peace."

Berengaria stared at her. Richard, with his terror of illness and anything unclean, had been in the same room as Baldric, the Leper King? That, more than anything convinced her that Isabel was speaking the truth.

"And Richard has gone? Gone without me? Gone without saying a word? What did you tell him?" She said bitterly. "That I was dead?"

"No. It wasn't like that." Isabel said earnestly. "The whole castle was in uproar. Everybody was rushing about, but at the same time it was if they had all been expecting it and knew what to do. The King came to see you, but…. but you were shouting in pain and he wouldn't come in. You screamed at him to go away, ma'am." Berengaria looked at her incredulously, but Isabel nodded, her face pleading. "You were pouring with sweat and threshing about and the King seemed to think that you were trying to warn him. He stood outside the door and demanded to know if you had the sweating sickness, and before I could explain anything one of the knights ran up to him and they went away together."

Berengaria stared past her. The sweating sickness. It had been at court in Navarre when she was a child and it had been unstoppable. Men and women who were well in the morning were dead by the same night, and none of the apothecaries had been able to even offer a hope of a cure. The very thought of those dreadful times made her shiver with terror, and she could almost understood why Richard had left her. He had already tempted fate by meeting with Baldric; he would not risk it again.

"Has Johanna gone as well?"

"No, she's still here. The King left a letter for you, ma'am." Isabel was holding out a folded piece of parchment, sealed roughly with red wax, stamped with what Berengaria recognized as Richard's signet ring.

She took it in shaking fingers, fumbling to break the seal.

Richard's writing was ragged, the words uneven. He had clearly folded the parchment without sanding it, as some of the words were smeared. The letter was brief.

"Dearest Wife,

I'm most sorry that I cannot be here to see you, to explain myself what has happened. I know that you'll be well soon, and when you are recovered you can follow. I must leave now, or as soon as I can make it so, or all will be lost. The Crusade is lost already. I believe Saladin is an honourable man, but I have no faith in those who are under him. I have made arrangements for your travel, have no worry. Johanna is to go with you. You are both bound for Rome, where you'll be safe. I hope Eleanor may still be there, if she is, she will look after you both. I have left my knight Stephen de Tancred to escort you both. Trust him, he is a good man.

Take time to rest in Rome, and then go to your lands at Poitou. Once I reach France, I will find you there

I will explain all when we meet again.

Richard"

She laid the letter down and stared at Isabel.

"He says he had made arrangements for me to travel to Rome, with the Lady Johanna. But if everybody has gone, how can we escape?"

Isabel spoke quickly.

"Not everybody's gone, Ma'am. I understand that the King and the knights and the soldiers had to go at once. Saladin himself granted them safe passage, but I believe that the King thought that the hotheads in Saladin's camp might decide they did not like their Master's clemency towards the Christians, and if he lingered it would be too late. A few men remained here at Haifa, waiting for you to recover but they can't wait for much longer, it's too dangerous. Once you're well enough to travel, you and the Lady Johanna must take ship. If the Saracens who were against allowing the King to go in the first place realised that you were both still here, they'd take you both prisoner, hold you to ransom, for sure."

Berengaria turned the parchment between her fingers.

"How long has Richard been gone?" She said quietly. "How long have I been asleep?"

"You were in labour for three days," Isabel said evasively. "You were exhausted, and still the baby wouldn't come."

"How long?" Berengaria demanded.

"I feared for your life. I gave you something to calm you, and you slept, but not so deeply that the baby couldn't be birthed. She was born on the third day, but you'd lost so much blood, had so much pain, I had to make you sleep. I had to stop the blood, give you some peace. You would have died otherwise."

Berengaria stared at her silently and Isabel dropped her eyes.

"You were gone from the world for six days." She said miserably. " The King left at the end of the third day."

Berengaria counted on her fingers. He would be at sea now.

"Rafe?" She asked quietly.

"Gone with the King."

"Johanna?"

"Packed and anxious to be off, ma'am. As soon as you're well enough to travel, she's ready. She wouldn't leave without you."

"I'm ready." She said quietly. "Find De Tancred and tell him I'm ready, and then tell Johanna we go, as soon as the tide can take us."

She sat for a moment, sending up a silent prayer that Eleanor might have got tired of Rome and left for England before they got there.

Chapter 15

Rome was breathtaking. Literally so, for Berengaria. Used to a court that overlooked the wide plains of Navarre, Rome seemed to her to be without rest; choked with heat, with people, with noise – and often stenches as the sewers hummed and even the Tiber churned sullenly in the heat. There was no peace for her in the court itself. Always, no matter how or where she sought solitude, there were people demanding her. After the long sea journey, Johanna was in her element, almost purring with pleasure. The more so as they found that Eleanor had left for England weeks before they arrived; neither woman bothered to hide their relief at the old queen's absence.

They had slunk out of Acre harbor under cover of darkness, and raced quickly along the coast with a brisk following wind. For once, even Johanna had been too worried to be sea sick. But fortune had not smiled on them for long. After the first day, the pleasant breeze had turned into a howling gale and they were forced to put ashore until it abated. Time and again the storm forced them to run for land, and Berengaria felt huge pity as Johanna knelt and kissed the earth with gratitude for their deliverance each time the weather got the better of them. She helped her sister to rise tenderly, understanding that the theatrical gesture was made from the bottom of Johanna's heart.

De Tancred apologized for the delays constantly, but Berengaria smiled wanly and put his distress aside. They were alive, that was all that mattered.

Lost in reminiscences of the journey, she blinked and gathered her thoughts quickly as she realised that Johanna was talking to her.

"Do you know what they call us?" She asked. Berengaria shook her head, barely listening. It was easy, she had learned, to keep Johanna sweet tempered. A rise of the eyebrows, a slight inclination of the head to indicate interest and she would rattle on until forced to pause for breath. "The court calls us 'The Two Queens.'

" She laughed delightedly and Berengaria shook her head in puzzlement.

"So? I suppose that is what we are, aren´t we?"

"Yes." Johanna tutted impatiently. "But they mean it as a compliment, don´t you see? Rome sees more royalty than anywhere in the world, I would think. Queens and kings are nothing new to them. But we are. We are the Two Queens! Isn´t it lovely?"

Berengaria nodded slowly. She pursed her lips, tasting the words. "The Two Queens". Slowly, she realised that she agreed with Johanna. It was lovely. It was only since coming to Rome that she had felt like a queen. Not just the daughter of a King of Navarre, or the wife of the King of England, but a Queen in her own right. Surely, this was a good omen! It couldn´t be long, now, before she saw her kingdom, before she set foot on English soil. She made a prayer for it nightly, but still found it difficult to really believe.

"Oh, you!" Berengaria glanced up at Johanna in surprise. She was on her feet, marching back and forth across a ray of sunshine so that one moment her face was in shadow, the next bathed in rich, golden light. Her fingers clicked an impatient rhythm.

"What?" Berengaria asked. "What is it? A moment ago you were so happy, now look at you."

"It's you, isn't it?" Berengaria raised her eyebrows in surprise and pointed to herself as if to say, "Me? What have I done?"

"You see? You're doing it now!" Berengaria shook her head uncomprehendingly. Johanna threw herself into her chair but her foot kept tapping, as if it could not restrain itself. "You sit there, all sweet and smiling and … and accepting. As if nothing could touch you. As if nothing could have any effect on you, ever. As though you're just above everything and everybody. They love you for it, you know. All the courtiers are mad for a word from you, for a smile. 'La Donna', they call you. 'The Lady'."

"Johanna, you're just being silly. Didn't you just say the court calls us the Two Queens? Two of us. If they like one of us, they like both of us."

"You just don´t see it, do you?" Berengaria stared at her, bewildered. "Yesterday, Giancarlo was flirting with me. Oh, so very prettily."

"Which one is Giancarlo?"

Johanna closed her eyes wearily.

"One of the many who usually clusters around you. You must know him – he has very blue eyes and very black hair; he reminds me of Rafe."

"Oh, him." Berengaria said.

She opened her eyes wide to keep the tears back. Every sight of Giancarlo – who did remind her of Rafe – was a physical pain, as if a sharp skewer had been rammed between her breasts. Rafe, Richard, her unbaptised babe, the unholy Trinity that haunted her every waking moment. Johanna had picked up her tiny, precious Venetian glass hand mirror – a gift from one or other of the courtiers - and was peering in to it, pursing her lips and turning from side to side to inspect her profile carefully. How could she – another woman, her sister at that – how could Johanna fail to see, Berengaria wondered? Even the worldly, self-absorbed courtiers understood instinctively there was something untouchable about her, something she could not, would not share, but how could Johanna not notice, not wonder why Berengaria would suddenly leave the throng, needing to be alone; alone with her memories?

"Oh, him." Johanna mimicked, finished with the mirror. "So you do actually notice somebody, then? Giancarlo was flirting with me, beautifully. He praised my eyes, my skin, my hair. My queenly bearing. Oh, how I was enjoying it! Then I realised, that ever so subtly he was turning the conversation to you. Did La Donna like Rome? Did I think she could be persuaded to stay in Rome a little longer? Did I not think that there was something so sad, so very beguiling about La Donna? Something that made a man want to giver her comfort, to try to make her smile?"

Curious, Berengaria asked,

"And what did you say?

"Say? I told him he was a wretch, and to leave me alone. To go and seek the company of La Donna, if he thought that much of my dear sister. He laughed, and tried to touch my waist."

"See?" Berengaria said quickly. "It's all just nonsense, you know it is. All the young bucks at court are desperate to try their hand at this new idea of courtly love, and who better to practice on than us two? Here, but not really available. Two Queens, indeed!"

"I suppose you're right." Johanna shrugged. "It's amusing, though, isn't it? I could almost forget that I'm betrothed, that I'm to be a married woman again very soon."

Something wistful in her voice made Berengaria look at her closely. Instantly, she was filled with remorse; all the many days she had spent feeling sorry for herself, she had been too busy to notice that Johanna was unhappy. She had lost weight, Berengaria realised, and there were dark shadows under her eyes.

"You must be happy, sister. To be married again, to have your own court?" She asked tentatively.

Johanna shrugged.

"I suppose so." She said quietly. "I was a child when I married William you know, barely eleven. And it was no forward contract; he took me to his bed the day we were wed. And I was never really a queen, not like you.

I was always the "Queen Consort". I would like to have been queen." She added wistfully. Berengaria stared at her, astonished. "I had a babe, you know. A son. We called him Bohemund – a fine old name. No more came, though. And my lovely Bohemund died when he was two." She stared at the wall, her nostrils flaring with remembered anger. "There might have been more babes, but William was always too interested in his damned concubines to come to my bed overly much. He passed them off as wives of his knights, absent from court by way of their duties, or widowed ladies of the court, under his protection. Tried to tell me it was his kingly duty to look after them. Doe-eyed Arab women, the most of them. They used to cast their gaze down before him as if he was God on earth. Oh, how he loved that! His harem. It took me years to wake up and understand what was going on. I was just a child, you see. Just a child. And I had no one to talk to. I had my ladies of the court, of course. A dozen of them, all hand picked by Mama Eleanor, and all reporting to her to make sure I kept in line. Not one of them was my friend."

She fell silent, and Berengaria reached for her hand, stroking it gently.

"But this time will be different, I promise you. You're not a child now. You'll have your own ladies around you, ones that you've chosen yourself, that you can trust. And I understand Raymond keeps a great court, and in your beloved France, at that."

"Sometimes I think that I would have been better married to Saladin's brother after all." Johanna said sadly. "At least I believe that he was a cultured man. Raymond – my dear husband to be! – I have heard about. He is famous, indeed. A famous barbarian. A man who cares for hunting, and drinking and eating, and not much else. He has no thought for dancing, or singing. No taste at all for compliments or even a little flirtation. They say he has to be dragged to mass on pain of losing his immortal soul, and that he can neither read nor write. Do you really think I will be happy with him, Berengaria? Really?"

"Of course you will." She said firmly. "There will be more babes, I know there will, and you can bring some civilizing influence to Raymond's court."

"Aye." Johanna sighed. "Perhaps I can. They are all the same, under the skin, aren't they? All men, all the same."

Berengaria nodded.

The Two Queens stayed silent for a long minute until Johanna giggled suddenly, her serious mood forgotten.

"I thought Clementine would be different, you know."

"*He* isn't just a man." Berengaria said gently. "He's the Pope. God's emissary on earth."

"Aye? Do you know, before I went in to confess to him, I was terrified." She nodded vigorously. "I was literally shaking in my shoes. All my life, my confessions have been made to some little priest who was too frightened of my rank to do more than give me a blessing and a couple of Aves, no matter what I confessed. But this was the Pope!"

"And what did you have to be so worried about?" Berengaria smiled. "Did you confess that you poisoned your first husband? That you had always wanted to poison Eleanor? And Richard?"

"I thought he would be able to look into my heart, and read every bad thought I had ever had." Johanna said simply. Berengaria grinned, understanding immediately.

"I felt exactly the same." She admitted.

She flushed as she remembered her confession. Clementine had been seated on a great throne of a chair, and she had sunk to her knees to perch on the low prie-dieu that was before his feet. The Pontiff had smiled gently at her, laying his gnarled hand softly on her head in benediction. All the sins in all of her life had risen before her. His voice murmured softly, words she had heard a hundred, a thousand, ten thousand times from the mouths of priests, but this was different. This time she could not toss a handful of minor sins into the game, and walk away with a blessing. This time, God's man was seated before her. This time, all her sins would be taken up and examined. She realized that the Holy Father was waiting for her response, and the words tumbled out just as she had been taught.

"Bless me father, for I have sinned."

After a moment, the age old formula took control of her halting tongue. Confessions missed, or skimped.

Time spent amusing herself, when she should have been on her knees at prayer. Curses uttered lightly, and barely regretted. Jealous moments when she had wished her life as easy and light – if only she had known! – as Johanna's.

The sun shone through an embrasure on to the Pope's arm and shoulder. The room was silent apart from the murmur of her confession and the buzz of a lone fly, circling languid in the heat. Berengaria closed her eyes and felt the words flow from her lips as she spoke of Richard and Rafe and her unbaptised babe, the babe that could have been the child of either man. She stumbled as she confessed that she still thought of Rafe, still longed for him in spite of everything. Caution stilled her tongue at the memory of Rafe in Richard's arms, and she didn't speak of that, telling herself that that was a matter for their conscience, their confession, not hers. And in any event, was she really sure that it hadn't been her imagination, playing tricks on her? Wasn't it more likely that she had simply seen comrades, close comrades, embracing but nothing more?

Her confession finished and she exhaled with a gasp. All was out, all was said. Her knees hurt and her left foot began to curl in cramp, but still she waited for the Pontiff's words. A sound nudged at the edge of her consciousness and she glanced up under her eyelashes and saw that the annoying fly – which turned out to be a vast, ugly bluebottle – had landed on Clementine's hand and was following the course of a raised blue vein towards his wrist. She dithered, wondering whether to flick it away, and raised her eyes to the Pope for guidance.

Clementine's eyes were closed, his chin fallen on his chest. A bubble of saliva drooled from the corner of his mouth. Unbelieving, Berengaria realised that the Pope was asleep. She coughed softly and shuffled on the low stool, and he blinked awake immediately. With the practice of sixty years, he raised his hand – the bluebottle flew off, disturbed by the motion – and began to intone the sonorous words of the benedicte. Berengaria listened, hardly believing, as he blessed her and gave her an indulgent penance of three Aves. She lowered her head as he put his hand on her hair, and rose quickly.

"You'll come back to see me, you and your dear sister?" Clementine smiled fondly at her. "I may be old, but I do like to see you gay young things about the place."

Johanna laughed at her rueful face.

"Did he fall asleep during your confession as well? I didn't know whether to laugh or cry afterwards. Do you think the absolution actually took, if he didn't hear a word we were saying?"

"I hope so." Berengaria said ferverently. "I really do hope so."

"So do I." Johanna shook her dice cup alluringly. "Come, sister. Enough of this gloom. Will you have a game or two with me?"

"That I will not. You cheat, Johanna." Johanna pretended to look hurt, her eyes wide. "You do, and we both know it. Go and see if one of your tame courtiers will play with you. They'll pretend not to notice, and you can take their money with a clear conscience."

"And shall I give them your greetings, sister?" She asked cheerfully. Berengaria made to throw her book at her, and Johanna left without a backward glance, her laughter floating on the air behind her.

The room was very quiet without her. There was a whisper of bees, murmuring in the honeysuckle that folded around the window embrasure, and very far away, the shouts and laughter of the young men of the court at some game or other. Heat fell in strata from the ceiling, humid and heavy. Berengaria felt the pressure on her head, and wondered if there would be a thunderstorm later. She sat back in the chair and closed her eyes, dozing and comfortable.

A vicious crack of thunder, straight overhead, awoke her. She jerked up with a start, and looked around, unsure for a moment where she was, what was real and what was dream. Her heart was pounding with the sudden transition from sleep to consciousness.

"Mistress," Isabel was in front of her, bent slightly from the waist. She had to speak loudly to make herself heard above the yell of the storm. Thunder rolled again, and the rain started; a torrent that fell with the row of rolling barrels. "Mistress, I'm sorry. I knocked twice, but you didn't hear me, so I came in. I'm sorry if I've disturbed you."

Berengaria shook her head, still half asleep. Isabel looked well, she thought idly. The Roman sun had gilded her skin gold, and she had put on a little weight. Although her gown hid most of her figure, it was obvious that her breasts were fuller than they had been in the Holy Land. All in all, she looked remarkably pretty.

"Yes, Isabel. I was asleep, but it doesn't matter. What is it?"

As she came awake, she noticed with a tremor of unease that Isabel looked anxious. Her hands were clenched in the folds of her gown at the waist, and her fingers were working back and forth, pleating the linen. No, she thought. No, Isabel. Whatever it is, I do not want to hear it. Leave me alone. Go away, and tell your news to somebody else. I have had enough. No more. Please. No more.

Aloud, she spoke kindly.

"What is it?"

"Ma'am, there are rumours."

"Rumours?" Berengaria relaxed. "There are always rumours at court. What is it this time?"

"My lady." Isabel paused and wet her lips with the tip of tongue. "It's about the King. About King Richard."

Berengaria shook her head. No. No, don't tell me. I don't want to hear.

"He's dead, isn't he?" Her voice shook so that the words trembled. Her nails dug into the palms of her hand so tightly that later she found half-moon shaped indents, flushed with blood.

"No. Not dead. Nor injured." Berengaria closed her eyes and whispered a wordless prayer of relief. "So far as I know. But the word is that he was blown off course when he left the Holy Land and instead of landing in France, he ended up in either the Low Countries, or the Germanic States, it's not known for sure. It's said," she paused and Berengaria held her breath. Said? What is said? Tell me! "It's said that he has been taken for ransom, and by now he is probably in Austria."

Austria? Leopold of Austria, she remembered, was no friend to Richard. There had been bad blood between them, Richard had said, something about the Crusades.

But still, no one would harm a king. Certainly not a King of England. No one.

"Ransom?" Berengaria picked eagerly on the salient point. "If he is offered for ransom, then we can get him back."

Isabel avoided her gaze, staring at her feet. Berengaria spoke slowly.

"How much?" She asked quietly. Isabel shook her head. "How much Isabel? If you know everything else, you know that as well."

"I understand that they're asking 150,000 silver marks. And I have been told that Leopold has already sold the King to Germany, so that no one knows where he really is. I'm sorry, mistress. I really am."

Berengaria's mouth opened and closed soundlessly. 150,000 marks! No, that was impossible. Such a sum had never been asked for any king ever born, ever taken. And how could it not be known where Richard was being held; if it was known he was in Germany, then it must also be known exactly where he was, surely? It was all wrong. It had to be. Isabel was mistaken. The thought gave her hope.

"Isabel, these are just rumours, you said so yourself. It can't be true. Have you spoken to Sir Stephen about this?" Isabel shook her head. "No? Then we will speak to him now – if anybody knows the truth of it, then it will be him. And surely, if he did know, he would have told me. Go and find him for me."

Isabel bobbed a curtsy and nearly ran from the room. Berengaria stood and paced back and forth, the rain lashing down outside wetting the wall beneath the windows. She clutched her elbows in her hands, shaking her head as she walked. It could *not* be true. If it was she would have known. And yet ….Isabel always knew. Isabel heard rumours so faint they were barely a murmur in the distance. Isabel knew things before other people. Knew things other people did not know. Berengaria drew a stuttering breath and began to pray silently.

"Your Majesty?" De Tancred loomed over her. A fatherly smile turned up his lips. " Isabel said you wanted to see me urgently."

"Richard. Is he taken?" She said sharply, without preamble.

She knew immediately. De Tancred's smile stayed, but it was at odds with the rest of his face. His eyes bulged and beneath his ruddy tan, his skin flushed a bright, ugly red. Every muscle in his body seemed to tense and he swayed towards her slightly.

"When? How long have you known?" Berengaria demanded.

"This past fortnight." De Tancred said. He wilted under the fury of her stare and rushed on, filling the silence with desperate words. "I could not tell you, my lady. Queen Eleanor forbade it. She said that you were not to be worried until something was resolved."

"Queen Eleanor?" Berengaria fastened on the words and her anger grew, unwinding like a snake in the pit of her stomach. "Queen Eleanor forbade you? Strange, I thought that I was the Queen, not Eleanor. I thought it was I who was married to King Richard, and Eleanor who was the Dowager Queen. As Richard's wife, and Queen of England – and Cyprus," she added as an afterthought, "I would assume I was entitled to know that my husband had been imprisoned." Fear dowsed her anger and she reached out and grasped De Tancred's tunic, trying to shake him into a response, even though she might just as well have tried to shake the palace walls. "Is he injured? Is that why Eleanor told you not to let me know? Is that it?"

De Tancred shook his head.

"No, Your Majesty. As far as we know he is well, and uninjured. For certain, it would not be a good thing for him to be hurt before he is ransomed. He will be well looked after, be assured."

Berengaria fought down her anger. With an almost physical effort, she loosed her grip on De Tancred's tunic and forced her hands into her lap. When she was sure she could speak without stuttering, she said quietly;

"Tell me all. Never mind what you think I already know, start from the beginning and tell me everything. How did you find out?" De Tancred paused, licking his lips nervously, and she shot him a look that had him racing into speech.

"The Que… The Lady Eleanor sent a message overland which reached me some thirteen or fourteen days ago. She had found out a further twelve days before." Berengaria was about to demand how Eleanor had come to know, but bit the words back. Eleanor's diplomatic routes were famed throughout Christendom; it was said that she knew the dreams and aspirations of every king in Europe before they knew themselves. Some said in reality she was a witch, who used a special scrivening glass to see into the future; into men's hearts. Although no one dared say that to Eleanor's face, it didn´t matter – she knew anyway. "At some point after he set sail from Acre," De Tancred explained, "King Richard must have realised that there was a very real chance that he would not be able to get to either England or France, as the weather was so bad. When he understood he was being blown off course, and might land in a hostile country, he borrowed the clothes of some of the slaves on the galley and disguised himself as a poor pilgrim."

Berengaria choked back hysterical laughter. Richard, disguised as a poor beggar. Richard, who stood a head taller even than his own knights; Richard with his golden Angevin hair and healthy, well fed body. Richard, with the arrogance of bearing born of being feted and feared since he first stepped out of the cradle …. Did he really think anybody would believe he was a poor pilgrim? Yes, she thought grimly, he was conceited enough to believe he could get away with it. Stupid, stupid man!

De Tancred had paused uncertainly, and she waved at him to carry on.

"We don't know for sure where he finally made landfall, but it appears that somehow he was taken, and ended up with Leopold in Austria." She nodded and De Tancred stared respectfully at her, obviously surprised that she knew so much. "Leopold in his turn, having need of ready money, passed him on to the Emperor Henry. We don't know how much Henry paid, but we do know how much Henry is demanding for Richard's release."

"150,000 silver marks." Berengaria said. De Tancred smiled grimly.

"Aye. 150,000 silver marks. And fifty first line galleys. And the release and return of one hundred captives, taken for ransom from either the Germanic states or Henry's allies, and kept at various courts around Christendom."

Berengaria gawped at him.

"There isn't that much wealth in the whole of England!"

"There would have been, before the Crusades. But now …no. John could not raise it alone. But you must remember. The whole of Christendom will be expected to contribute to the ransom. Who knows? Next time, it could be their prince, or their king who is taken."

Berengaria nodded. So much wealth; but as De Tancred said, if each king could be persuaded to part with a little, then it could be found. Would be found.

"Where is he? Where is Richard being kept captive?" For some reason, it suddenly seemed of great importance that she knew where he was.

"We know the castle he's being held in. It's formidable, it would be no use to try to recapture him by force."

"How did you find him?"

De Tancred shuffled his feet, clearly uncomfortable.

"As soon as Eleanor heard the rumours, certainly before she knew for sure what was true, she sent out men to start searching. Richard's troubadour, Blondin, insisted that he would go with them. He persuaded

Eleanor that it was sensible, that a skilled jongleur would be welcome at any castle, no matter what the country. I don't know if she agreed with him, or if she simply didn't care, but she let him go anyway, and as luck would have it, it was Blondin who found him." Berengaria's mouth set in a thin line; Blondin, Johanna's 'meaching toad' was the one who had found Richard. "According to Blondin's own account, he worked his way through the Germanic states, staying no longer than a day at any castle or palace he thought likely. As he had insisted, he was welcomed warmly and by God's own luck, he found Richard quickly. He says that he knew at once he was in the right place, as the particular castle was very well fortified, and he was searched for weapons before he was allowed into the court. He saw no sign of Richard, but wandered around the place anyway, singing quietly to himself all the while. He says many doors were locked, and he tried many a one, but singing all the while and eventually, just as he was about to give up and go on his way, his song was answered. By Richard's voice."

Berengaria sighed, remembering that long ago night when Blondin had leaned at Richard's knee and the two voices; Richard's deep tenor and Blondin's lighter tones, had mingled so well. So. The Toad really had found him, after all.

"He wasted no time but made his farewells to the court and got a message back to Eleanor at once. It arrived long before he did. As soon as Eleanor was sure who had the king, she set the wheels in motion. She's already contacted every member of the nobility throughout the known world, and has asked them to contribute. It will not be a fast thing, but the money will come in."

"And when was I to be told?" De Tancred shrugged, unable or unwilling to reply.

Berengaria rose abruptly, forcing De Tancred to move out of her way.

"Come with me. Both of you."

She swept out, leaving De Tancred and Isabel to follow.

The cleric outside the Pope's apartments stared at her in astonishment. Yes, the Pontiff was in his chambers, and yes, he was alone. But was he expecting her? No, she said. He was not. But she was going to see him.

Now. The cleric's jaw dropped in astonishment, but he wilted beneath her glare and shuffled to his feet, closing the door firmly in her face. Berengaria decided she would count to ten before entering anyway, but the door was thrown open in a few seconds.

"The Pontiff will see you, Your Majesty." He sounded surprised but bowed Berengaria and her companions in anyway.

"My dear Berengaria." Clementine smiled at her. "Always so very good to see your beautiful face. And your retainers, of course." He nodded approvingly at Isabel, and spared De Tancred a vague glance. "But you look troubled? What is it that has sent you to me so urgently?"

"Don't you know?" A sudden premonition made Berengaria forget her manners. "Don't you know why I have come to see you?" Behind her, she heard De Tancred gasp at her rudeness.

Clementine sighed and his gaze dropped to his great ring of state. He twisted it gently between gnarled fingers.

"Ah. So you have found out. I'm sorry, my dear. I would have told you, I assure you, but Queen Eleanor forbade it, and she insisted it was for your own good. And even I find it easiest to agree with Eleanor, you know."

Berengaria trembled with fury. Her hands locked, the fingers splayed wide. The sight of her wedding ring, the thick gold symbol of her position, soothed her enough so that she could speak without shouting.

"I'm the Queen." Clementine looked up, startled at her tone. "Eleanor is Richard's mother. Nothing more. I'm Richard's wife. Do you understand that, sir?"

Clementine rubbed his chin. In the total silence, Berengaria heard the rasp of stubble against his fingers. She stared at him, made brave by her anger. Later, she would feel sick when she remembered how she had defied a Pope, but at that moment she felt nothing but rage, rage that buoyed her up and carried her on.

"I'm sorry." Clementine said quietly. "You're quite right. It's just ... Eleanor has been Queen for so very long. She is so, how can I put this? So very, very sure of her position. Even I find myself just a little in awe of her." He chuckled ruefully and Berengaria felt her anger begin to ebb. This may be the Pope, she thought, but he was, in truth, an old man. And Eleanor could bully anybody.

"You'll help, me then? Help me to raise Richard's ransom?" She pleaded.

Clementine stared at her, his surprise obvious.

"But my dear, it's already done! As soon as I heard from Eleanor, I called a Council of my Cardinals, and sent notes to all who could not attend, and they agreed that in turn they would speak to their Archbishops, and the Archbishops in turn to the Bishops, and so on. It is happening even as we speak, I assure you."

Berengaria choked out her thanks and bent to kiss the Pope's ring. She stayed, head bowed, as he gave her benediction, his voice wavering slightly. She was aware, dully, that he was relieved that the interview was over. She rose and turned, walking away without a further word. De Tancred and Isabel scuttled after her.

Johanna looked up and sniffed as she entered their apartments.

"I've was waiting for you for ages." She whined. "Where have you all been?" She glanced from Berengaria to De Tancred to Isabel. "What is it? What's happened?"

Berengaria felt a grim satisfaction at her ignorance. At least Richard's sister had also been kept in ignorance. She thought that she would not have been able to bear it if Johanna, too, had known.

"Tell her." She said abruptly to De Tancred.

Johanna interrupted only once, when he talked of Richard disguising himself as a pilgrim. In spite of the seriousness of the thing, Johanna hooted with laughter.

"Richard? A poor pilgrim? Of all the silly things to try!" Berengaria nodded her agreement and gestured to De Tancred to continue.

The room fell silent as he finished.

"I have a letter from Eleanor." Johanna said finally. "I had just read it when you came back in. She said nothing of Richard." Thank the good Lord, Berengaria thought acidly. At least she views her own daughter with the same contempt as she views me. "But she does say that everything is finalized for me to marry Raymond.

She says that I should leave Rome as soon as possible, as all the arrangements are already made for the wedding. My dowry is paid. How could she not tell me about Richard? How can I marry Raymond when this is hanging over our heads?" Her lips trembled piteously as she stared at Berengaria.

Berengaria laughed shortly.

"It appears, dear sister, that Eleanor has everything in hand. You have nothing to worry about. She's already made sure that all the great kings and princes, aye, and all the great clerics too, have made their pledges. She's no need to worry about Richard anymore, so she can turn her attention to you, instead."

Johanna pursed her lips, considering.

"I suppose so." She said grudgingly. "Mama could always think and do three things at once. Oh, well. If it's done, it's done. Will you come with me? Please?"

Berengaria caught the anxiety in her voice and melted. What good could she do in Rome, after all? The Pontiff and Eleanor between them had done everything, probably more, than she could have done. Still she hesitated.

"Johanna, I´m sure it is nothing. An idle rumour. But, I have heard…" She paused, searching to make her words as delicate as possible.

"You mean about Angela, I suppose?" Berengaria blew a sigh of relief, and nodded. Johanna shrugged. "Yes, I heard the gossip as well. You probably heard it before me, as I assume people were trying to keep it from me. Tactful of them. But I heard anyway, and wrote to Mama to ask if she knew the truth of it. She was quite blunt about it; never one to be mealy mouthed, dear Mama. She said that it was quite true that Raymond had entered into some sort of liaison with dear Angela, but that for sure it had never been sanctified by any priest. Nothing legal about it. Not really surprising, I suppose. After all, Angela is a blood royal, a princess of Cyprus. Quite suitable, if she had anything like a dowry, or even influence at court. Of course," she added, "She is remarkably pretty, if you like those sort of simpering, sweet good looks. She took Richard in, didn´t she?" She added spitefully. Immediately, she was apologetic. "I´m so sorry, sister. That was uncalled for."

Berengaria shook her head ruefully.

"It´s already forgotten. We go to Toulouse together, Johanna." She said quietly. "As soon as possible."

Chapter 16

Arrangements were made so quickly, so smoothly that Berengaria guessed that Clementine had already received his instructions from Eleanor and was acting on them as promptly as possible, so as not to incur the wrath of the Queen. De Tancred was to go with them to Toulouse, and Clementine insisted that they also be accompanied by one of his Cardinals. Berengaria wondered cynically whether this was to ensure their spiritual welfare, or whether Clementine wanted to appease Eleanor by bestowing some prestige on their raggle taggle little party.

The seas were kind, but as always Johanna turned green and began to be seasick the moment their ship left port. Sighing, Berengaria found what had become her normal station on deck, and sat basking gently in the sun. Isabel, a gilded shadow, sat close by, silent until her mistress chose to speak, but a constant presence. Ever and again, Berengaria glanced at her but spoke little. Isabel appeared to be occupied by her own thoughts and barely seemed to notice.

De Tancred approached her on the third day out. He cast his shadow across Berengaria and she looked at him, surprised that the big man had moved so silently. He stood before her quietly, head bowed, his fingers twisting in his cap which he held against his stomach. He glanced sideways at Isabel and she stood immediately, bobbing a curtsey before she clambered awkwardly down the ladder to below decks.

"I came to apologise." He paused, and then the words came in a rush. "It was wrong of me, I know, not to tell you at once about the King. It's just that Eleanor's always been the Queen. And," he added frankly "She's always terrified me."

Berengaria smiled.

"I know." She said. "She used to terrify me, as well."

De Tancred laughed with relief.

"Sir." Berengaria paused, selecting her words carefully. "I wondered if … if you had heard anything of

Rafe? He looked after us so very well, I would be unhappy to think anything had happened to him."

She felt her cheeks glowing at the lie, but managed to watch De Tancred's face, searching his expression for something. Anything.

But he shook his head.

"I'm sorry, but I've heard nothing of him. But that in itself is probably good news. If something had happened to him, then I would surely have known."

Berengaria nodded and dismissed him. Left alone, she watched the waves shouldered aside by the passage of the sleek ship. Sea birds bobbed in its wake, hunting for refuse, and so suddenly and quickly she thought she was seeing things, a pair of dolphins broke the surface at the prow and leaping exuberantly appeared to lead the ship onwards. She watched them, enchanted, for a moment until they disappeared and then remembered, with a surge of uneasiness, that the sailors said that dolphins were the souls of drowned sailors.

The dolphins had spoiled her mood. Whilst she was still deeply glad to be away from the crowd and stench of Rome, abruptly her sense of gentle content evaporated and she was filled with a sense of deep foreboding that she could not shake off.

Johanna remained below for the whole of the journey, retching constantly and eating only when Berengaria forced her to. Berengaria scolded her, demanding what she thought Raymond would say to the sight of a skinny, whey-faced bride. Johanna shrugged, her mouth puckered.

"I don´t care." She wailed. "I hate the sea. Hate it, hate it, hate it. When we get to Toulouse, I shall never, ever leave the land again."

True to her words, as soon as she had the earth beneath her feet again, Johanna brightened immediately. She spent the whole of the land journey to Toulouse chattering happily about her plans for the future, and Berengaria let her talk, answering absently.

They were met by Raymond as they came in sight of Toulouse. He immediately enfolded his wife-to-be to be in his arms. He was a short, stocky man with an abundant head of hair and many missing teeth and Berengaria took an immediate dislike to him. His fine velvet tunic was smeared with rows of grease, and she guessed that was where he had wiped his hands after eating. Her dislike wasn't helped by the lecherous glance he gave her over Johanna's shoulder.

Once settled at her new court, Johanna was surrounded by a clutch of noble women, all cooing and chattering and vying to be heard at once. Berengaria's head was soon pounding and she fled to her own quarters, sure that Johanna hadn't even noticed she had gone. Isabel had already hung her gowns up on the wall, and was in the process of shaking out and refolding her linen from the great trunks.

"Well, Isabel? What's the gossip saying?" She asked idly

"I've heard that your cousin, the Duke Sanchez, is here, ma 'am. I believe that he is to escort you to your lands at Poitou, when you're ready to go."

Berengaria smiled to herself. She had not, she was sure, ever discussed her plans to move to Poitou – the French lands she had acquired when she married Richard, and the place he had told her to go to, to wait for him – with Isabel, and yet somehow she knew. It took a moment for the rest of Isabel's comment to register.

"Sanchez? Sanchez is here?" Isabel nodded. "That's odd. Sanchez and my father haven't spoken for years; Sanchez is Castilian and there's bad blood between Castille and Navarre. But if he's really going to ride with us to Poitou, it's past time old quarrels were mended. Could you find him for me, please?"

He stood before her, smiling as if the long years had never passed.

"My dearest ." He took her hand and kissed it. "How marriage does become you! You're positively blooming."

She stared at him, wondering how it was possible for him to have changed so much. He had been little more than a boy last time she saw him, now he was a man, and a handsome man at that. And he was hiding something. She could sense it.

"Why are you here, Sanchez?" She asked bluntly.

He wet his lips with his tongue, not to meet her gaze.

"I'm sorry, Berengaria." He said softly. "I'm so sorry. I had hoped to give you time to settle a little before I found you, but I decided that would be unfair. I have been sent to take you to Poitou, which I understand is your wish?"

She nodded, and said tersely, "And?"

"I'm sorry, cousin, that after all these years I should meet you again with bad news."

More bad news? She thought wildly. What, in God's name, was there left to go wrong?

"Tell me."

"Your father, I'm so sorry, your father is dead."

She stared at him her mouth opening and closing soundlessly. Suddenly, greyness swept over her vision and she swayed. In a moment, Sanchez and Isabel were at each side of her and she leaned into Isabel, grateful for her sturdy support. When she opened her eyes, Sanchez was kneeling before her, her hands clutched tightly in his fingers.

"I'm so sorry." He repeated. "So very sorry. We tried to get a message to you in Rome, but you'd already left. It's entirely wrong for me to have to give you this news on what should be a happy occasion, but I had to tell you."

"How?" Berengaria choked on the word. "How did he die? My father was always so healthy, he never had a day's illness in his life. Did he suffer? Tell me!"

"He fell from his horse during a hunt. His mare reared at a snake, and he was taken by surprise." Berengaria stared at him fiercely, trying to make sense of the words. Her father, thrown from horseback? No, surely that was nonsense; he was one of the best horsemen she had ever known. "He was thrown and landed on hard packed clay, on his head. But he got up at once, and insisted it was nothing, that he was well and had taken no hurt. But after dinner, he complained of a headache, and took himself to his bed. When the servants went to wake him the next morning, they found him dead." Sanchez started at her stricken face and went on quickly. "I've been told that he seemed very peaceful, and it's thought that that he went quietly, in his sleep. I'm sure that he didn't suffer. Sure of it."

"He is buried?"

"Aye, I'm afraid so. No one knew when it would be possible to contact you, and it could be left no longer. The heat." She blanched "Your Aunt Constanzia asked me tell you that everything was done just as you would have wanted it. He lies alongside your mother, as he wished."

"Thank you." Berengaria swallowed, trying to shift the husk in her throat. "Leave me please. Both of you."

Sanchez lingered, but she waved him away with a gesture. Isabel held the door open for Sanchez and closed it gently behind both of them.

Berengaria sat, staring at her hands. She wanted to cry, to rage, to scream, but her eyes were dry and no sound came from her parched lips. She cleared her throat and stared into space. I´m sorry, father. She thought. I should have been with you. I wouldn't have been able to help you, but I should have been there anyway. You would have known I was there, and it would have been good for us to have been together. As it is, I shall have masses said for your soul, and perhaps you will find my daughter in your travels in purgatory. It would be good for you to see your grandchild. She found the thought comforting.

She went and lay down on the bed, and after a while, she slept, seeing her father´s face in her dreams.

Sanchez handed her the letter from Eleanor the next day. Awkwardly, he said;

"I would have given it to you yesterday, cousin, but it wasn't the right time."

She turned it over in her fingers, inspecting Eleanor's great seal. The fat gobbet of red wax seemed inappropriately festive. She was about to ask if he knew if Eleanor had heard of her father's death, but she didn't bother. Of course Eleanor would know. She knew everything.

She broke a finger nail trying to prise the wax away. She stared at the bleeding nail dully, wondering if it was an omen to the contents. Turned the parchment over and over and over in her hands before finally wrenching the doubled sheet open.

She had been right. Of course Eleanor had known of her father's death. She started to read the scant sympathies with burning anger, only to find the anger evaporating at the honesty of Eleanor's crabbed words.

> 'It may seem to you, daughter, that I do not grieve enough for your father's untimely death. I assure

you, I do. He was a great friend to me in life, and I will think on him often. But you must remember, I'm an old woman and I have seen so many friends taken from me that death no longer has any great fear for me.'

Of course, one forgot how old Eleanor was. She had always been there, had been Queen for so long that everybody assumed she was immortal. Everybody, it appeared, but Eleanor herself.

Eleanor wrote that she had already taken all necessary steps to raise the ransom for Richard. It would, of course, not be a swift task to amass such a huge amount, but it could – and would – be done. Berengaria could rest easy on that count. In any event, Eleanor understood that Berengaria wished to go to Poitou. She felt this was an excellent idea, she had always been fond of the place herself.

Berengaria laid the parchment down carefully. Eleanor had everything in hand, then. How kind! At least, she thought, Eleanor had done her the courtesy of assuming that she knew all the details of Richard's capture and ransom demand. But not one word that even hinted that Berengaria might like to take up her rightful place in the English Court as Queen. Had Eleanor not even thought of it, she wondered? Or thought of it, and decided that she would simply sweep over any intention Berengaria might have had, tossing her ideas aside like breadcrumbs strewn before sparrows.

Thoughts of Richard and her father mingled, and tears slopped down her cheeks at last. She pushed the parchment away with a sudden gesture in case it got wet. Even in the midst of her grief, ingrained teaching said that parchment was far too precious to be ruined by tears, no matter how deeply they were felt. She cried for a long time, then wiped her cheeks with her hands over and over before she got to her feet. She had sat for too long, and her knees protested at the movement. I'm getting old, she thought sadly. Not as old as Eleanor - God forbid! - but older. Hard on the heels of that thought followed another; if only my babe had lived! Even a girl child would have meant so much; proof to the whole world that she could bear children. Proof that she and Richard could make babies. She shrugged off the inconvenient knowledge that her babe had probably not been Richard's child. It didn't matter. Not now. Would Eleanor have treated her with such contempt if her babe had lived? She thought not.

She shook herself like a dog coming out of water and went in search of Isabel.

Chapter 17

Johanna's wedding was very splendid. Johanna herself, recovered from her journey and restored to happiness, looked beautiful. Berengaria smiled for her as she watched her sister-in-law make her vows proudly. The feasting and celebration lasted for the best part of a week, and by the end of it Berengaria felt she was only too ready to set out for Poitou. She embraced Johanna fondly, and Johanna wept in the middle of her happiness to see her go.

"Can you not stay here?" She asked. "Must you go to Poitou? You'll be lonely there. You'll have no one. Stay here with me, and be happy with me."

She freed herself gently from Johanna's grip.

"I must go. I can't hang about here, relying on your charity. And anyway, you know Richard told me to wait for him at Poitou. I'm not far away, you know. We can write, often, and visit with each other, once I'm properly settled."

Johanna sighed, her face a mask of misery.

"God be with, you, sister." She said softly.

Berengaria fell in love with Poitou at first sight. The winding road that led to her castle reminded her instantly of the vista opening up before the court at Navarre, but rather than making her homesick, she felt instantly welcomed. The castle servants had been expecting her, and the doors were thrown open, the servants themselves lining up to greet her. Sanchez raised his eyebrows and leaned towards her.

"You'll really stay here? Virtually on your own? If you wish, I can take you to Navarre. Your aunt would be delighted to see you, and at least you would have some comfort. This place can never have been more than a grand hunting lodge at best."

Berengaria shook her head.

"I'm staying here until Richard comes to take me back to England." She said firmly. "Will you stay a few days before you go back to Castille?"

Sanchez eyed the towering grey walls and algae-green moat, and shook his head.

"I will see you settled, Berengaria. And take any messages you have back to Navarre." He was about to ask again, if she was sure she wanted to stay, but a glance at her face silenced him. Women! Who knew what on earth went on in their minds? She could have stayed at Toulouse with Johanna. Gone back to Navarre. But Poitou! Who had even heard of the place? Back of beyond, he thought.

Berengaria was glad when Sanchez went. He was gallant, to be sure. He flirted beautifully. But he reminded her of Navarre, and all she had lost, and she found it difficult to respond to his light-hearted teasing.

She wrote to Johanna, and to Eleanor. Both letters said the same thing, that she was arrived and settled and content. Eleanor she begged to tell her if there was any news of Richard. Johanna she asked – for she knew her sister would expect it – to let her have all the gossip of court, and to assure Berengaria that she was truly happy with her new husband.

And then she sat, and thought. And the more she thought, the more she knew what she had to do. At first, she shrugged the idea away as too fantastic. The thing could not – should not – be done. Was without any doubt a mortal sin. But the more she brooded on Eleanor's letter, the more she came to consider it the right thing, the only thing that she could do. Richard need never know what she was about to do for him.

She looked at the idea from all sides, and decided, finally, that it was right. That she was right.

Isabel glanced at her, and smiled herself, pleased to see her mistress happy.

"You are well, ma'am." She said. "The air here agrees with you, I think"

"Aye, I think that it does. And you, Isabel? You are also well?" Berengaria asked softly. "And your babe? How is that?"

Isabel's smile froze. Her lips parted and she shook her head, but did not speak. Berengaria stared at her, her expression full of tender concern.

"My babe?" Isabel's cleared her throat and tried again. "I ... I have no babe. You're mistaken. Are you still unwell? Can I get a cordial for you?"

Berengaria spoke quietly, but her voice was firm.

"Don't bother lying to me, Isabel. I know. Whose is it? Do you know who the father is for sure?"

Isabel's face had turned a curious green beneath her normal olive complexion. Berengaria stared at her in open curiosity, waiting quite patiently to see if the girl would lie again.

"Tell me." She commanded, and Isabel succumbed to habit.

"One of the King's men." She whispered.

"Ah." Berengaria nodded, satisfied. "How far gone are you?"

"Perhaps five months, maybe a little more." Isabel choked out. "How did you know?"

"I felt it here." Berengaria said simply, and put her hand on her belly. "Where my own babe should have been. But tell me, did he promise you marriage, this King's man? Did he say he would take you back to England with him? Did he tell you he loved you?"

"No." Tears trickled silently down Isabel's cheeks, soaking the neck of her gown. "No, he promised me nothing. Nothing at all."

"Oh, you stupid, stupid bitch." Her tone was almost tender, but Isabel's head jerked back as if she had slapped her across the face. "Did you think yourself in love with him, I suppose? Still do? Even though he has slunk off and left you here? Does he know you're expecting his child?"

"No. I ... I didn´t have time to tell him."

"Just as well." Berengaria smiled. "God really is good, isn´t he? Since we came here, I´ve had time to think. I thought that He had deserted me, at first, but now I realise that losing my baby was just a setback. It was only a girl, anyway." Her voice trembled as she said it; *Oh, my daughter, forgive me*! she thought, but carried on anyway. She had to. Her daughter would understand, she knew. "Richard would not have been pleased with a girl child." She reached out and stroked Isabel's belly gently. Isabel flinched from her touch. "But now I understand that the good Lord has given me a second chance. Your baby, Isabel, your sweet little bastard, will want for nothing, I can assure you. Richard – just the same as your own lover, in that way – had no idea that I was pregnant. It will probably be many months before I see him again, and by that time your baby – my baby – will be birthed. Sublime, isn't it?"

Isabel swallowed and shook her head.

"No." She croaked. "No. This is my baby, mine. You can't take him. He is mine, not yours. You're mad."

Mad? Berengaria considered her words. Perhaps she was mad. But what did it matter? She was the Queen; a queen with neither husband nor lover, a queen who had never set foot in her own kingdom. But a queen who would have her baby, by hook or by crook. Already, she noticed. Isabel was calling the baby "he." Her baby. The future King. Everything would be right, now. *Forgive me, daughter. I must do this. For both our sakes.*

"I may well be mad, Isabel." She conceded sadly. "But it really doesn't matter, does it? I am Queen of England, and if I say that your babe is mine, then mine he shall be."

"I'll run away." Isabel jerked to her feet as if she would run at that moment. "You can't watch me all the time. I´ll get away from you, one way or another. You can´t stop me. And you can´t hurt me, because if you do, you'll hurt the baby. My baby."

Berengaria shook her head, her expression puzzled.

"Hurt you? How could I ever hurt you when you are carrying our baby. Of course not. But I don´t think that you´ll run away, Isabel. Tell me, how long is it since you have seen your family? Seen your father, your brothers and sister?"

Isabel's eyes rolled like a cornered animal. She stared, not understanding this sudden change of direction, but deeply suspicious of it.

"Eleanor took you when you were, what, twelve? Nine years ago? Ten?"

"Ten."

"She owed your father money, didn´t she? Money she couldn´t pay?" Isabel nodded, her gaze fixed on Berengaria´s smiling face. "And what was it your father – Isaac, isn´t it? – told Eleanor? "Please. Take my daughter. Take her away from York. It isn´t safe here for us Jews. She is my favourite daughter, she is clever – she can read and write, sew, she is skilled with herbs.

She will pay you back for her keep a thousand times over. And in return for your promise that you will keep her safe, why then we will forget your debts to me, my Lady Eleanor. See – I will burn your promissory notes. Just take my girl Rachel, and keep her safe." Isn't that how the conversation went, Isabel? Or would you prefer your given name, Rachel?"

Isabel stared at her, her lips moving soundlessly. Berengaria wondered if she was mouthing a curse, or a prayer..

"And did you really think, the pair of you, you and your so very clever father, that Eleanor, the all-wise, the all-seeing, Eleanor believed a word of it? She didn't, you know. And she told me. Explained to me that you were a cunning little bitch, and that I must never trust you for a minute. Showed me a couple of your letters to your father; disentangled your neat little code for me so that I would know for the future. Of course, you never expected that your letters would be intercepted, did you? But just in case, it was as well that they should look harmless. And they did, didn't they? Eleanor told me that it had taken weeks for her best men to be sure of the information that you were passing; information about the Royal household, about finances, about politics. Because as Eleanor's little servant girl, you could go everywhere, see everything, and no one ever suspected, did they? In fact, wise old Eleanor encouraged you, didn't she? 'Isabel is my eyes and ears' she told me, right at the beginning, but you thought you had fooled her, didn't you? You thought that because you passed the gossip to Eleanor she trusted you. Oh, you silly, silly little bitch. She knew everything, right from the start. But she tolerated it, because it gave her power. Power over you, and through you, power over the Jews, back in England."

She watched as Isabel crumpled in on herself, fragile as a blown leaf. The girl's prettiness deserted her and her face looked as old and withered as an apple that had been stored for too long. Berengaria wanted desperately to reach out to her, to hold her hand and explain that she had to do this, that it was out of her control, that she was deeply sorry, but she steeled herself to stay still. If she showed a single sign of weakness, she knew that she would never be able to go through with it. And she had to. So she spoke cruelly, as if she had not a care for Isabel, for her family and all she had left behind.

"You never knew, did you? Right from the very first, every letter that went to your father was carefully changed by the Royal spies, changed to ensure that your father heard exactly what Eleanor wanted the Jews to know, and nothing more. You've spent the last ten years lying to your father, Isabel. Ten years of nothing but deceit."

"I'll kill myself." Isabel said flatly. "It's all I deserve. And I'll take my baby with me."

"I don't think so." Berengaria shook her head. "I daresay it's not a mortal sin for you Jews to commit suicide, like it is for us Christians, but I don't believe you quite understand your position. You're guilty of treason. You can't deny it. If I wanted to, I could have you burned alive just like that." She clicked her fingers crisply. "And not only you. It's not just you who's guilty of treason, but so is your father. Each of your brothers and your sister has been spoken of in your letters, so not only your father, but your whole family are equally guilty with you. Would you really like to die, with their deaths on your conscience? Or see them all burn in front of your eyes, and know that it was all your fault? Would you? Could you stand that? "

"I saved your life." Isabel choked. "If I hadn't been there, you would have bled to death. Have you no pity, no mercy, at all?"

"But of course. I have … infinite mercy. Just think, not only am I letting you – and your family – live, but I´m going to put your bastard on the throne of England. Is that not mercy enough for you?"

Isabel fell to her knees. She was crying silently, her mouth stretched wide. Berengaria stood carefully, and stretched, her face turning towards the sun that streamed through the window. With Isabel unable to see her, she blinked away tears and walked away, hardly able to see where she was going. Walked away before she could change her mind and lift Isabel up and tell her she had been mad for the moment, that she could never hurt her. Still less hurt her unborn child.

She watched Isabel hungrily as the weeks rolled by. Isabel ate little, drank less. Eventually, Berengaria found herself standing over her, forcing her to eat, much as she had done with Johanna, a lifetime ago. And to her joy, it gradually became obvious that Isabel was definitely with child. Her waist thickened, and her skin took on a bloom of health and wellbeing that a blind man could have seen.

Slowly, the two women fell into a rhythm. Isabel seemed more resigned than angry, concerned only with the welfare of her growing child. The autumn leaves fell, slowly at first, and then thicker and thicker. Both women walked out daily, shuffling almost companionably through the litter of gold. If only she had gold in such quantities, Berengaria thought sadly. Richard would be freed, and all would be well in the world. Unconsciously, she found herself mimicking Isabel. She rose carefully, and stretched, her hands firm in the small of her back, just as she had seen Isabel do. Walked leaning backwards slightly. Sat with her hands spanning her ribs. If Isabel noticed, she said nothing.

The weather turned bitterly at the beginning of December. Berengaria woke with the dawn, but lay huddled in bed. Her hands – outside the covers – were frozen, and she rubbed them together to get some feeling back into them. Once warmed, she pushed her hands back under the bed linen and ran them over her belly. Sometimes - and this morning was such a time - she awoke sure that her baby was still with her. That it had all been a terrible nightmare. Only by feeling the flatness of her belly did she know the lie.

Awake, she spoke softly to herself, *it's no good, is it?* Tears stung her eyes, running down to her mouth. She licked them away and they were bitter. "I have no babe. My babe is dead. And I can't steal Isabel's child. It would never take the place of my own babe. I would know, always. I could fool Richard, but I could never fool myself. How, in God's name, could I ever live with myself?"

She sat up in bed and sank her head in her hands and rubbed her face as if she was washing it. Over and over again. Smearing away the tears. Isabel found her sitting there and sat quietly at the foot of the bed, saying nothing. Watching. After a few moments, Berengaria leaned forward and stroked the other woman's hair silently. After a while, she realised that Isabel, too, was weeping silently.

"You were right, Isabel." She whispered. "It was madness."

Isabel said nothing, but shook her head sadly.

She never found the words to apologize to Isabel. Could not; no matter how hard she tried, the words choked in her throat. How was it possible to apologise for such an overwhelming wickedness? Hating herself, sick to her very bones, she knew she could never hope to make it up to her.

And yet, it seemed to her that Isabel understood. Although she said nothing, she was there. Even as her belly grew larger, making it difficult to bend and lift, she insisted on doing everything she had always done for Berengaria; kneeling to fit her shoes. Fetching and finding. Caring for her clothes, brushing her hair. At certain times, Berengaria had to send her away so Isabel couldn't see the tears of regret that her mistress wept.

And neither could Berengaria bring herself to make a full confession of her sins. All during the terrible journey to France, she had told her Rosary time and time again, and had ached for a priest to take her confession and absolve her of her sins. Now that one was available, she found it impossible to tell him more than the most venal of her sins. He was a smug, fat cleric who simpered and oiled around both the women, bowing almost permanently in Berengaria's presence. Isabel, on the other hand, reported that he was offhand with her, except when they were alone when his hand lingered a little too long in the benediction and his gaze rolled over her body greedily. Berengaria suggested that she should accidentally knee him in the groin when she was rising from prayer, and both women collapsed in helpless laughter. Berengaria relished the moment, grateful that Isabel could still laugh.

Accepting at last, she felt the loss of her daughter in her very bones. Sometimes, she woke in the night and – for a moment of sheer joy, just as happened sometimes upon waking in the morning – forgot that she had lost her child, that her babe was dead and buried in the Holy Land.

Both women waited quietly for Isabel's child to be born. Try as she might, Isabel could not give an accurate date for the birth. The babe would come when it was ready, she said. Not before. Berengaria was anxious, but

Isabel shrugged her concerns away; she was young and healthy, there would be no complications. Embarrassed by her own lack of knowledge, Berengaria nodded.

Two letters came for Berengaria, and she read them eagerly. Johanna was firm – Berengaria must come to her in Toulouse. And soon. She would not take no for an answer. Berengaria could leave word, and Richard would find her when he was finally ransomed. Had Berengaria heard as to how much ransom had been raised? She, Johanna, had asked Raymond but he insisted he had no idea. How she was looking forward to seeing her dear sister again! Berengaria sighed; it was a temptation, to be sure, for all she had longed for the peace and quiet at Poitou, now that her trickle of visitors had ceased, there were times when she longed to be at court at Toulouse, surrounded by nobles, all respecting her as Richard's Queen. But she could not. There was Isabel, and Isabel's baby – for a second, she had to force away the renewed upsurge of longing to take the baby for her own – to consider. And Richard would expect her to be at Poitou when he was released; reluctantly, she admitted to herself that she doubted if he would go to Toulouse to collect her, unless it suited his plans anyway.

The second letter came from Eleanor, and made her bite her thumb nail to shreds in fury. She knew Eleanor's handwriting, and knew instantly that this had been written by a clerk, not the Queen herself. Eleanor presented her compliments, and was pleased to tell her that the campaign to raise money for Richard's release was going well. Berengaria must be sure that all that could be done was being done, and she had no need to worry her head about it. Eleanor was pleased that Berengaria seemed to have settled in Poitou, but she understood perfectly that she might, at some point; wish to come to court in England. If this was the case, then Eleanor would ensure that King John would make her most welcome. Berengaria seethed. King John would make her most welcome? How dare she? She was the wife of the rightful King, and as such would expect to take her place as Queen of England as and when she chose. Ousting Eleanor as Queen into the bargain. King John, indeed!

She decided that she would reply with pleasure to Johanna, but at the same time plead fatigue and a slight fever as excuses not to travel to Toulouse at present, but she would not reply to Eleanor. Let the old woman make what she would of her silence; once Richard returned and they went back to England together, then both John and Eleanor would understand where the true power of the throne lay. Once she was crowned, then the world would acknowledge her as England's Queen.

Her anger had barely cooled before Isabel came in. The woman stood silently as Berengaria read Eleanor's letter yet again.

"Listen to this, Isabel." She said. "Listen how my dear relatives would make me welcome in my own kingdom." She read Eleanor's letter out loud. "Can you believe how they treat me?"

Silence greeted her remark, and she glanced up to ask Isabel if she had been listening?

"Isabel?" She whispered.

The woman who stood before her bore no resemblance to Isabel's normal elegant appearance. Her hair was loose, falling almost to her waist in a tangle of waves. It looked as if it had been grabbed and tugged and mussed, time and time again. Isabel's face was ghastly white, smeared with wood ash. Her eyes were wild, staring and her lips bloodied.

"Dear God, Isabel. What has happened to you! Has somebody attacked you? Are you hurt? Speak to me woman, what is it? Your baby? Is that it? Has something happened to your baby?"

Berengaria jerked to her feet but before she could touch Isabel the other woman held out a scrap of parchment and as Berengaria grasped it, Isabel slid to her knees and put her arms around herself, rocking back and forth, back and forth. The horrible silence was broken by her howl of pain, heart-breaking in its intensity.

Berengaria moved to put her hand on Isabel's shoulder, but she shrugged the gesture away, almost flinching from the touch. Bewildered, Berengaria focused on the parchment, holding it up to the light to try and read the scrawling handwriting better. Her lips moved as she tried to make sense of the words. After the first sentence became clear, the rest was easy. She shook her head in pity and horror.

"All of them?" She whispered. "Every one?" She slid to the floor beside Isabel and put her arm around her shoulder. Isabel stopped her relentless swaying and leaned against her mistress, boneless as a sack of straw.

Her voice was hoarse, broken by torment and choked with tears.

"All of them. My father. All of my brothers and my sister. Nieces and nephews. Cousins. Friends. Men and women and children and babies. They spared none of them. Not one. All of them, everybody I loved. Children I played with. All of them. My people. And I never knew. There was nobody to mourn them. No one. If I had known, I could have said Kaddish for them. But I didn't know. How could I?" She lifted her face and stared appealingly at Berengaria, beseeching her to agree. Berengaria stroked her hair gently.

"You couldn't have known." She agreed. "None of us knew."

Even as she spoke, Berengaria felt her stomach lurch with horror as she realised what she had said. 'None of us knew.' But wasn't this exactly what she had threatened Isabel with? Immediately, more important even than comforting Isabel in her grief, the most important thing in the world was to make her understand that she had truly known nothing of this terrible thing, that she had had no part in it.

"Isabel, I didn't know. I would never ... never have done it. You must know that. It was just a threat. I had no idea. None. You must believe me."

Isabel raised her head from her shoulder and stared at her. When she finally spoke, Berengaria had to strain to understand her; Isabel's voice was her own, but suddenly her accent had changed, become coarser and thicker.

"I believe you." She said wearily. "You might a' done it, at t'time, but it would a' been too late, anyway, wouldn't it? De Tancred says they all died over a year ago. Rounded up by t'good citizens' o' York, and taken off to Clifford's Tower. Every single Jew in York. Old and young alike. Taken from t' ghetto and prodded through t'streets like cattle to be burned to death. Mebbe a merciful end. There must a' been hundreds on 'em. If they hadn't burned, then I daresay they'd a suffocated to death." She drew a deep, wobbling breath. "Well, no matter any more. It's done, innit? I'm going now." She shook Berengaria's hand off and stood. Staring down at her, she smiled grimly. "They always reckon you've got to be careful what you ask for, y'know. You might not like it when you get it, so they say. Odd, innit, when you think about it? All those years ago, me father asking the old Queen if she would tek me and keep me safe. Makes you wonder if he knew something, dunnit? With your permission." Abruptly, her accent was genteel again and Berengaria reared back as if she had been slapped hard in the face. "With your permission, I will go. I must sit shiva for my people. Say Kaddish for them. It is only right."

Stunned, Berengaria let her go without another word. She wanted to cry for Isabel, release the pain she felt for her, but no tears came. She picked up De Tancred's scrawled note and read it through again automatically, finding questions she had not even thought to ask were answered.

"My Dear Lady Isabel,

I am sorry to give you the news you asked me for on the journey. I thought perhaps you had some little knowledge of this thing, as it was widely known at court, but perhaps it was kept from you by kindness." Widely known at court? And what did Isabel, or for that matter, Berengaria herself, know of the gossip of the English court? "I have been telled that Lord Richard learnt of it soon after the event, and expressed great unease for as you know he has had many dealings with the Jew usurers, and has said often that without their aid he would not have been able to raise muster for his Crusade. But I must tell you that all the Hebrews in York were kilt some fourteen months ago. I was told that the people of York took it on themselves to pay no more money to the usurers, and that anger grew until a few hotheads took charge and a mob started, as sometimes happens. All of the Hebrew Jews, regardless of man or woman or child or infant or old persons were rounded up in a great mass and taken to a fort on a high point, I believe called Clifford's Tower or Fort and there were burned. None were spared, my Lady, so I must think that your friend from your childhood was amongst the unfortunates. I am sorry to be the bearer of such news, but can but hope that both you and my Lady the Queen continue well.

I remain your obedient servant.

Stephen De Tancred."

Berengaria sat very still. The parchment clutched tightly in her fingers fascinated her; she read it again and again and again. She longed to weep for Isabel, as proof that she shared her pain, but could not. Beneath the grief throbbed one selfish thought; did Isabel really believe that neither she nor Richard had had anything to do with the terrible massacre? Were both completely innocent? As innocent as the babes that had burned? It mattered so much, to her – at least.

The parchment blurred in front of her, and she realized that the tears had come, at last. She threw the parchment from her and staggered to her feet. She guessed where Isabel would be, and used the wall to guide her to the tiny room used as a chapel; the room that had always been empty, always quiet since the visitors had ceased, save when either she or Isabel wished to use it.

Isabel was crouched in front of the altar, on a low stool. Her arms were crossed across her breasts, and she was rocking back and forth, back and forth, back and forth, crooning the same words in a foreign, guttural language in time to her rocking. Berengaria knelt in front of her silently until she paused.

"I must say Kaddish for them." She whispered. "There's only me left to help them. For each of them I knew, I shall name a Kaddish for them. For those I did not know, for those who were born after I left York, I shall say Kaddish."

Having no idea what she was talking about, but understanding that it was important to Isabel, Berengaria simply nodded and left her.

She told the servants that Isabel suspected that she may have a bad fever, and had quarantined herself in the chapel. The servants drew back in horror and crossed themselves when Berengaria said that she would nurse Isabel and take her food to the chapel herself, but not one of them offered to help her, or take her place. Wryly,

Berengaria wondered if they would go if she ordered them to do so. Looking at their faces, she doubted it.

Berengaria selected food for Isabel herself, not trusting the servants to do it. Fever of any sort was greatly feared; she tried not to blame them for their instinctive horror of the unknown, but she was unable to push away the thought that had she been in Isabel's place, and had truly been smitten with a deadly fever, then she would have starved before any of them would have come near her. But Isabel would have looked after her, she knew. In spite of all that had happened, Isabel would have nursed her. And now, she would look after Isabel. Her friend. Her one true friend.

As an afterthought, she looped a wooden pail over her arm and balanced herself precariously to the chapel, food and wine on a tray in one hand, pail looped over her other wrist. She knocked courteously on the chapel door, but pushed it open anyway when Isabel did not answer. Isabel was asleep on the bare floor and Berengaria stood over her, overwhelmed with pity at the sight of the dirty, exhausted figure. She placed the food at the foot of the altar and the pail some way away.

She continued her duties for seven days. Isabel was sometimes awake, sometimes asleep, sometimes whispering prayers with her eyes closed, when she entered. Berengaria set her food down silently and crept away, sure that Isabel hadn't even noticed her. The pail was always empty, and Berengaria guessed – gratefully – that Isabel had emptied it herself in the house of easement in the night, when everybody else was asleep.

Isabel was calm and somehow noble in her terrible grief. Berengaria, guiltily, wished she would break out; rant and rave and scream at the injustice of it all. Hurl insults at her. Blame her for what had happened, at the very least blame her for wanting it to happen. Anything but this unbearable, enduring dignity. But Isabel was dedicated to her prayers and her mourning, seeming unaware of anything else.

Berengaria watched her closely, worry for her gradually yielding to concern for her unborn child. But Isabel gave no outward sign that she was in distress or pain, so Berengaria tried to shrug aside her own worries.

Finally, on the eighth day, Berengaria awoke to find Isabel walking about her chamber. Her hair was clean and braided, her skin clear of ashes. She had changed her dress and was quietly shaking out clean linen for Berengaria as if the past seven days had never happened. Instinctively, Berengaria's gaze moved to Isabel's waist, but as she turned and was silhouetted against the light she saw with overwhelming relief that her figure was still thickened, and that she moved carefully and more slowly than usual.

If the servants wondered at Isabel's miraculous return to health, Berengaria heard no gossip about. Shrewdly, she guessed the ever efficient Isabel had dealt with that issue.

Grateful as she was for Isabel's return to daily life, Berengaria became more and more uneasy as no news came from outside Poitou.

She had no word of Richard, but eventually a letter came from Johanna. After a page of her normal gossip about life at court, and a complaint that Berengaria had not been to see her, Johanna said – with more tact than Berengaria would ever have expected – that she assumed that neither Eleanor or John has given any thought to how she was managing, all alone in the middle of nowhere? That being the case, Johanna rather wondered if she might be able to use this?

Berengaria tipped the coins out of the sealed casket that came with the letter and stared at them in surprise before finishing Johanna's message.

Johanna had added acidly that if and when she needed more, Berengaria would have to apply to John, in England, as she had had to beg her husband to advance this amount for her. If it had not been for her promises that Richard would pay, of course he would, as soon as he was released, then Raymond would have refused outright. She, who was once a Queen, had been reduced to begging her husband for money! Johanna's indignation shone through in her written words.

Berengaria weighed the money in her hand, faintly bewildered. She had never had any need of money; no noble woman ever did. First her father had taken care of such things, and then, when she had married Richard, his officials had taken care of money matters. It had never occurred to her to even consider it. But now, apparently, she had to.

"Damn you, Richard." She said aloud.

She shouted for Isabel, and when she arrived poked the casket towards her. Isabel face lit up as she hefted the silver in her hand, and Berengaria felt a tiny glow – not so much of hope, but rather of relief that Isabel might understand what was needed.

"We are saved, then." Isabella said with satisfaction. She glanced at Berengaria´s bewildered expression and sighed. "Have you spoken to your Reeve, my lady?"

Berengaria shook her head.

"Should I?" She said tentatively. Isabel nodded firmly.

The Reeve seemed pleased to have been summoned. He was a tall, handsome man with a fine head of dark hair, and Berengaria realised she had seen him about the castle without questioning who he was, or why he was so much better dressed than the rest of the servants. Her cheeks burned as it began to dawn on her exactly how little she knew about almost everything to do with the estate. She drew a deep breath and held up her hand, stopping the Reeve in mid sentence.

"I´ve never had need to concern myself with accounts, or money at all for that matter." She said simply. The Reeve stared at her, his expression deeply worried. She glanced at Isabel and realised that the other woman was leaning forward, every inch of her body itching to take hold of the Reeve's accounts. Deeply relieved, Berengaria nodded. "Discuss these things with Isabel, if you will. I'll listen, and try to learn."

Berengaria watched the two dark heads lean towards each other over the parchments. After nearly an hour, the Reeve gathered up his papers and bowed deeply to both women before departing. Berengaria looked desperately at Isabel, who was counting the coins into piles and making a note on a scrap of parchment that was already covered in figures.

"Your Reeve is a good man, I think. And an honest one." Isabel smiled.

"Is he?" Berengaria said. "I'm pleased to hear it. But what's the answer? Do we have money, or none?"

"This," Isabel prodded the little piles of silver gently "Is already spent."

Berengaria's mouth dropped ajar in an "O" of disbelief.

"Spent?" She squeaked. "Spent? How can it be? I've only just received it!"

Isabel chewed her lower lip and then spoke slowly and carefully, as if to a child. Berengaria bridled for a moment, but listened. And as she listened, her shoulders slumped with worry.

"The castle and estate are yours, ma'am, by grant of the King, I believe?" Berengaria nodded – Richard had said Poitou was part of her marriage settlement. That Eleanor still chose to style herself "Duchess of Poitou" was of no importance. That was one of the many things that would be settled on Richard's return. "That's one good thing, then. But you have servants, who have to be fed, and must also be paid. Once a year they also get a new set of clothes. We must all eat, and drink. The estate provides some food and wine, but not all of it. You have no skilled artisans so they must be hired in. You have no fishponds, so the fish you ate yesterday was bought from local fishermen. The linen on our beds, the rushes on the floor – all must be paid for."

"Why doesn't the estate provide enough?" Berengaria frowned.

"If it was run properly, it would. But there's been no money put into the estate for years; the Reeve has done his best but Richard ignored his pleas for money. The poor man has been at his wits' end. He hasn't even been paid himself this year. This," she nodded at the money, "Will pay most of your debts and your servants' wages. But there will be nothing left. Now you are here, the Reeve thinks that the local merchants will be happy to give you credit again, once they have been paid. But you must have more. And soon. Will you petition Prince John?"

"Petition him?" Berengaria felt anger shoulder aside her helplessness. "Petition him, for what is rightfully mine? I shall demand, not ask!"

Isabel nodded and smiled widely.

"I'll tell the Reeve." She said cheerfully.

Chapter 18

The Reeve found a decent sheet of vellum, together with a stone bottle of iron-gall ink and some quills for her. Once begun, she found the words flowed easily enough and she signed the vellum with a flourish, "Berengaria, Queen of England", moved almost to tears when she realized that this was the very first time she had signed herself as "Queen". Isabel dripped wax on the carefully folded sheet, and Berengaria affixed her seal firmly. The Reeve assured her that he would make sure that it would reach the English Court and she took his word for it.

Once the message had gone, the two women sat together quietly. Berengaria watched Isabel covertly as she sat in silence, staring into space, and Berengaria sensed that her thoughts were far, far away.

The days drifted and as each day passed, Berengaria found that she was more and more unsettled. She couldn't concentrate, couldn't sleep, barely tasted her food, drank wine with no more pleasure than if it had been water. The longer she watched Isabel, the more worried she became.

When Isabel was gone on an errand, she counted on her fingers, the figures flying through her head. The days and months since they had left the Holy Land rattled in her mind until they were no more than a hopeless blur. When Isabel was with her, she watched the other woman closely, seeing that she no longer sat with her hands comfortably resting on her belly, no longer smiled to herself as she felt her babe move. Her voluminous skirts concealed her belly, but even so Berengaria was absolutely sure that the babe was still there. Isabel gave no sign that anything was wrong; she was as quiet, as caring of Berengaria's comfort as ever. Yet still Berengaria worried, until the moment came when she could no more.

"Isabel." The other woman turned her head enquiringly; her brows raised a little, perhaps in surprise at Berengaria's tone. "Isabel, your babe. Is it not past due? I've counted the days over and over again, and I m sure you're past your due date."

Isabel said nothing for so long that Berengaria itched to shake an answer from her. Finally she sighed and turned to face her.

"My baby is dead." She said simply. "I have said Kaddish for him." Berengaria raised her hands, clenched into fists. She shook them mindlessly in the air in front of her, the gesture saying "no, no, no, no" more eloquently than words.

"It is so." Isabel's voice choked and tears dripped down her cheeks. She made no move to wipe them away, even though they must have stung as her eyes reddened. "I felt him die on the day the news came about my family. He has not moved since. I knew, here," she thumped her heart with her fist, " but I hoped I was wrong. Hoped and hoped and hoped. But what's the use?" She stared hopelessly at Berengaria and for the first time in weeks put her hands flat on her belly. "He's dead. My baby is dead."

Berengaria fell to her knees and shuffled across the floor to Isabel, the reeds rucking beneath. Frustrated, she went on her hands and knees and crawled forward, dragging herself up with the aid of Isabel's skirts. The two women folded in to each other and their tears mingled as they hugged. Berengaria knew that Isabel was in her arms, and both their tears wet on her cheeks, but at the same time she was not sure, not sure at all, whether her own tears were for Isabel, or for herself. All the sorrow and pity and despair she had kept walled up in her own heart since her baby had died spilled out and she wept and wept and wept. For Isabel. For Isabel's baby. For herself. For the love she had lost, for the love she had never really known. For Richard. For Rafe. The salt tears tasted bitter as they ran into her mouth.

"He's gone." Isabel choked. "My baby's gone to join the rest of my family. At least the poor bairn will not be alone, he will have found them waiting for him. They'll comfort him, look after him. They won't care that he's a bastard." Her voice rose into a wail. "My baby, oh my baby."

Berengaria rocked Isabel in her arms as if the other woman were herself a child, in need of comfort. She spoke softly, words that made no sense at all, spoken for comfort. Comfort for Isabel. Comfort for herself. The women clung together until Berengaria's knees ached so much that she could hardly move. She shuffled and Isabel moved slightly away from her. As if the separation had restored her senses, quite suddenly, through the clouds of her grief, Berengaria had a thought that made her feel physically sick.

"Isabel, no matter whether your babe is alive or…or," she could bring herself to say the word "dead", "Or not, he must be birthed."

"I know." Isabel swallowed. "I think he's about two weeks overdue. If I'm right," And her tone of voice told Berengaria that she was sure. "If I'm right, then he died over a month ago."

Berengaria shook her head in a daze, unable to understand how Isabel had kept this dreadful thing to herself for so long. What would she have felt like, she wondered, if it had been her baby? Would she ever have been able to contain herself with such dignity? No, she thought with absolute certainty, she would not. She would have gone mad, the instant she was sure. How could any woman know she was carrying a dead child, and not go insane?

Isabel was speaking again, very quietly, and Berengaria listened in dawning horror.

"I have waited, hoping he would come himself. But it's not going to happen, not now. He must have some help, or I'll die and go to join him." Berengaria blurted "No" and Isabel grimaced. "Don't worry." She said quietly. "At first, I welcomed the idea. It would be wonderful, I thought, to go with him, to be with him and all my family. To be with all those who loved me, and who I loved. To go into the darkness and never to look back. I was happy. But as the days passed, I became frightened. I always thought – my religion told me – that beyond death there was something else. Something better. A place where there was happiness, forever. But what if there isn't? What if there's …. Nothing? Nothing at all?" Her face was as white as chalk, her dark eyes huge. When she spoke again, Berengaria sensed she was speaking to herself. "If I had been able to keep my faith, here." She pounded her fist against her breast "I would have died happily. I would have taken something that would have sent me to sleep, something that would have made sure that I never woke up again. But then I began to wonder, what if he isn't dead? What if I was wrong, and he was just sleeping? What if I killed myself, and him with me? After a while, I was in such a state I couldn't do anything. So I just waited. But now, I know that no matter what happens, my baby must be born. I owe him that. Alive or dead, he must be birthed." She clutched Berengaria tightly, thrusting her face close to hers. "You'll help me, won't you? You must."

"I 'll help you. I'll do what I can. But," helplessness tied Berengaria's guts in a noose. "But I don't know what to do. I've never even seen a baby born."

Isabel shook her head and choked on a laugh that was half a sob.

"No, of course not. But I need help. There's a woman in the nearest village who's a skilled midwife. She'll be able to help me." Berengaria stared at her, surprised. It had never occurred to her that Isabel would need a midwife. She flushed, ashamed. How could she not have thought about it? Did she really think Isabel was so very capable, that she could deliver her own child? She cursed herself for her stupidity, and as if Isabel had read her mind, the other woman put her hand on her sleeve and patted her arm. "You weren't to know. You said yourself you'd never even seen a baby birthed. Please, shout for Marie for me."

Stinging with guilt at Isabel's understanding, Berengaria ran and opened the door and called for Marie. The maid came in seconds, but not fast enough for either woman. Isabel spoke to her in rapid French and the girl nodded, lifted her skirts and departed at a run.

The midwife was a shock. Berengaria had been expecting a wrinkled crone, a capable old woman who had seen every babe in the village born, and probably most of the animals as well. Instead, this was a tiny woman, barely five feet tall even in crude wooden pattens that lent inches to her height. Berengaria's first impression was that she was like a Jenny Wren, for slim as she was, she had heavy breasts that made it seem she would overbalance at any moment. And she was young, certainly not out of her twenties. She bobbed a curtsy at

Berengaria, but her eyes were instantly on Isabel. At Berengaria's nod, she moved quickly to her patient.

Berengaria wrung her hands in an agony of impatience as Isabel and the midwife talked. They spoke in a strongly accented French dialect, and she understood barely a word.

Needing to do something, to help in some way, Berengaria scrabbled in her purse for one of the few remaining coins from Johanna's hoard and held it out to the midwife. The woman stared at it curiously and shook her head, speaking rapidly. Isabel translated for her.

"She says that's no good to her. Nobody in the village would be able to change such a huge amount, but that wouldn't stop somebody stealing it from her. She asks if she can have a skin of wine, and perhaps some wheat and – if we can spare it – a little salt beef. That will do her better than silver."

Humbled, Berengaria put the coin away and nodded agreement, watching the midwife go about her work with a tenderness that appeared at odds with her workworn hands and face, After what seemed like hours of talking and nodding, the midwife pushed Isabel back gently, and lifted her skirt. Berengaria coloured, but watched fascinated as the woman ran her fingers over Isabel's belly, pushing and probing, stopping every few moments to ask Isabel a question. Finally, she bent and laid her ear against Isabel's stomach, moving her head up and down every few inches, listening intently. When she spoke again, her voice was very gentle.

"What's she saying?" Berengaria demanded.

Isabel paused and shook her head. When she spoke, her voice was so quiet that Berengaria had to strain to hear her.

"She thinks I'm right, the baby is dead. It's not going to come on its own. She says that it wants me to be with it, that if she doesn't help me, then I will die as well. She says that we must persuade it that it's not yet my time."

Berengaria's hand flew to her mouth. She shook her head mutely.

The midwife looked at her curiously and shrugged. Glanced at Isabel, who nodded. Slowly, she began to run her hands over Isabel, starting at her breasts and working her way rhythmically down to her belly, and back. At the same time, she began to rock back and forth, back and forth, crooning softly, the same words over and over again. Berengaria understood that she was calling the baby forth, charming it from Isabel's womb.

After perhaps fifteen minutes, the midwife straightened and put her hands to her back, easing away a crick. She frowned and spoke to Isabel, who nodded.

"She's going to break my waters." Isabel said. Berengaria stared at her, perplexed. "It'll help the baby to come."

The midwife bent quickly, and her hands busied themselves beneath Isabel. Before Berengaria could really understand what she was doing, her fingers plunged into Isabel's cunny and worked their way upwards with astonishing speed. Isabel shouted in pain as liquid gushed between her legs, soaking the straw of her pallet. Immediately, the midwife began her crooning again, her wet fingers moving to massage Isabel's belly with increasing firmness. Isabel tried to sit up, but the midwife pushed her down again.

Suddenly, Isabel gave a deep moan of pain. Instantly alert, Berengaria stood and tottered across to the bed, her feet prickling with returning circulation.

She held Isabel's hand as she rocked too and fro. Her moans became more and more frequent and sweat drenched her face. Berengaria clutched her tightly, as the midwife shouted instructions. Isabel strained and gave a great cry and the midwife thrust her head down below her belly, Isabel's shoulders tensing as she tugged.

"Again!" Berengaria cried. "Isabel, again. He´s nearly here. I can see the crown of his head. Push. Now!"

The baby slid out so suddenly that the midwife had to lunge to catch it. All at once, there was a flurry of activity and Berengaria was thrust aside without ceremony as the baby was turned and the cord snipped by the midwife's teeth. She retreated to the window embrasure, worried she would be in the way, but neither the midwife nor Isabel seemed to notice that she had moved.

Isabel lay still, panting but silent. Berengaria twisted her hands in her gown in a frenzy of fear and hope as the midwife scooped up the baby and bent over it, sucking mucous from its mouth and nose gently, spitting the residue on the rushes. She turned the babe and smacked it, not on its bottom, but on its back, again and again. She raised it to her face and blew into its mouth: pinched its tiny nose and tried again. Finally, she glanced at Berengaria and shook her head silently.

Very gently, and slowly, as if all urgency had gone from the matter, she soaked a cloth in the waiting ewer of water and wiped the baby clean. She wrapped the child in a clean shawl, and laid it gently, so very gently, in the crook of Isabel's arm. Isabel's eyes were closed, and her arm fell away as if she did not have the strength to keep it raised, never mind hold on to her baby. After two attempts to lodge the babe safely, the midwife gave up and walked over to Berengaria, pushing the shawled bundle towards her impatiently. Trembling, Berengaria grasped the baby in her arms, clutching it tightly to her breasts and rocking it from side to side, crooning nonsense words very softly, over and over again. The midwife stared at her for a second, and then bustled back to Isabel.

With all her attention on the babe in her arms, Berengaria was only vaguely aware that the midwife was lifting Isabel up from her pillow, and forcing her to drink. The liquid must have been bitter, as Isabel gagged and retched. As soon as Isabel had lain down again, the midwife seized a handful of clean clouts, wet them, and began to scrub her down briskly, chattering all the time. Isabel strained again, and for one horrified second Berengaria thought another baby was on the way, that they had all been wrong, and it was twins. But nothing came but a mass of bloody matter, which the midwife scooped up and threw to one side with evident satisfaction. This, she supposed, must be normal. Please God!

Deciding reluctantly that Isabel was in safe hands, Berengaria turned to the window slot. The late afternoon sun was low, but still streamed in golden glory. Gently, so very gently, she pulled aside the shawl from the baby's face and stared at him, unable to believe that such perfection could be lifeless. His eyes were wide open, appearing to stare at her and understand that she loved him as well as if he had been her own. His skin glowed gold; every feature from the slightly puckered little mouth to the well-delineated eyebrows were beautiful. She gasped and hope so strong it hurt wrenched her body as a single curl, drying from the midwife's attentions, sprang to attention on the baby's head. She waited, even shook the little body very slightly, but there was no breath of life, no movement from the babe himself. Trembling, she unfolded the shawl slightly and touched each tiny finger, wondering at the beauty of each miniature nail.

She felt cocooned, as isolated from the world around as if she had been knocked unconscious yet could still see and hear, but could say nothing. A noise from Isabel started her out of her trance and she turned to see that the other woman was trying to push the midwife aside so that she could climb out of bed and reach her babe. Isabel held her arms out to Berengaria, and she almost slipped and fell in her hurry to reach her side. Very tenderly she laid the baby in Isabel's arms, almost shouting at her not to hurt the child as his mother's arms tightened fiercely around him. Berengaria felt sick as she suddenly remembered that nothing could ever hurt this baby.

Isabel's skin was grey, apart from two fierce spots of red that burned over her cheekbones, and her eyes were sunk back in her skull. Her normally beautiful hair was plastered to her skull with sweat. She was breathing deeply, almost panting, and her breath was sour. Horrified, Berengaria stared at the midwife and gestured towards Isabel, raising her eyebrows in question. The midwife shrugged and rattled out a few sentences in guttural French. Without knowing how she understood, Berengaria nodded.

"Marie." She said and waved her hand towards the door. The midwife nodded and walked off briskly to the kitchen to claim her fee. Berengaria turned back to Isabel.

"I was right, wasn't I?" Isabel spoke wearily, every word an effort. "He is dead. My poor, poor baby." She hugged the child to her shoulder, rocking back and forth gently. Berengaria nodded, swallowing the lump in her throat, and suddenly words came.

"He has gone to be with my daughter, Isabel." She said firmly. "It's fate that it is so. My child went first, to prepare the way. Now they are together, and will look after each other."

For a moment, she thought that Isabel had not heard her, but then she realised that the new mother was nodding her head, almost imperceptibly.

"It is so." She said softly. Tears trickled down her cheeks and she licked them away with the tip of her tongue, so they did not fall on the newborn. "That's good. Neither of them will be alone, then. May I hold him for a while?"

"Of course. I must go for a few minutes, to make arrangements. Will you be alright?" As soon as she had said the words, Berengaria felt foolish. Alright? How could Isabel be alright? Would she ever be alright again? Isabel said nothing, concerned only with the silent and still baby in her arms, but nodded. Berengaria guessed that she wanted nothing more than to be alone with her son, and tiptoed out. Finding a gaggle of maids standing outside the room, she rapped out orders to them briskly. The girls scattered and within an hour, Isabel had been helped to another chamber and the apartment was being cleaned and scrubbed and new rushes put down

"Tell the Priest I want him here in the morning, as soon as we have broken our fast." She instructed firmly.

Berengaria lay awake all that night, running over her plans in her head. Isabel slept a little, but awoke frequently, the babe clutched in her arms. At intervals, Berengaria heard her whispering to her baby; singing the same lullaby to him over and over again.

"Lullay, mine Liking, my dear Son, mine Sweeting,
Lullay, my dear heart, mine own dear darling"

When she could bear it no longer without her own heart breaking forever, Berengaria called out to Isabel quietly, telling her to sleep, so that she could regain her strength. Isabel obeyed as if she was a child herself. Twice during the night she rose and walked over to the pair to check that Isabel, at least, was breathing, and both times she returned to her own bed, her mind working grimly as she thought about what needed to be done in the morning.

The Priest was clearly deeply uneasy. He stood before the two women, licking his thick lips, his gaze drifting constantly to the shawled bundle in Isabel's arms.

"My lady." He bowed with his usual unctuousness to Berengaria. "I heard that all was not well with the babe, but obviously I´m wrong?" His voice rose hopefully.

Berengaria stared at him until his gaze dropped. She waited in silence until the Priest began to fidget with his robe, rubbing his stole between his fingers miserably.

"Isabel's baby must be christened." She rapped. The Priest stared at her, his mouth working silently. "When you have christened him, you will shrive him. When he has had the Last Rights, we will bury him. In a proper Christian grave, with all due ceremony. Do I make myself clear?"

The Priest's face had turned purple. He cleared his throat loudly, his lips moving but uttering no sound. Losing patience, Berengaria snapped "Now."

He shook his head, his eyes rolling wildly.

"My lady." He croaked. "My lady, I can´t. I can´t! The maids told me the babe had been born dead, is that not so?"

"He was born." Berengaria said evenly. "He has come into this world, by God's good grace, and he will leave it in the same state."

"I can't! I can't christen a stillborn child, still less shrive him. And if I can't do that, then I can't give him a Christian burial. I would be excommunicated in this life, and would burn in hell in the next!"

"Come," Berengaria smiled coolly. "Where is your charity, man? Where is your Christian feeling? If you can't – will not – baptize this child and give him a Christian burial, then surely it is he who will burn in hell, not you. And we wouldn't want that, would we?"

The priest stared wildly from Berengaria to Isabel, to the babe clutched in Isabel's arms. Suddenly, his fat, cunning face lit with an idea.

"I can't baptize him. He must have Godparents, and there are none present. Were it otherwise…" he held out his hands, palms upward, miming sorrow.

"Nonsense." Berengaria smiled sweetly. "I'm to be his Godmother and the King will stand as his Godfather. My Reeve shall be the King's proxy in his absence."

Realising his last straw had failed him, the Priest lowered his head but remained stubbornly silent.

"Come, good father." Berengaria coaxed. The words nearly strangled her. "You have no choice, you know. If you continue with your silliness, then I shall write to the Bishop and tell him that you came to me and volunteered to christen the baby, even though you knew he was stillborn. I will tell him that you asked for silver in exchange for your part." The Priest's mouth dropped in disbelief; he began to stutter a denial, but Berengaria raised a regal hand and silenced him. "I shall tell him that I was so disgusted by your actions, that I want you removed from my house and sent to some far parish, where it will do your soul good to minister to the poorest of the poor. On the other hand, if you do what is right, then I shall give you this." The coin Berengaria had offered to the midwife winked between her fingers. "And never a word to the Bishop. You may be damned in the afterlife, but at least that way you'll be able to enjoy the fat of the land in this."

The Priest's mouth closed with a snap. His hand snaked out and snatched the coin from Berengaria's fingers, secreting it quickly on the folds of his sleeve.

" I see that you are right - it appears that I have no choice in the matter. And so I can't be blamed. Do we do the work here, or in the chapel?"

Isabel found her voice for the first time and spoke hesitatingly, addressing Berengaria rather than the priest.

"I think that if we are to do this, then it should be done properly. The chapel?"

"The chapel it is." Berengaria agreed readily.

She supported Isabel tenderly on their short walk to the chapel, and the other woman leaned on her gratefully. The Reeve walked at their side, shooting worried glances at Isabel.

The priest ran through the baptism ceremony at a rattling pace, only slowing when Berengaria gave him a reproachful look.

"Who gives this child?" He asked, and Berengaria smiled and held out her arms for the babe. For a moment, she thought that Isabel would refuse to hand him to her, but finally, trustingly, she gave Berengaria the silent bundle. "And his name?"

Berengaria drew a breath and paused, glancing at Isabel.

"He is named for his Godfather." She said strongly. "His name is Richard."

For a moment, she thought the priest was going to faint, but he rallied and poured the holy water over the baby's head, making the sign of the cross over his forehead. He stared at Berengaria pleadingly, and she raised her eyebrows.

"It is done?" She demanded. The Priest nodded. "Correctly?"

"Yes."

"Then shrive the poor little mite, give him his Last Rights, and we will bury him as a good Christian."

The tiny grave looked lost in the castle graveyard. Richard was buried in the shawl that Isabel had wrapped him in, and the Reeve – that good man – shoveled the soil back in to the pitiful mound of earth himself.

Berengaria nodded her thanks to the Reeve, and the two women walked back to the castle slowly, Berengaria with her arm around Isabel's waist. The Priest scuttled away as soon as he could, and Berengaria watched him go with a feeling of relief, as if something distasteful had gone from her presence.

Chapter 19

Winter came early, and fiercely. Snow started to fall – first as sleet, then thick, floating flakes – at the beginning of November, and carried on, day in and day out, through to Christmas. Berengaria gave orders that Christmas should be celebrated by the servants, and ensured that Jean Reeve had enough money to get a bolt of cloth for new clothes for each and every one of them. She and Isabel, she explained to the Reeve, were in mourning for Isabel's son, and would not celebrate this year. Jean Reeve glanced at Isabel, his expression unreadable, and nodded his understanding before melting away discreetly.

The two women huddled in their thickest clothes, wearing dense woolen clothes even indoors. A fire blazed in the centre of the hall and in the solar, day and night, but it did little to shoo away the wicked chill. Close to the flames, the side facing the fire roasted whilst every other part of their bodies froze.

As well as worrying about Isabel, Berengaria constantly wondered about Richard. She had had no further word from either Johanna or Eleanor, and had got to the stage where even an acid letter from Eleanor would have been welcome. Neither did any further money arrive from John; Berengaria wrote to him weekly, alternating between pleasant requests and firm demands. Finally, in desperation she took the risk and told him that if he did not send her the money she needed – the money she was entitled to – then she would have no option but to leave France and take up residence at the English court, assuming her rightful position as Queen of England.

"Let's see what he has to say about that," She said vengefully to Isabel. "Richard warned me never to trust him, and now I understand why."

First as a distraction, and them with rapidly growing real interest, Berengaria asked Jean Reeve to explain the workings of the estate to her. Slowly, she began to understand the annual rotation of life on the estate; the endless roll out of nature, of crops planted and harvested, lambs born and reared and sheared for their wool, goats kept for their milk, cattle for milk and salt and fresh beef and hides. Vines planted and pruned and harvested, wine made and kept and drunk. But with understanding came increased puzzlement.

"I don´t understand, Jean." Firelight threw shadows over her face, deepening her frown. "From what you´ve shown me, the estate should not only produce enough food to feed and clothe the castle and all the villages, but there should even be a little left over for harder times. Is that not so?"

The Reeve fidgeted uncomfortably and pulled a sour face.

"It used to be so, my lady." He said heavily. "In my father's time, this estate was the most prosperous for miles around. It was even possible to sell some excess grain and wool." He paused, and Berengaria raised her eyebrows waiting for his response. "But times changed. The old King," King Louis, she thought, who had been married to Eleanor. "The old King decided that all of the Holy Land must be bought back to Christendom again, and he stirred the whole country up to follow him on the Crusades. At first, everyone thought it was wonderful, that the Holy Land would soon be ours again, but it didn't happen. In any event, all the young men who were capable of holding a weapon up and went off to fight for God in the Holy Land. That was the start of it all; the older men who were left were not enough to farm the land and tend the cattle, so things began to go down hill. Then the King began to demand that every estate contributed to his war chest, and every spare penny disappeared. Soon, there was no money to buy grain to sow, no sheep left to give us wool. When the young King - King Philip - went on the latest Crusade alongside King Richard, the country round about groaned in pain. We had nothing left to give, but still it was wrung from us." He paused, clearly afraid that he had overstepped the mark, but Berengaria was nodding in understanding. Memories of her journey across Spain and France came flooding back; the poverty of the countryside, the peasants hungry everywhere. Wryly, she thought of the contrast with Louis, in his magnificent clothes and clearly not a thought for the country he had left behind. Just like Richard. She was surprised to find that the comparison caused her no pain at all, just a grim determination that when she was the rightful Queen, she would make sure that things were very different.

"What can we do?" She asked aloud. "This can't be allowed to continue. The people have suffered for far too long, over something that's not even their quarrel."

"You are doing all that you can, my lady." Jean Reeve responded eagerly. "The estate needs money, it needs investment. If you can get that money, then I know exactly where it can best be spent. Now the last Crusade has crumbled, the young men will begin to drift back to the land, and we will have a workforce again, at long last. It will be hard for them at first, but they'll have their womenfolk to welcome them back and they will become peasants again, not soldiers."

The Reeve's words echoed in Berengaria's head. I'm doing all I can to help, she thought. pleased. A stray butterfly – a Red Admiral – basked in a ray of sunlight that shone through the window slot, its vivid colours a welcome splash of colour against the dreary landscape outside. For once, the solar was quite warm, the log fire was beginning to burn down and spat and hissed suddenly as a knot in the wood ignited.

Isabel stood behind Berengaria, tugging an ivory comb – one Berengaria had had since childhood, and had bought with her from Navarre – through her unbound hair. The comb caught on a snag, and Isabel coaxed the comb through gently. Berengaria spoke softly, almost without thought. There never would be a good time, but this time was as good as any.

"Did he know you were expecting his child, before he left? Did you tell him, Isabel?"

For a moment, Berengaria thought she was going to lie, to deny that she knew what Berengaria was talking about, and she was deeply disappointed. But then she felt Isabel relax and knew she was wrong, and was glad of it. Isabel spoke quietly, matching her mistress' matter of fact tone.

"No. He had no idea. I knew before he went, of course, but I didn't tell him. I just couldn't. It wouldn't have made any difference, anyway. He would still have gone."

"I suppose so. It was his duty, after all." Berengaria said thoughtfully. "How long? How long were you … together?"

Isabel continued to pull the comb through with long, rhythmic strokes. They could have been discussing something minor, something that did not matter at all. In a flash of understanding, Berengaria realised that Isabel was glad she had asked, pleased that at long last she could confide in somebody. To herself, she wondered almost absently why she had chosen this precise moment to ask. But it didn´t matter, really. Questions, like babies, chose their own time. And it seemed that this was the time.

"I loved him, you know." Isabel said, instead of answering Berengaria´s question. "I loved him from the first moment I saw him. I would have done anything for him, anything he asked. I know that's no excuse, that it was wrong, but I couldn´t help it. I just couldn´t."

"It was for him that you went to tie the cloth on the Jericho Tree in Cyprus, wasn't it?"

"Aye." Isabel said simply.

"It started then? Tell me Isabel, please. I need to know. You understand that, don´t you?"

"I understand." She paused, and then sighed. "Not then. Not until we were aboard ship for the Holy Land.

You – all of you; Lady Johanna, Angela, you – you all made it so easy for us. You spent most of the time on deck. Lady Johanna was sea-sick every time a wave struck, and Angela had a fancy for one of the sailors, and took every opportunity to be with him." Berengaria snorted with surprise, and Isabel laughed shortly. "You didn't know that, did you? "

"I think there's much I don't know." Berengaria admitted ruefully.

"Rafe came to see Lady Johanna often, at least at first. She doted on him and was delighted that he was there. She didn't see – or perhaps she did see, and just didn't believe that a great knight like Rafe could be interested in a serving woman – how he looked at me. How he touched me as often as he could, pretending he had lurched against me with the sway of the ship. I knew he wanted me. I waited as long as I could, I kept telling myself that I was probably wrong, that I was in danger of not only making a fool of myself but causing trouble if Rafe was unkind and reported me to you." She paused for breath and Berengaria itched to speak, to tell her to get on with the tale. She pressed her lips together and made herself wait. "Eventually, I couldn't stand it any longer. I thought of some pretence or other, and went to his cabin. I remember, when I stood in front of the door I was shaking so hard my teeth were chattering. I had just raised my hand to knock when he swung the door open and stood there, smiling at me."

Ah, that smile. Berengaria blinked away tears as she recollected how Rafe had smiled at her, and how that smile had made her feel. She felt a spasm of deep pity for Isabel; if Rafe had conquered a queen without effort, what chance did a servant have?

"He stood to one side and swept me a bow, just as if I was a great lady. Then as he stood up, he hit his head on the deck – it sloped down towards the door – and he swore. Somehow, that made everything easier. We both laughed and before I could get frightened again, I was inside the cabin and the door was shut."

"You became lovers then?" Isabel sighed.

"No. Not that day. Nor for the rest of the voyage. He … he made me mad for him. I told you, I would have done anything for him. Anything he asked. And I did. He would not make love to me, but rather, he showed me how to please him, as he put it. How to touch him, caress him. With my hands. With my mouth. He taught me things I didn't know existed. I was crazy for him, but he never did more than kiss me in return for all I did for him."

Isabel stopped combing and came around to sit at Berengaria's knees. She clasped her own knees in her hands, and looked at Berengaria appealingly, begging her silently to understand. Berengaria stroked her head gently, as if she was a child, asking forgiveness for some minor transgression.

"I know." She said softly. So clearly, she could remember Rafe's touch. His mouth close to her ear, his breath hot on her cheek. The tenderness in his hands. The knowingness in every contact of his body. And she had responded to him, just as Isabel had. Neither of them had had any choice, any chance.

"When did it change? When did you actually become lovers?"

Isabel closed her eyes at the question. When she opened them, Berengaria saw tears ready to fall.

"Not until the Holy Land." She whispered. "Not until after he had begun to love you."

Berengaria turned Isabel's words over in her mind.

"Love me? No, I don't believe he did. I thought he did, but I was wrong. He didn't love you, and he didn't love me. But you knew? You knew that Rafe and I were lovers?" Once spoken, the words seemed to unleash something in both women. All pretences were gone, all walls between them finally taken down.

"He told me." Isabel said. "He told me that he was going to make you fall in love with him. I was nearly mad with jealousy, but he just laughed at me. You were a woman, I said. Were you so much different to me? If it came to that, wasn't I more like him than you were? Didn't we share far more than you and him ever could? You were the queen, I said. You had everything, the world at your feet. Why did you have to have more? Have him? He sneered, told me I would never understand. Said that I was a pebble on the beach, and that you were a diamond to my pebble. I cried. Ranted at him. Promised to make him want me so much that he would never look at another woman, but it was no good.

He told me that he had to do it. Had to make you love him. Make you want to go to his bed." She paused and looked at Berengaria with pleading eyes. "I tried to hate you. Oh, how I tried. But I knew, you see. Knew what you didn't. And I couldn't hate you. Instead, I pitied you."

Berengaria's throat went dry and she coughed before she spoke.

"Tell me, Isabel. I have to know. If Rafe didn't love me, why did he have to make me love him? Why Isabel?"

"Because of Richard." Isabel spoke quietly, so quietly that Berengaria had to lean forward to hear her clearly. "Rafe told me. He said Richard had told him to take you. He said that Richard had told him that he had to have an heir, that without a son to follow him, John would sweep in and ruin everything he had ever worked for. Rafe said….." She stopped and bit her lip.

"Tell me, Isabel. Tell me. Let me hear it. I promise you, it can't be worse than I've imagined. Worse than the all the nightmares I've been living with. Tell me, please. If you love me at all, tell me."

Isabel closed her eyes.

"Rafe said, Richard told him that if he himself couldn't get you with child, then somebody had to. And because he loved Rafe, then it would be better him than any other."

Berengaria sat, silent. A sense of relief so profound that she could not explain it even to herself spread through her body, leaving her shaking with weakness. Isabel was crying, snuffling apologies through her tears. Berengaria patted her gently, only vaguely aware of the irony that it was she who was comforting Isabel.

"Did you know that he and Richard were lovers?" She felt sick as she said it, as she finally acknowledged the truth to herself.

Isabel nodded. Her voice was thick and hoarse when she spoke.

"I knew almost from the start. Rafe told me. Dangled it in front of me, gloating. My lover, the King! He used to say. Mine! In spite of everything, my lover! Richard said this, Richard said that. At first, I thought he was just doing it to upset me, but after a while I realised he was telling me because he had to talk to someone about Richard, and I was the only person he could speak to. It's often that way, isn't it?" She smiled bitterly through her tears. "When somebody is so deeply in love, they have to talk about their lover every chance they get. Even if it's only commonplaces, it's enough that they can mention their name. And he did love Richard, you know. He told me once that Richard was the only person he had ever, truly loved. Told me that – just as I would have died for him, then he would willingly lay his life down for Richard. I tried, I tried so hard. I did everything he wanted, everything I thought he might like. I … I even gave him love philters. They should have worked, but they didn't. The last day I saw him, he told me casually that he was following Richard wherever he landed after he left the Holy Land, and that I might well not see him again. Just like that, and he was gone. I thought about telling him about the babe, but it was too late. Before I could say anything, he had turned on his heel and gone." She paused and raised her head to look at Berengaria. "I'm sorry, I have to ask. Is that how you felt about him?"

Berengaria stared into space. Had she really been so deeply in love with Rafe as all that? Would she, like Isabel, have laid her life down for him? Done anything for him? At the time, she would have said yes, but now? She shook her head slowly.

"I thought I loved him." She said sadly. "He was gentle and tender and gave me everything that I wanted from Richard, but never got. And," she thought for a moment and then shrugged; how stupid to try and keep secrets between her and Isabel now! "And he was exciting, so very exciting. He aroused me in ways I didn´t understand, had never even dreamed of."

"I know. It was the same for me. I´m sorry. So very sorry. I couldn´t help it." Isabel spoke almost to herself. "And I didn´t know that you knew about him and Richard. Oh, how much that must have hurt you. And I suppose it must have made it even worse, you knowing that Richard had chosen somebody he was supposed to despise, over you."

"What?" Berengaria frowned. "Richard loved him. I can understand that, if nothing else."

Isabel stared at her, the colour draining from her face. Her lips opened and closed, but she made no sound. She cleared her throat.

"You must have known. About Rafe. He was your lover."

"I don't know what you're talking about." Berengaria said, bewildered.

Isabel closed her eyes and spoke carefully

"Rafe. You didn't know, didn't realize? He was – is – a Jew. Or at least, his mother was Jewish, and in our religion that makes him a Jew. He didn't worship in the Temple, but he thought of himself as Jewish. I often wondered if it was something he gloated over, knowing how Richard felt about us."

Berengaria stared at her. She began to shake her head and then remembered the thing that had always puzzled her about Rafe; the thing she had never mentioned to him, in case it upset him. He had not been whole. Unlike Richard, the hood of his penis had been missing. At first, it had worried her greatly. She had wondered if she could arouse him, but had stopped worrying when it became clear that she could. After a while, she had stopped thinking about it at all, and Rafe himself had never mentioned it.

One of the nobles at court in Navarre had been rumoured to be from a Jewish family. From a long, long way away she had a memory of the ladies giggling between themselves, and saying there was only one way to prove it. Of course. She remembered discussing it with Blanche, and how they had sniggered about it. Had she been so very much in love with Rafe that it had never entered her head? Probably.

Even if she had known, it wouldn't have mattered. Not at the time. Still wouldn't matter now, if it hadn't been for Richard. Christ, how much had Rafe really meant to him, that he could take a despised Jew as his lover?

"Will you send me away now?" Isabel said quietly.

"Send you away?" Berengaria echoed. "Why? It wasn't your fault. None of it. We were both foolish Isabel, both silly little girls. Me twice over. And we've both paid for it, haven't we?" Isabel watched her face anxiously and nodded. "In any event, hurtful as it all is, it's not as bad as I thought it was, I promise you. None of it is as terrible as the thoughts I've lived with since I realised that you were pregnant. As soon as I saw your babe, I knew straight away that it was Rafe's. I suppose you know that at first, when I knew you were expecting, I thought it was Richard's?"

Isabel stared at her, and shook her head. She laughed shortly, almost a snort of amazement rather than amusement.

"The King? But he hated me! You knew that. It would have killed him to even touch me."

"But he touched Rafe, didn't he?" She flushed, wondering if Isabel thought she was insulting her. A glance at her face reassured her. "I knew he hated you. Or he said he did. But I thought ….. When I lost my baby … Oh, I don't know. I thought that perhaps," she paused and then the words came in a rush. "I thought that Richard had decided I was barren, and he said, so many times, that England had to have an heir. And you look so much like me, our skin is the same colour, our hair the same. I thought that he had got the idea into his head that if you had his child, then he could claim it was ours, and if it looked like you, nobody would notice the difference.

That's where I got the idea from, that I could pass him off as my babe. At the time, there seemed to be some dreadful rightness about it. Richard would have his babe, after all, and so would I. Just as he had planned. He would be happy, and he need never know that his plan had worked."

"And you kept that to yourself, all this time?" Isabel whispered. "You really thought I was expecting the King's baby? Was it a relief, then? When you saw my son, and knew he was Rafe's? If he had been the King's son, would that really have been better than knowing that we shared a lover? Because if he had been the King's child, then the only way it could have happened was through hate, not love."

Berengaria smiled sadly. Just as Rafe had felt compelled to speak to Isabel about Richard, she wanted to tell Isabel everything, to empty all the pain that had raged within her. Not to confess, but rather to share. To explain.

"I thought" She said softly, "That Richard had been playing some dreadful, hurtful game, just to amuse himself. If he had managed to get a baby on you, that would have been a bonus for him. But it seemed to me that all he wanted – not just from me, but from all of us, from you, from Rafe, from me as well – was the triumph of having it all. The King's man, the Queen, the serving girl. When I saw your son, saw he was the image of Rafe, I thought my heart was going to stop. At least then I knew that Richard was blameless, that I had damned him in my heart for nothing. That it was Rafe who had led us all on; the thought made me feel sick, but at least then I knew that I was wrong about Richard. And at least Rafe loved Richard, and – in his way – Richard cared enough about me to want to have my child as King of England. He could easily have had me set aside, you know, on the grounds that I was barren. Could have taken you, if he wanted. You, or anybody else he took a fancy to. Even Angela. But you Isabel, you're the only one in this sad and sorry affair that has been left with nothing at all, not even a memory that hasn't been soured. And I'm sorry for that."

"You're wrong." Isabel spoke gently, but her voice was jagged with pain. "Rafe did care about you. Not in the same way as he loved Richard, but he did care.

Alongside tales of Richard, he would talk to me about you. Tell me how beautiful, how regal you were. How there was not another woman in Christendom like you. And it was not said just to spite me, I could tell. I was his amusement, nothing more. You, he treasured."

"How you must have hated me." Berengaria said. "And I never knew. How did you hide it all so well?"

"You forget, I was taught discretion by my father. Taught to keep a closed face at all times. I did hate you at first. Hated you so much I was tempted to feed you poison. I could have done it, you know, and no one would ever have known. But I couldn´t. You have always been good to me, better I think than anybody has ever been. And when I found out about Richard, I no longer hated you. I pitied you, with all my heart."

Both women fell silent, the only noise the spit and crackle of the falling logs. The butterfly stretched its wings and took flight suddenly, flapping almost with a sense of purpose into the fading light. Berengaria felt sorry for it, thinking sadly that the cold would kill it quickly; just as it had hatched before its time, so would it die.

"So here we are." She said softly. "Two women who have been treated badly by the same man. Bastards that they are!" She broke out suddenly and Isabel turned to look at her anxiously. Suddenly, both women began to giggle and with a few seconds the amusement turned to almost hysterical laughter.

"No more secrets between us." Berengaria wiped tears that could have been either pain or laughter or both from her eyes. "Whatever the world has left to throw at us, we will face it together."

"Aye." Isabel slid her fingers into her mistress´ hand and Berengaria squeezed them gently. "For surely, we have weathered the worst between us."

Chapter 20

"You knew nothing, either?"

"Nothing at all. I've had no word, none." Berengaria watched as Johanna swished past her. As if from far away, she could hear the chatter and laughter of Johanna's ladies, and she thought – irrelevantly – that the women sounded like caged birds chirping. Johanna suddenly took offence at their levity and bawled at them to shut up. Silence followed instantly.

Johanna had arrived unexpectedly, with her full retinue of ladies and a handful of courtiers. The ladies had immediately made themselves at home in the solar next to Berengaria's own apartments, and the courtiers were lounging in the great hall, dicing and gossiping and calling for wine and food. Berengaria hoped they would soon be off hunting, as a snatched moment of conversation with Jean Reeve had confirmed her worst fears about the state of the larders. But she had had no more than a few minutes before Johanna had swept her into her own apartments and shut the door firmly on her gossiping brood.

"Fifty eight weeks he's been captive. Over a year. You heard nothing from him. Nor did I. Nothing! Mama must have been in contact with him – he wouldn't have dared not write to her." Berengaria smiled briefly at the image of the great King, still boy enough to be cowed by his mother. Then she thought of Eleanor, and the image ceased to be amusing.

"You're absolutely sure, Johanna?" She asked quietly. She was deeply hurt; hurt and worried. Surely, even in the midst of all that must have been happening, Richard could have got word to her? Just one letter in all the time he had been held to ransom? She had waited and waited, but had finally persuaded herself that Richard's captors had not allowed him to get word out. But obviously she had been wrong, Richard could have written to her, but he had chosen not to. The hurt deepened and became a weight pressing on her chest until it was painful.

"Oh, I'm sure. He's free. Even my dear husband Raymond knew before I did. In fact, it was Raymond who told me. Quite casually – "Oh, I see your dear brother is back in England, then." I tell you, I gawped at him, I really did. I was so confounded, I actually said, "Which brother?" And he laughed his damned head off at me."

Berengaria shook her head, not wanting to believe. Richard was not only free – he was in England? Surely, this couldn't be possible. He would have come for her, taken her with him. She was his wife. His Queen!

"Johanna, sit down. Start at the beginning. Tell me."

Johanna sat abruptly, but every limb was trembling. To make sure she didn't start pacing again, Berengaria reached across and grasped her hand.

"When? When was he released?"

"About a month ago." A month! A whole month! And nobody had told her? Richard himself had not thought it worth while to even write to her, still less come to her himself? She shook her head in disbelief "It appears that the last installment of the ransom was paid, and he asked Mama to go to him, to bring him home."

"Well, I suppose Eleanor was the one who raised most of his ransom. And they always were very close…" Berengaria's voice tailed away miserably.

"Don't bother." Johanna said harshly. "Don't bother trying to make excuses for him. You've not heard the rest of it, yet."

"I don't want to know." She said. And then, immediately, "Oh, Johanna. Go on, tell me."

"Raymond took great pleasure in informing me – and he knew this all along, mark you, but didn't think it necessary to mention it to me until now – that as soon as Richard could get word out, he wrote to Maria. Maria!" Berengaria stared at her helplessly. "Maria of Champagne, our half-sister. She always was his favourite." Johanna said darkly. "You've never met her, have you?"

Met her? I've never even heard you mention her before. But yes, of course I've heard of her, in the same way that I know who has married whom throughout the Christian world.

"She's married to one of the Counts of Champagne, isn't she?"

"Aye, that's Maria. Sweet Maria. Patron of the arts, but can't bother to read and can barely write. Lover of fine verses, but can't string two sentences together herself. Great aficionado of music, but her attempts on the lute make you wince. But she's got the whitest skin, and the blondest hair and great big blue eyes. Tiny, she is, like some sweet little creature of the romances. She always had a habit of looking at Richard as though he had just ridden up and rescued her from a dragon or some such, all wide eyes and sighs. He loved it, of course. Lapped it up. Raymond says he even wrote poetry to her, lamenting his captivity; "J'a nuns nons pris" if you please."

"The bastard." Johanna blinked at her, so surprised that even her flow of indignation was stopped for the moment. "How could he? He could write to her, write poetry to her, but not to me, his wife! Not one word in all this time. He could have been dead, and I wouldn't have known."

"Not one word to me either." Johanna said sourly. "I hesitate to speak ill of two of my siblings in one breath, but I have always wondered if there was something going on between those two." Berengaria's head jerked back as if she had been slapped. "Don't tell me you're really surprised? You know the great King as well as anybody on earth. Do you really believe there's nothing he wouldn't try, if he thought it might amuse him?"

"No." Berengaria admitted sadly. "I suppose it comes of him being a great king. He thinks that normal rules don't apply to him. That it doesn't matter, because it is him. That God will forgive him."

"He probably will, at that. If Richard turns on the charm, he'll manage to squeeze past St. Peter somehow. But," she paused and Berengaria stared at her wildly. No more, she thought. No more bad news, please. "But, I really am sorry, dear. But someone has to tell you this, and I don't suppose anybody else will have the courage. Except Mama, of course, but you don't want to hear this from her, I know."

Berengaria closed her eyes and tensed, physically braced for the next blow. Get on with it, Johanna. Whatever it is, get it over with.

"Go on."

"Apparently Richard arrived back in London to a hero's welcome. In spite of the fact that he bled England dry for his Crusade, in spite of the fact that he's said more than once that he would sell London itself, if he could find someone willing to pay a decent price. In spite of all that, the crowds cheered him home. Threw flowers at his feet. Tried to kiss his hand. Would have lifted him on high, horse and all, if they could. Even dear brother John is said to have kneeled before him and proffered his crown as if he had just been taking care of it. And Richard raised him up, and embraced him. I don't know which of my two brothers disgusts me most, they're both as two-faced as Janus."

Berengaria shook her head. Go on, she urged silently. This isn't the news you're going to tell me, is it? Go on.

"Perhaps it was just to please the mob. Or maybe to please Richard's sense of theatre. Or to make sure that everybody knows he *is* the king. Or perhaps all those, I don't know. But he was crowned again, Berengaria." Berengaria's eyes flew open and she stared at Johanna in silence. She was beyond words. "In Westminster Abbey. He was anointed king again. And Raymond says that the crowd cheered until they were hoarse, and when they were tired of crying on Richard, they shouted for Eleanor as well. Even John is forgiven for his greed and ambition, and is now thought of fondly. Raymond said Richard made a speech to the mob after his coronation, and even though they couldn't understand a word he said, they still screamed for him. I'm sorry, Berengaria. I really am."

Berengaria stared into space. She felt calm, as though she was listening to something that did not really concern her. Perhaps a story about an acquaintance; amusing, but no more than that. Not something personal, at all.

"Have you been listening to me, Berengaria?" Johanna's voice was distant, coming from far, far away. "Richard is ransomed. He is back in England. He has been crowned king again. Without you. You should have been at his side, crowned Queen with him. Do you understand?"

"Yes, of course." Berengaria said calmly. "I understand perfectly. But I also understand that whether I have been anointed or no, I'm still his wife. Still Queen of England. He can't put me aside, Johanna. He can't."

Johanna pursed her mouth, watching her carefully.

"Don´t be too sure he can't put you aside. It´s happened before." She sucked air through her nose. "You´re barren." She said bluntly and Berengaria jerked her head back as if she had been slapped. I´m not, she thought fiercely. Oh no I´m not. But I can´t tell you that, Johanna, can I? Johanna was watching her closely, and for a moment Berengaria was so sure that she knew, that she almost confided in her. But Johanna was speaking again, and the moment was lost. "I don´t suppose he will put you away, even though he could. You know, of course, that he has at least one bastard he's owned to?"

She looked closely at Berengaria, who shrugged. She had heard rumours, of course. Years ago when she had still been at court in Navarre. Tales of indiscretions abounded at court, it was normal. In any case, such rumours didn't agree with her romantic vision of Richard, and so she had simply refused to believe them. And of course, no one had thought to mention it to her after her marriage; who would dare? Satisfied that she was not breaking bad news to Berengaria, Johanna continued relentlessly.

"So he could put all the blame on you, say it was you who was barren, but it still wouldn't reflect well on him. No, his vanity wouldn't let him do it. He couldn't ever tolerate the thought that he, Richard the Lionheart, couldn´t get his own wife with child. So no, I don´t think he´ll put you aside. But what will you do? Just supposing – I don´t think for a moment that this will happen, of course - but just suppose he doesn´t send for you. What then?"

Berengaria turned the words over in her mind. It was impossible, of course. Naturally Richard would come and get her, as soon as things were settled in England. She would write to him immediately, and congratulate him on his safe return. And then he would send for her. She would see her kingdom at last. Set foot in the land she had long come to think of as home.

"He will send for me." She said firmly. "He will."

Chapter 21

Understanding came so gradually that had she been asked to pinpoint a week, or even a month, when she fully accepted that Richard was not, ever, going to send for her; that she would never reign at his side in her rightful position of Queen of England, she would have thought carefully, and then shaken her head in defeat.

She wrote to him immediately, as she had told Johanna she would. The letter was worded carefully; she had heard that he had gained his freedom after so many, many months of captivity, and rejoiced with him. As he was now King of England in fact as well as name, would he name a day when she was to set off to join him, to reign at his side? Or better still, would he come himself to France and reclaim his bride? He knew, of course, that she was still here at Poitou, waiting for him?

Nothing, he replied promptly, could give him greater joy. However, the time was not yet right. He had been gone from his kingdom for so long, first fighting in the Crusade and then cruelly imprisoned by the Emperor Henry that much had gone wrong in his absence. John, he hinted, had been far more interested in feathering his own nest than ruling England in a fair fashion, and action was needed in so many areas at once, that he was distracted. She must forgive him, but his duties as King came before any personal inclination. He also sent a fat purse full of gold, which Berengaria handed over to Jean Reeve in silence. Bitterly, she decided that Richard was probably trying to console his conscience with the gold.

Still, she let matters rest for a couple of months before writing again. This time, the reply took longer and Richard's tone was vaguely hurt, although Berengaria was sure she had taken care not to upbraid him in any way. She must understand, he explained, that matters were still difficult. If the decision was his, and his alone, he would have flown to her side long before, but he could not. The times were unsettled; once the first golden glow of his return had worn off, the citizens of

England had begun to be restless. The peasants were moaning that there had been yet another crop failure, the great nobles were demanding a greater say in affairs of state. She must wait awhile, and all would be well. In the meantime, he remained her most affectionate husband.

She threw the letter in the fire, and felt her dreams burn with it.

To her surprise, Berengaria realized that she was glad that Johanna was close. Slowly, she realized that infuriating as her sister-in-law could be, she had gradually become a true sister to her. Johanna obviously felt the same as the two women visited each other often, but Berengaria began to worry when she noticed that Johanna seemed happier to come to Poitou, rather than for Berengaria to visit Toulouse.

Berengaria herself was far from unhappy about it, as she hated Raymond. He smelled of sweat and stale wine; she wondered how the fastidious Johanna could stand him close to her, and she was reluctant to even shake his hand – which was always grubby – and flinched from his kiss. Unfortunately, he had taken a fancy to Berengaria and constantly patted her hands and face, touching her waist and neck whenever she was too slow to dodge his attentions.

As if summoned by Berengaria's thoughts, Johanna arrived unannounced, supported by only two of her ladies and a small army of servants. Berengaria smiled at her, immediately relieved that all her worries had been nothing.

"Is it the air at Toulouse that suits you, sweetheart? That makes you look so well?" She asked slyly.

Johanna slithered to the ground awkwardly, with the help of two grooms. She embraced Berengaria warmly, and it seemed to the other woman that her embrace was longer and more ferverent than was usual. She led her inside, walking slowly and allowing Johanna to lean on her.

"So, Johanna." She said as soon as they were settled with a goblet of wine and a plate of sweet cakes. "Tell me; when is my nephew to be born?"

Johanna sighed and smiled.

"Oh, that it is a boy! For myself, as long as the babe is healthy, I don't care a fig, but Raymond is worried. He got a soothsayer in, and she hung a bodkin over my belly on a string, and it went from side to side. Every time she did it, it went from side to side, and she said that was an inevitable sign of a boy baby. All his babies from his other wives died very young, so he's pinning all his hopes on this one. Do you think it will be a boy, Berengaria, really?"

"How do I know?" She laughed. "I'm no soothsayer. But come on, let's get Isabel's advice. She knows more about babies than either of us put together, and she will not lie to you."

Isabel listened carefully to Johanna's story of her pregnancy, then, after asking Johanna's permission, asked her to stand up and ran her hands over Johanna's belly, pressing here and there. Finally, she rocked back on her heels, her head on one side.

"I can't be sure." She cautioned. "But the baby is sitting very high, and it's big. I think that it is a boy."

Johanna whooped with delight, and Berengaria beamed.

Berengaria sat and listened as Johanna chattered on. She ran out of breath eventually, and Berengaria repeated her earlier question.

"When is my Godson due?"

"About two months, perhaps a little more."

Berengaria stared at her in surprise.

"So soon? But what are you doing here? You should be confined, resting quietly."

Johanna scowled and stared down at the floor, stirring the sweet rushes with her toe.

"Aye, as soon as I get back to Toulouse. But that's why I came to Poitou now. Will you come back with me? Stay with me until at least the babe is born? Bohemund was a difficult birth, I nearly died then. And I was younger when I had him." Tears blurred her eyes and she looked at Berengaria piteously. "Please? I have no one at Toulouse that I could trust."

"Of course." Berengaria said immediately, touched. "And would you like me to bring Isabel with us? She's birthed many babes, and she's more skilled than any local midwife. Besides, you know her."

Johanna clutched her arm tightly.

"Oh, yes, please."

In the event, Johanna's babe was born without any trouble. She laboured for hours, rather than days, and her baby slid out so quickly that Isabel fumbled to catch him. Berengaria watched, her heart in her mouth, as Isabel sucked mucous from the child's mouth and slapped him – for it was indeed a boy – briskly on his back. The boy sucked in an aggrieved breath and gave a great roar of indignation. Almost as bone tired as Johanna, Berengaria left her sister nursing the child and slept for eight hours without waking.

She sat beside Johanna next day, watching the babe enchanted as he sucked hungrily at his mother's breast. His little face was wrinkled contentedly; Johanna detached him with a wince as his toothless mouth hung on, and he burped loudly and immediately fell asleep. Both women laughed.

"You are well?" Berengaria asked anxiously. Johanna nodded.

"Sore, and very, very tired. But happy, Berengaria, happy. Raymond has seen the boy, and he's also very happy. He claims he looks just like his father, but I myself think he has more of a look of Richard about him." She glanced slyly at Berengaria. "I've already spoken to Raymond about it, but if you're not unwilling, would you be happy for us to call him Richard?"

Tears welled in Berengaria's eyes. She blinked them away but they clung to her eyelashes, blurring her vision.

"I would like that above anything." She managed to say, and held out her arms to take the baby. Johanna handed him over willingly, wriggling against her pillows to ease her back, and Berengaria cradled him in her arms, rocking him softly too and fro. Woken by the movement, he reached hungrily for her breast and both women laughed.

"Would I have some milk for you, Godson." Berengaria said, muffling kisses on his bald head.

"There'll be babies for you." Johanna insisted. "As soon as my stupid brother comes to his senses and realizes that his own wife and his kingdom come before fighting gallantly in every corner of Christendom, there'll be babies enough to keep you happy."

"Aye?" Berengaria raised her eyebrows and looked down at the Richard in her arms. "I loved him, you know." She said sadly. "From the first day I saw him at court in Navarre, I loved him. He was so tall, and handsome, and witty and …. oh, every inch a king. And such charm he had, such charm."

"And now?" Johanna said shrewdly. "You said you loved him, do you love my dear brother still? For if you do, I consider you a saint in all but name. Mad, but a saint nonetheless."

"No." Berengaria shook her head. "No, I don´t love him now. All through the time in the Holy Land, even when we were in Rome, I convinced myself that I still loved him. That he loved me, and that it was only affairs of state and then his imprisonment that stopped him being at my side. But gradually, I realised that I really was a fool, and that he had never loved me. If he ever loved anybody other than himself, it was Eleanor. I doubt anybody else ever spent more than a moment in his mind."

Apart from Rafe, she thought. Apart from him.

The two women fell silent, both gazing adoringly at Richard, who slept in Berengaria´s arms. Eventually, Johanna stirred and stretched luxuriantly.

"How long can you stay with me?" She asked. "Forever would be good; between us we could make Toulouse the most elegant, the most sought after court in the whole of France. Can I tempt you?"

Berengaria considered. The idea was attractive. She would have Johanna, who would make her laugh and furious by turns. There would be baby Richard. And, as Johanna said, between them they could make Toulouse wonderful. But even as she thought of it, she knew she couldn't stay. Poitou was her home, the place she had made for herself, Poitou was hers and hers alone, no matter if Eleanor did still style herself – amongst her many titles – Duchess of Poitou - and it was to Poitou that she would return. Where she would live out her life if, and for the first time she allowed herself to give real consideration to the idea, Richard did not choose to send for her. Poitou would be her refuge. Her home. For she knew, quite suddenly, that she would never ask Richard again to come for her, to send for her. If he chose to come, that would be different. Then, she would take her place by his side in her own kingdom. Gladly. But she would not beg.

She shook her head finally.

"I must go back. It's my home, Johanna. And it needs me to look after it. But if it will make you happy, Isabel and I will stay until after you're churched, and Richard is baptized."

Much to her relief, in the six weeks before Johanna was deemed pure again and allowed back into church, and back to normal society, Berengaria was astonished to find Raymond much changed. He no longer leered at her openly, and restrained his more lascivious attempts to rub against her. Isabel, too, reported that he had kept his hands to himself, and it was Isabel who had an explanation for the sudden transfiguration from sinner to saint.

"It's young Richard, my lady." She said. "Not the babe himself, but Raymond's hopes for advancement through him. I just know that as soon as Lady Johanna suggested naming him after the King, Raymond's mind would have started calculating. Here was his only son, not only named for the great and glorious King of England, but with the Queen of England standing as his Godmother. What a future the child would have, if only he could manage to keep his lecherous hands to himself while we were still here!"

Berengaria laughed.

"And there was I thinking that fatherhood had improved the rat's morals! But it's time we were going back to Poitou, Isabel. Will you be sorry to leave here?"

"No." Isabel said simply. "The court here is very fine, but it's very crowded and very noisy, and there's no time and no place to be alone, to think. Poitou is better."

Berengaria remembered Isabel's words as their farewells were made. Johanna held baby Richard up and he waved his podgy little fist in farewell, but although Berengaria smiled and waved in return and blew kisses to baby and mother, she was glad to be gone. She had no premonition that it would be the last time she would see Johanna well and happy, and later she would think often of that merry parting and wish that she had not been so secretly happy to leave.

Poitou basked in the autumn sun, gold and dappled and welcoming. Isabel disappeared as soon as they arrived and Berengaria sat back, tired from the journey but overwhelmingly content to be home. She had only moments to savour that pleasure as Jean Reeve bowed before her and murmured that she had a visitor, who had been at Poitou for some days and was very anxious to see her. She sat up astonished as De Tancred bowed his head to clear the low door to her solar.

"My dear Stephen!" She half stood and clasped his arm for support as her travel-weary legs refused to support her properly. He lowered her down solicitously, and towered over her, smiling. "How long have you been here? I'm so sorry I wasn't here to greet you – we've been at Toulouse with Johanna and her new son. You heard, no doubt?"

"I did, ma'am. I did. I was unsure whether to set out to Toulouse to find you, but was told you would return soon, so waited for you here. I was en route to Aquitaine, you understand, so was able to come to see you." He fell silent, and stood quietly in front of her.

Berengaria's content drained away as though her body had been punctured by some dreadful wound. He was en route to Aquitaine? Aquitaine was nearly a week's ride from Poitou. De Tancred was here because he had bought bad news. Otherwise why go so far out of his way? Why wait, rather than leaving a note for her?

"Tell me." She demanded. "What is it? Richard? Is it Richard?" Her hands clenched into fists.

"No, ma'am. No. The King is well."

"Eleanor, then?" For a moment, Berengaria found herself hoping that De Tancred had indeed bought news of Eleanor. Bad news. Calling herself a spiteful bitch, she pushed the thought away.

"No. My Lady Eleanor enjoys good health, as always."

Berengaria shook her head in frustration. If not Richard nor Eleanor, then who? What could be important enough to cause this good man to ride so far out of his way? To wait for days for her to return? The answer came to her in a flash of instinct.

"Rafe." She said softly. "Rafael de Valencia. It is, isn't it? Anybody from the family, and you would be here with a retinue, with documents, with all the panoply of state. But Rafe …. Rafe is just your friend."

De Tancred cleared his throat loudly.

"I'm sorry. I knew nobody else would think to tell you. But Rafe was a good friend to me, as well as you, and I could not leave you not knowing."

She nodded her head.

"Thank you. Tell me, what happened? Did he die in battle?"

"No. Not at all. Such a stupid way to die for the bravest of men." She saw that De Tancred had tears in his eyes and she looked away tactfully. "He was out hunting with King Richard. The hounds flushed a magnificent stag, and the two of them hared away after it. Both of them shot at the stag, and it came down with both arrows in its side. Rafe was first there; he beat back the hounds and was about to cut the beast's throat when it turned and thrashed at him, and punctured his arm, here." De Tancred held out his own forearm and placed his fingers on the inside, just below the elbow. "The King laughed at him, said he was clumsy and Rafael made light of it. It was, in truth, a very small wound. But it didn't heal. No matter how many salves the surgeons put on it, no matter how many times the King ordered Rafael bled, it just got worse and worse until his arm was swollen to twice its usual size, and oozed pus and blood fit to make your eyes water with the stink. The surgeons were all for taking the arm off. But the King would have none of it, said it would heal on its own, given time, and of course Rafael agreed with him, in spite of the pain he must have been in. Anyway, just as everybody could see that amputation was the only way, Rafael came down with a terrible fever and he died, ma'am. I think he would have preferred that to losing his arm anyway." He shrugged and was silent.

"Thank you." She said simply. "Does Richard know you're here?"

"No. He's in Aquitaine, with Lady Eleanor, and I was sent back to London to take various documents to the Lord Chancellor. If he asks why I've been so long, I'll tell him that the weather was bad, and my ship was delayed. I doubt if he'll bother to ask. He's been very upset, since Rafael died."

I would imagine he has, she thought cynically. But probably not for long. He'll recover. Find a new lover. I suppose I should be grateful he hasn't found a new wife. The news that Richard was in France, with Eleanor, and hadn't ridden to see her stung. But not as much as she expected.

Having delivered his news, De Tancred fidgeted to be off. Berengaria dismissed him kindly, telling him to ensure that the Reeve gave him provisions and wine and a change of horse for the rest of his journey. He was a good man, she thought absently, a better man than either Richard or Rafe deserved.

She sat silently, listening to the afternoon unwind outside the window. She thought of Rafe. Her lover. Probably the father of her child. But her thoughts constantly slid away, refusing to focus. Distressed, she realised that she could not recall what he had looked like. Certainly, she could remember his black hair and blue eyes; that he was tall, that his hands were large and well formed. But try as she might, she could not bring the elements together, could not recall the whole man. She thought of his touch, his kisses, how they had roused her, excited her beyond reason. The memory was pleasant, but nothing more. Faded like a tapestry bleached by too long in the sun, she was left with only the shadow of something that had once been very beautiful.

Stirring, she called Isabel and told her the news, gently but bluntly.

Both women sat in companionable silence for many minutes until, curious, Berengaria said;

"Will you sit shiva for him? Will you say Kaddish for him?"

Isabel frowned, and looked carefully at Berengaria.

"Will you have masses said for the good of his soul? To help him out of purgatory? If that's where he is."

Berengaria considered before replying.

"I don't believe he had a soul." She said eventually. "Or if he did, it was in thrall to Richard and will remain so through all of eternity. No, I will not have masses said for him."

"Nor will I say Kaddish for him" Isabel replied quietly.

"Amen." Berengaria said softly. "Amen."

Chapter 22

Poitou became her support, and her family. Her life. She smiled at the antics of her courtiers and their ladies, but couldn´t quite bring herself to join them in their games.

Richard's notes became fewer; fewer and both shorter and curter. He spoke increasingly of matters of state and she began to feel that he was writing to her as he might to an advisor, or a member of his clique. Nothing as intimate as a wife. Several times he wrote of things that he obviously assumed she was aware, when she knew nothing at all of the matter at hand. But each letter was accompanied by a substantial sum of money, so she shrugged and accepted what she was offered, neither asking nor expecting more.

Time drifted past pleasantly enough, and she thought herself content. It wasn't the future she had looked forward to, but it was good, for all that.

She took more and more of an interest in Poitou; not just the court, but the estates. These, she knew, were hers. Bestowed upon her the day she married Richard. Eleanor may continue to style herself Duchess of Poitou and whether she did or not, Berengaria neither knew nor cared. These green, fertile lands were hers, and with every day that passed she cared for them more. Cared for the peasants who tilled her fields, the grape growers who produced the wine for her, the miller who put bread on her table. She spent more and more time with Jean Reeve, learning how the land worked and lived, understanding that there was so much more to it all than she had ever known. It became her pleasure, and she looked forward to the quarter day accounts, after which she made a point to sit and chat with Jean Reeve, discussing things that had no place in the accounts. Births and deaths, quarrels and family feuds, pestilences and celebrations.

The Michaelmas accounts dispensed with, she waited for Jean Reeve to rise and take his leave, but he did not. Instead, he hovered, not quite straight, not quite meeting her glance.

"Yes, Jean? We have something further to discuss?"

He shuffled, pursing his lips in a show of hesitation that was almost comical.

"My lady, there is something. Something that I must ask you."

She waited patiently, watching him squirm. This was so unlike the normal, quiet, self-contained Jean Reeve that she was intrigued.

"What is it? Have the crops failed? Or have you lent all our money on some hare-brained scheme that has seen us bankrupt?" Jean shuffled his feet, refusing to rise to her teasing. "Oh, out with it, Jean. Tell me."

"My lady, I want to ask you." His courage failed, and he looked at her for all the world like a little boy who wanted to ask for a treat, but did not dare to speak. She nodded encouragingly. "I want to ask you if … if I can marry Isabel." The words came in a final rush and he stopped at once, looking at her beseechingly.

Berengaria stared, her mouth hanging open. For once, she was totally lost for words. Taking her silence for anger, Jean babbled on.

"I have asked Isabel, and asked her. Time and time again. But she says that she can't marry me, or anyone, for she is bound to you and cannot, will not, break her vow to you. But I know that she's fond of me, and I would make her very happy. If only you'll allow it?"

Berengaria took a breath and forced herself to be calm. How had she had not foreseen this? She, who had been as close to Isabel as if she had been her sister? Her immediate reaction was to say no; no, Isabel could not marry Jean, or anybody else for that matter. They had been through too much together, had shared and suffered so very much. She needed Isabel. The pure selfishness of the thought jerked her with shame. Taking the gesture as rejection, Jean Reeve's face crumpled into misery.

"No. I mean, yes. I'm sorry Jean, I'm taken by surprise. Does Isabel want to marry you?"

"I think so." Jean nodded. "I know she cares about me. It is just that she cares more about you."

"If Isabel wants you, then she shall marry you." Dimly, Berengaria remembered thinking – so very long ago – that she would ensure that Isabel would marry any man she wanted. And the time had come at last. "You may tell her that not only does she have my blessing, but that I will disown her if she's fool enough to say "no" to you."

Jean Reeve babbled his thanks, but she shooed him away with a clap of her hands.

"Go talk to Isabel. Go. Now."

Alone, she wondered at the agonizing pain of jealousy deep in her stomach. She could, she supposed, have dismissed it to herself as hurt that Isabel wanted to leave her, but she knew it for what it was. Envy, pure and simple. She might be Queen, at least in name, but she would have traded her very crown for the sort of love that Jean Reeve was offering to Isabel.

As if summoned by her mistress' thoughts, Isabel entered quietly, her face glowing. She slid silently to Berengaria's feet and took her hand, leaning against her legs like a child clinging to its mother's skirts. Berengaria said nothing, but patted her shoulder softly, and both women cried; the one through joy, the other through dreams that had been broken into a thousand pieces, long ago.

"I will never leave you. Never. If you go from Poitou, then Jean and I will go with you."

"Does Jean know this?" Berengaria smiled through her tears.

"Aye. He does. He knows…everything.. Not about you." She added hastily. "But about me. He knows I was born a Jew. He knows that I spied for my father. He knows about Rafe, and of course he knows about my baby."

"Then he is the best of men, and you are lucky,"

"I am." Isabel spoke simply. "I am."

Jean and Isabel's wedding was a bright torch that flared in the winter greyness. Both were well liked at court, and there was more than one courtier who looked on Jean Reeve with envious eyes. The wedding celebrations went on for three days, and Berengaria was glad. Glad for Isabel and, in a strange way, relieved. What was the old superstition? Things always came in threes; one birth, one death, one wedding. That, then, was her three. Surely, now, she could throw off the mantel of nagging worry that had haunted her for months on end.

Surely.

Chapter 23

Berengaria opened her arms wide in welcome, and ushered the Abbess inside. In spite of her astonishment, she was pleased to see the elderly woman. She had never met her before, but had heard of the good works she did at Fontrevault.

"Welcome to Poitou, madam." She said, ensuring the older woman was seated and comfortable. "You've had a long journey. Will you take some wine? Can I get you some food? Or are you tired? Would you like to rest?"

"You're very good, child." The Abbess looked at her piercingly. "And very beautiful. Not what I had been told to expect, at all."

Berengaria started back. The words set a whole train of thought in motion, as she realised that the Abbess was not simply breaking her journey at Poitou, but had come her for a reason. And for the Abbess to be here herself, it was an important reason. She watched the other woman in wary silence, waiting.

It appeared that the Abbess was in no haste to part with her news. She glanced around Berengaria's chamber with apparent approval, taking in the simple hangings and furnishings, and nodding approvingly at the plain crucifix that hung above the prie-dieu. Finally, her gaze came to rest on Berengaria again.

"You don't know why I'm here? You've had no word?"

Berengaria shook her head. In spite of the warmth of the early spring sunshine, she was suddenly chilled. Her teeth chattered, and she knew she would not be able to speak, so simply shook her head from side to side, unable to stop once she had started until the motion became little more than a tremor, as of palsy.

The Abbess leaned forward and touched her hand.

"I'm sorry, child." Her old voice was still firm, still in control. "I'm sorry to bring you ill news. The King. Richard. Richard is dead."

Berengaria sat still. So very still that the Abbess cocked her head on one side, the better to see if she was still breathing. Satisfied that she was, she started to speak. She told her tale with the calmness of old age, the perspective that saw that death came to all, sooner or later. That it might not be so long before it came for her. Berengaria heard, but the words might have been spoken about somebody else, some casual acquaintance, for all the impact they had.

Richard, the Abbess said with more than a hint of disapproval, had hared off to Limousin after rumours began to circulate that a peasant had turned up a fabulous horde of ancient gold in his fields. Having no use for the gold himself, the peasant had taken his find to Aldemar, his Lord. On his arrival in Limousin, Richard had demanded the whole of the horde from Aldemar, although, she added critically, he had no right to it at all. Aldemar, not wishing to offend the great Richard, had insisted that he had nothing but a jar of ancient coins, and those he offered to Richard unreservedly.

"A good man, Aldemar." She added. "I know him and I think he would have told the truth of the matter." Berengaria nodded dumbly. If her mouth had not been so dry that her tongue felt as if it was stuck to the roof of her mouth, she would have implored the Abbess to get on with her story, not to waste time on trivial asides. As it was, she crossed her arms to stop herself taking the old woman by the throat and shaking her to make her continue.

"Now, where was I? Oh, yes. Aldemar. In any event, Richard chose not to believe him and the King having with him a great force of men – did he anticipate trouble, I wonder? Or would he have had soldiers with him anyway?" She met Berengaria's imploring glance and hurried on. "No matter. Richard laid siege to Aldemar's castle and attacked him. I have been told that Richard was in the front line, urging his men forward, apparently treating the whole thing as something of a joke, when he was struck down by a crossbow bolt, fired by one of Aldemar's foot soldiers. And that, of course, was that. The attack ceased instantly. Aldemar threw his doors open and Richard was taken inside. A surgeon was summoned, but the man was maladroit, and the bolt broke off in the King's shoulder." Berengaria moaned, her fist balled into her mouth, and the Abbess paused. "I'm sorry to give you pain, child." She said gently.

"I'm not skilled in these things; perhaps I have lived too long and become inured to other people's distress. I shall make a point of saying an Ave for it after my next confession, and shall try to be more sympathetic in future. Shall I continue?" Berengaria nodded. "As I said, the bolt broke off in his shoulder. In spite of their former differences, I'm assured that Aldemar gave the King the best of attention, but to no avail. The wound went from bad to worse, and the King obviously realised that he was about to meet his Maker."

She paused, rubbing her lips with her hand and Berengaria frowned, suddenly realizing that something was not right. If Richard had died in Limousin, then why was the Abbess of Fontrevault, Fontrevault that was in the Department of Maine-et-Loire, the one who had come to bring the news to her?

"Forgive me," her voice was hoarse and she cleared her throat and tried again. "Forgive me, Reverend Mother, but I don't understand. How did you come to be involved in my husband's death?"

"Ah. I was not, directly. But when the King realised he was dying, he sent word to Queen Eleanor to come to him." Berengaria stared at her unflinching. Eleanor, or course. Who else would Richard have sent for? "At the time, Eleanor was in retreat for Lent at my abbey. As soon as she heard the news, she flew to her son's side, as was only right, and she told me, with tears in her eyes, good woman that she is, that he died in her arms on the eighth of April."

Berengaria raised her hand, palm out.

"He is buried? Already?"

"I'm sorry, child. But he is. We entombed his poor clay at Fontrevault on Easter Sunday, as he had asked. No doubt the best of omens for his immortal soul."

Irrelevantly, Berengaria thought; what? Nothing for England? Not even his body for the country he reigned over as King?

"Thank you." She said aloud. "Thank you for traveling all this way to tell me."

"Eleanor requested it." She said simply. "I could not refuse her."

A thought struck Berengaria, and she spoke anxiously.

"Do you know what happened to the man who shot Richard? I would not have him punished for it. I can't believe it was anything other than an accident, or a lucky shot that proved to be unlucky."

"He is dead, I believe." The Abbess' face puckered with distaste. "I heard that, as soon as Aldemar realised that the King was beyond help, he had the man flayed. Alive. It was only to be expected; had he not been seen to inflict a suitable punishment on the guilty man then Richard's followers would have torn his castle down to the foundations. Possibly if Eleanor had arrived in time, she might have interceded, but she did not."

"Possibly." Berengaria said, not believing it for a second. Eleanor, she was sure, would have wanted her revenge on the man who had killed her darling. She would have shown no pity, none at all. The Abbess smiled at her, a small, tired smile, and said that she thought she would take some wine, now her task was completed. And some bread and meat if Berengaria would be so good. Lent had seemed unusually long this year, and she was heartily sick of the sight of fish. Berengaria realised suddenly that the Abbess was an old woman, and had undertaken a long journey with no promise at the end of it except bad news. She hurried to provide the Abbess with a hearty meal, and got a chamber ready for her.

As soon as the Abbess had departed – in a litter drawn by fresh horses, and with baskets of supplies and wine – Berengaria launched automatically into performing her last tasks as Richard's wife. She did so with neither heart nor soul, simply issuing orders without caring. Endowments were to be made to various Abbeys in France – amongst them Fontrevault – and England, so that masses could be said in perpetuity for Richard's soul. To further hasten his journey through Purgatory, doles of small amounts of money and food, in the form of fiches of bacon together with skins of wine and ale, were provided for annually to a number of poor families, who would be expected to include Richard in their prayers. The court was officially plunged into mourning, and all amusements and hunting banned.

Berengaria took refuge from the constantly mumbled sympathies in her own apartments. She spent the long hours simply staring out of the window, vaguely surprised – when she thought about it – that the world seemed to be going on just as always. She found it difficult to think of Richard as dead. Although it had been nearly four years since she had seen him last, still she could not shake the idea that one day he would fling the door wide and stride in to her apartment as if nothing had happened between them, larger than life as always, bellowing commands and taking over her life as he had done, truly, in life. She willed herself to cry; dwelling on the days when she had loved Richard with all her heart and all her soul. Oddly, she could remember how he looked the first day she had seen him at Navarre as well as if he stood before her, and that was the image that remained with her, whenever she thought of him. But the tears would not come, and she simply sat, vaguely sad, and could find no tears even in self-pity for her own situation. Was Eleanor weeping, she wondered, for her favourite son? Or was the old Queen so adamantine that she would spare no tears for the dead, no matter who they were, what they had been to her in life? For sure, she thought sourly, Eleanor would spare no tears for her bereaved daughter-in-law. Indeed, it was more likely that Eleanor would rejoice – although privately, of course - that Richard had died childless. For if Berengaria had borne Richard's children, then she would now be taking her rightful place as mother of the next ruler of England, and how Eleanor's elegant nose would have been put out of joint at that. John had children. The knowledge was bitter; now, she would never be Queen. Would never take her place as monarch of England.

She surprised herself by cursing Richard's memory, and then laughed out loud and found that next second she was weeping.

Isabel came and sat at her side, silent, and she found her presence more comforting than words could ever be.

"I loved him, you know. Not now, not for a long time. But at first." She said.

"I know."

"Do you think he ever loved me, even a little?"

Isabel made a rocking motion with her hand, but didn't speak. Berengaria sighed.

"No, I don't think so either." She agreed sadly.

But in the event, Berengaria had little time to mourn. Just as she had marveled that the world rolled on, in spite of the death of kings, soon something much nearer to her poor, bruised heart lifted her. In early summer, a letter came from her sister Blanche. She turned the parchment over in her hands, puzzled. The seal was Blanche´s; she had seen it too many times to mistake it. But the knight who bought the letter was French, from Champagne, and Blanche had returned to her father's court at Navarre when she had been widowed some years before. She dismissed the messenger with a smile and broke the seal eagerly.

A few minutes later, she smiled even more widely. She re-read the letter quickly, needing to be sure. Blanche sent her deepest regards and sympathy for her dear sister's bereavement, but wasted little precious parchment on too many condolences. Berengaria would not have heard her news, but she – Blanche – was to be married again. And this time, not only land and fortune was the basis of the match, but she was truly fortunate in that her bridegroom was Thibaut of Champagne. Berengaria frowned slightly at this, a shadow laying across her pleasure at Blanche´s good fortune. Maria, she remembered, the half-sister to whom Richard had dedicated verses during his captivity, was also married to a nobleman from the Champagne house. She shrugged away the thought impatiently. Every noble in Christendom was in some way related to each other; it was hardly surprising that Blanche was to marry in to the same noble house as Richard's half-sister.

Thibaut was a man who she had known for some years, and she was very fond of him. She was to be married in July; no disrespect to Richard's memory was meant by the haste, she assured her. But there was much unrest in parts of France, much rumbling of discontent between the various ruling houses, and both she and her future husband were anxious that the marriage should take place quickly, in the event that Thibaut was forced to ride to war before the summer was out. Berengaria was lucky, she added, that Poitou seemed to be safe from such wrangles.

So, to the point of Blanche's letter. Would Berengaria come for her wedding, be witness to her marriage? If Berengaria felt that it was too soon after the King's death, then Blanche would understand. Perfectly. But dear, dear, dear sister, please come!

Berengaria laid the letter aside and laughed quietly to herself. How like Blanche. Always the beauty of the family, always the spoiled baby. Always so very sure that not only would she get her own way, but that she deserved it. Quite suddenly, the tears she had been unable to shed since Richard's death spilled down her face and Berengaria let them flow unchecked, not even sure herself whether they were tears of pleasure or grief or both.

She wrote at once, a short note saying simply that she would not miss the wedding for the whole world and entrusted it to the knight who was waiting for her reply. Once he had gone, she passed the good news amongst her court, and let it be known that the period of mourning could be lifted as soon as she set out for Champagne. Isabel pointed out to her that a family of magpies had nested in the tree outside her solar window embrasure, and had two exuberant chicks in the ramshackle nest.

"One for sorrow, two for joy." Isabel said firmly. Berengaria smiled at her superstition, but in spite of it, wondered if the eternal cycle of birth and marriage and death was starting yet again. If it was, then whose would be the birth? She stared at Isabel with interest.

The journey to Champagne was serene, and Berengaria wondered if Blanche had exaggerated the tales of imminent war. Once with her little sister again, she forgot all about it anyway, and the two women spent days closeted together, reminiscing and giggling like young girls, rather than the widows they both were. Thibaut was obviously enchanted with both his new bride and his good fortune in wedding her, and Berengaria had no doubts about their future happiness. Blanche, too, was glowing with delight and Berengaria envied her frankly, and told her so.

"You'll marry again, dear sister. I know it." Blanche said. "I have a very good fortune teller at Court. He's also a good hand with the lute, and a witty fool, but he's famous for his foreknowledge, and it's a fact that his fortunes are always correct. Shall I ask him to make a fortune for you?"

Berengaria shook her head.

"I don't want to know." She said firmly. "What will be, will be. Let it lie."

Blanche stared at her in surprise, but did not insist.

"In any event, I must leave you." Berengaria said. "As I'm so close, I intend to visit Johanna before I go back to Poitou. I've had no word from her in many months, and I'm anxious about her. What? What's the matter?"

She stared at Blanche in concern. Her sister had put both her hands over her mouth and was shaking her head from side to side wildly. As Berengaria stared, she took her hands away from her face.

"No, Berengaria, no. You can't, honestly. You don't understand what it's like here at present; you're tucked away in nice, peaceful Poitou, but even so, you must have heard the rumours about the unrest in Champagne. I told you, when I wrote."

"Yes, you said something about trouble here. But everything is peaceable at the moment, isn't it? You have no problems at the moment?"

"No." Blanche shrugged, obviously reluctant to agree. "Not yet. But there's been fighting to the south of us, and it grows closer every week. Thibaut has made preparations so we're ready if it does spread to us. And as far as I know, Raymond and Johanna have no serious issues at the moment. But for you to ride, unescorted, in that area would be madness. Thibaut would lend you some men at arms to get you to Toulouse, but they couldn't stay and I doubt that Raymond would be generous enough to ensure you had safe passage back to Poitou. You're forgetting, you would be a ripe prize for somebody to take for ransom. I'm not having it, and that's all there is to it."

She stared at Berengaria defiantly and Berengaria almost laughed at her younger sister's bullying. But she could see that Blanche was serious and agreed, reluctantly, to go straight back to Poitou.

"Although why anybody would think me worth taking for ransom, I have no idea. It's been many years since I was worth anything. John would be delighted to get rid of me, and I don't suppose Eleanor would be particularly upset either."

"I would be upset." Blanche said stoutly. "I would never forgive myself if something happened to you."

Chapter 24

Blanche's warnings echoed in Berengaria's mind as she sat, eyes closed, mentally urging her horses to go faster, faster, faster. The carriage swayed alarmingly and she was thrown from side to side but she clung on and shouted to her groom to make better speed still. His reply was lost to her, but she thought that he had coaxed a little more speed from the sweating horses.

Why had she listened to Blanche? Why hadn't she gone south, not north? If Blanche would never forgive herself, then how was she, Berengaria, ever going to be able to make up for her neglect of Johanna? She had felt that something was wrong, that it was strange that Johanna had not visited or written in so long but she shrugged the concern aside, assuming that her second pregnancy was occupying her. And of course, as her pregnancy advanced she was less likely to want to travel. But this! In spite of the rumours about the growing unrest in Champagne, she had never thought that any harm could overtake Johanna. She was protected by a husband, ringed by armed men, in a good castle. She should have been safe.

Jouncing about in the closed carriage, Berengaria tried to pray, to ask the blessed saints to take care of her sister, but the words mumbled and jumbled in her brain and became nonsense.

The nuns at Rouen welcomed her courteously. Anxious as she was to see Johanna, Berengaria had to summon all her reserves of courtesy to allow herself to be taken to the Abbess first. The elderly woman looked at her kindly, taking in her travel worn clothes and dusty face and hair, and made her sit down and drink a goblet of wine.

"Please." Berengaria said urgently. "Please, may I see Johanna? I have been told that she is very ill. I must see her. She has asked for me."

The Abbess steepled her fingers under her chin.

"She isn't ill, child." She said gently. Berengaria stared at her wildly, her first thought being that the Abbess was trying to tell her that Johanna had died.

Understanding immediately, the Abbess repeated, "She's not ill, but she is very badly injured. Do you know what happened to her?" Berengaria shook her head mutely and the Abbess sighed. "Drink your wine."

Quietly, Abbess Matilda told Berengaria the terrible truth. The unrest in Champagne had come to a head in the last couple of months. Raymond had been forced to leave his wife behind in order to suppress a revolt in Languedoc, where he had substantial lands. Taking advantage of their lord's absence, a group of Barons in St. Felix also revolted. Johanna, refusing to be cowed in spite of her advanced pregnancy, had stirred up as many supposedly loyal followers as she could, and had led them herself, laying siege to the castle of Cassee at the head of her men. Berengaria, in spite of her frantic worry, smiled. How like Johanna! Nothing on God's earth would make her change her mind once it was set, and her courage was amazing. The Abbess nodded, clearly following Berengaria's thoughts.

"I never saw her in health, but I think she is a very strong, very determined woman."

Berengaria smiled, proud of the praise for Johanna.

"That she is." She said.

It was at Cassee that Johanna was hurt. Her supposedly loyal followers, obviously realizing that they were in a weak position, had turned coat on their mistress, and had set fire to the camp. Johanna had escaped by the skin of her teeth, but had been badly burned.

Berengaria whimpered, hardly daring to ask.

"Will she live?" She whispered.

Matilda reached forward and took her hand gently.

"My child, I'm sorry. You must prepare yourself for the worst. Dear Sister Johanna was sent to us by Queen Eleanor, who was at Niort. Johanna went to her there, seeking help, but the Queen knew she could not help her and sent her to us, as we have a reputation for healing."

Berengaria stared at her blindly. Eleanor *sent* Johanna to the nuns? Sent her own daughter rather than taking her? Dear God, was the woman so blind, so selfish, she could not be troubled to help her own daughter in her time of need? Could she not see that Johanna was badly hurt, was dying, or did she simply not care? Of course, she thought bitterly, Johanna was just a girl. Eleanor had dashed to Richard's side to be with him when he needed her, but Richard was a man, Richard was the King. Johanna was just another girl child.

"You can't help her?"

"We can't. I'm sorry, we've done all we could. Had it just been the burns, we might have been able to save her, but the baby…. the baby came early, no doubt as a result of the shock and terrible injuries Sister Johanna suffered. The poor child lived long enough to be baptized, but it was too much for her mother." She stopped and looked at Berengaria gently. "She is still alive, I think perhaps she's determined to wait until she sees you before she goes to her Maker. She's called for you constantly for the last few days."

Berengaria stared blindly into space. She would not cry, she determined. What right did she have to cry, when Johanna – dear, mercurial, effervescent Johanna – had suffered so much, so very much? Was still suffering.

A sudden thought distracted her, and she raised her head to look at the Abbess.

"Reverend Mother, you called Johanna "Sister"?"

"Aye, she has taken the veil. I know." She raised her hand to stop Berengaria's confused flood of questions. "I know, as a married woman with a husband still alive, it should not be possible. Canon law forbids it. But", she added simply "But, it's her dying wish, and it's in my power to grant it, so I have done so. If God wishes to take me to task for it when my time comes, then so be it."

Berengaria shook her head in disbelief. Johanna, who had always insisted she didn't have time for religion, a nun?

"Did she say why?"

The Abbess looked at her with tired eyes.

"Sister Johanna told me that her life has always been lived without giving much thought to God, but that at least in death she could make up for the neglect." She smiled. "Anybody else, and I would have refused. I would have explained that God sees through the clothes on our back to the soul within, and he wouldn't be easily deceived. Sister Johanna wouldn't be the first one to try and sneak into heaven in disguise! But it seemed to me that her request was different, that it really mattered to her, and I decided that God would understand. I hope so."

Berengaria stared into space, remembering Richard – so many years ago – disguising himself as a pilgrim to escape detection. That hadn't worked; she prayed that Johanna would be more successful.

"May I see her?"

"Of course." The Abbess got to her feet with a groan, and Berengaria felt her pain as she watched the old woman unknot her knees as she stood, carefully.

At first sight, she thought the nuns were wrong. Johanna lay, clad in a nun's simple habit, with her head turned to one side, towards the wall. Hope sprang quickly to Berengaria; surely, Johanna could not look so peaceful, so …so comfortable, if she was about to die? Then Johanna turned her head slowly and Berengaria knew she was wrong. So very wrong. The left side of her face was a mass of burns; her scalp was a blistered mess, and totally hairless as far as her centre parting. Her neck and shoulders glistened with salve, but were red raw and weeping. Berengaria shuddered as she realised that the rest of her body was probably in the same dreadful state.

The beauty that was still obvious in the other side of her face, together with her beautiful, abundant hair made the terrible wounds all the worse.

As Berengaria moved towards her, she was met with a strong smell of roasting meat and had to swallow repeatedly as her gorge rose. Johanna whispered something, she had no idea what, and then she sat at her sister's side and put her arms around her, gently, so very gently, and her scalding tears fell onto Johanna's burned flesh. If the tears caused Johanna greater pain, she made no sign. Silently, she fell into Berengaria's embrace and the two women stayed locked together for many minutes.

Berengaria laid her back on the pallet when she felt Johanna try to move. Johanna remained mute for a while, and then muttered something so softly that Berengaria was forced to put her ear nearly against Johanna's lips to hear her.

"Richard." She whispered. Her voice was hoarse and raw, and Berengaria realised with huge pity that her throat, as well as her body, must have been burned. She reached blindly for a cup of wine mixed with lettuce sap opiate that the nuns had left ready, and helped Johanna take a tiny sip. The soporific mixture must have helped slightly, as Johanna reached her hand out and grabbed Berengaria's sleeve with surprising strength. "Richard. Please. You must look after him for me."

Berengaria's stomach churned and she suddenly felt sick. Richard? Was it remotely possible that Johanna did not know that he was dead, dead and buried at Fontrevault? How could she tell her? She licked her lips, scrabbling for words, but before she could say anything, Johanna spoke again.

"Look after him for me, please. Tell him what his mother was like. Tell him I loved him, and would have never have left him of my own will. Please, don't let Raymond turn him into a monster, like he is."

Tears trickled down Johanna's face and Berengaria hastened to give her another sip of the wine mixture. Her hand trembled so much that she tipped the goblet further than she had intended and Johanna choked. Berengaria wiped the wine from her chin tenderly with her fingers and found herself whispering in response, so relieved she was almost crying herself.

"He is my Godson, Johanna. I will look after him. I will, I promise you. He will be like my own son to me."

Johanna's eyes closed and she sighed, but Berengaria sensed that she was content.

She rallied once more, but only to ask Berengaria to make sure that she was buried at Fontrevault, with Richard, and after that she was silent, only her rasping breaths breaking the quiet.

Berengaria stayed by her side, dozing and waking by turns. Whenever she thought that Johanna was able, she gave her more wine and lettuce sap as the soothing liquid seemed to give her some small relief from her intense pain. On the second day, unable to deny the demands of her body, Berengaria slept for an hour and woke to find that Johanna had gone, that the body that lay next to her was nothing more than an empty shell, bereft of life and spirit and all that had made her Johanna.

Berengaria detached herself gently and went in search of one of the Infirmarian Nuns.

"She waited until I was asleep." She said sadly.

The nun glanced at her and nodded.

"It's often that way." She said very gently. "I have seen so many that have waited and waited until a loved one could come, and then drifted away as soon as they had spoken to them. The dying know when it is time for them to go to God, and she waited until you were asleep to spare you any more pain. I think that she was a good woman."

"She was my sister, and I loved her." Berengaria said simply.

She explained Johanna's wish to be buried next to Richard, and the Abbess assured her that she would make the arrangements.

"You will not go to Sister Johanna's funeral." She said, and it was a statement rather than a question. Berengaria shook her head, perplexed.

"Of course I will. Why not?"

"It's not safe for you." The Abbess said firmly. "I'm astonished you managed to get here in safety, but to travel to Fontrevault would be tempting fate too far. The countryside is full of warring factions, and you would be seen as a choice prize for ransom."

Berengaria laughed shakily.

"No me, I assure you." Absently, she wondered why everybody except her thought she was worth anything? "I pity anybody who thinks me worth taking. Richard is dead, King John has no love for me. In fact I have no doubt that he would be delighted to be rid of the thorn in his side. I'm worthless as a prize, I assure you." She glanced at the Abbess to see if she was shocked, but Matilda had lived too long and seen too much for that.

"Worse still, then. If you were taken and it became obvious that no ransom was forthcoming, then you would be killed, or at best thrown into a dungeon to rot. No, you must go back to Poitou, and as soon as possible."

Reluctantly, Berengaria allowed herself to be persuaded. She had to choke down hysterical giggles when the good Abbess produced a nun's habit for her, plain and voluminous and hiding her face. Shades of Richard's disguise as a pilgrim, she thought. And then, more soberly, came the thought that if it had been good enough for Johanna, then it was surely good enough for her.

She had cause to be grateful for Matilda's caution. She was stopped twice on the way back to Poitou by roaming bands, and on both occasions was allowed to continue when she said, simply, that she was on pilgrimage to Compostella. One of the leaders of the bandits even had the cheek to ask for her blessing, and she gave it, hoping he did not notice how her hand trembled when she made the sign of the cross.

Never, she thought, never, never, never had she been so glad to see anywhere as Poitou. And she would be well content if the good God let her rest there until the end of her mortal days.

Chapter 25

"I haven't been invited, but I'm going."

Berengaria paced up and down the great hall. A dog yawned and stretched in her way, and she pushed it aside with her foot. Isabel scurried to keep up with her, also pushing the unfortunate dog to one side at it moved out of Berengaria's way. It looked at her reproachfully before sitting to scratch behind its ear.

"You're sure?" Isabel watched her uneasily.

"Wild horses wouldn't stop me." Berengaria said firmly. She glanced around the hall, and seeing nobody but the dog, added, "I want to makes sure she really is dead. Sixty-odd years she was a Queen, Isabel. Queen of France, Queen of England. I thought she was going to live forever. If I don't see her in her coffin with my own two eyes, then I will still not believe it."

"Amen to that." Isabel grinned. "Are you going to take young Richard? She was his Grandmother, even if he really didn´t know her very well."

"No. That I will not. Richard is nicely settled at the Court at Castille. As you say, he never knew her well."

She paused and stared out of the window embrasure, thinking fondly of her Godson. Richard had grown into a sweet natured child, more and more like Johanna with every day that passed. He had an excellent singing voice, and a tender hand with the lute, and all of his mother's ready wit and ease of laughter. As soon as the trouble in Champagne had faded a little, Berengaria had gone to Raymond, to plead with him to allow the boy to come to Poitou with her. But he had refused so bluntly it was rude.

"You can do nothing for the lad." He said dismissively. "Now King Richard is dead, you have no influence, no power. In any event, I don´t want him raised by women."

But as the years had gone by, Raymond had remarried and had more children. Richard annoyed him; he had no great taste for jousting or swordplay. He was, to be sure, a wonderful horseman, but what was the use of that, when he didn't even care to ride out to the hunt? His skill with music meant nothing to Raymond, and he had been grudgingly pleased when Johanna had used all her contacts to get him a place as a page at the great Court at Castille. Cousin Sanchez, after so very long, had come in useful after all. Richard was happy, as was his aunt.

And now, finally, the old Queen was dead. Berengaria watched her body lowered into the tomb prepared for her, between her son Richard and her husband Henry and had to choke back an almost insane desire to laugh. Poor Richard, she thought, poor Henry, with Eleanor between them for all eternity! She returned to Poitou weary from the journey, but glad, as always, to be home.

Isabel looked at her questioningly.

"All went well? Did you have the chance to have words with John?" Berengaria smiled softly, grateful for the tact that had made Isabel refrain from calling her brother-in-law "The King"

"It went as well as one could expect, I suppose. As I had not received an official invitation to my dear mother-in-law's funeral, I was late. They wouldn't even let me in to the cathedral, until one of the knights recognized me and was kind enough to usher me down the aisle to a place of honour in front of the altar."

"No!" Isabel gasped.

"Aye. I must have been imagining it, of course, but it seemed to me that John was quite composed until he saw me, and at that point his feelings overcame him absolutely, and he was forced to bury his face in his sleeve to hide his tears. So upset was the poor man that he had to hurry away straight after the ceremony, but he left word with one of his courtiers that he would, without doubt, be delighted to see me at noon the next day."

"And did he?" Isabel asked shrewdly.

"Did he hell." Berengaria spat bitterly. "When I went to his apartments, I was told that urgent matters of state meant that he had had to leave for London, at once. He was sure I would understand. But John would undoubtedly write to me, as soon as he had the chance." She shook her head. "Do you know Isabel, on the journey back home, I found myself thinking on Eleanor and I realised that I felt sorry for her."

Isabel shook her head in disbelief.

"After the way she treated you? And me!" She added.

"I know, I know. But she has buried the best of her children - Richard and Johanna - and it is not right that that should happen to any mother." Both women fell silent, thinking for a moment of their own dead babies. "And look who has survived her. John, the child she could barely stand to own as her own son."

"I suppose so." Isabel pulled a sour face. "But I'll not say I'm sorry she's dead, for I'm not."

"Neither am I." Berengaria admitted. "Neither am I."

Berengaria was surprised. John had promised he would write, and she had doubted that he would even do that. Still less had she expected that he would actually send his representative to see her, and so soon. Barely a month after Eleanor's funeral.

John's man smiled at her. Jean Reeve had given his name when he ushered the man into to her, but she was so surprised she had forgotten it instantly.

"I'm deeply sorry, my lady, to have to come to you so quickly after your return." Don't, then, she thought cynically, but said nothing, simply inclining her head politely. "But I must return to the King as soon as possible. Affairs of state can't wait."

"And what, pray, do affairs of state have to do with me?" She asked courteously, even as worry began to roll in her stomach.

He was smooth-faced and expensively dressed. Even though he had ridden many miles to get to Poitou, his tunic showed no trace of dust. His hair, she thought critically, must have been done in the latest style by skilled hands. She took an instant dislike to him, more so than was justified by the fact that he had been sent by King John. She guessed Jean Reeve had felt the same, as he hovered protectively until she had nodded him away. And then he went reluctantly, with many a backward glance.

"The King has asked me to convey his most sincere compliments. He was unable to attend you at his dear mother's internment. I'm sure you appreciate he had to return to London, as there's much unrest in England at present. However, he's asked me to present his sincere compliments and hope that you will accept his apologies. If he could have stayed, he would. But the parlous state of the kingdom had to take precedence over his personal wishes."

It was a smooth speech, smoothly delivered. Berengaria felt her hackles rise.

"Indeed? I had no idea that my sweet brother-in-law was so fond of me. Oh, be done. Come on man, tell me. Why are you here? What's so damned urgent that it couldn't be told to me tomorrow, or next week, or by means of a letter?"

He passed his smooth hand over his even smoother chin. Berengaria guessed he had been thrown off balance by her abruptness, and was pleased by it. She raised her eyebrows in question and waited patiently, as though she had all the time in the world. For the first time, she sensed his hurry.

"The King conveys his compliments. He would have you know that as the widow of his dear brother, you are constantly in his thoughts." As a pebble in the shoe will constantly be an irritant, she thought cynically.

"However, he wishes me to explain to you the difficult position he finds himself in since Queen Eleanor's death."

Taken aback by the unexpected words, Berengaria frowned. Eleanor's death? What did Eleanor's death have to do with her? Seeing his chance, John's man spoke quickly.

"You are aware, of course, that Queen Eleanor was also Duchess of Poitou?"

"Of course." Berengaria said warily. "But it was merely a courtesy title. Poitou is mine, gifted to me by Richard on our marriage. Gifted to me by my husband, the King." She emphasized.

"Alas, my lady. That is not so. The grant of Poitou was not in the gift of Richard, nor of any other King of England. The lands of Poitou form part of the Crown Lands, and can't be given away at the whim of any king."

"You're wrong." She said scornfully. "I have the deeds of Poitou in my possession. Poitou is mine. On my death, certainly, it may return to the Crown, but not until."

He shook his head in pretence of sorrow. But Berengaria saw the gleam in his eyes and her heart beat so hard that she could hear the boom, boom, boom of her pulse in her ears. No. She thought, no. Please don´t let this be so.

Lips pursed, he shook out a document from a silk traveling bag, and spread it before her.

"You may well have the deeds in your possession. But they give you no right of ownership. See, here. This letter is from Richard, sent to Queen Eleanor not long after he was released by the Emperor Henry."

Berengaria´s hands shook so hard, she could barely focus on the words, written in Richard's unmistakable bold scrawl. Richard, it said, understood Eleanor's concern. He knew that she had always had a fondness for Poitou, and he assured her that it would always remain her domain. Berengaria, he said, understood that it was only hers on a grace and favour basis, and that it could be taken from her at any time that it was needed. No, she thought, that was not right. Poitou was hers. Hers by right.

She shook her head.

"No. This is nothing. Poitou was given to me on my marriage. I have the marriage settlement here; I will show it to you."

She rose and walked to her trunk, throwing back the lid against the wall with a crash. The settlement document was safe, right at the bottom, and she threw the top layers of lavender and slips of silk and less important documents aside regardless.

"Here." She threw the bulky, sealed parchment in front of him. "Read it for yourself."

She sat and tapped her fingers on the table, watching his face carefully as he read through the document quickly. By the time he had finished, she could hardly breathe for anger and fear.

"I'm so sorry." She saw the mock sadness in his expression and felt sick. "Poitou is mentioned, but it is on the basis I have already explained to you. It is yours for life, unless and until the King of England has need of it."

She snatched the parchment from him angrily. Read and re-read the clause he was indicating. The words danced before her, refusing to make sense. Over the pounding of her heart, she heard him speaking.

"My Lord the King regrets the necessity of taking Poitou from you. But with the death of Queen Eleanor, he has need of the title. It is promised by him. And of course, with the title of "Duchess of Poitou" also goes the Duchy of Poitou. My Lord feels that you would be very happy at Le Mans, in Maine. You are, of course, Countess of Le Mans, and that property is undoubtedly settled on you. King John has authorized me to make an offer to you, to defray all your moving expenses, and he has also agreed – and I'm sure you'll acknowledge how generous an offer this is – to give you an annual allowance of one thousand marks." He paused, licking his lips. "Providing you agree to give up all title to those lands in England that were settled upon you at the time of your marriage. Together with Poitou, of course, which we have agreed you have no legal title to anyway."

Beneath the table, Berengaria curled her fingers into tight fists. Coincidence, perhaps, but barely six weeks before, she had asked Jean Reeve to go through the accounts of all her properties with her.

Poitou, mainly thanks to Jean's dedication, made a small surplus each year, providing God was good and the crops did not fail. Her other properties in France were so-so, but not beyond saving with much care. But her English lands….she knew so little about them; was barely aware of even where they were, what her tenants were like. Nothing. But what was clear was that the English property was taking money rather than making it, and it would remain so while ever she could not be there to take look after it.

It isn't my fault, she thought angrily. Why had this terrible neglect happened? Because I wasn't there. Because I wasn't allowed to be there. Because the country that should have been my home has always been barred to me. Damn you Richard, damn you, damn you, damn you.

Wrenching her mind back to the current horror with an effort, she wondered; was it a co-incidence that John had suddenly decided to take an interest in her English affairs? Or was it simply a case of the King that had been known for so long as "John Lackland" deciding that now he would have his land. As much of it as he could possibly – rightly or wrongly – claim. From whoever he saw as weak and vulnerable.

She was aware that John's man was watching her carefully and smiled icily.

"King Richard was very generous in his endowments at the time of your marriage." He said quietly. He closed his eyes and began to speak from memory, ticking each property off on his fingers as he went through them. "You have no fewer than twenty-nine endowments in England, ranging from land in Kent and Sussex, which are in the south of the country, to Lincolnshire which is further north. You also have land in Devon, which is in the toe of England, and property in London itself."

Berengaria raised her eyebrows. Richard may have been generous, but not to her. Richard and Eleanor between them had not thought of her at all, but of the heirs that would follow Richard. Heirs that had not come, but neither Richard nor his mother were to know that, at the time. She gathered her drifting thoughts, realizing John's man was waiting for her to speak.

"And if I refuse?"

"Ah, then matters would be .... difficult. For you. You know that many of the so-called Wool Barons, men who have made their wealth and obtained a place in society through trading, are unhappy with the status quo in England?" She nodded, impatient for him to get to the point. "These men believe that it is only through their wealth that England remains prosperous. They believe that they should have a voice in the running of the country. All nonsense, of course. The King is the King, and his position as God's representative on earth is carved in stone. But it is a sad fact that the Crusades and several years of bad harvests have left England in a poor state."

"What's any of that to do with me? I have never even set foot in England! Never taken my rightful place as Queen." She added bitterly.

"Indeed, and that is part of the problem. There are many amongst the barons who speak against you. They say that it's not right that a woman who has – as you so rightly say – never even stayed one night in her own kingdom should own such great swathes of England. There are those who have estates where you hold lands that are unhappy, but most vociferous of all are those nobles who live in the parts of London that you own. "

Berengaria stared at him incredulously. All the warnings Richard had given to her about John came back to her, but beneath them came an even harsher thought; if what the man was saying was true, then it was not just John she had to fear, but his nobles as well. And the ordinary people, what did they think about her? Did they also think that she was an absentee landlord, by choice rather than circumstance? Did they wonder why she did not help them, why she took from them but appeared to give nothing at all back? Did they hate her for it? Sadly, she guessed that they did, and the knowledge decided her even as it broke her heart.

"A thousand marks, you say? Each year? Guaranteed?" He nodded. "And how much to allow me to move my Court to Le Mans?" He named a sum that surprised her in its generosity; that much would fund Poitou for a year. Affecting shock, she shook her head sadly. "Nay, I would need at least twice that amount."

"Agreed." She stared at him in disbelief. Would he have agreed to almost any sum she named? Had she sold herself – and Poitou – cheap? "I have two copies of the contract ready. I will witness them now, and King John will sign both when I get back to London. I will ensure that a copy that has been fully signed is sent to you immediately."

She was dazed. How had this happened, and so quickly? How was it possible that her whole world had been turned inside out, in a matter of minutes? But he was taking no chances that she might change her mind. He witnessed her shaky signatures and sanded the documents carefully, before placing them back in his silk sack. It was only then that she realised that John had been so sure of himself, that the documents had been drawn up without her knowledge, ready for her to sign.

"I had no choice, Isabel." She said, close to tears. "None at all. If I had fought back and insisted that I kept my lands in England, then he would have thrown us out of Poitou without a penny. And they didn't want me, the English, he made that clear. The English people and the nobles both. I can tell them that it wasn't my fault, that I wasn't given any choice, that I would have been there with them years ago, if I could, until I'm hoarse, but they won't care. They probably think of me as just some foreign upstart who cares nothing for them or for their country. They're probably convinced I'm not in England because I don't want to be, not because I've never had the chance."

"Probably." Isabel agreed calmly. "All they know is what they see. They know you've never set foot in England, and so they think you don't want to. I'm sorry, but what else are they to think?" She shrugged. "No matter. It can't be helped. So we go to Le Mans."

"You don't care? You don't care about leaving Poitou? Don't care that you will not be going home, to England?"

Isabel placed her knuckles on her lips and spoke quietly.

"I care, of course I do. I have dreamed of seeing England ever since I left it. And I – and Jean – have been very happy here at Poitou. But it's not the same for us. All my life I've moved when I've been told to. I expect it. Jean has spent his life here, but he's just as much at your beck and call as I am. He'll understand. Poitou has been home to us, Le Mans will become home to us."

"I hope so." Berengaria said sadly. "I hope I've made the right decision. For all our sakes."

Isabel shrugged her mind already on the minutiae of the move.

"It wasn't your decision to make." She said quietly. "It was made for you."

Chapter 26

The court seemed to feel little of Berengaria's bone-deep sorrow at leaving Poitou. And it would be forever, she knew. Even if by some miracle John – and the new Duchess of Poitou – allowed it, she would never be able to bring herself to return to the place she thought of as home, only to find somebody else in her place. Somebody who cared nothing for the land, or the people, someone who – she had no doubt – would care only for the title of Poitou.

Her retinue meandered along in the early summer sun. Berengaria in the lead, shadowed by Jean and Isabel, the courtiers and ladies following behind in a gossiping, giggling straggle. Behind them, the servants; some on mules, some on foot, some leading carts piled with her possessions. Behind them all, the beasts – oxen and horses and a few cows that had escaped the winter cull as they were either too young or too thin to be slaughtered for meat.

The courtiers seemed to approve of the new countryside; she could hear them talking happily of the hunting prospects. There were densely wooded areas, spaced with thick, tangled maquis and open areas that showed signs of being tusked by wild boars, searching for food. She guessed that there would also be deer, and probably wolves; possibly even bears in the autumn, coming in to forage for food before their winter sleep. She noticed that fields were few, and the even fewer peasants they passed on the tracks stared at the passing parade sullenly. In Poitou, the ordinary people would have bowed and called out to her, held their children up for inspection and run alongside her, knowing that she would have alms for them. But here, there was nothing. Not even any curiosity.

Funds for the move had arrived from John; exactly half the amount she had finally agreed. She tossed the purse to Jean Reeve, who assured her that there would be enough, and to spare, to see them settled. Still, worry gnawed at her over John's deception. If he was ready to bilk her now, how safe was her annuity? Would he really part with a thousand marks each year? And what if he didn't? How would they manage?

Isabel's touch on her sleeve distracted her.

"Ma'am." She nodded. "Le Mans."

Berengaria looked up, shading her eyes to stare into the sun. Wavering slightly in the heat, she made out grey walls, appearing to rise sheer out of the landscape. Unlike Poitou, there was no home farm clustering around the walls like chicks around a hen, simply a gaunt and ugly castle.

She sighed and pulled a face, sick at heart.

The castle's thick stone walls made it cold, and it was as bare within as it was outside. Berengaria wandered through the rooms, mapping out her new home. The courtiers were flitting about like moths, the nobles uttering little cries of amusement at each new corner discovered, the servants carrying and and removing things as their masters changed their minds.

Berengaria drifted around like a ghost in her own home, unable to settle. She wished she could go away until Le Mans could be lived in. Until she could begin to think of it as her home. For a few minutes, she considered traveling to see Blanche, much nearer here than she had been at Poitou, and she even got as far as planning the journey before she gave in and realized she couldn't. Her court could have elected to stay at Poitou, to move their loyalties to their new lady – or lord – but they had not. They had chosen to follow her here, and she couldn't abandon them now, just because she was less than happy. Le Mans was her new home, and she had to make the best of it.

Listless, she allowed Isabel to choose her apartments. She smiled at her courtiers, and congratulated the servants on making the place so comfortable, so quickly, but it was all done politely, without heart. On the third day, she took Jean Reeve with her and rode about her new estate as far as Jean felt comfortable in taking her. The countryside itself was wild, far less farmed than Poitou. The people they encountered spoke a strange dialect that she could barely understand; she gave them alms, and they bit the coins suspiciously and stared at her with almost superstitious fear, as if they could not believe that anybody would give them money and ask for nothing in return. She felt their eyes on her back as she rode away from them, and was relieved when Jean decided it was time to get back to Le Mans.

Could she ever make anything of this dreadful place? Even Isabel, who took everything in her stride, was flustered. She had engaged some locals as servants, to help out in the kitchens and to do the heavier work needed to make the castle habitable, and they had rapidly driven her to fury.

"I tell them what to do, and they stand there and look at me as if I hadn't spoken." She said. "I was reduced to getting some of our own servants to actually show them what I meant. Silly things, like – here is a broom! This is what you do with it! Here is the well, draw water in this – this is called "a bucket" – and put it in this cauldron. And the food! We have already had to slaughter some of the cattle from Poitou that should have been kept until much later. I don´t know what people here eat. Each other, probably."

Berengaria smiled reluctantly.

"The courtiers will hunt." She said. "And then at least we will have meat."

"Hunt? Hunt?" Isabel said scornfully. "Oh, they are hunting already. But nothing we can eat! There are wolves in the area, and a thriving colony of otters in the river, and that is their prey. They're so excited, they're like little children. I have tried to explain to them that we need meat, that there are stags close by – I've heard them roaring to each other - and there are surely boars, but they shrug me away. There are always boars, they say. They're bored with hunting boars. And stags are difficult to hunt in this country. But wolves, now. There's game for a man to hunt! And they're already mad to obtain a pack of otter hounds, on the grounds that the otters eat the fish, which leaves less for us. As if they would even know a fish if it wasn't dressed and cooked and on a platter in front of them!"

Berengaria closed her eyes. This trivial thing, the thought of grown men, excited as children over the fact that they had something new to kill for sport, nearly reduced her to tears. Did they care nothing for the fact that they had been evicted as easily as if they had been mere peasants, with neither rights nor privileges? I was Queen of England, she thought miserably. My husband was the greatest King in Christendom, and now I'm reduced to this. Turned out of my own home; forced to move where I was told to go, to this sour, miserable countryside where nobody knows me, and cares even less. She watched Isabel as she wandering around the room, tutting over the disarray of the furniture; turning oddments this way and that until she was satisfied. She felt a sudden, painful stab of deep envy. Even Isabel had more than she had; Isabel had a husband – a good husband – she had the chance of children, of happiness. Isabel had a future. And what did she have, who was once the great Queen of England? Nothing. Nothing at all. Neither husband nor family. No land except this miserable tract of nothingness, in the middle of nowhere. No future, only a past that would make her more unhappy still, if she thought about it. She who had had everything, now had nothing.

It had gone, and none of it had been her fault. None of it.

She sat quietly, waiting until Isabel had clucked and fussed herself into silence and then watched her go, no doubt to shoo yet more servants about the place. And yes, that was something else that Isabel had that she did not; Isabel had a place in life. She had something to get up for each morning, something to keep her brisk and alert. Oh, she would mutter about it, and complain, but in her heart, she would, Berengaria knew, thoroughly relish her task. She would look forward to each new day, and at night she would sleep well, in the knowledge of a job well done, of something accomplished. And what do I have, the Lady of Le Mans? The woman who was once Queen of England? Why, I have dusty memories and hopes that were never fulfilled. Ambitions that were never realised. Joys that died and turned to dust. Joys as dead as my baby. Dust that nobody will mourn or even think about, unless Isabel remembers to pay to have masses said for my – and my baby's – soul when I am dead as well.

She clenched her teeth to keep the tears back and rose to her feet jerkily. The chair crashed to the floor behind her, but she ignored it and walked from the room half-blinded by her unshed tears. Somewhere in the castle, somebody was picking out a tune that she did not recognize on a lute; she paused to listen, but it was a melancholy melody and made her feel sadder still. She walked blindly, meeting no one. She passed door after door, all closed but it did not matter, she had no desire to open them, to see what was inside. Finally, her way was blocked by yet another closed door, at the end of a passage. Unable to summon the energy to retrace her steps, she leaned against the door and it creaked open, swinging with her weight.

The room beyond was thick with fluffy dust, speaking of years of disuse. The four high windows were glazed, but very small, and very dirty. The light they let through had the quality of fog rather than sunlight. The stone floor was bare of rushes, and there was no furniture at all, except for a single table raised on a dais at the far end. A table surmounted with a plain, ebony cross, bearing a tormented Christ nailed to his last resting place.

Wearily, Berengaria realised that she had found the castle's chapel. She stared at the bare room, and felt as empty inside herself. Close to despair, she remembered her beloved chapel at Poitou, the windows tall and bright with coloured glass, the light that flooded through sending rainbows of joyful colour over the floor, illuminating the faces of the worshippers raised to the richly dressed altar. Only the cross was the same.

She walked slowly down the centre of the chapel – nothing to mark it as the aisle, but she thought of it as such – and sagged to her knees on the bare stone. The cold burned into her knees like fire, but she barely noticed. Head bent so that her chin bit into her breastbone, she wept.

Wept great, snorting, noisy tears. For herself. For Richard. For Rafe. For her dead babe. For her father. For Johanna. For Poitou. For this dreadful, cold, dirty chapel. For what had been, and now would never be again. For the love she thought she had had, and now knew had always been false. For the past that had been, and the future that now would never be. For the Queen that had never been, the wife that had never been. The lover who had been false. The mother who had never had a chance. The country that had been hers, yet which had betrayed her without her setting foot in it.

And for herself. Above all, for herself.

She sobbed, rocking back and forth, hugging herself. After a while, the stone began to hurt her knees badly, but she did not move, relishing the pain, almost pleased that she had something else to add to her woes. Nothing would ever be good in her life again, she knew. Ever.

"Why are you crying, dearest?" The question was asked from straight in front of her, and stopped Berengaria's tears as if she had been slapped. She wiped tears and mucous from her face with her fingers, and strained to see through her bleared eyes.

Johanna stood in front of her, her head dipped as she stared down at Berengaria. The breath caught in her throat but try as she might, she could not speak. She caught a sob between her teeth, but it broke loose and she could do nothing but wave her hand in supplication. Wait, the gesture said, please; wait for me.

As she fought for breath, it never entered her thoughts that the Johanna who stood before her, apparently restored to both beauty and life, could not be real. She was here, and that was all that mattered.

"Why are you crying?" She repeated.

Berengaria shook her head, lost as to where to begin.

"Why am I crying?" She held out her hands wide, gesturing at the filthy chapel as though that gesture encompassed everything that was wrong. "Why shouldn't I cry? I've lost everything. Everything I ever wanted, everything I ever loved, has been taken away from me. And none of it was my fault!" She wailed like a child. "I have nothing left, and you're asking me why I'm crying? I thought you, at least, loved me. That you would understand. But if you don't, then I've truly got nothing and nobody left."

Johanna tossed her head impatiently. The gesture was so like her that Berengaria managed a smile through her tears.

"I do understand." She said briskly. "I understand that you're full of pity – for yourself." Berengaria gasped at the injustice of the words. "Are you hungry? No? You've got a roof over your head, haven't you? Got an army of servants to look after you, haven't you? Got a good friend in Isabel? And above all, you're alive and well. What else do you want?"

"I want to be loved." Berengaria mewed, and even as she said it, realized how pathetic she sounded.

"And what makes you think you're not loved? You, who have an entire court who have followed you without even being asked? And Isabel and her husband – they could have stayed at Poitou, lived an easy life for they would have been the only ones who knew the running of the place. And your sister Blanche, who thinks about you constantly, and prays for your welfare in the midst of her own troubles? And me, sister? You weep constantly for me now, don´t you? But how often in life did you tell me that you loved me? That I truly was your sister? And now you dare to tell me that you have none who loves you? Look at me."

Johanna commanded, and Berengaria raised her eyes, unable to refuse the power of that voice.

Johanna stood, ramrod straight, before the make-shift altar, her hands spread wide, mimicking the crucified Christ on the altar behind her. Although her clothes were the simple nun´s habit Berengaria had last seen her wearing, she was transcended. Her presence lit up the grey chapel. Beautiful as Johanna had been in life, now Berengaria was struck dumb by her magnificence. She had none of the trappings of power, no jewels, no rich clothes. Yet Berengaria knew and recognized in her a greater power than anything earthly could assume.

"Listen to me, sister." She commanded. "You feel sorry for yourself, because you think God has taken everything you cared about. Your husband. Your lover. Your baby. Even me. But I tell you, God does not take. He only gives. Once, I, too, cursed God. Cursed the God who took my son away from me, cursed the God who made me cry out in terrible pain, and refused to help me. But I understand, now. God does not inflict evil on us. We make our own choices in life, and must suffer the consequences of them. God can only watch and suffer for us, and hope that in the end we come to Him. And I tell you now, my sister, all that has happened to you has led you to this place. Here is where your salvation lies, where you'll find your true vocation. You are a woman, and it is only truly women that can know the sorrows of this world, and yet not give in to them."

Berengaria shook her head, tears flying from her eyelashes.

"Johanna, I thought …. before Richard came … I thought then that I would end my days in a convent. Is that what you are telling me? That I should take the veil? Like you did?"

Johanna shook her head.

"And what good would that do for anybody?" Her words were so tart, so much the old Johanna, that Berengaria smiled through her tears. "Forget your self-pity. Get on with life. With the life God has given you. You loved Poitou because it was a green and pleasant place, because your peasants adored you and the living was easy. Look around you, at your new found land of yours. Look at the scrub that's lying idle, because there's not enough knowledge to know how to clear it. Look at the woodland that's going wild because nobody has tools enough to turn it into houses. You despise the peasants here because they're suspicious of you. Look again. Look at their faces, and see how they fight the land every day of their lives, trying to scratch a living. Then wonder why they view this magnificent noblewoman who's suddenly appeared amongst them with such worry. Look at the rows of unmarked graves alongside each village; tiny graves, children buried by people who could not afford to leave even a wooden marker for them. You're daring to tell me you've got nothing? Look at them, and then tell me." Her nostrils flared and she bent forward, so close that Berengaria could have touched her. "And above all, sister. Remember. You're alive."

Stunned, Berengaria rocked back on her heels and asked the question, the one question, above all others, that she needed answering.

"What should I do?"

Johanna smiled and told her what she was going to do.

Chapter 27

Berengaria stood on the hill that looked down on L´Epau. Isabel stood beside her, her youngest son hand-in-hand with his mother on one side, and his Godmother on the other. He was a good child, and stood quietly whilst the women watched the work progress.

"I will not live to see it finished." Berengaria said softly. Isabel shrugged.

"Neither of us will." She said. "But little Jean here will, and he and his sons in turn will worship in the abbey at L´Epau. And he will be able to tell his sons, and his grandsons, and they will tell their sons and grandsons in turn, about the greatest lady who ever lived in Maine, who built this abbey by hook and by crook." Tears welled in Berengaria´s eyes and she gestured at Isabel to be quiet, but she carried on anyway. "He will tell them the tale about the greatest Queen that England ever had, the Queen who came to this place and turned it from the devil's own ground into somewhere where people can live and worship in peace and plenty."

"I did all that on my own, did I?" Berengaria smiled and wrinkles creased around her eyes and mouth. "If it hadn't been for your Jean spending every moment he could find with the local farmers, explaining to them how best to clear the ground, and sow and harvest efficiently, then there would be no prosperity here. And I suppose you had nothing to do with it, either, teaching the women to sew and cook and use the herbs hereabouts to cure the illnesses that used to kill them?"

"Aye, we helped. But if it hadn't been for you," Isabel gestured with her hands at the small army of masons who were laying the foundations of the great abbey below them, "None of this would have been able to happen." She let Jean's hand go and waved for him to go play. The child ran a few steps and that sat down, gazing absorbed at a brightly coloured lizard sunning itself against a rock. "Didn't you ever despair? All those years when King John," She spoke his name like a curse. "Didn't get around to sending you your money? All those times when you had to beg him for money to put bread in the mouths of your people?"

"I found threatening to go to London, dressed in rags, tended to work very well." Berengaria said cheerfully. "And when that failed, promising that I would have to desert Le Mans and go to live at Court with him in England worked wonders."

"Bloody man." Isabel said rudely. "And what did you do with the money, when you had prised it out of him? Gave half of it away in alms to the peasants, of course. I remember that dreadful winter, when you even had to sell your pearls to keep the wolves and the bears from the door. Our door and the peasants' doors alike."

"It didn't matter." She shrugged. "You can't eat pearls, they'll never keep you warm. One way or another, we never actually went hungry, nor cold."

"No. But how many winters was it a close run thing? And no matter how close the devil danced to us, you always managed to raise funds for the Abbey, didn't you? And no matter how often Jean, or I, appealed to you, you would never use any of that money for Le Mans."

"I couldn't. I just couldn't." And what, I wonder, would Johanna have said if I had? The thought made her smile. "It doesn't matter. We managed." She broke off to tell Jean not to lick the lizard and then fell silent. Eventually she turned to Isabel and spoke softly.

"Do you really think that I will be remembered fondly, by your children and their children and grandchildren?" She asked awkwardly. "There was a time when I thought that all I would have after I died would be masses said for my soul by priests who did not even remember me, but said the words because they were paid to do it."

Isabel blinked at her and then laughed out loud.

"Remembered?" She said incredulously. "Your name will ring down the years forever, you'll never be forgotten. In a thousand years' time, mothers will tell their children the story of the most courageous, the wisest, queen who ever ruled England. The most beautiful, as well. There will never be another queen like you, never. Whilst ever England exists, then people will have your name on their lips. And here, the Abbey will be your legacy. Forever and a day."

"I hope so." Berengaria said softly. "It would be good to think that I will be remembered kindly. I would give everything I ever had, even," She waved her hand at the activity below them, "Even this, to have spent one day, just one day, in my Kingdom. In England."

Isabel put her arm around her mistress´ waist, and the two women looked down at the construction works below for so long that young Jean grew bored, and bellowed for attention. Isabel scooped him up on her hip, and Berengaria helped her walk back along the narrow path, ensuring that neither mother nor child stumbled along the way.

Made in the USA
Middletown, DE
26 January 2019